ARCHAEOPTERYX

ALBUQUERQUE TRILOGY / BOOK 1

DAN DARLING

D1400778

CURIOSITY
QUILLS PRESS

A Division of **Whampa, LLC**
P.O. Box 2160
Reston, VA 20195
Tel/Fax: 800-998-2509
http://curiosityquills.com

© 2017 **Dan Darling**
www.dandarling.net

Cover Art by Eugene Teplitsky
http://eugeneteplitsky.deviantart.com

All rights reserved, including the right to reproduce this book or portions
thereof in any form whatsoever. For information about Subsidiary Rights,
Bulk Purchases, Live Events, or any other questions - please contact
Curiosity Quills Press at info@curiosityquills.com, or visit
http://curiosityquills.com

ISBN 978-1-62007-007-9 (ebook)
ISBN 978-1-94809-933-2 (paperback)

Dedicated to the people of New Mexico

CHAPTER ONE

'll get to the point: one day, ten thousand birds fell dead from the
New Mexican sky.

The next morning, I toiled away in my little lab behind the Reptile House
of the Rio Grande Zoo. I worked on a cute little guy named Terrence, a
horned lizard. I'd rescued him a few weeks ago from an elementary school in
Albuquerque's south valley, where a bunch of kids had taken him hostage in a
cardboard box and tried to feed him sticks for a week. Horned lizards eat meat.
A teacher called the zoo when she found the lizard cowering in a corner of the
box, and they sent me to collect it. Horned lizards have gray bodies stippled
with craggy scales and heads armored and horned. They look like miniature
dinosaurs lost in our modern world. I have a soft spot for misfits.

A horned lizard's only defense is staying low to the ground and hoping it
doesn't get noticed. I stayed low to the ground myself, in a metaphorical sense.
I'd been born with gigantism, and after nearly forty years of a raging pituitary
gland, I stood eight feet tall. The disease elongated the bones in my face, and
my hands and feet had grown disproportionately huge. I looked like a statue
of a gaunt titan from an old, dead civilization.

I'd been feeding Terrance ants—their venom would help rebuild his ability
to autohaemorrhage. Horned lizards aren't fast or mean. They just try to
hunker down and blend in with the desert around them. If a predator comes
after them, they puff out their bodies and hope their horns and armor put off
their attacker. And if everything else fails—if the damned world just won't
leave them in peace—they shoot a stream of blood from their eyes, called

autohaemorrhaging. That was life: you eat poison day in and day out, hoping to be left alone, until you get pushed and pushed and end up doing something truly horrific.

As I dribbled a few ants into Terrence's terrarium, the phone rang. I picked it up. "John Stick."

"It's me." The slurred voice belonged to Melodía Hernandez, my friend, whose speech contorted around tumors in her face. I could count my friends on two fingers. I'd made my other friend as a kid and met Melodía in college. In the fifteen years since, I'd shied away from getting to know anyone else.

"This better be important," I said. "I have a no-human policy before noon."

"You haven't heard. Of course not. How could you? Spiders and snakes don't report the news."

"Heard what?"

"New Mexico could have seceded from the union and you wouldn't know it." Melodía had a nice, middle-ranged voice, always edged in sarcasm. After a conversation with her, you came away feeling cut up. "Aliens could have come to back to Roswell. An earthquake could have knocked down the Sandia Mountains. John Stick would be sitting in his dark room, miserable as ever."

"I'm hanging up. Call me if we get nuked. I might care."

"I need you to do me a favor."

I chuckled at her.

"I'm serious. I need you."

I pushed out another laugh, but her plea gave me that warm sick feeling. The feeling when I first saw Terrence huddled in his box. The feeling when I came home from work every day to find my pet tarantula tickling the side of his terrarium in his excitement to see me. I had a tough outer shell, but Melodía made me warm and gooey.

"Tell me about this favor," I said.

"Yesterday, at exactly noon, every bird in the Bosque Del Apache fell out of the sky. Dead. Thousands of them."

The Bosque Del Apache, a nature reserve a couple hours south of Albuquerque, put my state on the map. The Bosque was particularly renowned as a winter nesting ground for migratory birds. Imagining all those birds dead sank my guts with a totally different sick feeling. In late February, tens of thousands of birds would have been nesting there.

"They can't all be dead," I said.

"Every single one. At exactly the same second. Geese in mid-flight. Cranes wading through the marsh. Bald eagles eating snakes. Ducks quacking. Boom. Dead."

"That's—" I searched for a word but didn't find one, so I let the miles of empty phone line do the talking.

"Yeah," Melodía said. "It is."

"I suppose you're doing the post-mortem." She worked at the University of New Mexico as an ornithologist.

"I need you to drive down to the Bosque. Get some samples and bring them back to me."

Normally, if somebody called me at that hour making demands, I'd have hung up on them. Melodía, however, was not normal. She'd been born with a mass of tumors in the left side of her face that swelled it to twice the standard size. Normal people gave her a hard time when she went outside. I'd seen the stares, the snickers, and the gasps. She'd had garbage thrown at her from passing cars, cruel normals called her ugly, freak, and mutant, people followed and harassed her. I'd suffered the same treatment my whole life. It had turned my shell extra hard, but pummeled Melodía into a jelly. Every jab hurt her ten times more than an average person. After a few decades of abuse, she'd developed a bad case of agoraphobia. She practically lived in her lab in the basement of the university's biology building. In the old days, we would both have been carnival spectacles. In modern society, we tried to stay out of the way. She was the kind of friend I couldn't refuse.

I groaned into the phone.

"It sounds like an earthquake when you do that," she said. I had a very low voice.

"You want me to drive hours for you, shovel dead bodies into my truck, and haul them back to your lab so you can study them and publish findings and get awards for being a genius? Fine. But first, the magic word."

"Please," she sung. "Pretty please."

I gave her my best resigned sigh.

I donned my Rio Grande Zoo jacket and cap, and hit the road. Interstate 25, a raised freeway that cut through the city like an axis, suspended my truck high above Albuquerque, a wide, flat city that stretched from the foot of the Sandía Mountains on the east side to a string of five dormant volcanoes on the west. Beyond, the tortuous mountain desert spread in every direction, from Mexico to Colorado and Arizona to Texas. A human could map that desert, but they couldn't fathom its scale: the diversity of life it held, the pine-scaled mountains, the river valleys cut by eons of current, the llano nodding with sienna grasses, the red cliffs, the lattice of caverns beneath it all. I'd lived in that desert all my life.

As I drove south, the sun crested the mountains and sprayed the city with light, as if the dusty collection of adobe plaster and strip malls were the Seven Cities of Gold finally discovered. The ice blue sky hung above the freeway as it traced Isleta, Los Lunes, Los Chavez, and Belen, a line of villages with McDonald's signs across from two-hundred-year-old adobe churches, dirt alleys meandering along the black top Interstate, chicken pens beside driveways with well-washed hotrods. Past the villages' perimeters, the rough desert lay dotted with clumps of scrub and low-lying cacti. These towns clung to the banks of the Rio Grande, the river that flowed from Colorado through New Mexico to Texas, where it formed the border with Mexico for a thousand miles before it reached the Gulf.

It took me an hour to reach the Bosque del Apache. I didn't speed since the birds would stay dead. The Bosque boasted fifty thousand acres of mountains, woods, desert grasslands, and floodplains irrigated by the Rio Grande. The park consisted of driving loops, hiking trails, picnicking spots, and paved paths that led tourists from their parking spaces to observation platforms where they could ogle the birds and maybe read an informative plaque or two.

At the entrance to the park, a ranger piled corpses beside the welcome sign. Their white plumage twitched in the desert wind. Emerald and black ducks hung from the rain gutters of the visitor's center. Birds of all stripes lined the dirt road, as if someone had snowplowed the way clear. I could have collected my pick of dead bodies without even entering the reserve.

The road carried me in a loop around the marsh. It dipped low over soft ground with billowing brush on both sides. After a few hundred yards, the left bank dropped away and the marsh spread a quarter mile to the west. The gray Chupadera Mountains loomed beyond. State and county vehicles packed the observation parking lot. Humans in earth-toned uniforms and wading boots milled around in the water, taking tall, careful steps. The entire marsh, from one shore to the other, bobbed with feathery death. The waders lifted sodden bodies from the water and cradled them back to shore, where other rangers loaded them into the backs of pickup trucks. They'd already filled one with a gray mound of corpses.

A ranger or two gave my vehicle a brief glance as I drove on, but to the casual observer, I was simply another normal person in a pickup truck with dark windows and an extended cab. They couldn't tell that I'd removed the driver's seat and sat in the back, where I'd tilted the seat so that I could sit relatively comfortably and still reach the steering wheel and pedals. The lower position also gave my neck a little relief, though I still had to hunch.

I parked beside a quiet stand of spruce pines that screened me from view of the marsh and its crew of normals. I gathered up a couple of northern shovelers, ducks with broad, flat bills and iridescent jade heads. Their bodies hung heavy with death. I slipped them into sample bags and noted their location with a black marker. I found a dove dead in its nest and bagged that too, and a few steps farther into the brush, a Canada goose with its wings tangled in a thicket. While I worked to free it, the weeds rustled behind me.

A man leaned against the trunk of a cottonwood in an olive windbreaker, with clean new hiking boots and a shiny watch. Each leg of his khakis sported a crease down the front. He was an average looking Anglo, not too bald, not too old, not too skinny, not too muscular. He had eyes and hair the color of your average dormouse.

"You the mortician?" he asked. "*Dulce et decorum est pro patria mori.*"

"What was that? Greek?"

He gestured at the insignia on my jacket. "A zoo man who doesn't know his Latin." He shook his head in a dumb show of sadness. "What is the world coming to? Where have our values gone? And all that garbage."

"I don't use the Latin names for animals. It's rude."

"Touché," he said. "I like your style."

"I don't have a style. I'm working a job."

"Zoo keeping dead animals now? Can't afford to feed the live ones? Kidding."

I glanced at his white-collar outfit. "You're not a ranger."

"Nice sleuthing." He crossed his arms and watched me.

I bagged my goose, marked it, and walked it back to my truck where I nestled it in with the other bodies before opening the driver's side door.

"Leaving?" he asked. "Got everything you need?"

"No offense"—I let my giant's voice rumble the air—"but why don't you go find another state park to lurk in? Nobody here wants to chitchat today."

"I'm here on business," he said, "just like you."

I gave him one of my unfriendly giant stares.

"Your business has nothing to do with the zoo," he said.

"Is that a fact?" I asked.

"It's a guess."

"I'm doing a favor for a friend. As far as anybody should care, including you, I'm not even here."

"You're a good friend," he said. "You wanna be an even better friend? You'll follow me."

I slammed my truck door. "First, tell me who you are and why we're talking to each other."

"I'm Jacob Charon. Chief biologist at a genetics research lab east of the city. Typhon Industries. Mass deaths are pretty interesting to us."

"Never heard of you," I said.

"That shocks me. We're big-time. We study animals, just like you. As far as *avialae* go, we harbor a certain type of rare finch. Indigenous to the Galapagos Islands. Drinks blood. *Geospiza difficilis septentrionalis*. Common name of vampire finch."

"I'm a reptile and arachnid guy," I said.

He shrugged. "As to the second question, we're talking to each other because at times like this, people shouldn't just go about their business. They should take a moment. Death on this scale—it should give us pause."

"Like I said, I'm just collecting samples for a friend."

"You're not a person of your own." He nodded as if we were in staunch agreement. "You're just your friend's friend. You don't feel anything unless your friend tells you to."

"Death is normal," I said.

"Ten thousand birds falling dead at the same second. That's not normal. It's either the biggest scientific coincidence in history, God's wrath has gone Old Testament, or we humans did it. Which one is your money on?"

"Didn't you say you had something to show me?" I didn't really care if he did or not. I just wanted to get back in my truck and go find a quiet place to harvest dead birds.

"You have to earn it," he said. "It's the diamond at the bottom of this bloodbath. I won't hand it over to just anybody."

"And how do I earn it? Do I follow your tracks through the leaf litter? Because that sounds pretty easy to me."

He grinned, showing me teeth neither straight nor crooked, too white or too yellow. He didn't have dimples, and his smile was as unremarkable as everything else about him—besides his personality.

"You're feisty. I like that. I'll tell you what. We're colleagues. I study animals; you study animals. I'll scratch your back. You scratch mine."

I didn't study animals. I fed them, cleaned their cages, and watched over their young. But I didn't argue. "Sure. Absolutely."

"When my back itches," he said, "you'll be there?"

I tried not to glare at him. "Whatever you say."

He grinned again and waved for me to follow. He led me down a shallow ditch, knee deep with bramble and weeds. My feet found mud at the bottom. Charon clambered up the opposite bank, and I took it with a deep bend of my knee. At the top, in a small raised clearing, lay a white-plumed whooping crane, as tall as a normal, the most endangered bird in North America.

"You don't want this for yourself?" I spoke quietly, without meaning to. The clearing with the white downy body at the center felt holy even to a cynic like me.

"Nah." Charon shoved a stick of gum in his mouth and smacked his lips. "You keep it. I'm here doing another type of study altogether. Just give me a ride back to my car."

I lifted the crane's body, as light as a fossil, into my arms, and slipped it into a bag before marking it.

Back in my truck, he directed me around the southern loop and past the western side of the marsh, lined with trees. Feathered clumps hung from the limbs like Christmas ornaments. A sandhill crane with sienna wings and a red crown lay across a picnic table like a pagan feast. Near the table sat a rich person's shiny car.

I pulled in beside it. Not far away, a tumult erupted. Men yelled. What sounded like a rabid sheep brayed and bleated. As a zookeeper, I'd heard it all, but never a sound like that in all my years. Something beat against the insides of a van or truck, rocking it on creaky shocks. Glass shattered. A few more yells rang out before quiet settled over the preserve.

Charon stared out the window with a veiled expression on his average face. "Curious." He shifted his eyes to me.

"What the hell was that?" I wondered aloud.

Charon shrugged. "Who knows? *Arbor eram vilis quondam.*"

"Enough Latin," I said. "This is your stop."

"That it is." He cracked his door and sprang from the truck. "Thanks for the ride, zookeeper. Looking forward to our next meeting."

I didn't tell him that I didn't make a habit of meeting people—that this pure-chance encounter broke my routine and would never happen again. I wanted him out of my truck. "Thanks for the bird."

After he'd shut the door, I drove toward the northern loop, which wound around a small farm. I figured I'd find some different species there, maybe even spot a live bird or two to show Melodía that there had been a few survivors, proving the whole thing wasn't as bad as she thought. I didn't want to prove her wrong so much as I wanted to demonstrate that the world wasn't completely awful. It was just pretty bad. We'd been in a fifteen-year long debate about that distinction.

At the intersection of the north and south loops, I passed a white cargo van set back in a thicket of shrubs and trees. The front windshield had fissured into a web of cracks and both front doors stood ajar. Something had ripped the upholstery of the front seats to shreds. The stench of carnivore musk leaked in through my vents.

Two men stood nearby: one middle-aged and thin with a lot of loose skin on his face, the other meaty and young with broad shoulders. They wore black uniforms, Kevlar vests, and sidearms. The older one wound a bandage around the younger one's forearm. Beside them, a pile of bloody gauze sat in the dirt.

I'd found the source of noise Charon and I'd heard earlier. It looked like the two soldiers—or security guards, or riot police, or military mercenaries, or whatever—had been carting a wolverine around in their van and it had finally snapped and turned the tables. I wished the beast well and drove on by. I had enough weird events to ponder already.

CHAPTER TWO

returned to Albuquerque with a truck bed full of samples: ducks, geese, a sandhill crane, a couple herons, a dozen larks and finches. A roadrunner I'd found on a fence post, as if it had been struck dead in a classic Southwest tableau. A bald eagle with the egg goop of another bird crusted on its beak. But the best—in other words, the worst—was the whooping crane.

In the 1980s, the forest service tried to save the endangered whooping crane by taking eggs laid in captivity and putting them in the nests of wild sandhill cranes. The sandhills run about five feet tall with brown plumage and red crowns. Whooping cranes are six feet tall and pure white. Somehow, though, it worked. The sandhills raised the whooping cranes as their own. At the Bosque, you could see a vee of long brown birds flying north with one white body among them.

Cranes are less prejudiced than humans. Hating people who are different is a special thing we have going.

This whooping crane I'd found probably represented in the realm of one percent of her entire species. Melodía would be happy I'd found her and would probably do all kinds of things to the body to determine why it died. When she figured it out, she'd write an article about it. People would read the article, and then they'd throw it in the trash. Eventually, the bird and the article would end up in the same landfill. But at least the humans would be able to say, hey, we understand something.

I packed all the little birds I could into my duffel and tied up a few bundles of long-bodied wading birds. It took me a few loads to get them all down to

Melodía's lab in the basement of the university's biology department. By the time I'd schlepped the last haul, she had the whooping crane laid out on a metal table and peered into its feathers with a magnifying glass like some old-fashioned sleuth.

The bird stood as tall as a man—meaning a couple feet shorter than me—with long, slender limbs. Melodía was also tall and slender, with brown skin and dark brown curly hair. She had curvy hips, a tapered waist, and long hands. The right side of her face featured a narrow jaw and high cheekbone; the left looked as if it had been stuffed with plums.

"Any clues?" I asked.

"Too much dander," she muttered. Talking to oneself was a habit of people who spend a lot of time alone.

"I didn't see any external marks," I said.

She gave me a look. Shut up and let me work, that look said.

I leaned back against the wall and hit my head on a projecting vent. I constantly hit my head. Human beings tended to hang things at the height of my chin, especially in labs. Scientists needed lights, scopes, scales, instrument racks, and cupboards. It made for lots of things to duck.

Melodía treaded her gloved fingertips through the birds' feathers. Every few minutes, she'd take a razor blade and shave away a dime-sized area of skin.

It's hard to sit and watch a person do minute work. "Watcha looking for?"

She met my eyes. "You don't need to be here." The slur in her voice was a little more pronounced than usual. Her tumors stretched her lips tighter in moist weather.

"Thank you, Stick, for bringing me the birds," I said.

"Yes, Stick. I'm very grateful." She didn't sound grateful.

"I'm happy to share my findings with you, since you were happy to be my errand boy in a run to the forest of death," I said.

"You've got a thousand hours of flex time," she said. "You could take a month's vacation and still have time left over."

She knew too much about me. "C'mon. Call it professional curiosity."

"You're a reptile man. What do you care about birds, besides that they're an evolution or two more sophisticated than the animals you handle?"

"Mine and yours: they're cousins." I almost added *just like us*, but I didn't. She didn't like to acknowledge our freak status made us friends. She still envied the normals.

She sighed. "I found bites."

That took me aback. Most insects would have been dormant for the winter. "Like bug-bites?"

"See for yourself." She held the magnifying glass out to me.

I made it over to the table without bonking myself, took the tiny magnifying glass in my giant fingers, and leaned way down. She'd shorn the feathers away from half a dozen abrasions, upraised like mosquito bites, but with a jagged slice at the center instead of a pinprick.

"Well?" she asked.

"No insect bite like I've ever seen." I'd seen quite a few. The reptile house at the zoo also housed arthropods—insects, arachnids, myriopoda, and the like. I'd dealt with every critter in New Mexico that bit, stung, spat, or clawed.

"A tick?" she asked.

I shook my head. Not many ticks lived in New Mexico, and they left a crater, not a welt.

"Wasp sting?"

No again. The tear at the center didn't fit.

"Horsefly?"

I shrugged. Horseflies used their mandibles to slice the skin before lapping up the blood that poured out. "Have to be a hell of a horsefly. Biggest horsefly in New Mexico."

"But you're not ruling it out."

I held up my hands. "Don't let me rule anything in or out. I'm a simple zookeeper."

She scoffed. "All you do is read books and watch nature shows. You know as much as anybody."

"You need an insect guy," I said. "I'm sure you have one here."

The skin around Melodía's right eye flexed downward and the right side of her mouth tightened. Her left side stayed largely immobile. She hated admitting she had colleagues. It meant she might have to talk to them. "Don't you know someone at the zoo?"

"Not a PhD," I said. "We're amateurs."

Melodía's body drooped like a wet garment on a clothes hanger.

"I'll get somebody to take a look, if that's what you want," I said. "But they won't be a scientist. They'll look at the bite, but they won't be able to run tests like one of your university types."

She collapsed onto a stool and stared at the dead bird. Two Melodías existed: the playful, sarcastic Melodía who'd been here when I arrived—and the one weighed down by anxiety. She'd built up a phobia of meeting people face-to-face like others do a fear of snakes or heights. It paralyzed her. She'd been that way since we'd met in college twenty years before, and she'd only gotten worse with age.

"There's Dr. Ramón." She kept her eyes on the bird. Her left eye was slightly bloodshot and stretched at the corner by her tumors. "He's one of those popular professors who gets called 'doctor' and his first name. Everybody loves him. A harem of undergraduate girls follows him around pretending to be fascinated by cockroach behavior."

He sounded like my enemy.

"I hate him," Melodía said.

"Tell you what. I'll find this Dr. Ramón and ask him to take a look. Save you a trip."

"No," she said.

"I don't mind."

Melodía raised her head and looked at me. Her face was half beauty and half travesty. "Goodbye Stick."

I left.

I tried not to think any more about the dead birds. I wanted to enjoy my day off.

My truck felt twenty degrees hotter on the inside than the outside. In the New Mexican winter, the sun made the interior of a truck paradise, like a greenhouse for one person. I sat there for a few minutes enjoying it. Then I drove home.

I lived in the Northwest Valley, where I rented the bottom half of a house. It was technically a basement, half above ground, half below. A set of cement steps led to a garden and patio sunken into the ground at the level of my entrance, hidden by trees and shrubs. Fresh out of college, I'd only been able to find one place that would fit my height and budget. The widow who lived in the main level had given me a great deal, probably because she sensed a kindred spirit. Like me, she never had guests, rarely went out, lived a quiet life. I'd settled in. Now, many years later, I was nearing forty and she'd dwindled into an old woman.

Ralph, my tarantula friend, waited for me when I got home. He stood on the tips of his eight legs, his many eyes gleaming. He'd doubtless sensed me coming through the vibrations in the ground. I'd adopted him from the zoo, which displayed only female tarantulas because of their longer lifespans and larger size.

After I'd liberated Ralph from his terrarium so that he could run around the apartment, I made myself some breakfast: avocado on toast with tomato slices, a spritz of lemon juice and a hefty dose of black pepper over it. I sat at my bar to eat, which to me stood at about the height of a kitchen table.

I'd designed my life in this house below the earth to scale. I drank from big glasses. I ate with cooking spoons and salad forks. I sat on a brown sectional couch with extra sections so I could recline fully. I slept on two beds laid end to end. I owned custom made clothes and shoes, of which I took special care. To small objects, like my toothbrush, I'd attached long, fat handles. Handling tiny objects made my joints hurt. My condition had side effects: joint pain, brittle bone disease, and an enlarged heart to name the worst.

When I finished eating, I sat and watched my garden through the bay window. Life abounded in the shadows beneath the branches of willow and cottonwood trees that grew in my landlady's yard. I'd planted apple, peach, and cherry trees long ago. The unpaved sides of the patio housed dirt planters, where I raised ferns, holly, and hydrangea. In the darker parts, I cultivated stands of mushrooms. If I'd ever invited guests to my home, they would have wondered why I didn't grow vegetables. I'd point to the fruit trees.

However, in the spring, I let a good bit of the fruit drop and fester. I harvested and ate about half, brought some to my aging father who lived in the South Valley, and dispersed the other half back out into the garden over time. It makes good compost, a guest might say. True. But the real truth is that I didn't grow plants in my garden—I grew animals. Worms, centipedes, earwigs, millipedes, fruit flies, gnats, common houseflies, horseflies, honeybees, wasps, hornets, a dozen types of beetle, crickets—they all love rotting fruit and moist topsoil. All of those animals draw predators: spiders, scorpions, garter snakes, toads—as well as birds and mice. I liked animals. I could sit on my patio in my lawn chair and watch the food pyramid in action.

I could also catch a wide array of prey for Ralph.

I'd turned my living room into a gladiator's arena by sealing all the baseboards, allowing no cracks, crevices, or other avenues of escape. The doors had rubber skirts that hugged the doorframe. The bases of the couch and cabinets were similarly skirted and sealed. Every evening, I released a hapless victim—a cricket, a wolf spider, a millipede, a tiny garter snake or mouse—into this coliseum. Every evening, I lifted Ralph from his terrarium and let him loose to stalk and kill his prey. It made for an engrossing home life.

Ralph was a prisoner. Hunting kept him occupied. Many of the zoo animals received live prey. However, their small enclosures didn't allow for a satisfying hunt. My apartment roughly equaled the size of Ralph's natural territory—except should he have gone in search of a mate. New Mexican desert tarantulas could stride miles in search of a mate. Ralph would never have that pleasure. We'd both embraced bachelorhood, trying to keep each other the best company we could.

I didn't think much more about the bird corpses I'd dropped off that morning. I handled dead creatures all the time. The scale of the death was horrific and it had occurred in the worst possible place, during the worst possible season—in summer, spring, or fall the birds would have been far away. Nature, however, powered itself with calamities. We New Mexicans lived on a soil dense with bodies.

My earliest memory is of seeing a dead body: the archaeopteryx fossil. My mother had taken me to the Albuquerque Natural History Museum. The creature lay spread flat on a slab of rock, the bones of its four-limbed skeleton long and thin. It had the head and tail of a lizard. Imprints of feathers, light as brushstrokes, surrounded the skeleton of the bird-lizard, a hybrid of two beings. It marked either a moment of transition from one form to another or a moment of indecision by God. Its body had struck me as light, fragile. It looked as if you could crumble it to pieces between your fingers and throw the dust into the wind.

After we saw that fossil, I thought to myself that my mother was just like it. She had gigantism as I did. She wore away over the years, her bones breaking, healing, and breaking again, until they wouldn't knit together anymore. The small bones in her ears crumbled until she went deaf. One morning, her bones simply turned to dust, and she ceased to be.

Maybe if I stayed below ground, I'd either disappear forever or the world would change. If I stayed out of sight long enough, one day I might emerge into the sun and find a whole world of stooped eight-foot men with gray beards and crackling knees, all deaf and sad.

I entertained myself with thoughts like these during my long hours of solitude.

I'd begun to nod off around eight, when a pickup truck lumbered to a stop outside my house. I said earlier that I could count my friends on two fingers. That muscle truck belonged to number two.

A door slammed. Jackboots clomped down my stairs. Tree branches and bush fronds rustled. The spring in my screen door contracted, and it slammed open. Knuckles hammered on my inner door. Ralph, who'd been standing at alert since the truck arrived, scurried into a corner. Only one person in my world moved with such frustrated violence.

"Stick." His voice growled like a back-alley mutt—small, bullied, hungry, and frustrated from always losing to the bigger dog. "Old buddy. I know you're there."

My door opened on Spartacus Rex, a short, wiry man with the big grey mustache and unruly graying hair of a long-haul trucker. Dandruff plagued his scalp, and twenty years of acne muddled his face. The child of a drunk and a mail-order bride, Rex was an outcast before he'd even left the womb. As fellow outcasts, we'd formed a quick friendship that spanned all the way back to elementary school.

"Stick," Rex said, the smell of boilermakers radiating from him.

Before we met, everyone had called me Johnny. On our first day of friendship at the age of six, Rex had issued the proclamation that we call each other by our last names. He'd wanted to be in the military and soldiers often called each other by their last names. It had stuck. "You are the man."

"Thank you," I said as we shook hands.

Rex took in a deep breath and let it out. "Normals." He shook his head and furrowed his immense brow ridge. "I've been up to my neck in them. They're scumbags and liars. Buddy, after a whole night with normals, I'll tell you how it feels to see you." He teetered on his heels as he searched for the words. "It feels like home."

I stepped back and gestured with my arm. "Get in here."

"Okay, pal." He walked by me and leapt atop one of my bar stools.

I pried the caps from a pair of Tecates. I set one in front of Rex and leaned on the bar between my kitchen and living room. "You went out."

"It's Tuesday," Rex said. "You know Tuesdays."

Rex worked weekends, as I often did. Sometimes, he bounced at the Atomic Cantina or worked security at the El Rey Theater whenever they had a concert bound to be unruly. He was also a substitute doorman at a strip joint downtown called Knockouts. He celebrated Saturdays on Tuesday, a day he reserved for self-defilement.

"A night out with the normals. Tell me about it." I understood why he did it: he still had hope. He was too close to being one of them. I'd never be a normal, and I'd come to grips with it.

"They're rubes," he said. "It's not that they don't like me." They didn't.

"They like me fine. They just don't understand that this"—he gestured around at my apartment—"this is all bullshit."

I nodded. I liked my apartment, but I understood he meant society.

"They don't get it."

"They do not," I said.

"We live in a system." Rex's mustache quivered with intensity. "I try to tell them. *We live in a system.* That's what I say."

"We do," I said.

"You have to see beyond the system to understand."

The clock read just shy of eight. Rex was the drunk guy at the bar ranting about the system before most people's evening had even begun—on a Tuesday.

He took a deep drink and leaned his forehead on his clenched fist. "There was this girl."

Rex always mooned over some strange girl and appealed to the normals to understand the system of oppression. Love and subjection ravaged Rex's existence. He'd never solve either one of them.

"Tell me about her." I never had a girl on my mind. I'd dulled my desire for a mate over the years as a matter of emotional survival. Rex's crushes never went well, but at least he tried.

"Some pale, black-haired girl. Tattoos. Piece of metal through her lip."

Rex had a type. We all gravitated to people as wrecked as we were.

"Listen to me rattling on." The lines of his face had fallen, and he looked like a tired old man.

"Rattle away," I said.

"How was your day? You should go to the bar with me, once in a while at least." He threw a hand in the air. "Open invitation."

I chose not to go to bars or any public spaces unless absolutely necessary. "Flowers go with you?" Leon Flowers, the third man in our triumvirate, was the odd man out—he and I never spent time together unless Rex led the way.

"Had some gig," Rex said. Flowers performed as a birthday party clown and drove an ice cream truck.

"So, this girl," I said.

Rex sighed. His posture drooped. "We're not talking about me anymore. We're always talking about me. That's not how friendship works."

My boring life—even I didn't want to talk about it.

"So, tell me."

I shrugged.

"Nature documentaries," Rex said. "About what."

"Aphids." I'd watched a video on aphids the night before.

"Aphids." He laughed. "Tiny little bastards. Tell me about them."

"Less than one percent of them survive to maturity," I said.

He shook his head. "That's depressing. It's about right for life in America, too. The Dream is dead to all of us little aphids down here in the dirt." He barked out a laugh.

I felt childish telling Rex about the things I'd learned from reading or watching documentaries. I'd shared a passion for animals with my mother and had spent hours of the day talking to her about them before her death. As an adult, I didn't do much besides think about animals, read about animals, feed animals, clean up after animals, nurse animals back from sickness, dispose of the bodies of animals.

"More about your day," Rex said.

I got us two more beers from the fridge and pried the caps off. "Sleep on my couch. No sense in wasting a Tuesday night."

"Alright, buddy."

"I insist," I said.

"Fine, but more about your day!"

"Got a call early this morning."

"Jesus Christ," Rex said.

"Mass bird death at the Bosque Del Apache."

"Cranes and ducks—that kind of thing?" he asked. Everybody in Albuquerque knew about the Bosque. It amounted to a holy site.

I nodded.

"How many died?"

"Ten thousand at least," I said. "They were still counting. Looked like damn near every bird there."

Rex searched for words. He groped at the air with his oversized hands. "That's nothing short of a tragedy."

Tragedies slid off my back. Tragedy was a human word. In nature, we called it reality. Animals died by the million every minute. Every creature had to destroy another creature to survive. Constant death formed the nucleus of our world. Still, the Bosque deaths sat like a thorn in my mind. I could still feel that whooping crane's delicate bones resting in my arms.

"They know what caused it?" Rex asked.

I shook my head. "Not yet. I gathered samples for UNM."

"Hernandez is looking into it?" Rex waited for me to nod. "She'll figure it out. Any guesses so far?"

"Who knows?" I said. "Mass trauma. Lightning storm. Wind surge. Disease."

Rex winked at me. His crows-feet stood out like etchings. "C'mon."

"Fireworks or even a spotlight can cause mass confusion. Birds crash into each other. Birds crash into trees. Birds go blind and fly straight into the ground."

"You're not thinking what I'm thinking?" Rex asked.

I sipped my beer, bitter and ice-cold. "They're near enough White Sands. A stealth flight or missile test could have caused enough turbulence. Strange sounds, bright lights. Who knows?"

"You're not thinking UFO?" Rex squinted up an eye.

"I am not." Many New Mexicans believed in UFOs. I didn't.

"It's only a hundred miles or so from Roswell." Rex shrugged broadly, as if conceding a point to himself. "Aliens are always messing with our wildlife."

I drank my beer.

Rex drank his beer and leaned his elbows on the bar. Even on a stool, the bar's height made him look small.

We hadn't seen each other in weeks. I assumed he'd been busy with odd jobs and booze. A woman may have come and gone. One of his 'business ventures' may have taken up his time, eradicated his savings, and gone south. Meanwhile, when Rex and I fell out of touch, I settled into my delicious routine. Sunrises and sunsets. Work and tranquility.

It didn't matter how long we went without seeing each other; our bond went back too far. As children, we had a lot in common. I was a freak with a dead mother, a father in perpetual mourning, and nothing but time to kill. The teachers gave me a lot of pitying looks and little help. Rex raised hell: he put ants down girls' shirts, spent a lot of hours outside the principal's office, and couldn't do math. His dad hit him on the ears a lot. He couldn't get the ringing in them to quiet down long enough to concentrate on anything. His teachers never flunked him in their eagerness to get rid of him. Our peers cast us out—children have innate freak-radar and ruthlessly mete out prejudice—and our teachers handled us with two fingers. In first grade, we'd banded together out of a will to survive.

"Thank God for you, Stick." Rex raised his beer bottle. "Saving the animals and solving mysteries."

A smile grabbed hold of my mouth before I could think of anything depressing. Few people could make me smile, but Rex had a knack for it. I tilted my bottle toward his. "Here's to you. The most loyal friend."

"My promises never die," Rex said. "That day your mom passed on—God rest her—I promised to be your brother. Thing is, I'm on to something. It's big."

Rex always had a scheme.

"You know the Minutemen," he said. "They're looking for ex-military guys."

The Minutemen, a group of vigilante rednecks who hated Mexicans, claimed to be defending the U.S.-Mexico border from drug-muling illegals. In reality, they mostly sat in the backs of their off-roaders with the floodlights on, drank Bud, and shot at coyotes with sniper rifles. Rex becoming one of them came as no surprise to me. "I thought they were volunteers."

"They have a new project," Rex said. "They're flush with cash through a partnership with some company that specializes in border security tech. Government contractors. And they need guys to help deploy it."

"So," I said, "a private government contractor is hiring a vigilante group to help them test a security system on the Mexican border." That combination sounded as absurd as anything else our society had coughed up.

Rex nodded. "I could get you in on it."

I held up my palm. My father was Chicano.

"They asked, do I have friends might be interested," he said.

I clinked my bottle into Rex's again. "Cheers. Glad you've got a new job."

"Sorry I haven't been around."

I shrugged. "You're busy. Not a big deal."

"This Bosque thing. You find out why all those birds died, you tell me. I'm interested."

"It's not my thing," I said. "I did my part."

"Too bad," Rex said through a yawn. "You're the right guy to get to the bottom of it."

"I'm the wrong guy." Our beers were gone. "I'll get you a blanket."

"Thanks, pal."

I got a quilt and a spare pillow from my bedroom closet and tossed them on the couch. I retrieved Ralph from where he crouched in a far corner of the living room and dropped him in his terrarium so Rex wouldn't accidentally step on him during the night. I rinsed each empty beer bottle and set them in the recycling bin. By the time I stretched out on my bed, Rex already snored on the couch.

CHAPTER THREE

The mass bird death occupied the front page of *The Albuquerque Journal* two days in a row. It probably made national news, for all I knew. I didn't use the internet much. I didn't read anything except the local paper, and I didn't talk to anybody who did.

I'd told Melodía that I didn't know a bug guy, but I did. I'd just forgotten about him. He came to the zoo's reptile house once a week to check on our invertebrate collection. Most of the time, he worked at a private biomedical lab somewhere. His name was Simon Marchette. A skinny bald Anglo with thick glasses, he had the yellowed complexion of something that spent too much time in florescent light. He showed up at the zoo on Thursday—not his usual day. I hadn't heard from Melodía since Tuesday, but I took the initiative to talk to him anyway.

Marchette had his head in the Madagascar hissing cockroach terrarium. Imagine tickling three-inch long cockroaches onto their bellies to check for mites. They scuttle and wiggle their antennae and hiss. Then you turn around and find your face in the stomach of a giant. Marchette took it in stride. He was alright.

"Zookeeper Stick! You seek an update on the *gromphadorhina portentosa*, I presume."

"I do not," I said.

"They thrive! They thrive! What do you feed them?"

I'd been feeding the hissing cockroaches fruit leftovers pilfered from the monkey enclosures. A rotten tangerine here, a mushy banana there. The cockroaches loved it. "I'm not here about the cockroaches."

"Ah-ha! Other business." Marchette bowed. "Proceed."

"You've heard about the birds?"

"Of course." The scientist wagged his head. "Tragic. Of course, millions of insects die every minute of every day. No one thinks twice about it. But birds, I suppose, are another matter."

"One of the birds has a bite," I said.

"An insect bite?"

I shrugged.

"An arachnid bite?"

I shrugged.

"It couldn't be a bat bite?" Marchette asked. "Could it?"

I stood there.

"You don't know what type of bite it is. You wish me to examine this bite and determine its origin."

I nodded.

"Ah! Of course, you only need send me, via electronic mail, certain details: fang-span, envenomation, etcetera. Any photographs would be helpful. Of course, out of professional curiosity, I should like to behold the victim myself, if possible. Is it here?"

I shook my head.

"Well, where is the victim of this bite stored? Let us sally forth to examine it at once. Tally-ho!"

"It's in the lab of Dr. Melodía Hernandez," I said. "She's a biologist at the University."

"Excellent! I have a luncheon to attend. Would she be receptive to a professional visitation in the after-noon?"

"I'll call her," I said. "Thanks, doc."

He gave me the double thumbs up.

Melodía didn't answer her phone. I left a message and considered my good deed done for the week.

After work, I didn't drive home. Thursday night marked my weekly visit to my father's casita in the South Valley. He still lived in the neighborhood where I was born, one of the old, poor barrios of Albuquerque. To its west flowed the Rio Grande. To the east, the abandoned rail yards lay like relics of a forgotten America. Fifty years ago, my old neighborhood had been a manufacturing and shipping district. Now, the adobe houses crumbled, the factories loomed dark and hollow, and the rail lines led to nowhere.

My dad was the only one on our street who cleaned the trash out of his yard. He kept his adobe patched and his roof relatively sound. He managed to sustain a couple of fruit trees, despite the ongoing drought. His faded blue Chevy pickup still ran.

I parked where the cracked asphalt met his dirt yard. Mrs. Chavez, an old woman in a threadbare apron and ratty housedress, froze in her driveway. She'd known me for over thirty years and still stared at me as if some new monster were invading her neighborhood.

My father's house was neat, as always. The front door opened on the kitchen to the left and the living room to the right. Both small rooms had wooden floors that the years had warped and scratched, but that my father swept clean. A woven red rug lay as it always did between the small green lazy boy my father used and the large rocking chair I managed to fit into. TV trays flanked each chair. The bare walls bore two shelves. One held an icon of the Virgin Mary and a few candle stubs, the other held my father's radio.

My father, small, brown, and white-haired, stood at the double-burner stove. He wore tan slacks, brown shoes, and a white shirt. His reading glasses came from Walgreens. He shaved every morning and again before he cooked dinner. On the stove, two pots steamed—one with rice, one with beans. I didn't have to see inside. He ate the same thing every day, except Christmas, my birthday, The Day of the Dead, and Cinco de Mayo. On those days, he made chicken enchiladas with mole sauce that took an entire afternoon to prepare. In the old days, he'd kill the chicken himself from the coop we once kept in the back yard. Nowadays, he bought it prepackaged from the Super Wal-Mart.

"Hi Dad."

He blinked at the pots, a wooden spoon in his hand. He'd stand like that until the food was done.

The ceilings hung low. Growing up, my spine had been flexible enough to stoop around. As an adult, his ceilings were agony. I always tried to time my visits so that I'd arrive as he finished cooking. Otherwise, I'd have to stand there with him for half an hour—his kitchen was too tiny for a chair, as were so many in old Albuquerque casitas—and my neck would pay the price the next day.

"Have a cold beer," my father said. He rarely used Spanish—and had never taught me a word of it—but he spoke with the accent typical of an old Chicano man raised in rural New Mexico.

I got a beer from the fridge. My father never drank.

I leaned my back against the wall, pushing my feet out and slanting my legs to reduce my height as much as possible. By tilting my head against the ceiling, I could almost straighten my spine.

The pots steamed. Two plates sat on the small table opposite the kitchen sink, each holding several tortillas. A jar of homemade salsa, two forks, and a paper napkin sat beside the plates. My father used a pocket-handkerchief to wipe his mouth after he ate. He bought the paper napkins, the beer, and the salsa as special considerations for me.

"You can turn on the radio," my father said.

I went into the living room and flipped the switch. He kept it tuned to an AM station that played Mexican polkas. That tinny accordion music sounded like home to me. A lot of families have stories they tell each other over and over, or old jokes they repeat. My father and I were both men of few words. We had his Mexican polka music.

We ate about fifteen minutes later. He sat in his little green lazy boy and I made do with the big chair he'd bought for me when I was twelve. At that age, I'd been six feet tall. The chair had been comfortable. A year later, I hit my teenage growth spurt. By fifteen, I'd grown a foot. At my high school graduation, the longest gown they had stopped above the knee. My father had never bought a bigger chair. On his custodian's salary, he could barely afford to keep me clothed and fed.

We finished our food. My father extended the footrest of his lazy boy. He crossed his legs at the ankle, and his eyes drooped half-closed. He'd drift off within the next half-hour. I'd do the dishes, put any leftovers in his fridge, and head on home. This was our Thursday routine.

"Little Rex came by," my father said.

"I saw him a couple nights ago."

My father and I sat in our chairs listening to an announcer rattle off rapid-fire Spanish. I couldn't understand a word of it. The next song started up, a ballad, not the usual high-energy polka. A slow-pumped accordion and a woman with a deep voice shared the melody. I couldn't understand the lyrics, but the woman's voice brimmed with sadness.

"What did he want?" I asked.

"He came by to see if I needed any work on my truck."

"And?"

My father shrugged. "I keep it in tip-top shape. He said he'd clean my roof. Take a look at my cooler. Do some weeding. Said he didn't want to do it for money. I told him thanks and gave him a cold beer."

Rex liked my dad. His father had been a bastard.

"I think he comes around here because he's lost." Spanish staged a coup in my father's mouth when he got tired. His vowels rounded out and his consonants drifted toward his old language. "You can tell the way he looks up and down the old street, like he thinks it'll say something to him. Show him what to do with his life."

Rex had waited too long to find meaning in his life. We all had.

My father's blinks got longer and longer. With his feet elevated, his arms on the armrests, and his eyes staring straight up at the ceiling, he looked like a patient in a hospital bed.

My mother had spent the last three years of her life bound to a hospital bed. Her body'd become too fragile for anything else. After my mother's death, my father shipped every one of her things out of the house. I don't know if he sold them, gave them to relatives, or took them to the Goodwill. My seven-year-old self simply saw our house emptying its contents. She'd done all the decorating. She'd hung our drapes and our family photographs. Her rugs and side tables and shelves full of knickknacks had filled our little space. When her things vanished, we ended up with a barren house.

He'd kept it that way. I used to think my father, a simple man, didn't see the need for ornamentation or clutter. He'd been a janitor by trade, after all. Much later, I discovered that my father's blank house matched his state of permanent retreat.

I'd learned that from him. I'd also learned it from the staring, hooting, whistling, gasping, mocking, hollering hordes of normals. I couldn't buy a goddamn grapefruit at the grocery store without it becoming an event.

My father's eyes finally closed and he began to snore. I wondered what having a giant for a wife and a giant for a son had done to him. Asleep, he looked like a cute little old Chicano man who could've been a garrulous jokester, a storyteller, a wise old man that people sought out. Instead, he lived like a hermit. What had we done to him?

I went to the kitchen and did the dishes in his low sink. It took me ten minutes and would give me two hours of back pain. Over the past few years, my joints had plummeted downhill like my mother's. My knees squeaked. My rounds at the zoo of plucking up crickets and dropping them into the enclosures of reptiles, amphibians, and arachnids set my thumb joints on fire. My vertebrae ground like the rusting gears of an old clock. My body was moving toward its first big break.

My mother's brittle bones had started in her early thirties soon after she gave birth to me. At thirty-eight, I was overdue. Once my skeleton started to disintegrate, I knew what life had in store for me: a slow, crumbling death. I'd made a pact with myself. I stored it in a small safe in my closet loaded with hollow-point bullets, and it wouldn't miss.

I had my future planned out.

I spread a knitted blanket over my father before I left.

CHAPTER FOUR

My home below the earth sat in darkness. Ralph slept in his terrarium. The old woman upstairs had retired for the night. Everything was as it should have been.

Until I saw the red light blinking on my answering machine. I never received messages—certainly not more than one every month or two. I sat at my bar and watched the light blink. I didn't like it. My life didn't need blinking lights. It angered me. It ruined my perfect subterranean darkness. My father hadn't left me a phone message. Rex hadn't left it—I'd seen him only two days ago. That left only one possibility.

I opened a beer and drank it all the way down as I thought about the light. My answering machine had a tape. Even if I unplugged the machine, the tape would hold onto that message. The machine might forget the tape had ever been recorded upon, but I would know that the message sat there, imprinted on that magnetic strip. I could erase it.

Or I could listen to it.

I did.

Melodía's husky voice spoke in fragments. "Stick. I need you to come back to the lab. The whooping crane—Dr. Marchette found something. The crane—you won't believe—just come see me tomorrow morning." The tape ran quiet for a few seconds. "It's Melodía. You'll want to see this."

I didn't. I wanted to wake up at dawn and go through my routine. I wanted to set up my coffee machine the night before and let its automated brewing cycle rouse me from sleep. I wanted to sit and sip my first cup while the world turned orange. I wanted to eat toast and a grapefruit and drink a glass of calcium-fortified skim milk in the first quite moments of the day. I wanted to take my calcium and vitamin D supplements on a full stomach and then drive to work. I had a rare blond tarantula there. I was trying to get her to mate. It was difficult. That was the day I'd set out for myself and that was the day I'd earned.

Tumors. I'd had a tumor on my pituitary gland. My mother had one, too, I imagine. She'd never been to a doctor who'd bothered to check. She was too poor. I was too poor until I got my health insurance at the zoo. After a few years of wrangling with my insurance company, I'd hired some doctors to cut it out of me. My growth stopped, though by then I was twenty-five and bumped my head on the sky when I went outside. My doctor said that removing my tumor might save me from the disease that killed my mother. I had no faith he was right.

Melodía's tumors couldn't be removed. They were entwined with her muscles, nerves, and vascular system. Whenever Melodía asked me for something, I said yes.

I kept my own hours at the zoo, which were very regular. I had a routine and I intended to act it out, day after day, until my death. My routine left nothing around the corner. It left no room for my enemy, loneliness, to ambush me. I'd spent my twenties as the loneliest man on Earth. I took long drives around the most depraved parts of Albuquerque and lamented. I sat in my dungeon and wept like a Cyclops with his only eye gouged out. I tore my hair and asked: why? Back then, I believed a God existed to scream questions at. In those days, I realized a good life is a life every moment of which is planned, predictable, and safe.

I didn't break my routine lightly, and I sure as hell wouldn't have done it for anyone besides Melodía.

I showed up at the university around seven the next morning. The campus was sparsely populated. Still, a couple of girls in cargo pants and pixie cuts stopped smoking their clove cigarettes to drop their jaws at me. A skateboarder crashed into a bike rack. I didn't check to see if he was okay.

The door of the biology building was plastered with a poster promoting the Gamut Circus and Freak Show. It featured rearing horses, women in feathered blue sequins, and a girl with lobster hands. I tore it down and balled it up in my fist. I hunched down the sterile hallways of the biology building where I found Melodía in her lab. She stood at a microscope amidst a dozen birds in various stages of dissection. With the right side of her face in profile, she looked like a normal. Her lab looked like the den of a psychopath.

"You should have told me you were coming," she said.

"I'll just leave then." I headed for the door.

"Get in here. You have to see this." She had the white-feathered corpse of the whooping crane stretched out beneath her microscope. It had lost patches of feathers and appeared shriveled. The whole room smelled like a morgue. "Come over and get a look."

"My people don't like formaldehyde," I said. "It reminds them of all the wrongs done to them."

She looked up from the scope. The bulging left side of her face still surprised me after all the years I'd known her. "Your people?"

"Frogs," I said.

She snorted.

"How many frogs have we slaughtered for the sake of biology? And for how many years? Ancestral memory," I said. "They know that smell."

"Get over here."

"I feed them. I help them mate. I look after their tadpoles. They trust me."

"How do you help a frog mate?" she asked.

"I show up smelling like formaldehyde, and they're going to think I'm fattening them up for some classroom of sweating, acne-riddled, pubescent normals."

"You like frogs more than people," she accused.

I grinned.

She stepped away from the microscope.

I bent way down and looked through the lenses. Low magnification centered on a close-up of a wound, similar to the sliced-up flesh she'd shown me when I'd dropped the birds off. This one was bigger than the others riddling the crane's corpse. The wound went deep and had a coating of pus.

"Pus like that," I said. "That's a reaction to a sting."

"That's what Marchette said."

"Short duration, though. Not the kind of pus you see in reaction to an infection or the kind of venom that could kill a bird." I raised my eyes from the microscope and looked at Melodía. "Marchette said that, too, I bet."

She nodded.

I poked around a little bit, increasing and decreasing the magnification. The wound had been scraped. At the bottom, it looked particularly manhandled. "You take some tissue out of here?"

"I removed something I found at the bottom." Melodía looked like someone trying not to betray her excitement.

"What?" I asked.

She motioned to another microscope.

"Use your words," I said. "What did you find?"

She shook her head and motioned at the microscope.

It hurt my back to bend over and peer through the instrument at a single slimy insect egg, a little lopsided, but moist and healthy. It hurt my neck, it hurt my shoulders, and it hurt my feet. I did it anyway, but I wasn't enjoying myself.

"An egg." I straightened, careful to avoid hitting my head. "What's in there?"

"You tell me," Melodía said.

"Marchette already told you," I said.

She shook her head.

"Cut it open," I said.

She stared at me.

"You want me to tell you what I think without being influenced," I said. "I'm not a scientist. I'm not a scientist for good reason. I don't want to be consulted, collaborated with, or recorded for publication or presentation. All I want is to go to my Reptile House. I want to figure out how to tantalize a girl tarantula into meeting a boy tarantula, for her to fall in love, and for them to make beautiful, hairy, eight-legged babies."

She stared at me while making her right eye big and needy. The left one stayed crumpled at the corner and stretched at the bottom. Her tumors had been playing tug of war with it since we were kids.

"That's what I want."

She fluttered her eyelashes.

I sighed. "You've got a bite that looks like it was inflicted by a goliath of a horsefly."

Her mouth spread into a smile as I talked. I could tell that she'd already heard everything I told her. She'd already researched it. She probably had articles from scientific journals on her computer. She had digital photos. Those eyes: they sparkled beautifully with excitement. Beauty and excitement both annoyed me.

"You know all this already."

She stood there.

"The bite's too big for a horsefly," I went on. "Maybe some horseflies got too near the Trinity Site. They're giant mutant horseflies now. They're on the loose. Did you find bites on all of the birds I brought you? Is this a hypothesis for Birdmageddon or am I just entertaining you?"

"This is the only bird with a bite," she said.

"Well," I said. "Good day."

"What else?" She grabbed my elbow as I turned to walk out. Her touch felt good and it was an invasion of my routine. I'd scheduled intimacy with females out of my life. I didn't need any of them touching me and making me feel an emotion.

I pulled away. She noticed. It was awkward and I didn't care. People deserved to feel awkward.

"What else?" I said. "You have mutant horseflies and you want more."

She remained close, her long curly hair smelling of lavender and formaldehyde.

"Horseflies don't sting," I said. "This wound was inflicted by horsefly-like mandibles, but a wasp's sting has penetrated the center. Horseflies also don't lay eggs in birds. They like disgusting piles of horse feces or any other kind of excrement. Brackish water. Rotting vegetation. That's where they lay their eggs. And they lay egg clusters. Scores of eggs. Not a single egg."

She looked up at me, keeping a grip on her excitement. Like every person, she was small and far away.

"Judging from the pus on the walls of the wound," I said, "that bird was alive when stung. Judging from the amount, the venom wasn't lethal. No limb or skin discoloration. Non-lethal venom. I only know one animal that stings prey to stun it then lays a single egg under the flesh of the still-living victim."

She mouthed the name of the animal as I said it.

"The tarantula hawk wasp." It was the New Mexican state insect, a two-inch monster with an excruciating sting.

She finally let the excitement shine out of her. Half her face lit up. The other half stretched and twitched under the casement of tumor. It made me feel emotions.

"Are you saying," I said in a high-pitched mimic of her voice, "that I've discovered a mutant half-tarantula hawk, half-horsefly? A hematophage and a hymenoptera?" I switched back to my own voice. "No, I'm just a simple zookeeper."

"Marchette is very interested," Melodía said.

"I'm sure he is. I'll bet he'd take that egg off your hands for big bucks."

She smacked my arm. "I'm a scientist. It's not for sale."

"You're going to hatch it."

"You bet I'm going to hatch it," she said.

"That should be either very science fiction, or very horror movie," I said. "Either way, I'm sure you'll have your hands full."

She smiled her most charming smile and cocked her head to emphasize her good side, flipping coils of dark hair from one side of her head to the other. Her nose crinkled and her eyelashes did something charming.

I groaned.

"I need two things from you," she said.

"Of course you do."

"Pretty please?"

"Out with it!" I may have bellowed it too loud. I meant it to be a playful bellow, but Melodía's expression lost its glee.

Her gaze flicked over my face. "Two things."

I tried to look kind. I didn't have much practice at it.

"One. Incubate this egg for me."

That would be tough. I would have to simulate the warmth of a living being. I would have to monitor the pupa within the egg and provide it with proper nutrition when it hatched. If it was, indeed, the egg of a tarantula hawk, the larva would need a lot of sustenance. Tarantula hawks implant their eggs in living tarantulas. When the larvae hatch, they burrow into the body of their host, devouring flesh and organs until they mature into full-grown wasps. The tarantula was a cocoon of sustenance that sheltered the wasp until it metamorphosed. It was like the caterpillar-butterfly thing, only from your worst nightmares. Taking care of this egg and whatever emerged would be a challenge for any caretaker.

"Okay."

"Two," Melodía said. "Go back to the Bosque."

"No way. All the birds are dead. Nothing to see."

"You need to find the creature that laid this egg."

It was probably just a big coincidence. An abnormally large horsefly bites a nearly extinct whooping crane and drinks its blood. A tarantula hawk wasp stings the bird through the incision that the horsefly cut into the bird's flesh. The wasp mistakes a five-foot white-feathered wading bird for an eight-legged arachnid. It implants its egg and flies off. Then, in a freak lightning storm, wind-swell, missile test, radiation surge, alien experiment, or stroke of God, the bird participates in a mass death. The laws of probability stated that even the most unlikely series of events happen.

I shrugged.

"Can you go today?" she asked.

I shrugged again. I could buy a coffee on the way. I could listen to my Tom Waits CD. I'd be back by noon. My tarantulas only mated at night, anyway.

"You'll do it!" she said.

"Can you hold onto the egg until I get back?"

She smiled like a kid who'd forgotten all the evils of the world for a few precious seconds.

A question distracted me as I walked back out into the land of gawking hipster girls and fragile skater boys. How do you track a horsefly?

I walked through the university parking lot. A campus security vehicle rolled past. The two pale normals inside showed me their tonsils. A young couple on the sidewalk froze in their tracks. A scattering of solitary walkers craned their necks over their shoulders. The whole city contorted its body to get an eyeful, except for one person: a small man sitting on a bench not thirty feet away reading a newspaper. He didn't even look up. I wanted to salute him. Instead, I gave the security guards one of my evil giant glowers and got into my truck.

An hour later, I turned off at the exit for the Bosque Del Apache and drove around the marsh loop to the spot where the average man—my brain had already erased his name—had led me to the whooping crane. The sanctuary was nearly deserted, except for a couple of park ranger vehicles. The dead birds had been cleared away. The water in the center shone like blown glass. A casual observer would have said that the most fertile land in New Mexico was going to waste, that it was a damn shame, that they hoped new flocks of birds would come back to populate the place.

I would never say that. Birds occupy the top of the food pyramid. The lower tiers of that pyramid teem with fathomless numbers of beings. Those tiers were throwing a party. Fewer monsters were trying to eat them. The crayfish, the frogs, the dragonflies; the wasps, the garter snakes, the blue-tailed lizards; the slivery minnows, the earthworms, the whiptail lizards—all of them were probably beginning to realize that they could poke their heads out without being devoured.

I was after one of those little creatures. Humanity was the worst monster in the world. I was a monster among men, and I had ways of catching my quarry.

The usual method for taking a biological sample of flying insects is to set traps. Netting. Sticky traps. You can bait either one with scents that attract the insect you're after. You can get the males by baiting your traps with the pheromones of females and sometimes vice-versa, depending on the insect. You can bait your traps with live bait. That works well for wolf spiders and some types of ants. For web-dwelling spiders, you go find their web. The spider will be lurking nearby. The same goes for any other trap-dwelling insect. For hematophagous insects, you bait your traps with fresh blood. For pollen-collecting insects, you bait with pollen or set traps near food sources. Insects and their cousins, the arachnids, are the most successful beings on the planet. You can kill a thousand and know that they've already laid ten-thousand eggs to replace themselves. So, you catch them dead. That's just how it is. Especially flying insects. Taking a sample of a population of flying insects is a euphemism for murdering a representative number and studying it.

I wasn't equipped with bait, traps, or any other murderous gear. It would have taken me a week to set it all up, a week longer to gather specimens, and a month to sort through them all. Never mind the permitting doing so in a national wildlife refuge would require. For some reason, I'd volunteered to come down here anyway. My blinders came on when I was with Melodía.

Still, there were ways.

I sorted them out in my head as I pulled onto the shoulder of the road near where I'd found the whooping crane and where a woman now poked around in the bushes. She wore a tan button-up top and high-waisted khaki slacks with the cuffs tucked into her knee-high rubber boots, coated in fresh mud. Her safari hat had one side snapped up, and a strap dangled beneath her chin. Her straight black hair hung in a ponytail. The insignia on her rain slicker told me she worked for US Fish and Wildlife.

I pulled onto the road, figuring I'd come back later. But she'd spotted me. When she saw me leaving, she dashed through the brush, and leapt in front of my truck like a jaguar cornering prey.

"I know you!" she yelled. She had dark skin, dramatic cheekbones, and a complexion that looked airbrushed. Her eyes sparkled like black suns. Her body curved and tapered in the proportions TV said we should value. She could have been a model for safari wear. I'd never seen her before—I would have remembered meeting a new person.

"I recognize your license plate!" She recited the digits, as if that should have impressed me.

I honked at her.

Before I could do anything about it, the woman clambered on top of my hood. Sitting back on her heels, she slipped a business card under my windshield wiper, facing inward. It read: *Tanis Rivera, Animal Theologian.*

She bounced to the ground, circled to the driver's side door, and rapped on my window. I slapped my zoo ID against the glass.

"I already know it's you, John Stick." She stood on her tiptoes hollering up at the crack in the window. She wore a grin that was half little kid and half carnivore. "Come out. I have a paradox for you."

"I don't believe in paradoxes." I left the window where it was.

"Open up anyway. It's part of your destiny to talk to me about the universe."

"I'm not impressed by the universe," I said. "It's a death machine."

"You're already exceeding my expectations of you, which were high. Come out. We need to talk."

I could have waited her out. I'd waited out society for going on forty years. I was good at waiting. But I also had a job to get to back in Albuquerque. I swung my door open and stepped onto the hard winter soil. The woman took a few big steps back, as if retreating from a dinosaur that might trample her.

"You"—she looked me up and down—"you're no disappointment."

I started to get back in the truck.

"No!" She held up both palms. "Don't go! We have a mystery to solve."

I paused with the door halfway open. "I'm not a detective."

"Yet here you are up to your knees in a mystery," she said. "Mysteries are like quicksand. Once you sink past your knees, there's no going back."

"I guess I should lift my feet and walk away."

"You could," she said, "but you won't."

"The only mystery I care about is how you know who I am."

"I saw you yesterday, and I said to myself, 'that man is part of this mystery.' "

"You're wrong," I said. "I'm doing a favor for a friend."

"No, *you're* wrong!" she yelled and poked my sternum. Human beings didn't touch me very often. Every now and then, an amphibian excreted defensive fluids through its skin onto me. I'd been bitten by several species of snake. The week before, an iguana had licked me for mysterious reasons. But people usually steered clear. Tanis Rivera's finger on my chest—it troubled me. I didn't like the way it made me feel.

"You're the most remarkable human I've ever met and this is the most remarkable event I've ever witnessed—even if only after the fact. There's a rule in detective work: when two events happen simultaneously regarding the same object of interest, we must pay strict attention."

"I'm not an event," I said. "I'm a guy with a plastic bag."

"You're modest. It's cute. I would pinch your cheeks if I could reach them." She pinched the air between us instead and made a cutesy face. "Two people meeting is an event."

"We haven't met yet."

She stuck out her gloved and muddy hand. I ignored it. She pulled the glove off and whacked it against her thigh, throwing mud everywhere. She stuck her bare hand out. I ignored it.

"Tanis Rivera." The woman mimed a handshake in the air. "I'm so pleased to meet you—now tell me everything about yourself!"

"I'm in a hurry," I said.

"I'll tell you a little about myself to break the ice." Tanis Rivera ticked off the fingers of her non-gloved hand with the muddy digits of her other hand. "I'm an animal theologian. I like ice cream. My dad was a seer and my mom was a truck driver. I have a doctorate from Harvard Divinity. My favorite color is vacuum."

I stared at her. I probably wore the same expression people did when they saw me for the first time.

"And I'm here to figure out why twenty thousand five hundred and sixty eight birds died for no reason at the same instant. And counting." She smiled, showing perfect straight white teeth. The wider she smiled, the more her eyes sparkled, and the more the world twinkled with goodness. She was the most beautiful person I'd ever talked to. I just wanted it to be over.

She held out a hand. "Now you."

"I'm a zookeeper," I said. "And I'm late for work."

"But this is your work. You are here to solve this great theological mystery."

"This mystery isn't theological," I said. "Animals die all the time. Didn't your mom tell you about dog heaven when you were little?"

She kicked me in the shin. "Of course it's theological! It's either random—they all happened to die at exactly the same time—or there is a single agent behind their deaths. Similarly, either you, one of the most unique beings on the earth, have also come here by pure chance, or there is some design behind your presence. Of course, the laws of probability state that anything can and will happen, however unlikely. But, given the nature of reality, it's very hard to tell chance from purpose. Distinguishing the difference and proving it—that's my job."

"Sounds like a tough job," I said. "I hope the money's good."

"Worldly riches are for moneylenders. I'll let the Lord handle them."

"So you're trying to figure out if God or chance killed the birds. Seems to me like you're missing the most likely culprit of all."

She nodded vigorously. "That's the obvious choice. Humans did it. But humans are a small part of a big question. Why do humans do what they do?

Are we part of chance or design? Is the universe, and thus humanity, fundamentally chaotic or fundamentally orderly? Is there a God or not? Is there good and evil? If the universe is fundamentally chaotic, implying that there is no God behind it all, does that mean that good and evil do not exist? Maybe this mass death is just a symptom of a chaotic, senseless universe with no rules and no purpose—a system that organizes itself by happenstance without a God-skipper at the helm. Maybe humans are just animals born of this chaos."

"All I can tell you is that behind every bad thing that happens on this earth, there is a white guy raking in a lot of money."

"A cynic," she said. "Of course, we know humans are selfish and bad. My primary investigative focus is this: Are animals also selfish and bad? Can animals commit acts of evil? If there is a God, then animals should be part of the moral design; if not, then animals are just part of the chaos. If we figure out whether animals are part of God's moral compass, we can figure out if God exists."

"You think an animal did this?" I asked.

"No, but animals are involved, so here I am."

I didn't like the idea of dragging animals into our moral rationalizing, but I didn't tell Tanis Rivera. Saying words to her was like poking fingers through a dam. But I felt I had to say something. "Things die. Whales beach themselves. Lemmings throw themselves off cliffs. Dinosaurs burn to death in lava flows. There's plenty of life on this planet to go around—and it'll keep on killing and dying until the sun blows up."

Her exuberance had gone behind a cloud. "Talking to you is no fun."

"I'm not here to have fun," I said. "And I'm not here to figure out if God exists."

"Then why are you here?" Tanis asked.

"I'm an errand boy."

"And what are you here to fetch?"

"A wasp. A crane I collected had some bites."

"A bug bite." Tanis crossed her arms over her Fish and Wildlife windbreaker. "That's what you're focusing on."

I shrugged. "You have to follow every lead."

"Ha!" Tanis rammed her finger into my sternum again. "You admit it! You're hooked! You're a part of this mystery just like me."

"Fine. You win. Can I do my job now?"

"Give me your phone number first," she said.

"Look it up."

"You're unlisted," she said. "I already checked."

"Call the zoo."

She smiled. Her teeth were too white and too straight. "I don't believe in coincidence."

I stepped around her. "I hope you have the evidence to back that up."

"I'm still in the data gathering stage," she hollered at my back. "It could go on for a very long time."

"Well, good luck." I walked into the forest. She didn't say anything else, but I felt her eyes on me until I was well into the trees.

Once I'd moved considerably away from her, I returned to the problem at hand: tracking and trapping a flying insect. I knew ways around using traditional trapping equipment. Many traps are built into nature.

I started for the line where the woods met the marsh. Along that line, I checked every spider web in the lower branches of trees, woven into stands of shrub, or between two rocks. The Bosque is temperate in winter, meaning that the bug population remains somewhat active. I inspected mosquitoes, a dozen species of fly, a few wasps and bees, a dragonfly that had collapsed half a web, and galaxies of gnats suspended in silver threads—nothing I hadn't seen before. I retraced my path at the water's edge, examining the gummy amalgamation of algae, vegetation, and mud that builds up at the edge of a healthy marsh. All sorts of insects had mired themselves there, but again, nothing unusual. Few horseflies. No tarantula hawks whatsoever. It wasn't a surprise. Tarantula hawks lived in the desert where their prey, tarantulas, were plentiful.

As I tramped through the last few yards of muck, I nearly stepped on a bullfrog the size of a cat. It lay on its back, bloated, the tongue hanging out, the eyes bulging from their sockets. All signs of a painful death.

Nature's traps: spider webs, bog-muck, an early freeze, even a heavy rainfall. All of these things could kill and collect specimens for a scientist. If these failed, nature provided you with an alternative: the stomach of every living animal. You want a specimen? Find out what eats the thing you're looking for, kill or capture that, and take a look in its belly.

I crouched. The air near the ground was cold and moist, shaded by the grasses that ringed the marsh. The frog's abdomen was taut with pent-up gasses, its limbs stiff. It stank of rotting death. I examined it for wasp stings, snake or spider bites. I flipped it over. The flesh of the frog's back was mucky with the early stages of decay. I had to turn my face away until I became accustomed to the stench. No abrasions on either side.

The frog looked like it had died from envenomation. I could have been wrong. Maybe it was disease or stress. Maybe it had died of the same mystery that had killed those thousand birds. Either way, it was the closest thing I had to a lead.

I took a sample bag from my backpack and slid the frog inside and strode back to my truck on a path that kept me concealed in the woods as long as possible. Normally, the woods would have been filled with the warbling of a thousand geese. Now, the trees stood silent. The wind scraped a few branches together and rustled some grass. Traffic droned on the interstate, far away. It would take decades for the bird levels to recover. Knowledge of wintering grounds passed ancestrally, parent to hatchling.

I made it back to my truck without anyone accosting me. It was not normal for people to talk to me. Usually, they stared. A baby might cry. A kindergartener might ask his mommy what I was. An old person might pronounce the name of God. But that was it. Tanis Rivera was an exception. I didn't see her either.

In the parking lot near the marsh observation deck, a middle-aged Chicano man sat in the driver's seat of a dark sedan reading a newspaper with a fedora on his head, a beard on his face, and spectacles over her eyes. He was the same man I'd seen reading a newspaper at the University. He stood out because he'd ignored me.

I drove on by. I got on the freeway and motored toward my city. After a few miles, a dark sedan eased into my rearview mirror. It held a distance of a quarter mile or so, but it was the same car. I tested it by slowing down and speeding up. It lingered far back, barely within sight.

No doubt about it. Someone was following me.

CHAPTER FIVE

had no idea how to react to being followed. I considered faking a
flat tire and hoping he'd pass me. A private detective in the movies would
probably lose his pursuer in a parking garage, trick them into driving over
one of those spiked barriers, or simply burn rubber and outrun them. I
wasn't a hero.

I drove to the zoo. In the parking lot, I smacked myself in the forehead for
not going straight to Melodía's. The man with the newspaper already knew I'd
been there. I sat in my truck and considered driving to her lab right then to
deliver the bullfrog and pick up the egg she wanted incubated. It would be
pointless. My pursuer already knew I visited the zoo. Maybe he knew before
any of this. Maybe he'd been following me for days—or longer—although his
motive was beyond me. Maybe he was doing a study on boredom.

Trying to be subtle about it, I got out of my truck and looked over the tops
of all the cars in the parking lot. I spotted the dark sedan with the telltale
rectangle of newspaper a few rows away. I thought about approaching it. I
thought about calling security. I thought about just going to work and hoping
it was all a coincidence—chaos, like Tanis Rivera had talked about.

As I stood there thinking, the man folded up his newspaper, started his
engine, and drove away. I stared after him until a school bus rounded a corner,
heading toward the zoo. Since the last thing I needed was a bus full of children
dropping their jaws at me, I grabbed the frog and made for the employee
entrance door to the back corridors that led to the Reptile House.

Marchette was in the front room. It was, again, not his day to be there.

"Mr. Stick!" he said. "Have you brought me a present?"

I brushed by him, retreating to the farthest of four rooms in the back area of the House. I'd staked that one out as my own, where no one would talk to me.

"Tally-ho!" he said at my back.

Some days I hated Simon Marchette.

Another of my coworkers was in the feed storage room. I walked by her and through the door into my lab, put my frog-bag into one of the large refrigerators, and hung my jacket on a peg.

My day should have been about two tarantulas: a blond female and a dark male. Tarantulas have a mating ritual that is highly contingent on geography. They mate only at night. The female stays below ground, feasting on whatever victim she's poisoned and dragged into her den. The male, come sundown, leaves his burrow and treks across the land. He can range up to a mile or more. He searches for the burrows of other spiders. The female can feel vibrations through the walls of her den. Anything that moves across the ground—she senses it. She can tell what kind of being it is, whether it's prey to be hunted or predator to be evaded. And when that distinct eight-legged creep comes tapping along, she knows it's a suitor.

Replicating that ritual in captivity was a challenge. My blonde tarantula's two-by-three-foot terrarium had no room for a trek. And since the male and female had to live separately—females tend to kill males they don't care for—one has to choose one's moment to place the male in the terrarium. The female must be well fed, but not be in possession of a corpse she's currently eating. The female must not be in a state of stress—which I'm sad to say is often the case at the zoo, where children yell and tap on the glass. The male must also be stress-free, or he'll hide in a corner of the female's terrarium instead of creeping around in exploration. Finally, there's that incalculable factor: love. When the female hears the male's legs tiptoeing around on her roof, she sticks her head out. If she likes him, she'll hover there, egging him on. If she doesn't like him, she'll retreat into her den. Often the male, enticed by the sight of her head, will venture to the mouth of the burrow. If the female doesn't like him, she'll spin a web in his face, barring him from entrance. If he tries to get through, she'll leap out and sink her fangs into his neck.

Then you have to find a new male.

I didn't like losing a spider. I was close with my spiders. I kept several males in non-display terrariums, all of which had gotten used to me and would quite happily sit on my shoulder or my knee while I worked. This meant that they didn't feel stressed when I transferred them from their terrariums to the female's. It also meant that I didn't want her to murder them.

I'd solved a few problems with getting my tarantulas to mate in captivity. The males trusted me. My female felt safe in her den. The design of the Reptile House allowed me to manipulate day and night. So, I didn't have to stay up all night to facilitate the mating process—an unacceptable break in my routine. Still, the blonde I was working with had exhibited only threatening behavior. I'd been forced to rescue every male I'd put in with her. Usually, they didn't even try: they took one look at her fangs and aggressive posture and cowered in a corner.

Lately, I'd been trying a new tactic: I'd place a cap over the mouth of the female's burrow. Then I'd put the male spider in her terrarium and let him walk around for a while. I thought that a few weeks of hearing the erotic tapping of male feet on her roof might tantalize and tease her to the point where she'd be desperate for a mate. Then, one day, when I left the cap off and lowered a male into her cage, she'd welcome him in.

I was getting all set for day three of my plan when the phone rang.

I ignored it.

A few moments later, Marchette walked into my lab. "Mr. Stick, you have a telephone call from, I surmise based on the vocal qualities of the speaker, Dr. Melodía Hernandez."

I growled. Several of the creatures in the non-display terrariums lining the walls twitched. Marchette shrank back a little, too.

"Stick," she said once I'd picked up my extension, "did you go to the Bosque?"

"I'm busy," I said.

"Did you find anything?"

"I found that I'd run down my gas tank."

"The University will reimburse you," she said. "Come to my lab and tell me what you saw."

"I have a couple hundred living animals here that rely on me to keep them alive. I can't just take the day off whenever you say so."

"You also need to pick up that egg and incubate it for me."

I growled again. The creatures arrayed around the room scampered for shelter. Marchette still hovered nearby, peering into the terrarium of my giant forest scorpion, a jet-black creature I'd acquired recently from Phoenix. I wanted the little scientist to leave.

"Stick," Melodía said, "I need you." Her voice broke. It made me feel emotions. This was probably a big deal for her. If she could figure out why all those birds had died in mid-air, her work might get real press. She'd publish in major journals.

Imagine you are an outcast. When you step out into the daylight, people stare. They are disgusted. They take sidelong glances at your face, but won't meet your eyes. Children ask their mommies what is wrong with you. You develop deep-seated trauma about it. You structure your life around avoiding people—their stares and their gasps and their whispers—at any cost. This means that there's no one you can rely on. Since you have few personal relationships—no lover, no children, one or two friends—you throw yourself into your work. It becomes your life. Then, one day you have a big opportunity that could make your career. It could catapult you into that next tier of achievement. The one thing standing in your way: it involves stepping out into that damned daylight.

I sighed. "I'll be over in a couple hours."

"Thank you," she said.

I hung up. I took my canvas cricket bag down from its hook and filled it with crickets. I bred them by the thousands and kept them in a cooled terrarium so they'd be sluggish. That way, they were easy to scoop into my cricket bag, but would liven up by the time I dropped them into the terrarium of whatever lizard, serpent, amphibian, or larger arthropod was going to eat them. I dispersed my bag of crickets and distributed some marsh flies. I checked to make sure everyone was alive. I fished out a few socks of shed scales. Most of the larger reptiles only ate once a week or so. They'd be fine if I stepped out for the afternoon.

As I leaned through the panel into the caiman lagoon, Marchette cleared his throat behind me. I turned and looked down at him.

"Excuse me, Mr. Stick?"

"Just Stick."

"Ah-hem. Stick." He pushed his glasses higher on the bridge of his nose. "I couldn't help but notice that you brought in a specimen with you this morning."

I closed the panel and faced him.

"Would you mind, you know, satisfying a fellow scientist's curiosity?"

"I'm not a scientist," I said.

He laughed. "Come, come. You know more about these creatures than anyone."

"That bag I brought in this morning isn't mine," I said. "It belongs to a friend."

"Ah-ha! Is Dr. Hernandez that friend?"

"I thought you were a bug guy? Since when do you care about frogs?"

He shifted from one foot to the other. "My guess is that any scientist in the state would be interested in Dr. Hernandez's work right now. She has a real mystery on her hands."

"I wouldn't know anything about that."

His face split from ear to ear in a smile a clam would have respected. "I see. Well, no matter! Ta-ta!"

I walked away. I should've just shown Marchette my bloated dead bullfrog. He was a good man. He kept a close eye on my insects. I didn't show it to him because it was a Friday. He wasn't supposed to be there on Fridays.

Then again, neither was the frog, which I retrieved from the refrigerator. I put on my jacket and made my way through the alleys behind the walls and buildings of the zoo, which I shouldn't have been doing either. These were normal zoo hours. In the parking lot, people were everywhere. It was as if a moose had gotten loose. Everyone stopped what they were doing and stared. It took eternity to get to my truck. Someone snapped a picture. I fumbled my keys and forgot to engage the clutch when I tried to start it, grinding a gear and almost killing the engine.

By the time I escaped onto the main roads, my face was hot. People always stared at me in the parking lot. Normally when I came and went, it was nearly empty. I could usually blow off the few who were present, but not this time. I shouldn't have been out there. It was not my routine. I wanted a drink, or better yet, a bar fight—I'd once ground out my anger in the dive bars of Albuquerque. I'd found my Zen place since then, or at least I thought I had.

I didn't drive to the university. It was one o'clock on a weekday and the place would be obscene with humans. Instead, I drove home. I entered my cool, dark space, closing and locking the door behind me. Ralph sat motionless in his terrarium. His calm bled into me. When I felt a little better, I picked up the phone and dialed Melodía's number.

"Dr. Hernandez," she answered.

"Your frog is in my refrigerator."

"My frog?"

"The result of my trip to the Bosque Del Apache," I said. "You may pick it up at your convenience."

"At the zoo?"

"At my home," I said. "I've gone home for the day."

She exhaled into the receiver. "Okay. I'll bring the egg—"

"Keep your egg," I said. "I don't want it."

"But you have to incubate it."

"Incubate it yourself," I said. "I've got my own eggs to look after."

The line went quiet. Across the room, Ralph tiptoed around in his terrarium. I'd woken him from his daylong slumber. Another link in the routine broken.

"Okay, I'll come by after work," Melodía said. "And Stick?"

I waited.

"Thank you."

"I'll see you tonight."

I stayed in my apartment the rest of the day, slow-cooking some beans for me and releasing a couple of small beetles into the living room for Ralph to hunt. I settled down in front of a documentary on Australian monitor lizards that I'd seen a half-dozen times.

A dead frog cooled its heels in my fridge. It was sealed up in several plastic bags, but the gasses released by the body during decomposition would swell those bags and potentially burst them. Then I'd have a fridge full of rotten frog. Still, I wasn't in a rush to see Melodía—or anybody. I'd had enough interruptions in my life.

The frog wasn't even a lead. I should have thrown it out. It was just a dead frog. It had probably died of disease or been bitten on the inside of the mouth by a spider. The bites on the whooping crane weren't a lead. The mysterious egg inside the whooping crane wasn't a lead. To be at all causally related to the death of thousands of birds, the bites and the egg would have to be common to all the birds. They weren't. Simple science. Case closed.

I tried to stop thinking about the dead birds.

Instead, I thought about Australian monitor lizards. They ate mammals, birds, eggs, other lizards, and insects. They loved carrion—my dead frog would entice one from a mile away. They climbed trees. They were good swimmers. I had a spiny-tailed monitor at the zoo. However, I'd always coveted the lace monitor, a dark-scaled creature which could exceed two yards in length. The lace monitor had been known to take down young kangaroos. It was a glorious desert monster. I wondered if Australia looked like New Mexico. I'd never get there to find out.

A car door slammed up at ground level where the normals lived. Melodía descended the steps outside and knocked.

"Enter," I yelled.

Her burgundy top hung loose at the neck and wrists, and her black slacks were wrinkled. Her curly hair was frizzy at the ends and flattened in the back. A bag hung under her darkened right eye and the small veins and arteries laced through the tumors stood taut below her skin. Her brown complexion had gone gray.

"You need rest." I didn't get up from my couch.

She sat on my love seat. "No time. Too many tests to run."

"Found anything?" I asked.

She shook her head, put her elbows on her knees, and dropped her brow into her palms. "What did you find at the Bosque?"

I shrugged. "I found a dead bullfrog. It's probably nothing, but I couldn't find any outward causes of death. Thought it might be related to the bird incident. If whatever killed your birds also killed an amphibian, it might narrow things down."

"Or broaden them." She groaned. "Where is it?"

I jerked my thumb at the refrigerator. I thought about telling her I'd been followed, but figured she had enough on her mind.

Melodía didn't get up. "What are you watching?"

"Documentary on goannas."

"What are those?" she asked.

"Australian monitor lizards."

She opened her mouth at the same instant the phone rang. The image of a toothy gray dragon clinging to a tree remained frozen on my TV screen. The phone rang again.

"Aren't you going to answer that?" Melodía asked.

"Absolutely not. I'm not even convinced the sound of the phone is real. You're here. You're the only one who calls me. Therefore, the phone is not ringing."

"You forgot to account for entropy," Melodía said. "The second law of thermodynamics. Nothing is static."

The machine picked up. It took me a minute to recognize the voice speaking uninvited into my apartment.

"I presume this is the residence of Mr. John Stick, employee of the Rio Grande Zoo," said Tanis Rivera. "I realize that I'm crossing a boundary of decorum by calling you at home after you refused to give me your telephone number. However, I feel a great urge to speak with you."

Melodía lifted her head from her hands and looked at me. Her pupils became hard and small. The arteries in her left eye burned red.

"I would like to share information with you," Tanis said. "I'll give you my insights, you'll give me yours. We're investigating the same mystery, though we approach it from different angles. I feel that we would benefit from working as a team." Her voice paused. "Please contact me. You have my card." She left her phone number for good measure and hung up.

The apartment fell silent.

"You met a woman," Melodía said, her voice flat.

"She's not a woman," I said. "She's a crazy person who accosted me at the Bosque. She thinks I'm a metaphysical detective."

Melodía snorted. "You're ridiculous. If you have a date, you can just tell me."

"This woman thinks I can help her unlock the secret of the universe."

"So, you admit she's a woman?"

"She's a fanatic. She believes animals conform to human codes of morality. Tree frogs are good. Tiger sharks are evil."

"I'd be happy for you," Melodía said, "if you had a date."

"Animal theologian. That's what her business card read."

"I'd cheer you on, is all I'm saying." Melodía held an imaginary glass in the air. "I'd buy you a drink and propose a toast."

"Is that your way of hinting that you want a beer?" I asked.

"God yes."

I retrieved two bottles from the fridge. They sweat into my palms. Melodía took a third of hers down before I could even sit. She heaved a deep sigh. Her eyelids fell like heavy curtains, and lifting them again looked like a Herculean labor. She smiled one of those gentle, genuine smiles that occupy people's faces when their guard is down, like a squatter taking over a vulnerable house. "You could have answered the phone."

"I couldn't have."

"I wouldn't have minded. I don't want you to miss out on a date just because I'm here."

"I don't have a date," I said. "That Tanis Rivera—I'm telling you—she's just a lunatic who only wants to talk to me because I'm a giant."

Melodía woke up. Her eyes got fierce and her mouth tightened. A hint of tooth gleamed at the stiff part of her mouth. "You shouldn't talk to people who are only interested in you because of that."

"I know."

"You're a great person, Stick. You don't need anybody thinking of you that way."

"Why do think I didn't answer the phone?" I said.

"Do you want me to call her and tell her to leave you alone?"

I held up a hand. I didn't have the heart to remind Melodía that Tanis had only run across me because I'd gone to the Bosque on her orders. I wasn't used to disclosing every little detail of my life to other people, so it was easy for me to hide things. When you say little, nobody notices when you're clamming up on purpose.

Once Melodía's work ethic had flushed her, along with one dead bullfrog, from my place, and I'd enjoyed a night of sleep on a clear conscience, I settled back into my routine. I'd rid myself of the frog. I'd fended off the responsibility of incubating a mysterious insect egg. I'd ignored the phone call from Tanis. The world had tried to get a bite out of me, but it had failed.

Four days went by. No one followed me, at least as far as I noticed. No one called. I consorted solely with animals that didn't have the complex brain functions to coax, ogle, or philosophize.

Tuesday came around again and found me reading a book about ants. Ants adhered to hierarchies. Some went to work. Others went to war. A select few queens lorded over the rest. Americans were supposed to be the opposite of ants: every individual took care only of itself, society be damned. Our system worked like gangbusters—the talking heads told us so every day.

I was deep into drone culture when Rex's truck roared up. The clock read shy of six in the evening. Two doors opened and slammed. A flap-footed tread accompanied the clomp of Rex's jackboots. That tread belonged to Flowers the Clown. Rex and I had known Leon Flowers since elementary school. Back then, he'd been a chubby, apple-cheeked kid. He'd been sweet and quiet. He'd been picked on mercilessly. As a fellow outcast, Flowers had become the third wheel of our friendship, always on the outside. I felt the kind of pity for him that only lasts until you see the object of your pity face-to-face—then they remind you how irritating they are.

Another car purred up. It sounded like it parked right behind Rex's truck. A car door opened and shut. Feet shuffled around and voices murmured. I couldn't quite catch what they were saying. Three pairs of footsteps marched down my stairs and crossed my patio, and Rex's fist hammered on my door.

I considered pretending not to be home. Strangers never visited me. My door was very difficult to find. It was not visible from street level. You had to venture into my vestibule of creepies, crawlies, and buzzies to get to it, by design. I did not want to meet this mysterious third person.

"Stick!" It was not in Rex's nature to be ignored.

I placed a section of snakeskin on the page I was reading and closed the book. Snakeskin made a beautiful bookmark. Every time a snake at my zoo molted, the snake got a fresh, sleek look, and I got a new bookmark. It was what you might call a win-win.

I opened the door. Rex was dressed as usual: jackboots, camo pants, heavy metal band t-shirt, leather jacket. That night he wore a baseball cap that cast a shadow over his deep-set eyes all the way down to his mustache. Flowers stood behind him in street clothes—dungarees, canvas jacket, and a button-up shirt with one button missing over his protruding belly—except for the orange clown shoes on his feet. He was pale-skinned, red-cheeked, with small eyes and a childish smile. He had a way about him that made me want to wrap my fingers through his hair and lift him up on his toes.

A white, middle-aged, short, bulky man with beefy forearms and very little hair accompanied them. He wore khaki on his legs and crow's feet around his eyes.

"Stick," Rex said, "meet the Captain. Captain, meet Stick."

The Captain's gray eyes bulged slightly out of their sockets. "Holy Toledo." He put the back of his hand against his forehead, as if checking himself for a fever. "You boys weren't kidding."

I gave the Captain one of my unfriendly giant glares.

The Captain stuck out his hand. "Mr. Stick. Pleasure's mine."

I looked at Rex. "I'm not calling him Captain."

The Captain laughed one of those good-old-boy laughs. "That's just a little nickname the men use. Call me Bruce." He stuck out his hand a little farther.

I ignored it. I wondered if I could have picked him up, carried him out my front door, and pitched him all the way to the bed of Rex's truck. He looked heavy, but my ire was riding pretty high.

Rex grinned at me. "Can we come in?"

Flowers hoisted a 30-pack of Budweiser cans above his head like an Olympic champion hefting a barbell. "We brought beverages!"

I groaned and stood aside.

It was like a parade. One body after another. By the time all three men had marched past, I felt like it would take a miracle to ever get my peace and quiet back. Rex leapt atop a bar stool and put his elbows on the wood. The Captain climbed onto the one beside him, one haunch at a time. Flowers threw open the refrigerator door and tried to jam the huge case of beer inside.

I didn't grab Flowers by the hair. I brushed him aside as gently as my temper would let me and took control of the beer. He hovered at my elbow, grinning like the Cheshire cat until I gave him three cans and explicit instructions to distribute them. I removed the case from the cavity it had violated in my orderly refrigerator and put the cans in a cooler covered in ice. After refilling the ice trays, I took out a beer.

The pinching sound that cut through my apartment as I popped the tab relaxed me a little. The icy first splash on my tongue helped a little more.

The three men chatted at my bar. They looked up when I turned to them.

"So, why do they call you Captain?" I tried not to growl out the words.

The Captain chuckled.

"It's not 'cause he owns a boat!" Flowers cackled and punched the older man's shoulder, not even moving him. The Captain may have been portly, but he was solid.

"He's with the Minutemen," Rex said. "He's hiring us."

The Captain held up his hands. "I recommended you. The Minutemen are volunteers. We don't hire anybody. Typhon Industries is hiring you."

"C'mon!" Flowers said. "That's the same thing in my book."

"Don't be modest," Rex said.

The Captain had his face turned down toward his beer. On his left, Flowers fawned over him; on his right, Rex beamed fiercely from beneath the bill of his cap. I felt sorry for the poor guy, even though he seemed like he was having a decent time.

"The Minutemen are volunteers," The Captain said to me. "These boys were hired by a private company that subcontracts with the government to patrol the border."

"Secret experimental surveillance technology and what-not," Rex said.

"We're riding shotgun," Flowers said. "For deployment. We're the hired military experts."

"When's your start date?" I asked, mostly to be cruel. I could tell by the way they were talking that any employment remained purely hypothetical. Once Rex actually started a job, he lost all enthusiasm for it.

"Soon's we get all the details ironed out," Flowers shot back.

"What did you do for the army again?" I asked, even though I knew perfectly well. Flowers and Rex had been glorified garbage men, driving trucks all over Kuwait and Southern Iraq during the Gulf War collecting American scrap.

"Stick here," Rex said to the Captain, "is an animal expert."

The Captain tilted his head up at me. The back of his thick neck bunched into folds, like a tortoise trying to find the moon. "That right?"

"That," I said, "is not right."

"He's a zoologist," Rex said.

"Zookeeper," I said.

"Goddamned expert in insects, spiders, snakes—all kinds of reptiles and poisonous monsters," Rex said. "The craziest fucking things. Stick knows 'em all."

The Captain raised his eyebrows. "You know desert animals?"

I stared at him.

"Stick knows everything in this desert and every other desert," Rex said.

"We could use a man knows the deserts of New Mexico." The Captain shrugged.

"Stick *is* the deserts of New Mexico," Flowers said.

"Stick"—Rex glared at Flowers—"is a local—what's the word?—resource. People find a weird thing under a rock, they take it to Stick. You know that bird thing, that incident with the birds?"

The Captain squinted. "You mean that event at the Bosque?"

"That's the one," Rex said.

"That tragedy?" the Captain asked.

Rex nodded. "The same one. They asked Stick to drive down there and give them his opinion."

"That right?" The Captain looked at me with something like admiration.

"That," I said, "is not right."

The Captain didn't seem to hear me. "You go down there the day after it happened?"

I sipped my beer.

"He did," Rex said. "I saw him that exact day. He went on behalf of the university to collect specimens and give them his take and whatnot."

"That right?" the Captain asked.

I sighed. "That's almost half right."

"We could use a man who knows the animals of the New Mexican desert," the Captain said. "You know critters—like mosquitoes, ticks, flies, bats, and such—from other places, too?"

"He knows it all," Flowers said. "He's got them in his zoo. He studies them all day long."

"A man who knows New Mexico, a man who knows all kinds of reptiles, insects, amphibians—critters of all types," the Captain said. "We'd consider such a man to be a valuable asset. I could very well have some work to throw your way."

"I thought the Minutemen didn't hire people," I said.

"I'd pass along a recommendation to a third party," the Captain said, "is what I'm saying to you. A well-moneyed party."

"I don't need a job." The last thing I wanted was to get on the crazy bus with Rex, Flowers, and this Captain.

"Oh, I know," the Captain said. "You work for the zoo. That's why you're valuable. We would ask one or two days a week. A Saturday of very well-compensated work."

"I work at the zoo on Saturday," I said.

"Your day off, then," the Captain said. "Our affiliate pays handsomely, especially for an expert. And an expert like you—you're a goddamned one of a kind." He guffawed as he looked me up and down. "We'd make it worth your while."

"I am not for sale."

The three of them laughed. I hadn't meant it as a joke.

The Captain reached across the bar and swatted at my wrist. "Think about it. We want to—the company I work with—wants to hire you. You're our man. We'll talk turkey another day. Right now, we're out on the town. We're having fun." He held up his beer can. Rex and Flowers rammed his can with theirs and the three of them sucked down whatever was left. I gave them another round. They cracked their cans open, chugged them, and erupted in snorts of beer-foam laughter.

I sipped my beer. I was the bitterness of the world.

It didn't take any prodding on my part for Rex and Flowers to fall over each other to tell me the Captain's story. He'd served in the army—just as they had—which had undervalued his vast talents and never promoted him past corporal. However, as they continued to tell me, after having served his tour and owned his own small roofing business for twenty years, he'd been a founding member of the Minutemen in New Mexico, which he'd joined both to relive the glory of his military days and out of a deep-seated fear of Mexican takeover.

An ex-brigadier general had dubbed the Captain with his unofficial rank. The general was also affiliated with the Minutemen, though too old to actually venture out to patrol the U.S.-Mexico border. The general did, however, get hoisted into the bed of an all-wheel drive vehicle every now and then and driven around the desert so he could brandish a shotgun at menacing juniper bushes and prickly pear cacti and such. Apparently—according to the gushing of my three guests—he was a visionary leader of American liberty.

I understood the Minutemen to be a bunch of beer-swilling Anglo gun-enthusiasts, who lived in a state of delusion that the entire region, from Texas to California, hadn't been stolen by force from Mexico. They tried to live out some Sons of the Revolution fantasy by hunting down poor families looking for work, scaring the devil out of them, and then turning them over to the special incarceration system that the United States used to house them before deportation—a system that didn't worry about treating them as if they had any human rights.

Not that I really cared. Mexicans, Anglos, Native Americans—I carried blood from all three groups, and regardless of race, they all treated me like something that had just crawled out of Loch Ness.

The case of beers wound down until the last dozen cans or so floated in lukewarm water that marked the demise of all my household ice cubes. At that point, I kicked everyone out. I knew they'd be over the legal limit and didn't care. Drunk driving was one of the great sports of Albuquerque. It put your abilities to the test and the stakes were high. I dumped the extra beers in a plastic bag and made Flowers take them with him.

The Captain was last out the door. He held out his hand. This time, to expedite things, I took it. It looked like a whale swallowing a dolphin. The captain's sleeve slid up his forearm, exposing a large, red welt with a gash in the center.

I gripped his hand bone-tight. "Wasp sting?"

He shrugged and pulled the sleeve down. "Dunno."

"Nasty... I can take a look."

"Just a mosquito bite." The Captain yanked his hand back. "Think about my offer."

I gave him the smallest of nods.

"Before I go..." He made both his hands into guns and pointed them at me. "Favorite animal at the zoo. Shoot."

"Painted box turtle." I didn't even have to think about it. "Name of Esposita. Unique white color pattern on her shell." I could look at her and feel content about everything else in my life. She could move an inch across her terrarium over the course of an hour, and to me it was high theater.

"Box turtle." He shook his head. "Incredible."

It wasn't incredible. That was the point. Any kid could own a box turtle. They were common, hardy, and lived a hundred years.

"Nice to meet ya," the Captain said and walked away.

It had not been nice to meet him, except for during that final minute. I recognized his wound. I'd seen it on a dead whooping crane only a week before.

CHAPTER SIX

spent the rest of my weekend in my apartment trying not to think about the twin welts I'd seen on the Captain and the whooping crane. It wasn't my business. I finished my book on ants, re-learning a bunch of stuff I'd learned years ago and forgotten. I ate a few meals. I tinkered with the pipes under my kitchen sink, which were draining more slowly than they might have, and made the situation slightly worse. I fed Ralph a couple of earthworms harvested from my garden. They weren't much sport for him, but it was winter. Not a lot of life was twitching.

On Thursday, the dark sedan followed me to work. I couldn't get a look at the driver. He hung back pretty well and didn't enter the zoo parking lot. I sat in my truck contemplating a course of action for about twenty minutes, then decided to try and forget all about it.

A Federal Express envelope lay waiting on my desk in the Reptile House. I read the label, hoping it was addressed to someone else and had ended up on my desk by mistake. No such luck. The world was after me. It was hell-bent on pestering me until I cracked. Its agent in this case was Melodía.

Inside the envelope, I found glossy eight-by-tens. They were not pictures of a beautiful woman or a vacation I had won to a faraway paradise, which was probably good since to me the beautiful woman would have to be blind to be interested, and paradise would be a desert island. Instead, I found a picture of a bullfrog splayed on its back, its skin incised from throat to crotch and staked to a dissection board. Its insides lay exposed like a dirty secret.

The next photo was a close-up of the frog's stomach. Frog stomachs were supposed to be pinkish-red, cylindrical, and circled by thin lateral bands of darker red. They were cute, all cuddled up to the liver. This frog's stomach was purple with green striations. A puncture wound drove right through the middle. It was not cute at all.

I flipped to the next picture, an incised frog stomach. A vague form lay within the digestive slime. It had several legs and a bulbous eye. The fourth and fifth pictures showed a half-melted monster washed clean of stomach fluids. Digestive acids had eaten away the left side of the head and most of the appendages. However, you could see that it once had six three-jointed legs, the front pair of which were tilted forward and probably used for manipulation. The most intact leg ended with a hooked claw. The half of the head that remained sported a wicked mandible. The head and thorax were short; the abdomen long and slender. Four wing joints flanked the thorax, the wings missing. The abdomen ended with a stinger, undoubtedly the agent behind the wound in the frog's stomach.

The creature was half-gone, its chitin digested to the point where I couldn't discern coloration. The fifth picture captured it next to a ruler: the thing was nearly two inches long—even after its body had shriveled in stomach acid. The only flying, stinger-bearing insect I'd ever known to approach that length was the tarantula hawk wasp. Tarantula hawks didn't have mandibles. Their front legs didn't tilt forward. Their heads and thoraxes were more slender than those of the creature in the photo. The position of the eye on the head was different.

I put the photos back in the envelope, slipped them into the bottom drawer of my desk, and tried to forget they existed. Trying to forget things was the order of the day, apparently.

Thursday was busy. I had animals to feed. I had supply requests to submit. I had terrariums to tidy. I also had to prepare my reticulated python for shipment. She was going to visit the Denver Zoo to be ogled by a whole new city full of normals. I'd fed her a rat on Monday. By now, she'd be as docile as a baby. Her whole body would have essentially shut down, save for the digestive system. In that state, she was travel-ready. I only had to prepare a kennel for her and print out care instructions. After closing, I walked back through the zoo, behind the walls, down the dark corridors and narrow alleys between animal enclosures. I stopped at the employee door that let out into the parking lot and half-kneeled so I could look through the small window.

It took me a minute. Then I found it: a dark sedan sitting by the curb next to Tingley Field, a park with a duck pond. When I squinted, I could spot the newspaper through the passenger window. It was him: Newspaper Man. For some reason, after several days off, he was after me again. I felt like walking over, rapping on his window and telling him that I wasn't worth the effort. I knew no secrets. I had no enemies or allies. No one should have cared about my comings and goings. I considered going back to the Reptile House and working until he left. There was always more to do. The Reptile House was my second home. However, as soon as 6:00 p.m. struck, my routine began to itch. It demanded I go home, cook something, and eat it.

I had an idea.

I walked back to my office and phoned Rex.

"Wha?" His voice was bleary, as if he wasn't fully awake.

"I need you to do something for me," I said, "right now."

"Course." Rex cleared his throat. "Whaddaya need?"

"Drive to the zoo."

"Car's broken down, eh?"

"No. I need you to drive to the zoo and park by Tingley Field. Wait for me to leave the parking lot. A man will follow me in a dark gray car."

"What kind of car?" Rex sounded alert.

"Four-door. Sedan. Inconspicuous."

"Got it," Rex said.

"I'll drive home. You see where he goes once I'm there."

The receiver rustled against Rex's mustache on the other end of the line. "Can do. Want me to call Flowers?"

"Why would you call Flowers?"

"Just in case."

"Do not call Flowers," I said. He'd likely show up in his ice cream truck. "Come by yourself."

"Be there in ten minutes."

The perk to having a friend who believed in UFO crashes and Mexican takeover conspiracies was that he didn't ask questions when you called him up and made a request that most people would think paranoid. I guess I was lucky.

I went back to the parking lot and waited inside the employee door. I let the minute hand on my watch track a quarter circle before I walked to my vehicle. Mine was one of only a half-dozen cars left. I tried to stride with my normal swift gait, as if unaware of Newspaper Man's presence. Once behind my truck's tinted windows, I scanned the cars parked on the street that ran between Tingley Field and the zoo. The dark sedan was still there. A hundred yards or so south of that on the park side, I spied Rex's truck. An extended cab, jacked-up muscle truck with a gun rack and spotlights didn't make a great tailing vehicle. I guess I hadn't thought my plan quite through. Still, Newspaper Man wouldn't likely expect to be followed.

I took a deep breath and drove home. For most of the way, I could only see Newspaper Man trailing discretely, intermingling himself with traffic. But on the trek up long, straight Fourth Street, I glimpsed the distant bulk of Rex's truck. He seemed to be doing a subtle enough job.

I arrived home and entered my apartment without looking back to see if Newspaper Man had parked a block or two away or had simply rolled on. I released Ralph onto the savannah of my living room floor where, according to my calculations, a cricket should still have been roaming. I pieced together some soft tacos for myself, but when I sat at my bar, I was too nervous to eat.

I decided to drink instead. A half-dozen Chama River Brewery beers sat cooling their heels in my refrigerator. I took one out, cracked the cap off, and drank it down. I opened another. I sat at the bar. All was quiet. No roar of Rex's truck. No footsteps. Even Ralph crouched softly in a crook of the wall and floor beneath one of my big bay windows. He listened for that cricket, hiding somewhere, too petrified to chirp.

My phone rang. I considered hitting it with a beer bottle, then realized that it was probably Rex. He had a cell phone. I answered.

"Did you get the photos?" Melodía asked.

"Nope," I said, trying to keep the disappointment out of my voice. "I don't accept articles from Federal Express. Government employee solidarity and all."

"Come to my lab," she said.

"I'm a USPS man. Until death."

"Come to my lab," she said. "I'll let you have the first look."

"Impossible! You've already looked."

"So you admit you got the photos." Her voice was bubbly and playful.

She had me. "Yes... That is a hell of a half-digested wasp."

"That's no wasp," she said. "If it is, it's a new species."

"What you need—" I started.

"A new species, Stick! Can you imagine? A new species of insect hasn't been discovered here for decades."

"What you need is a DNA test," I said. "Not a zookeeper."

"You're not excited," she said.

"I'm sure you can do a DNA test with all that fancy lab equipment."

"You don't want to come to my lab and look at a new species of giant wasp?"

I flinched at the word. Giant. Thankfully, she couldn't tell over the phone. "It's not a new species. It's just a damned big, weird-looking wasp. Every other month, some redneck claims to have shot the chupacabra. They peddle out a four-legged corpse with dermatitis and a scrunched-up face, and the internet goes crazy. One DNA test later: coyote."

"Come on, Stick. I've looked at the journals. The front legs aren't right. The eyes, or what's left of them, are not those of a tarantula hawk wasp. They're more like—"

"I'm very busy."

"They're more like fly eyes," she said.

"I'm in the middle of something. Good-bye."

The line went quiet. Ralph crept along the baseboard on the opposite side of the room. Did he smell that cricket? Could he feel the vibration of its little hops through the floorboards?

"Please," she said. "I need to share this with someone."

I could have told her a mysterious man with a newspaper followed me home. I could have told her that my best friend had brought a white supremacist into my house two nights ago and that they'd offered me a job persecuting people with whom I shared ancient blood. I could have told her that the next morning I was sending away my favorite python for six months.

Instead I said this: "I'll send Marchette over. You can share it with him."

The dial tone yelled in my ear.

I didn't hear from Rex until late. I should've been asleep, resting my body. My legs hurt all the time. My knees, hips, and ankles hurt. Every joint in my feet. Sitting in a chair stressed my bones. Walking to the refrigerator for a fresh beer jostled them. Pressing the pedals of a car made my ankles and knees creak like old pines. Over the course of a day, what began as a dull ache built up to a low-power flame that burned through the lower half of my body. We won't talk about my spine, neck, and shoulders.

I needed eight or so hours of horizontal time each day. Lying down hurt my joints in all new ways, but it also alleviated the pain caused by being up and about. So I awoke with a slow ache in my hips, elbows and fingers that ebbed over the course of a day's activity. That's right: sleeping hurt my fingers. Why?

What a stupid question.

The universe knew no why. It was a senseless, endless, cycle of destruction. I wanted to write that on a postcard and send it to Tanis Rivera, wherever she was. Just for fun, as I sat at my bar waiting for Rex and not resting my aching body, I checked to see if I still had her card. I did. The address was a P.O. Box in Tijeras, a suburb to the east of Albuquerque that lurked in a saddle of the Sandía Mountain range. No employer listed. I wondered what sort of eccentric zealot would hire an animal theologian.

A few minutes past midnight, my phone rang. I picked up.

"Buddy," Rex said. "You weren't kidding."

"Where are you?" I asked.

"That guy really was tailing you," he said. "What're you mixed up in?"

"Did you follow him?"

"I can protect you. The Minutemen are powerful people. We have a lot of guns."

"No guns," I said. "Where are you?"

"At the river. Seriously, I'll get guys outside your apartment. We have a shed. Enough AR-15s to take down—"

"Please tell me where you are."

"North Valley," he whispered. "South of Corrales. He turned down a side street and onto a dirt road. Led to the river. I didn't follow. It'd be too conspicuous. Anyway, I'm in the bushes. I'm watching. A blue van was waiting for him. One of those hippie vans that kids hang around in not shaving themselves and smoking reefer."

"Who's he meeting?" I asked.

"Two women. One with long gray hair. Face looks like it got tired of crying a long time ago." Rex said. "The other's dressed like a cowboy. Stetson and everything. You want me to take 'em?"

It took me a second to process this offer. "Go back to your truck."

"I only have the cowboy gun and a .22 rifle in the truck," he said. "Anyway, you point a revolver at someone, they'll listen to you."

"Go back to your truck."

"Bullets all do the same thing, no matter what type of gun."

"Come here. Drive to my house right now."

"I'm just saying." Rex's voice was fierce. "You don't follow my best friend."

"I appreciate that," I said. "All I want you to do is drive to my house and tell me what you saw in person."

"You don't follow the greatest friend I've had since we were six," he said.

There are moments when your routine has been fractured. During these moments, people say things they don't normally say, and do things they aren't normally called on to do. At that moment—when Rex offered to pull a gun on three people—I felt something. I didn't like it. It made me want to grab Rex and hug him and place my palm protectively over the top of his head. This was a brief glimpse into real human emotion. It made me feel a little drunk. I dampened it back down with a sharp dose of pragmatism.

"Rex, I need you to write down the license plate." Giving him a set of discreet instructions would trick him out of walking up to the trio and pointing his revolver at them. He was like all the rest of us raised in our poor Albuquerque barrio: conditioned to follow orders.

He cleared his throat. "Right."

"Do you have a pen?"

Shuffling echoed over the phone. "Pencil. Wendy's receipt. Got it."

"Come see me," I said.

He inhaled slowly. "Be there in ten."

While I waited, I realized I should have let Newspaper Man follow me around as long as he wanted. I could have led him to my father's house in the slums. I could have led him back and forth from the zoo, at exactly the same times, day after day. I could have taken him on my weekly Sunday 6 a.m. grocery run. He could have timed me. I was one of the most efficient shoppers this world had ever seen. I could have "accidentally" dropped my shopping list in the parking lot and the receipt in the gutter outside my house. He could have stumbled on each one, like breadcrumbs leading to the secret truth of my boring life. They would match exactly. I charted everything I was going to buy on my shopping trips and stuck to the list. No impulse buys. Nothing unplanned. That was my normal life. There was nothing in that life worth following me for.

Rex parked his truck outside and stomped down my stairs. I was waiting in the doorway for him. He brushed by me and paced the length of my big continuous kitchen and den. I shut the door and resumed my bar stool, where I drank beer and listened to my knees ache.

Rex stopped pacing and pointed a quivering finger at the window. "What's he following you for?"

I shrugged.

"I'm not racist," Rex said.

I sipped my beer.

"I'm not racist, but there's something going on in this city," he said, "with the Hispanics."

"Some people say they prefer to be called Chicanos." I didn't bother to remind him that I was, at least in part, one of them. My dad was about as Chicano as you could get.

"Hispanic, Latino, Chicano, Mexican—who the hell cares?" Rex said.

"They've got people sticking up for them all across the state. They're soaking up all sorts of welfare money. The country's in debt, and meanwhile, they're making their fortunes as drug-dealers, gun-runners, and job-stealers."

Rex liked to rant. One day he'd rant about banks, the next day about undocumented Mexican fruit-pickers, the next day about unions or Wall Street or the Federal government.

"Why?" he shouted. "Why are they after you?"

I walked to my fridge and got Rex the last beer. As always, as soon as he saw the glistening bottle, his face softened. The seams at the corners of his eyes and mouth relaxed a little. He lifted the beer a couple of inches above the bar and held it aloft there. His gaze, as if drawn to a lover, flicked down the bottle and back up. He brought it to his lips, swallowed a mouthful, and sucked the foam from his mustache.

This was how to tame a Spartacus Rex. Let him rant a little, let him pace, then drug him.

I sipped my beer.

Rex climbed onto one of my stools and leaned his elbows on the bar. Now that he'd exhausted his rage, every line of his face drooped. He looked ten years older than he was. "What could they want from you?"

I shrugged. "It's a mystery." The answer had something to do with the Bosque, the dead birds, Melodía, or all three—but I wasn't about to tell Rex that. He'd had enough excitement.

Rex sighed. The rush of air through his nostrils rustled his mustache. His eyes took on a faraway quality. "Remember when we used to camp?"

I smiled. I didn't plan it. I didn't rehearse it. The smile just happened.

"Just you and me," he said. "We used to pack up your truck."

There were memories you had. They made you happy. You didn't need even a second to think about it. You were just happy.

Rex smiled, too, in that fierce way he had. His voice was sharp like a can opener. "We'd buy all sorts of meat. Canned milk. You'd bring peppers and beans. You'd fry all day over the campfire."

I could smell those trips. Pine needles, dry leaves, wood smoke, the sting of peppers and the salty roast of meat.

"You'd cook everything over those fires. Spanish rice. Baked potatoes. Steaks."

"We'd go in the autumn," I said.

"The cold wind," he said. "That cold dusk wind. The sun would set and the air'd be ice."

I could taste that air. So crisp, so clean, like drinking ice water with your lungs.

"Remember washing your face in the river in the morning?" he asked.

I remembered washing the dishes in the river. I'd scrub them with sand and grit in the bubbling mountain current until my fingers were numb. It took hours to get them warm again, but the dishes were never cleaner.

"We need to do that," Rex said.

I nodded, knowing we'd never get around to it.

"No times like those," Rex said. "Let's promise: we'll go camping."

"It's a promise." I didn't really believe in promises. They were rooted in words. Without words, the concept of the promise wouldn't exist. A promise was an attempt to make words—the most transient of all things; you utter them and they cease to exist—permanent. In my experience, it never worked.

"Scout's honor," Rex said. We shook on it. Rex's eyes wandered across the room and found Ralph climbing up the seam between the refrigerator and the sink. "Your spider's going to fall into your garbage disposal one of these days."

I went over and put my hand in the air below where he clung. He climbed down into my palm. I carried him to the terrarium and put him inside. "I leave the plugs in the drains when I'm not using them."

Rex nodded. "Smart. So, are you going to tell me why this guy was following you?"

"Would if I knew," I said.

"People don't just get followed," Rex said. "There's always a reason."

I shrugged.

"You owe somebody money?" he asked.

I shook my head. I had no debt and a shocking amount saved. I was one of the few middle class people in the country with a bright future for my retirement—which I wouldn't live long enough to see.

"Normally, I'd ask if you made an enemy." Rex shook his head. "If you touched somebody's wife, or cheated at cards, or talked the wrong politics. But you—you don't do things like that."

"I do not."

"Any sort of union stuff going on at the zoo?"

"I wouldn't know," I said. "I stay out of it."

"Think. Has anything different happened lately?"

I pretended to think about it. "I met your Captain the other day."

Rex furrowed his brow at me. "No, the Captain's okay. He's a good guy." Rex glowered into space, tried to take a pull of beer but found the bottle empty. He turned to me. "You weren't followed before you met him?"

"Nope." I lied. I didn't need Rex turning private eye and going around harassing park rangers, asking questions at the zoo, and God forbid, poking his nose into Melodía's sanctum.

"What about the bird thing?" Rex asked. "That's new. Any reason anybody would follow you for that?"

"I can't think of a reason." I really couldn't. All I'd done was collect samples. I was an errand boy. "That was an act of nature, and no one knows I was involved."

Rex gave me a flat stare. "Let me tell you, good buddy. Everybody always knows when you're involved."

He was right, but I didn't like hearing it.

"It's time for bed."

"Right." The little man rinsed out the beer bottles, put them in my recycling bin, and pushed in his bar stool. He turned to me and stuck out his hand.

I took it.

Rex made his way halfway through the door before he turned back. "You should think about the Captain's offer. Make some money; make some new friends. The Minutemen are good guys. And they could help you with that Hispanic on your tail."

"I'm not working for the Minutemen," I said. "But I'm glad you're making some money off them."

His face sobered. "Fair enough."

"Good night," I said.

"Night." He clomped up to his truck and roared away.

The clock read 1:15 a.m. I would wake up, like it or not, in a little over four hours. My body was programmed. I was involved in nothing—no investigations, no plots, no paramilitary organizations or conspiracies of any kind. Still, when I lay in bed my eyes would not stay shut.

CHAPTER SEVEN

The next morning, I was too exhausted to feel bad about the way I'd treated Melodía the night before. Other people have described being tired to me. Their eyelids are droopy. Their minds wander. Their precious necks are stiff. When I'm tired, it constitutes a medical condition. I worry that every movement could crack something—a crack that could herald my slow, inevitable death.

I moved carefully during the day after a night of little sleep. I considered obstacles and planned my way around them. I drove at the speed of an old lady and with the heightened attention of a martial artist. I perceived threats and reacted to them well in advance. I took the back roads—I always took the back roads. Once at the zoo, I planned my day to maximize restful postures. I clustered similar tasks, so that every time I rose from my chair it was to accomplish as much as possible with minimal movement. With these precautions in place, I'd never broken a bone.

By the end of my work day, my body felt heavy, like it was made of very old oak. I set my wooden body in my chair. Sitting at my desk all by my lonesome, I got to feeling guilty. I sighed. I drank some water. I watched the painted box turtle, the wisest of all reptiles. She sat still. She blinked her eyes one by one, punctuated by very long pauses, as if every blink measured out one small unit of geologic time. I picked up the phone.

"I'm sorry," I said when Melodía answered.

Silence.

"I'm a bad friend." I didn't explain the details of my plight to her. When people are feeling upset, they don't need you telling them all the justifications for you treating them the way you did. They need a firm declaration of culpability. "It was selfish. It was late at night. I was grumpy. I wanted to go to bed, but I should have listened to you instead. I should have gotten in my truck and come over and looked at that monstrosity you've discovered."

The box turtle blinked both eyes at once. Anyone not versed in box turtles wouldn't have noticed.

"Are you even there?" I asked. "Am I spilling my guts to an empty line?"

"I'm here," Melodía said.

"I'm saying I'm sorry."

"I know."

"You deserve better treatment," I said.

"I do."

"Can I come over and make it up to you?" I was practically begging. The thought of Melodía throwing herself around her lab all alone was killing me.

She sighed. "Don't put yourself out. I know you're only doing it because you feel guilty."

"I'm Catholic," I said. "All of my good deeds come from guilt."

She stifled a laugh. "You're thinking of Irish Catholics. Our New Mexican church doesn't work like that."

"Let me come over anyway. I feel guilty because I've done wrong."

"I don't want you hanging out with me just because you feel like you've done wrong. I want you to want to."

"I do want to. You're one of the few people on the planet I actually like."

"I know that's true," she said.

I could hear the smile in her voice. It was remarkable how well telling the truth worked sometimes. "I'll be over in thirty minutes."

"Don't rush." The tightness was gone from her voice. "Come over after work. I'll order Chinese."

"How about Los Cuates?" I asked. Los Cuates was a local Mexican restaurant that had been in the city for decades. "I'll pick it up on my way."

"Okay, but I'll buy."

"I'll buy as part of my apology. This is America. Money talks."

She laughed.

After we hung up and I turned to my final tasks of the day, my head was fully in the game. Try it sometime: wrong someone, feel bad about it, apologize, convince them to forgive you. You'll feel better than you did even before you wronged them in the first place. It fills your head with all sorts of feel-good chemistry.

By the time I'd finished at the zoo for the day, called in the order to the restaurant, and walked to the parking lot, I'd temporarily forgotten about the night before. Maybe it was because I was exhausted. Maybe I was still high on forgiveness hormones. Maybe working all afternoon with the box turtle watching over me had lulled me into a Zen state. She was a hell of role model, our box turtle. Nothing much fazed her. And if it did, she'd just retract into her shell and chill out for a few days. I envied her.

I walked to my truck and ignored the odd pedestrians doing double takes. I drove to Los Cuates, picked up the food, and pretended the Spanish exclamations tumbling from the kitchen were about how hot the salsa was. It was easy since my father had been meticulous about sheltering me from the linguistic aspects of my heritage. I carried the food down to Melodía's lab without a significant fuss. I found the door, as usual, closed. I knocked and tried the knob. It opened to a pretty happy Melodía. She lounged back on a lab stool, her long legs crossed at the ankle, her feet atop a desk. She wore boot cut jeans and flat shoes. Her lab coat hung on the back of the stool and the top buttons of her white blouse were undone. Her hair was gathered and staked into itself with bobby pins to form a comely mass of black and chestnut curls atop her skull. Half of her face wore a contented smile.

"You smell good," she said.

"That's the sopapillas."

"I hope you remembered the honey," she said.

A sopapilla was a New Mexican fry-bread adapted from pueblo Native American fare that, when made properly, puffed up into a pocket that you could dribble honey into. Eating one was an experience worth living for.

I set the bag down on the highest counter in reach and hit my head on a florescent light fixture, cussing more than called for. I allowed myself to enjoy it—I let Melodía enjoy it, too. I hammed it up, rubbing my temple and scowling at the light as if it were a vexatious enemy.

We settled into our food. I'd purchased a couple of combo plates—blue corn tortilla chicken enchiladas, hard tacos with guacamole, beef tostadas—served with refried beans and Spanish rice. Melodía organized her food into little compartments on one of the dissection trays we used as plates. I piled mine all together. I enjoyed the collision of spice-levels, tastes, textures, and temperatures. We kept the conversation light as we ate. We talked about gizzards for a little while. She listened to me praise the merits of the box turtle. I complimented her on her hair. She explained that it was a result of her neck getting too hot and lack of a scrunchie. I told her that however it happened, it worked. We had a conversation like two semi-normals.

Once we'd finished our dinner and chased it with a couple of sopapillas, she put her feet back up on the counter and laced her fingers behind her head.

"Buy you a drink?" she asked.

"Hell yes," I said.

She opened a drawer in the desk behind her stool—the lab was full of desks, counters, tables, bookcases, and various sitting apparatuses—and pulled out a pint bottle printed with a picture of a barefoot woman wearing only bikini bottoms, a lei, and some voluptuous locks of hair. Sailor Jerry, it read. She poured generous shots into a couple of 500-milligram beakers. We clinked and drank. The rum was dark and sweet. I had a premonition of myself drinking too much of it.

"This feels like a celebration," I said.

"Maybe it is," Melodía said. "Whatever it is, I know it's breaking up your routine."

I shrugged one shoulder. "My routine can suffer for one night." Truth be told, I hadn't thought about my routine for an hour or so. But once the word left her mouth, my eyes developed a deep desire to find the face of my watch to see how far off this evening's fun had thrown my life. I forced myself to swallow some rum instead and push my beaker at Melodía for a refill.

She obliged. We clinked again.

"So," she said. "Do you want to see it?"

I nodded.

She gestured toward a wide magnification microscope set up on a nearby counter. I doubted I'd even need it. I could see the monster from ten feet away. It was as long as a normal's index finger. Melodía didn't get up. She let me go over and inspect the thing. That was her way: even on social occasions, she didn't want to taint my first impressions with her own bias.

I didn't get much new information by inspecting it in person than I had by looking at the photos. I zoomed in to inspect the joints of the forelegs. I spent some time on the eyes. I measured the proportions of the three body segments and looked at the wing stubs. The wings would've had a lot to say for themselves, if stomach acids hadn't dissolved them. Finally, I checked out the stinger.

"What is it?" Melodía asked when I straightened up from the microscope.

"It's a tarantula hawk wasp," I said.

She shook her head.

"What else could it be?"

"Explain the irregularities."

"Mutations." I wasn't sure at all about that.

"Those are some serious mutations," she said.

"She lived too close to Los Alamos."

Melodía gave me a flat look. "Ha-ha."

"Seriously. People born after the Chernobyl accident. People born in Hiroshima."

"Native Americans who drank the ground water near the Trinity Site," Melodía said.

"Yeah," I said. "Deformities. Look at the documentation. Kids born with four arms. Elbows that turn the wrong way. All sorts of skeletal malformations. Organs displaced or missing. Even the kind of proportional distortions present in our little lady here."

"She's a big lady," Melodía said.

"She's a Delphyne."

Melodía's face went blank.

"You don't know your Greek mythology." I shook my head. "And you call yourself an educated woman."

"I know more Latin than you," she said.

"Fair enough. My point is that your specimen may be mutated or deformed, but it's a tarantula hawk."

Melodía shook her head.

"That's the answer."

"Creatures that are deformed don't function well," Melodía said. "Their bodies perform awkwardly or break down altogether."

"How do you know this wasp functioned?" I asked.

"She lived out her life cycle," Melodía said. "She went through the larva stage, matured into an adult, mated, and implanted her egg. Given how tough life is for a flying insect, if she weren't functioning well, she wouldn't have lived that long."

"You're assuming she's the same one that implanted the egg in the whooping crane."

"She is. I can feel it. The birds, the bite on the crane, this wasp—they're all connected. I just have to figure out how."

"Assuming she did implant the egg, maybe she was lucky. Maybe in her case, her abnormalities paid off. Evolution in action."

Melodía sipped the last rum from her beaker and rested it on one of her upraised knees. "I've done my homework on this one."

"I'm sure your teachers are very proud," I said.

"To the untrained eye, she's a deformed tarantula hawk. Fine. But as somebody who knows something about insects, you should be picking up on a pattern."

I'd already picked up that pattern. I could tell that Melodía knew I'd picked up on the pattern. It'd been apparent from my first glimpse of the creature in the photo—even from the first glimpse of the bites on the whooping crane.

"You already know what I'm going to say. Admit it."

I didn't want to admit it. I took a slug of rum instead. It was delicious.

"The irregularities all correspond to a common horsefly," she said. "This is a wasp-horsefly hybrid. Deny it."

"I do deny it. I'll deny it all night long if you want, because it's impossible. Wasps and horseflies can't breed. Just like you can't get impregnated by a chimpanzee."

She slapped me. She was probably aiming for my arm, but ended up hitting my thigh instead. It made us awkward for a few seconds. "That's disgusting."

"So is the idea of a wasp and horsefly mating," I said.

"You're wrong."

"No. you are."

She smiled and stuck her beaker out at me. "Give me some more booze."

I poured her about fifty milliliters.

"Now pour yourself a little more," she said.

"I've had plenty." But I splashed myself some to make her happy.

"You know how we settle this," she said.

"I sure do. You admit that I'm right, then we drink to it." I held up my glass. She clinked. "Wrong."

"How, then?" I asked.

She pointed toward what looked like a small microwave in the corner of the lab.

"We put the thing in the microwave and blow it up like a baked potato?"

She slapped me on the arm. "That's an incubator, stupid."

We looked at it together. So that was where she was incubating the egg she'd found buried in the flesh of the whooping crane. "What are you suspending it in?"

"Nutrient solution. I plan on putting some raw meat in there when it hatches so it has something to eat."

That would probably work. The egg would hatch a creature that looked a lot like a maggot. It would have a ravenous mouth and a wormy body. Horsefly larvae loved to be born in any sort of organic filth. Tarantula hawk larvae enjoyed eating the organs of a living spider. If Melodía was right and the thing was a hybrid, it would probably be fine with raw meat for a cradle.

Melodía's eyes searched my face. "You don't like it."

I did not.

"What's the alternative? How would an expert zookeeper like you do it?"

I raised my eyebrows at her and let her put it together herself.

"You're not serious," she said.

I was serious.

The next morning, I proved it. I brought her a healthy adult tarantula. His name was Jones. I'd named him that because he looked like a businessman in a brown suit—not literally, of course. He was an eight-legged hairy spider the size of an English muffin. But I looked at him and my impression was the same every time: businessman, brown suit, mustache, working stiff's hunch.

I hauled him over to Melodía's lab in a roomy glass terrarium with a cedar chip floor, a water bowl, a hodgepodge of sticks and leaves for him to nest in, and a banzai tree in one corner for him to lurk beneath. It was a nice little home. I also brought a separate, much smaller terrarium full of crickets. I wanted him to stay well fed. He was about to go through a nightmarish ordeal, for which he would need every ounce of strength.

Melodía's eyes got pretty big when I'd set the terrarium on a table and removed the sheet. Jones stood in the exact center on high alert. He rotated ninety degrees clockwise, then ninety degrees counter-clockwise. The crooks of his knees ticked up and down like the type bars of an old-fashioned typewriter.

"So," Melodía started to say.

Jones spun a full 180 degrees to face her.

"Whoa," she said. "Can he jump out of there?"

I tapped the lid, which was closed tight.

"This is Jones. He's a friend of mine, so be nice to him."

"Hello Jones," she said slowly.

I shrugged out of my backpack, which held the box of crickets, a vial of halothane, a couple of cotton balls, a magnifying glass, two cotton swabs, a few slim tongue depressors, and a bottle of Elmer's glue—the kind that Flowers used to eat in elementary school.

"I don't know if I want to watch this," she said.

"Go get the egg."

She brought the egg from the incubator. It floated in a clear solution in a Petri dish. It looked the same as it had a week ago. I was surprised it hadn't hatched yet. If it hatched at all, it wouldn't take more than a couple more days—if it indeed housed a tarantula hawk larva. I put a dot of halothane on a cotton ball and dropped it into Jones' home. He pounced on it. A few seconds later, he fell to his belly and lay very still.

"Did you kill him?" Melodía asked. "Maybe you used too much."

I put spiders to sleep all the time. I knew what I was doing. I edged one of the tongue depressors under the egg and lifted it from the solution. It gleamed in the light. It was plump and healthy. I removed the lid to Jones' terrarium with my free hand and placed a dot of glue on the middle of the face-up side of Jones' abdomen. With great care, I lowered the egg into the terrarium and tilted the tongue depressor until the egg plopped into the glue, then pressed it in place.

I pulled my hands out of the terrarium, taking the cotton ball with me, and put the lid back on. "Done."

"That's it?" Melodía asked.

I nodded.

"So what do I need to do?" she asked.

"Wait. Throw Jones a cricket at dusk. Shouldn't take more than a few days."

"What will happen when it hatches?"

"If it's a tarantula hawk, the larva will burrow into Jones' abdomen. It'll eat around the major organs, saving them for last. It'll grow. It'll mature. It'll pupate, which only lasts a day or so, and then it'll become an adult."

"And then?"

"It'll rip through Jones' abdomen wall and emerge, wet and beautiful, into the world," I said. "Then we'll know what we've got."

"That sounds awful," she said.

"It is quite awful." Most of nature was awful.

Melodía stood with her head cocked, watching the sleeping spider. "Isn't there a kinder way to do this? Jones doesn't seem like he deserves to die in such a gross way."

"Death comes with being a spider," I said. "It won't be pleasant for him, but he's a predator. He's poisoned dozens of innocent little insects and sucked their liquefied guts out of them. This experience is part of his life cycle."

Melodía fell down on one of her swivel stools. "You work with some terrible things, Stick. I think they're beginning to affect your worldview."

I gathered up my tools and pushed the box of crickets toward Melodía. "That's his food. Be sure to fill his water. We want that larva to have a big strong body to eat from the inside out."

"Ugh." Melodía rumpled her hair with the palm of her hand. The messier her hair got, the better it looked.

"You look beat."

"Sleep is for the weak," she said.

"You should go home."

"I will when I figure out what killed those birds."

"You know, this egg has absolutely nothing to do with it."

Melodía frowned. "You've said that."

"You found bites on only one dead bird. There were thousands."

"You've said all that. You repeat yourself all the time."

"That's because you don't listen," I said. "Do you have any other leads on what happened?"

"Just the basics. Mass trauma. Heart failure. No sign of electrocution, no sign of impact, no disease. I'm pretty much stumped."

"Any other people involved in the study?" I asked.

She nodded. "I sent samples to Phoenix, Boulder, Calgary, Chicago. No dearth of corpses to spread around. Everybody's come up with the same thing: goose egg."

Neither of us laughed.

I thought about Tanis, the Captain, and the Newspaper Man. They'd all been after me since I'd become involved in the incident. Tanis worked for a mysterious employer interested in animals. The Captain had the same bite on his arm that I'd seen on the whooping crane. The Newspaper Man was interested in the dead birds—that had to be why he was following me. For a brief second, I felt like there was something behind the obvious facts, that there was a pattern I could almost perceive, but the feeling disappeared. But not before I opened my mouth. "What about a manmade incident?"

"You mean something intentional?"

"I don't know what I mean," I said.

"Like an experiment or something?"

I shook my head. "I'm just thinking out loud." I was beginning to worry that if we talked about it anymore, she'd wheedle my recent difficulties out of me. I didn't need her feeling guilty. "I'm tired, too."

"The Bosque is near White Sands." White Sands was a desert of fine ivory sand. It was one of the strangest and most beautiful landscapes in the world. The American government had built a missile testing range there, humanity's way of acknowledging nature's wonders. "Maybe some new missile flew close to the Bosque. Animals can die of fright-induced trauma." Melodía tapped her jaw with a finger. "Kirkland Air Force Base is close by. A fleet of fighter jets could induce that much trauma."

I nodded. I'd thought of those, and they sounded plausible. More importantly, they distracted her from any details about who was or was not harassing me. "Well, best wishes in your continued search for truth."

She caught my sleeve as I got up and headed for the door. The tips of her long slender fingers grazed my forearm through my shirt. They stayed there as she talked. "What's the timeline on this spider thing?"

"A couple days until the egg hatches." Those fingers felt good. It was a betrayal of my routine, but I was tired and far from my routine as it was. So, I stood there and enjoyed the touch of a beautiful, flawed woman. I wondered if she would have touched me at all if it hadn't been for the tumors bulging from the jaw to the hairline of her face. Probably not, but I was beyond complaining. "Then a week for the larva to mature, tops. You should be looking at an adult buzzing around Jones' terrarium in less than ten days. Probably sooner."

She wrapped her hand around my forearm. "Thank you, Stick. I had fun last night."

"I did too. Fun... is rare."

Melodía nodded. Our eyes had become locked at some point. Hers were deep brown with gold motes, below high slender eyebrows and long lashes. The left eye was pulled taught at the corner.

"I'm sorry again for being such a jerk the other night. I was stressed."

She squeezed my arm. "I'm sorry you were stressed. Want to talk about it?"

I tried to smile at her to show her the stress was gone. I probably failed. I wasn't good at smiling. "I'm good. It was just work."

She let her hand slip from my arm. "Okay. I realize you do a lot for me."

A more sincere smile emerged out from under my fake one. "No problem."

"I'm your friend," Melodía said. "You can ask me for things, too."

I did not ask other people for things. I was an island. "Thank you." I turned to Jones. "Good bye, friend. May you live out your destiny with dignity."

Melodía sat quietly and watched me walk out the door.

I thought about Jones on my way home. I, his keeper, had consigned him to a miserable fate. It was the way of nature, but it wasn't my way. I'd never thought about it much, but my role as a zookeeper was to hold the natural order at bay for my select group of animals. They didn't have to fear predation. They wouldn't die of exposure or due to an accident. They wouldn't starve. They rarely died of diseases. They were lonely, caged creatures, but they were safe from the kind of horror that Jones was about to endure—the kind that the natural world guaranteed.

CHAPTER EIGHT

The next morning I woke before dawn. I brewed coffee, boiled oatmeal, and butchered a grapefruit. I ate in front of my windows, watching the dawn edge over the mountains and trickle through the foliage into my patio. I finished my breakfast in a paradise of orange light. Birds tweeted. Spider webs turned platinum. You could feel each minute hang in the air before it quietly passed on into eternal nothingness. Being alone at dawn is one of the most important things you can do. It is the purest time, a time when you can peer into the face of the world and understand your absolute transience. You can realize it and welcome it because each moment is so peaceful and so long.

Dawn passed and I went to work.

At nine o'clock, when I was well into my paperwork and nearly ready to start feeding beings to other beings, I got a call.

"John," a gruff voice said over the line. It belonged to Dennis, an animal control guy.

"Denny," I said. "You got a snake?"

"We got a snake," he rasped. Dennis smoked two packs a day and had a voice like one of those ancient movie stars who sounded like they gargle sandpaper.

"Address." Every now and then, animal control got a call about an exotic snake—usually an escaped pet. They called me up to identify and capture it. I helped them with normal desert rattlesnakes, too.

Dennis gave me the address. I didn't care for him and he didn't like me much either. I didn't like his cigarette stench. I didn't like the way he drove all over the city kidnapping animals and euthanizing them. I didn't like the way he called me John.

"Be there in fifteen minutes," I said.

He grunted—which I didn't like—and hung up.

The address wasn't far from my house in the North Valley. It was in a rich new development in the Candelarias neighborhood called Matthew Meadows. The streets in the development were winding, with adolescent cottonwood trees, subterranean electrical lines, sidewalks flush with the asphalt, and houses with modern construction and fake adobe plaster in tones like lode and tope. I didn't like Matthew Meadows.

I found the house and pulled in behind Denny's truck. Denny was an Anglo guy with mussy white hair. He wore blue coveralls, yellow work boots, a lot of loose skin on his face, and burst arteries in his nose. He stood talking to a short Anglo woman with curly dark brown hair. She looked me up and down. Then she did it again, as if the first time wasn't enough. A skinny boy with her hair, darker skin, and terrified eyes stood nearby.

"Snake's out back," Denny said. "Kid here almost hit it with the lawnmower."

I blinked at Denny.

"Listen to this," Denny whispered at me before turning to the boy. "What kind of snake did you say it was, son?"

The boy stared at me. I was worried that his eyeballs might fall out of his head.

"Milk rattler," Denny sneered. Some people would have laughed or ribbed the boy or commented on how cute it was that he'd invented a new kind of snake. Dennis said it as if the boy was an idiot. Thankfully, the kid was too petrified of me to notice.

The boy had probably stumbled on an albino western rattlesnake, an escaped pet. Albinos didn't last in the wild; they were too visible to predators.

"Let's go get it," I said.

The woman led us around the side of the house through a rickety gate. Beyond lay a half-acre of lawn. The mower sat quietly at the spot where shorn grass met long grass.

The boy lingered behind us. His mom stopped at the edge of the lawn and pointed. "It's in front of the lawnmower."

Denny and I walked over. The grass was so deep that I didn't get a glimpse of the snake until we were nearly standing on the thing. Thick as an arm, it sported a wedge-shaped head and a rattle. Gold patches checkered its ivory scales.

The woman was one of those chatty types. "Daniel is never going to want to mow the lawn again," she hollered across the grass. "Last summer, he hit a toad. It exploded. It took us months to get him out here again, and this is what he finds."

We ignored her.

Denny threw his hands in the air. "Waste of a trip. Got a call from the West Side about a coyote and here I am looking at a dead snake."

I toed the albino rattler's head. Snakes could flail and even strike after death, but this one was far beyond that point. He was as limp as a dishtowel. I stooped and turned the body over. Something had mauled the underside of his neck. Bite wounds riddled his abdomen.

"Damn," Denny said. "Bit by something."

"Is it dangerous?" the woman yelled in a voice about twice as loud as it needed to be. "I can't bear the idea of my Daniel getting bitten by a snake."

Denny rumpled his calloused hand through his already rumpled hair. "Lotsa bite marks."

Pink flesh showed through the wounds, but no blood ran from them. I stepped closer, intending to screen the snake from the sun with my body, and leaned into a pungent cloud of ammonia. Viscous yellow dappled a patch of grass beside the body. The scales around the bites had faint pink patterns swirled across them, almost impossible to detect against the pale flesh of the snake, but present on every wound. Tongue marks. Some creature had bitten this snake to death, sucked the blood out of it, licked every drop from the scales, then urinated all over the place.

"Hey!" Denny yelled over my shoulder. "Are you ready to go, I asked."

I pawed at the grass, careful to steer clear of the urine. I worked out in a circle from the body, rifling clusters of blades until I could see the surface of the ground. The length of the grass made it tough going.

Denny groaned. "What are you looking for?"

"Tracks," I said.

"Good God, why?"

"Something killed this snake," I said through gritted teeth. I hated explaining myself to anybody, much less a normal like Denny.

"Who the hell kills a snake?" Denny threw his arms up in the air again, took five steps away, then took another five back. "I'll tell you who."

"I was wondering," the mother yelled at us from where she stood with her arm around the boy's shoulder, "if the snake is dangerous? Should we do something about dangerous snakes coming into our yard?"

Denny turned on her. "It's dead!" He turned back to me. "Eagle, that's who."

My search through the grass hadn't revealed anything.

"Eagle—he flies, John. He grabs rattlesnakes. He bites 'em. He flies away. You can't track eagle."

I didn't bother to tell him that I had recently tracked down a suspect mutant tarantula wasp—also a flier. I didn't tell him that eagles didn't suck blood. I didn't remind him that eagles didn't have tongues, and therefore couldn't lick wounds. Plus, there was no flying creature in New Mexico—in the world—big enough to kill a fat five-foot long rattlesnake and that also drank blood. "Denny, go to the West Side. Catch your coyote."

"I will just as soon as you tell me you're going to dispose of that snake, so I know how to fill out my paperwork."

I placed my palm in the spot where I was looking to hold my place in the sea of grass. I turned and gave him a malevolent giant glare.

He held up his palms. "Okay! You don't have to give me that look. Now I know how to fill out my forms. John Stick disposed of a dead snake that we should never have been called about."

I glared at him until he left, and went back to my search. A few square yards led to the feet of the short brown-haired woman, who'd obviously become tired of waiting for an explanation of what I was doing. Her son lingered at the edge of the grass. She smiled at me. She had a face pleasant enough for me to dislike.

"Can I ask what you're looking for?" She talked like a normal: instead of asking a question, she asked if she could ask.

"I'm looking for traces of the animal that killed this snake."

"What animal is that?" she asked.

I didn't have an answer for her.

"How important is it that you find it?" she asked.

I tried to figure out how to put it. "I have no idea what it could possibly have been. I'm a zookeeper. I know animals."

"Professional curiosity," she said. "Could it have been a coyote? There have been sightings."

"Coyotes are smart. I'm sure one could have dug under your fence. Found a gap. Snuck in and escaped."

"Do coyotes eat rattlesnakes?"

They did. A roadrunner could also take down a medium-sized rattlesnake. Eagles and hawks ate them. "Could be." I didn't mention the loss of blood—

no need to scare the kid.

"Well," the woman said, "I bet that's it."

That could have been it. A coyote might lap up blood that spilled out of the wounds of its prey—blood was delicious and nutritious. Then something might have scared it off before it could eat the flesh. It was a thin theory. A coyote would have left tracks, and I didn't think one would urinate so close to the kill. I'd know more when I got the snake back to my lab and checked the teeth imprints.

"Mister?" asked the boy. He still wouldn't step onto the grass. His thin, high voice made me feel pity for him, which I didn't like at all.

"What?" I asked.

"I heard a sound last night."

The corners of his mother's mouth twitched downwards.

"What sound?" I asked.

"I heard it at two in the morning," the little boy said. "I know because I got a clock radio for my birthday."

"Shouldn't you have been asleep?" I asked.

"I don't sleep at night," the boy said.

"He has trouble sleeping," his mother echoed. "He's been scared a lot."

Despite my best efforts, I felt sorry for the little guy. His body was tiny and fragile. He looked like he hadn't smiled in a year. "What sound did you hear?"

"A devil," he said.

"There are no such things as devils," his mother said to him.

"I saw one on TV," he said.

I stood. It hurt. My back had taken a lot of punishment during the past week. I walked to the kid and tried not to tower over him. "What show were you watching?"

"He likes nature documentaries," his mom said.

That was another reason to like the kid. "Are you talking about a Tasmanian devil?" I asked.

The boy nodded up and down the way little kids do.

"And that's what you heard last night?" his mom asked.

The boy nodded. "It was a screaming, grunting sound. Just like they made on TV."

The kid seemed legit. "You're sure you weren't dreaming?" I asked.

"I don't sleep at night," he said.

His mom circled behind him and put her hands on his scrawny shoulders. "We're thinking about getting him help."

I stooped down to get closer to the kid's level, despite the harm it did to my bones. "Do you know what the most dangerous animal on the planet is?"

"The Tasmanian devil?" he asked.

I poked him in the chest. "You."

He gulped. His dark eyes narrowed just a hair.

"Nobody messes with humans," I said. "We're the toughest living things on the planet." I straightened up. The boy's mother mouthed *thank you*.

I collected my snake and drove back to the zoo, to find Marchette waiting for me in my lab.

"Greetings Stick." He appeared a little yellower around the gills than usual. His bald head boasted a sheen and his eyes hung far back in droopy eye sockets. He wore rubber gloves and wielded a steel probe and scalpel. The opened body of one of the hissing cockroaches lay on a dissection tray. His voice was beaten down—it didn't annoy me as much as usual.

I nodded at him.

His eyes caught on the burlap sack I carried. "Pray tell, what's in the bag?"

"Dead snake."

He followed me into my lab. I upended the bag and dumped the snake on a table. Marchette blinked at it. "Albino rattlesnake. Quite rare."

"What can I do for you, Doc?"

"Ah yes." He jammed his glasses up his nose with a thumb. "Business." He opened his mouth. Then he shut it. Then he opened it, grimaced, and looked at the door. "May I?"

I gave him the mildest of shrugs.

He closed the door and rubbed a palm all over his cranium, as if polishing a light bulb. "This is awkward."

"Things with you are always a little awkward, Doc."

He giggled. "I suppose so. Social skills, and so forth." He cleared his throat. "I'm here about the egg."

I knew which egg he was talking about. "It seems healthy—"

Marchette held up his hand. "Please don't tell me. I'm not here to gather information about it. I'm here to tell you." He lowered his voice. "Keep it a secret."

Obviously, the doctor didn't realize how little Melodía or I went yapping around town.

"Has Dr. Hernandez told anyone about it?" he asked.

"I don't imagine so."

"Have you?"

I shook my head. I'd told Rex and my father, but Rex would have forgotten as soon as he left my house, and my father was probably asleep when I told him.

"I advise you: do not tell anyone. Give Dr. Hernandez the same warning. That egg has nothing to do with the death of the birds. It's just the egg of *pepsis formosa*. It's a false trail."

"I thought you told Dr. Hernandez it was more than just a tarantula hawk egg. That it didn't fit."

"Did I?" He cocked his head, as if trying to remember an event long past.

"C'mon Doc," I said. "You remember."

"I may have been swept up in the enthusiasm of the moment. An event such as that which wiped out so many birds at once will provoke excitement in even the most objective scientific mind, I dare say."

"So," I said, "you think the egg is normal."

He nodded too vigorously.

"Well, I guess we'll find out soon," I said.

"The egg is indeed normal," he said. "You both should let it go the way of the dodo—excuse me? Did you say you'd find out?"

I grinned at him.

"Why would you say that?" he asked.

"I would say that because I implanted the egg in the back of my friend Jones."

He cocked his head. "Who is Jones?"

"He's a tarantula I'm acquainted with."

"You're hatching it?" Marchette was a sincere guy. It was one of the reasons I liked him more than other normals. In our situation, it meant that he couldn't keep the panic out of his voice.

"Nope," I said. "Dr. Hernandez is."

He grabbed the collar of my zoo jacket. He had to reach above his head to do it. "You must tell her not to. It would be a mistake. Tell her to destroy the thing. Tell her to incinerate it."

I felt like I'd stepped into a movie. People in my world never grabbed each other and tried to plead sense into them. I almost laughed at him. Instead, I gently unlaced his fingers from my jacket and stepped away. "It's just an egg. An insect will hatch out. It may not even live. If it does, I'll buy Dr. Hernandez a flyswatter as a safeguard."

"You don't understand."

"So make me."

Marchette's shoulders slumped. His sallow face hung limp. "I'm afraid I can't."

I clapped the little scientist on the shoulder. "That's a defeatist attitude, Doc. Don't worry. I'm looking over her shoulder. She'll be fine. Tarantula hawks can't hurt anyone. Their stings are painful as hell, but never fatal."

He shook his head slowly. "You don't understand." His eyes wandered over to the albino rattlesnake. "Another innocent murdered."

"It's a dog-eat-dog world," I said. "This snake was slinking through the backyard of a little boy. The kid almost ran over it with the lawnmower. If something hadn't gotten to it first, it might have bitten him. With his body mass, he would've been a goner."

"What killed it?" he asked.

"Still have to figure that out."

"No blood." He fingered one of the bites. "Sucked out. How queer." The gears in his head were turning.

I propelled him toward the door with a whack on the spine. "Go get some lunch, Doc. Or better yet, sleep. You look like you need it."

He sighed, keeping his eyes on the snake. "What is that saying? I shall sleep when I am dead."

"It's your zoo day," I said. "Everything's in fine order here. I've got it under control. Go home and take a nap for twenty hours or so. If anyone asks—they won't—I'll tell 'em you were here probing the cockroaches and inoculating the dragonflies."

He smiled up at me. "You're a kind man, Mr. Stick."

"Just Stick."

"Unfortunately, my employer demands detailed reports that cannot be faked. I must do my rounds thoroughly and honestly, and bring the appropriate paperwork back to him."

It was strange to think about Marchette, a doctor and all, being anyone's poodle. "Where did you say you worked?"

His smile became bleaker. "I didn't."

I flexed my eyebrows and waited for more. I didn't get it. "Care to elaborate?"

He straightened my jacket for me. "Have a good day, Stick. I shall retire to the other laboratory, as I know you prefer to work in solitude."

As he walked out, I shrugged off that he wouldn't tell me who he worked for, and turned to my long, white, dead guest. The holes torn in his belly and neck were deep clean punctures. No chewing or gnawing. The assailant had powerful jaws. It had canines that were, from what I could tell, only slightly longer than the incisors, of which there were two on the top and two on the bottom. The mouth, from canine to canine, measured a little over an inch. That measurement was consistent in the lower and upper jaws. All this led me to one conclusion: I didn't know much about mammalian taxonomy.

Before putting the snake on ice so I could round up some books, I took a few digital pictures, with a ruler in the frame for scale, and printed them. I put the snapshots in a file, labeled the file with the address and date, and put it away in my filing cabinet, where it would sit for eternity. It was satisfying, filing something. It was comforting to know both that it would always be there and that you'd never look at it again.

The rest of my day transpired without any drama. I ate lunch at some point. I cleaned up my python's cage, being sure to leave every detail as she'd known it so that when she returned she'd feel no loss. I started thinking about what I would feed her on that day. It powered me through the remainder of my day until I went out into the parking lot a few minutes past dusk and found Tanis Rivera camped out in the bed of my pickup truck.

She sat in one of two fold-up lawn chairs flanking a small plastic table and drinking what looked like a piña colada from a tall, curvy glass. She wore a sun hat, white-rimmed sunglasses, and a winter coat. A grill with the lid down exhaled two spires of smoke, like a hippopotamus venting water vapor.

I was speechless.

"Good evening," Tanis said. "I made you a drink." When she held the drink out to me, her coat sleeve edged up, revealing a flower bracelet. A lei made of the same pink flowers peeked through her collar.

I stammered a little before I could find words. "You can't drink in the zoo parking lot. It's government property."

She tilted her head to the side. The starlight played a little game with her shining black hair. "Yet here I am, drinking in the zoo parking lot."

"Security will fine you," I said.

She smiled her too-white teeth at me. Her lips were full and painted a very tasteful shade of rose. "They were already here. I told them that I was arranging a surprise picnic for my boyfriend. They thought it was romantic. I cooked them each a hamburger." She smiled wider, showing even more of her perfect teeth. "I brought plenty of extra meat."

"I'm a vegetarian," I said.

"Liar," she said. "Take the drink."

The drink was delicious and strong, though a little cold for a winter night. "How do you know I'm lying?"

"Because you just admitted it." She set her drink on the table and opened the lid of the grill. A ball of smoke made a run for the cosmos. "Also because I went through your garbage, silly."

I almost spat out a mouthful of piña colada. "Why—" I had to stop so I could choke a little while. "Why would you go through my garbage?"

"Please climb on up and have a seat," she said. "I know that the chair may be a little small for you. I found the biggest one I could."

I snapped my fingers at her. "Garbage. Why?"

"Any good detective who is getting the runaround by a person of interest goes through their garbage. It's basic procedure. I also stole your mail."

I growled at her.

She put two patties of ground beef on the grill and closed the lid. "Don't worry. I steamed it open, sealed it, and returned it when I was done. You only had junk mail and bills, anyway. I learned very little about you."

"Have you been following me?" I demanded.

"A little," Tanis said. "Enough to know that someone else is also following you."

"Who?" I asked. "Why?"

She gave me one of her dazzling smiles. "Did you know that I'm wearing a blue bikini under this down coat and ski pants? I'm also barefoot inside of my boots and wool socks. And I have a nice tan, thanks to my Zuni heritage. Isn't a picnic at the beach pleasant?"

Tanis was obviously insane. I told her so.

"Wrong. I simply understand the world to such an extent that I realize all so-called truth is a social construction. The only reason that sitting under the sky, barbecuing hamburgers, and wearing skimpy clothes is considered a beach activity is because we've decided, as a society, that it is so. A polar bear would consider eating a seal burger in the moonlight by an ice floe to be about as wonderful as life could get."

"Show me your bikini," I said.

She shook her head. "Only once you've told me all your secrets."

"Who else is following me?" I asked.

"I'll tell you after you've eaten a hamburger with me and finished your drink. How do you like it?"

"Pretty rare," I said. "Not too rare, though."

She opened the grill and flipped the burgers. They were gorgeous, crisscrossed with grill marks, hissing with grease. "What have you discovered about the nature of the universe?"

"That it's nosey. Ever since I went to the Bosque—which I only did as a favor for a friend—I've been plagued by interruptions to my happy life. People following me. Scientists hassling me. Dead animals showing up without explanation, killed by mysterious beasts." I gestured at her. "Weirdoes going through my trash."

"Come up and sit in the lawn chair I brought especially for you." Tanis patted the chair. Her white sunglasses slipped a little down her nose, revealing big, dark, mischievous eyes.

I sipped my drink. It was half gone. "I'll stay down here."

"But I've arranged it just right," she said. "You'll notice that I have positioned the back of the chair up against the cab of your truck so you can stretch your legs all the way to the tailgate."

I leaned an elbow on the roof of the cab and took another slurp of my drink.

"Fine," she said. "Have it your way. What do you want on your hamburger?"

"Sauerkraut, avocado, and blue cheese."

"You may choose between ketchup, mustard, tomato, or lettuce," she said.

She opened the lid of the grill. The burgers were still sizzling and the outsides were brown. Tanis scooped one of them up with a steel spatula, put it in a bun and added fixings. She put it on a paper plate and handed it to me. I bit into it: perfection.

We didn't speak much as she doctored up her own and we ate. My burger was gone in five or six bites. It was the kind of meal that made you want to take a nap. Instead, I mixed both of us another drink.

"Do you read much literature, Mr. Stick?" Tanis asked as she dotted the corners of her mouth with a napkin.

"Just Stick," I said. "No, I do not."

"I consider myself to be a Renaissance woman. I study many forms of knowledge and art, not just those that apply directly to my field."

"What is your field exactly?" I asked, just to hear her say it.

"Animal theology."

"So you preach to monkeys? Stuff like that."

She gave me a smile that teetered on the brink between charm and mania. "I once tried to convert a school of dolphins to Roman Catholicism."

I couldn't tell if she was kidding.

"It almost worked. They liked taking the sacrament."

"You're full of it."

She placed a hand over her heart. "I spent two months in a wetsuit. The water infected both my ears. I had to go on antibiotics."

I didn't believe her. "Did they become good Catholics?"

"Why should religion only apply to humans? If God created the whole universe, including animals, shouldn't they get the opportunity to live in His grace, too? Why is it that, if God created us after so many billions of years of an Earth dominated by other beings, we are the only ones He cares about? I say that if religion can be brought to animals, then we'll know for sure that God is real. And for every animal I fail to convert, that's one more mark against Him."

"You don't talk like a normal theologian," I said.

"I am a true theologian," she said. "Theology should be about exhaustive critical inquiry. God gave me a free will and an extraordinary intellect. If I use them to disprove His existence, then that's His own fault. And if animals, who've outlived us and who outnumber us, aren't part of God's plan, then what kind of a plan is that?"

"What if God's plan is different for each species? He gave us an intellect and free will, and he demands that we use them both. Fine. He gave spiders the ability to spin webs and catch insects. He gave vampire bats the ability to navigate using sonar and to suck blood from cows. The way to worship God is to live out your life cycle, using the facilities that God gave you. Maybe that's it."

Tanis sat in her chair, with her piña colada in one hand and the fingers of the other pinching her chin. The night stars twinkled in the twin mirrors of her sunglasses. "Let's say we accept your hypothesis. What happens if a creature is born that was not made by God? What happens if a creature is created unnaturally and has no inherent life cycle? Is that creature inherently evil? Can we say that such a creature, having no purpose given to it by a benevolent creator, is of the Devil?"

"There is no such creature."

"Man creates animals all the time. The majority of our crops and livestock are either manipulated through husbandry techniques or directly genetically engineered. A chicken bred with no beak and no feet is no longer a chicken. It cannot peck. It cannot walk. Some chickens are even bred without wings. This is no longer an animal with a life cycle."

"So," I said, "you're suggesting the devil is a chicken."

She didn't laugh. "I'm suggesting that your measure of God includes, by proxy, an anti-God."

"You talk like a university professor. They think too much."

"That is a myth," she said. "You can never think too much."

"You can never think too little. We are beings born into a world of action.

The world doesn't think. It acts."

"By the world, you mean the universe."

"Fine," I said. "The universe acts. I don't know much about it. I do know animals: they eat, sleep, breed, and socialize. They don't sit around thinking. I live my life like an animal: I care for things. I grow things. I feed things. I don't philosophize."

She cocked her head. "You're an atheist."

"I am not."

Glee poured through her grinning face. "I just figured you out."

"No. You did not."

"My job is done for tonight, John Stick." Tanis rose from her lawn chair and dusted the crumbs from her thighs. Her tone became very business-like. "You are being followed by a member of a radical group of pro-immigration pan-Chicano militants. They call themselves the Good Friends. They're interested in you because they believe you're affiliated with the Minutemen."

"I'm not."

Her smile was a little bitter. "Don't lie to me. I've been following you, remember?"

"Rex is my best friend from when we were six," I said. "He's not a Minuteman. They're just paying him. He doesn't get much work. He's not a racist."

She leapt down from the truck. "You sound like you're trying to convince yourself as much as you're trying to convince me."

"I'm his best friend." I spread my arms. "Look at me. He's not a prejudiced person."

"Every human is prejudiced. It's in our genetic code."

"That's a cynical attitude."

"It's a truthful one," she said. "You're caught in a battle of prejudice. On one side are the Minutemen, and on the other are the Good Friends. Be careful. Both sides have guns."

"What side are you on?" I asked.

She removed her sunglasses. Her eyes were steely points in the slanting moonlight. "I don't have a side. I'm a free agent."

"So you're the only human without prejudice?"

She reached way up and patted me on the cheek. "Goodbye Stick."

"What about your bikini?" I asked.

She walked away into the night.

CHAPTER NINE

The phone rang as I left my house the next morning. Stress and lack of sleep throbbed behind my eyeballs, making the whole world pulse. My phone's constant ringing didn't help. Against my instincts, I answered.

"I've been robbed." It was Melodía. Her voice held that raw early morning tinge.

"By who?" I asked. "Are you hurt?"

"My lab," she said. "Jones has been kidnapped. The whooping crane is gone, too."

"That's crazy. Calm down. You'll find them."

"I didn't misplace a six-foot bird, you bastard. Get over here."

"Call the police."

The line went quiet. She didn't want to call the police. They were the most masculine, most judgmental, and least tactful people you could ever want to meet—the opposite of sweet, nurturing Stick.

"I really do have to go to work," I said.

"This is an emergency!"

I didn't tell her that the past week and a half had been nothing but emergencies. Instead, I put a gust of my wind in her ear.

"Thank you," she said.

I hung up.

Twenty minutes later, I stood outside the closed door of her lab. I knelt, hunched my body up at the doorknob, and inspected the lock. While I peered at it, Melodía pulled the door open.

"What are you doing?" she demanded.

I'd been checking for scratches, which I'd read in old detective novels were a sure sign that a lock had been picked. Melodía's doorknob looked as if it'd been scratched at for years. "Tying my shoe."

We spent the next half hour combing over the lab. Jones' terrarium was empty. A blank spot in Melodía's fridge marked where the whooping crane had been. The frog's corpse had vanished too. Otherwise, everything seemed intact.

"Someone stole those three things, and those only." Melodía's right eye was inflamed and her left, nestled between two tumors, pulsed visibly. The line of her scalp was flushed red.

"Why would they do that?"

"They're all connected to the egg," she said.

"What about the wasp you found in the frog's stomach? If someone were after the egg, and the wasp was really related, they would have taken that, too."

"So, you admit they're related?"

I gave her a resigned shrug. "Strange egg laid in flesh the flesh of a bird in the fashion of a tarantula hawk. Wound made with the mandibles of a horse fly. We find a creature with a tarantula hawk's stinger and a fly's mouth. I guess I'll concede the connection."

Melodía took a moment to look smug.

"The question is not who's right. The question is why didn't your burglar steal the half-digested wasp corpse as well?"

"No one knew about it. But no one knew about Jones either."

Something dawned on me. I felt slightly sick to my stomach. "I told someone."

Our eyes met. "Who?" She already knew the answer. I could tell by the betrayed look on her face that she was thinking of the same man I was: Simon Marchette.

"But why would Marchette steal anything?" I wondered aloud. "He's not the type."

"This is a once in a decade find." Melodía careened around her lab opening drawers and cabinets. "A new insect could get Marchette out of the zoo and back into the real scientific community. Hell, he could name it after himself."

It didn't seem right. Marchette wasn't a cutthroat biologist out to get famous. He was a sincere guy who tickled hissing cockroaches and handled centipedes as gently as newborn babies. Admittedly, he had been acting a little weird. "You should know something."

Melodía stopped roving around her lab and raised her eyebrows at me.

"Marchette and I talked yesterday. He said some stuff that, in hindsight, sounded wacky."

"Like what?" she asked.

"Well, you know how he is."

Her gaze wobbled away from mine and tentatively back.

"You met him, right?" It was an experiment.

Her gaze hit the floor and she turned half away.

"You never met him."

"I was busy." She still didn't look at me. "I left him instructions and had him dictate notes into a recorder. What does it matter?"

We both knew that she hadn't been busy. She'd simply not wanted to meet another human being and have him look at her face the way the normals did. I didn't blame her. Besides, it didn't matter—none of this really mattered. It was all just keeping me away from my quiet hole in the depths of the zoo.

"Well?" Melodía asked. "What did he say?"

"He said you should incinerate the egg. He said on no account should you hatch it."

"That's absurd. It's just an insect egg. Did he say why?"

"Nope. He seemed rattled though. He wasn't kidding."

"What'd you tell him?" she asked.

"I told him you were a big girl and perfectly able to handle an insect on your own. Then we talked about a snake, and I kicked him out of my office."

"A snake?" she asked.

"Yeah. We have lots of them. They're all sitting by their cage doors waiting to be fed right now. The one I was talking to him about was dead. Attacked and sucked dry of all its blood." I grinned at her. "Pretty gruesome."

"Looks like we both have problems with hematophages. A horsefly and—what kind was yours?"

"Jury's still out." I grabbed my forehead with my fingers and massaged it.

"What's wrong?" Melodía asked, touching my elbow.

"Marchette seemed pretty interested in that snake."

By the time I'd driven to the zoo, the snake was gone from my lab's refrigerator, of course. I called Melodía from my zoo phone. "Well, we know who did it. Only Marchette knew about the snake, the crane, and the tarantula. The cops should have an easy time."

"So, you're going to call them?"

"Yes, Hernandez, I'm calling them." My lab was an inviolate space. No one trespassed. "That pasty little scientist took some pretty important specimens."

"Are you going to tell them about my lab?" Her voice quavered. Her very slight slur deepened a shade.

"This is no time for your fear of people." As soon as I said the words, I knew they were going to cost both of us. Her fear, like her face, was taboo. She'd devoted her adult life to avoiding talking about them.

Melodía's breath came in bursts over the receiver, the rhythm of her rage, building. Like many recluses, she expelled her emotions at the wrong times, at the wrong targets. She packed them down into her psyche; they exploded out. I knew because I was just like her.

"Listen—" I said.

"People are bastards," she hissed. "People are sons of bitches. People are pure evil. After people have tormented you your whole life, come and tell me not to hate them. A cataclysm could wipe every last person from the planet. I'd celebrate. I'd be free to go out in the sunshine. I'd be free to walk through a field and smell the flowers. Songbirds would land on my fingers. Don't tell me not to hate people, you fucking bastard."

I probably should have exploded right back at her. I probably should have described my life to her in grave detail. I should have outlined my routine of solitude and then called her a heartless bitch or something. We could have screamed at each other and cried and apologized and realized that life was grand if you only had a friend. That was the way a couple of normals would have handled it.

I was a rock. "Go ahead and hate anybody you want. Whatever gets you through life. Hell, I'm convinced it's making you real happy."

I waited until after she'd hung up on me to hurl the receiver against the far wall. I waited until it was too late, and then I picked up the base of the telephone and crushed it in my fist as if it were an aluminum can. I let the remains fall through my fingers, and then I turned and punched a dent in my locker the size of a man's head. It fell loose at one hinge. That was the end of my locker. No one would think it was worth their while to repair. I'd been using it since I was sixteen. I'd moved it from the main locker room to my personal space after college. It was still an eighties shade of lime green, only now it was dead.

I didn't call the cops. My rage vanished, and afterwards something was missing from my body. I felt as if a vital fluid had been drained out of me and I'd lost the will to go through any of the motions that had comprised my life. I collapsed in my chair and thought I might slouch there for a few weeks.

An hour or so ticked by. My mind sat on top of my neck like an empty box. Then in its cold, post-rage objectivity, my brain snapped one and one together. A white snake. A white crane. Both were anomalies. It was a coincidence—until Melodía had pointed out that they'd both had the blood sucked from their bodies. Both had clearly been attacked by different hematophages, blood-eaters, and both had been stolen at the same time, by the same man.

Tanis' words returned to my ears: *When two events occur simultaneously with the same object of inquiry, we must pay strict attention.* Marchette had stolen both animals. He'd noticed that the snake had been drained of blood; he'd examined the crane's wounds. The two animals were related to each other somehow—and by proxy to the dead birds. I didn't know how, but if I could get my hands on that little bald scientist, I could find out.

Of course, I didn't know anything about Marchette apart from that he showed up once a week to keep the invertebrates healthy. I doubted many of my colleagues knew him, either, but I thought it might be worth a shot to talk to one of them—which showed just how weird my life had become. I was willingly seeking out a normal.

I found one in the bat cave, an annex of the reptile house. She was on her hands and knees, with the upper half of her body inside a back panel of the bat enclosure. When I rapped on a wall, she emerged and sat back on her heels. She was dressed in khaki slacks, tennis shoes, and a green zoo polo. She wore heavy work gloves and clutched a dirty, dripping sponge. She was short and plump, small-nosed, and with orange hair pulled back in a ponytail. Several strands had come loose and framed her face. Light perspiration stood on her forehead. A tag on her chest said "Abbey."

"Hello," Abbey said. A faint smile accompanied a flush in her cheeks. She rubbed a forearm across her forehead. "You've never visited me before."

"Hello."

She held up her gloved hands. "I'm cleaning guano."

"I understand it's the most valuable feces in the world," I said just to be polite.

Her smile got bigger. Her freckled cheeks and nose crinkled up.

A bat in a small cage on the far side of the room fluttered against the bars and then fell to the cage floor where it lay opening and closing its jaws.

"Is he okay?" I asked.

"That's just Ferdinand. He's having a time-out."

I decided to let that one go. "Can I ask you a couple questions?"

"Shoot," she said.

"You work a lot at night, don't you?"

She nodded. "Bats are nocturnal, after all."

"Did you stay late last night?"

She nodded. "I wanted to see how my Mexican free-tails would take to the new batch of mosquitoes I gave them. Matured them from larvae myself." She swelled her chest with pride.

"Did you see a skinny, short, bald scientist?" I asked.

"You mean Simon?" Her mouth softened at the edges and her green eyes twinkled.

"Yeah, Simon Marchette. When did you see him and what was he doing?"

"Is there a problem?" she asked.

"Maybe. I need to find him."

"We bumped into each other near the south entrance at 6:37 p.m. I almost knocked him over."

"Exactly 6:37?"

She nodded. "His watch happened to tilt in my direction and I saw the time."

"And you remembered?"

Abbey removed the gloves and laid them on the floor. She plopped down in a wheeled office chair, leaned back, and propped her boots on a cheap metal desk. "Yep. I have a photographic memory. Yesterday stuck in my mind because he usually flirts with me. Ramming into each other like that—it would have given him the perfect opportunity."

"But not yesterday," I said.

Abbey shook her head and blew a strand of hair out of her eyes. "It's cute when he flirts. It's harmless, but still flattering. Scraping up bat guano doesn't always make a girl feel pretty."

"What was he like yesterday? Was he headed in or out?"

"In. He looked paler and clammier than usual. His eyes were red. His hands were shaking—just a little. What did he do?"

I took a deep breath. "He stole my snake."

"Oh, no! It must have been a small one. I can't imagine him getting out of here wearing an anaconda around his neck."

"It was dead," I said. "An albino rattlesnake. About five feet long."

"Valuable?" she asked.

I shrugged. "Not in dollars. But scientifically, yeah."

"You want me to call security?"

I shrugged. "Marchette is a colleague."

"And a really nice guy," she said. "And a thief."

"If I can find him, maybe we can sort it out." A moment of our conversation the day before sprung back into my mind. "Do you have any idea where else Marchette works?"

Abbey squinted. "Some lab. Private, I think. Do you?"

"He wouldn't tell me," I said.

"The zoo subcontracts him through his other company. Human Resources would know the name of the company. They would tell you, if security gave them the okay. That'd mean you'd have to report him, though."

I mulled it over. If I told security, they'd tell the cops. If the cops got involved, it'd lead to Melodía. Despite our fight, I still didn't want a bunch of boots stomping around her lab against her will. The idea of Melodía dragged downtown and questioned at police headquarters was beyond terrible.

"You know," Abbey said, her eyes drifting toward the ceiling, "I've often noticed that Simon's shoes have dust on them. Not a lot and usually not on the soles. On the laces."

"We live in a desert," I said. "There's plenty of dust to go around."

"The dust is orange."

Orange dust. You say orange dust to any native of Albuquerque and they think of one place. "From the Sandía Man Cave?"

She nodded.

The Sandía Man Cave was a long, low-ceilinged, winding passage that led a few hundred feet into the side of the Sandía Mountains that flanked the east side of the city. Its antechamber had sheltered one of our ancestors 20,000 years or so ago. As a kid, I'd crawled to the back—as all Albuquerque kids did, only most of them could walk some of the way and crouch the rest. The Sandía Man, as he was known, was one of the earliest documented people in the area, which made the cave an interesting place for anthropologists. However, the thing that everyday folk remembered it for was the thick orange dust that coated your shoes, clothes, and hands when you emerged back into the sunlight.

"Are you saying that Marchette spends his free time spelunking?" I asked.

"If I thought that, I wouldn't be taking into account that there's not much dust on the soles of his shoes, just on the laces. It's harder to get dust out of the laces. You have to wash them. If you were stomping through the dust in the cave itself, it'd probably be on your soles, too. But if the dust was blowing around in the area you went to habitually, say to and from work, it'd stick in your laces, building up over time, while it would fall off the soles."

"You should go to work for the APD."

"And leave my precious babies?" She laughed, gesturing at Ferdinand. "Never."

"So what you're getting at is that Marchette walks by the entrance of the cave on his way to work. That's impossible. The cave is off in the wilderness. You have to climb a mountain slope to get to it. The entrance is sunk into the side of a cliff, practically."

"There are stairs now," she said. "But that's not at all what I mean."

"What do you mean, then?"

"Where does the dust come from?"

"The cave." Then I caught her drift. "The rock inside the cave."

"That means, that you find someplace nearby where excavations have recently occurred into the same kind of rock. You find your dust, you find your rock, you find your excavation site—and you find Simon's other employer."

Abbey was a genius. "I should talk to Human Resources first, to save myself some trouble."

"That's probably smart." She leaned farther back in her chair and laced her fingers behind her head. One of her pleasantly round biceps had a smudge of guano on it.

"Good work," I said.

She gave me a little smile and a shrug. "It's elementary."

"I guess I'll head over to H.R."

Her eyes flicked downwards. "You might want to put a Band-Aid on your hand first."

My right hand was dribbling on the tile. The first, second, and third knuckles were split and quickly turning purple from slugging my locker.

"Should I see the other guy?" Abbey asked.

"He's my front door. The thing's got a tightly-wound spring. Caught me as I was leaving the house this morning."

Abbey grinned. "I figured you punched a rhinoceros in the nose."

"I'm not that manly," I said. "Thanks again."

She gave me one deep nod. Ferdinand threw himself around his timeout cage. I waved at him and scrammed.

I didn't go to Human Resources. Instead, I went back to my lab and straightened things up. I tried to bend my locker door into shape. I swept up what was left of my phone and filled out paperwork to get a new one.

I couldn't figure it out. Why would someone of Marchette's status and education steal three corpses and a doomed tarantula? I didn't buy Melodía's argument about professional zealotry. He was a good guy, and other than some idiosyncrasies, pretty normal.

He was almost a friend.

CHAPTER TEN

The next day was my day off. I decided I'd enjoy it by taking a drive in the mountains—toward the Sandía Man Cave, to be exact. I left the city before seven to avoid rush hour, taking Rio Grande Boulevard north, which wound along the river beneath the gray winter limbs of the cottonwoods. The curling brown river flashed into sight intermittently in the shallow gorge beyond. I headed east on Alameda, a street named for the trees, across the northern suburbs of the city toward the mountains. The land grew dry, the trees disappeared, and gaudy strip malls sprung up in their place. I drove north on I-25 for about fifteen minutes to the small city of Bernalillo, got off the interstate, and drove a few miles east to Placitas, a satellite suburb that consisted primarily of big adobe-plastered houses peppered into the rolling folds of desert scrub and small trees. I turned south and left the village on route 135, which wound through the gentle eastern slopes of the Sandía Mountains into Las Huertas canyon—home of the Sandía Man and his cave.

I spotted what I was looking for before I even started looking. I remembered the canyon as a place of pine forests, trickling streams, and the occasional idyllic meadow. On the western side of the route, the up-slope side, that was still true. Near the base of the canyon, however, a huge swath of the lower mountain slope had been stripped of trees. Boulders had been cleared. What looked like a brand new prison facility stood in their place. It consisted of a small guardhouse projecting from a bulky central structure surrounded by high razor wire fences that sparkled in the sun. Upslope and separated by a quarter mile sat another stout building, smaller and without all the razor wire decoration. The east-facing side of the building featured a large rectangular extension three stories high, the size of a football field, and cased with greenhouse plastic. A few other buildings clustered nearby. The farthest one up the mountain's slope was the smallest—and the strangest: it was round with a domed roof made up of two half-spheres that formed a seam from the east side of the dome to the west. It looked like an observatory roof, which could open to give the interior a view of the sky—only you built observatories on top of mountains, not in canyons. A security fence ringed the entire complex, including a sea of asphalt parking lot. The fence must have measured a few miles in circumference. At the gate's opening, a massive marble block announced the complex's name: *Typhon Industries*. And below that in smaller letters, I could just barely make out: *Biogenic Research and Detainment Facilities*. It sounded like an absurd combination, but the whole world had been going mad since Christ died and came back.

To the south of the structure with the projecting enclosed football field lay a site of new construction. It was nothing more than a massive pit surrounded by bulldozers and cranes that looked like playthings from my high vantage point on the shoulder of the highway. But it was easy to see the exposed orange rock in the pit. I'd found the source of Marchette's shoelace dust—and by proxy the site of his other job.

As I sat pondering, a few cars trickled in and out of the parking lot. The bulldozers toiled away in miniature in their dusty orange pit. The sun blazed across the arid plains that ran east all the way to Texas. I stayed there for a long while. I rolled down my window. The crisp winter air sparkled with the chirping of mountain songbirds.

I hadn't driven all this way to enjoy nature.

I figured if Marchette worked for Typhon Industries, he'd be in whatever building held animals, which had to be the one with the big greenhouse enclosure. I drove down to the complex on brand new roads, the blacktop as smooth as glass. I had to pass through a booth with a gate and a security guard, but they both gave way when I flashed my zoo ID and said I was there on business.

The lobby was one of those grand foyer deals with a lot of black marble and glass and a fountain that trickled streams of water over a crystal double helix. It was pretty cheesy. A receptionist stood behind the kind of monolithic counter you might see in a five-star hotel. A couple of security guards flanked her, complete with sidearms and game faces. My presence made their stoicism slip but only for a second.

The receptionist didn't even blink. She wore a blue-skirted suit and a smile made of Teflon. Her teeth looked like they'd been mass-produced and installed. Her hair was a platinum helmet, and her figure looked like the template that they used to design mannequins.

"Welcome to Typhon Industries." Her voice was as slick as the rest of her. "How may I help you?"

"I'm here for a meeting with Dr. Simon Marchette."

"Your name?"

"John Stick."

"One moment." She chattered her fingernails against a keyboard and examined a hidden computer screen. She looked up at me. Her eyes were topaz. "I'm sorry. I don't see any appointment listed."

I looked down at her. I didn't say anything. I'd found that normals were uncomfortable with silence. Sometimes all you had to do was shut up, and they'd take care of the rest.

This normal wasn't that easy. She stared straight back at me. She didn't blink. With every second that passed, her eyes cut a sharper path between us and her smile became spikier.

I finally balked. I'd never been as hard as I pretended to be. "Can you call him? He probably just forgot to tell you about our meeting."

"I have no meeting listed. I have no record of your name—nor can I confirm that I have any knowledge of a Dr. Simon Marchette. None of this information is in my system. Were there such a person working here, I wouldn't even know—unless he appeared in my system. Which he does not."

"He works here." I said. "Call him. I didn't drive thirty miles to see the sights."

She folded her hands in front of her stomach and stood there. In the animal kingdom, her smile would have indicated that she was planning to eat me. On either side of her, security was getting itchy.

"He'll be glad I'm here," I said. "It's important."

She cocked her head just a hair, but otherwise didn't move.

She was beating me at my own game. I was about to retreat to my vehicle when something happened behind the counter, hidden from view. I couldn't tell if a sensor lit up, or an alarm went off, or if a mouse ran out of its hole and stole her donut. Her eyes flicked down. Her smiled cracked and an expression of brutal pragmatism flashed through. The guards twitched. They both wore earpieces—it didn't take an Abbey the bat-keeper to deduce something was going down.

One of the guards jogged through a back door of the room. As the door opened, the blare of an alarm echoed from the halls beyond. The receptionist picked up a phone, hit a button, and listened. I strained to hear what the voice on the other end of the line said, but failed—my hearing wasn't my strongest attribute. The woman's eyes lifted until they found mine. She held up a finger. After a few seconds, she hung up the phone. "You are to stay here. Someone is coming for you." The receptionist looked to the remaining guard. "This man is not to leave." Then she turned and stalked through the same back door the security guard had taken. Her skirt swished with the precision of glass being cut.

The guard walked over to me. He was a beefy guy with big shoulders in a black uniform over Kevlar armor. A gun, a can of pepper spray, a nightstick, and a whole lot of other contraptions hung on his belt. His head came up to my elbow.

I gave him a big, friendly smile.

"You're to stay here," he said in his toughest voice.

"It's a free country," I said.

"Not on private property, it's not," the guard said. "Anybody who steps onto our property is ours. I could cuff you and throw you in a room and nobody could say bupkis."

"I can't wait to see how that turns out for you," I said from my vantage point way overhead. It was all just talk. I was sticking around. Whoever was coming for me might spill something about Marchette.

I shouldn't have been shocked by the stocky, fifty-something, baldheaded man who opened and closed the door, letting the alarm do a loop around the room again. I wondered if it signaled a fire or an escaped lion.

"Mr. Stick." The Captain stuck out his hand. It was his thing. He couldn't get enough of shaking hands. "What brings you out here?"

"I'm on vacation." I took his hand. It was a small, dense lump in my palm. "I'm hitting all the hot tourist spots."

"Ha. You're a crack-up. You come here to take my offer?"

I scanned his arm. The welt, identical to the one I'd seen on the whooping crane, had healed, but it looked like it had been a nasty process. "Is this where I'd be working?" I asked. "Is this Minuteman Central Command?"

"Like I said, the Minutemen don't hire. You'd be contracting with

Typhon Industries."

"Doing what, exactly?" I asked.

He chuckled. "We'll give you the details when you commit. It's all a little hush-hush around here. So, you in?"

"I'm actually here for a meeting with a colleague. It's a pure coincidence that you work here. It's quite a surprise."

"There are no coincidences in the world, my friend." The Captain clapped me on the back and steered me away from the reception counter. The guard left us and returned to his post. "Everything's part of everything else. There's an order holding it all together."

"Tell it to the tornadoes, Captain." I regretted using his fake title as soon as my mouth made the sounds.

"That's what we Minutemen do," he said. "We're wardens of order. We keep the world working according to the rules."

"And I thought you were just Mexican-haters. Boy, do I have egg on my face."

"Mexican-Americans are part of our country," the Captain said. "I don't hate Mexicans. I hate law-breakers."

I didn't like the way we were pacing slowly across the foyer, his hand on my back, as if we were co-conspirators having a deep conversation. I was tired of deep conversations. I was tired of conspiracies. I wanted my albino Western rattlesnake back.

I pulled away from him and stopped walking. "Save it. I'm part Chicano. I think the Minutemen are delusional. They believe that range-roving around the desert toting assault rifles is some sort of patriotic act. I think it's idiotic. And maybe a form of terrorism."

The Captain's eyes got beady. He clenched his jaw the way men do to show how manly they are. "That's not nice talk. Not nice at all. If I didn't know better, I'd think you were calling my boss idiotic—and worse. He wouldn't like that. He also won't like it when I have to tell him that you're turning down his job offer—again."

"Tell him I'll put it in writing if he wants. I'll get a big tattoo of the word *no* if he wants me to. I'll hire a biplane to sky-write it for him. I'm here looking for a man named Simon Marchette. Where is he?" I was doing my own masculine pantomime. I loomed. I let my voice shake the earth.

The Captain gave me the stare-down. I'd seen it all before at the zoo. The spider monkeys liked to give that same look to each other when they were feuding over a favorite toy. He wasn't nearly as good at it as his receptionist was. "Never heard of him."

"That's sad," I said. "He won the lottery. I'm here to give him the good news. Guess I got confused about his place of business."

The Captain worked his jaw some more. He spoke through clenched teeth. "I guess that means you're leaving."

"Guess so," I said. "I'll let you get back to your fire drill."

He smiled. It was a little less inviting than his glower. "Guard! Get this guy out the front door." He walked away. His arms stood out from his torso the way men's arms do when they spend a lot of time lifting weight. It made him walk funny.

The guard escorted me to the entrance. I went willingly. As he held the door, I caught a glimpse down the collar of his shirt. He'd been bitten—just as the Captain and the whooping crane had.

"Nasty sting you got there," I said.

The real person broke through the guard's veneer—and I recognized him. He was the kid with the meaty shoulders I'd seen that first day at the Bosque. He put his fingers on the bite. He stretched his mouth and widened his eyes the way people do when they're recalling something painful. "Damnedest bite I ever got. Bled for a day. Swelled up like I was growing a second head."

"What the hell got ya?" I asked.

Meat Shoulders shook his head. "Some damned huge bug. Size of a dragonfly, but evil. They're all over the facility. We've got bug lamps, we spray the place down with poison, but they keep coming back. Must be breeding nearby."

I whacked him on the shoulder. "Heal."

"Thanks pal," he said. "Sorry about all the ruckus. Things are a little tense around here." He was a good guy. Once you broke him open, his pulp was soft and juicy.

"I've been on edge too. The bird thing. Down at the Bosque."

A guarded expression slid over his face like a visor. "Yeah."

"I saw you down there the day after it happened. Didn't I?" I was trying to make my tone casual and doing a shoddy job of it.

"Could be," he said. "We run patrols all over."

"Another guy was with you. He was bandaging your arm. Your van was torn to shreds."

Meat Shoulders' eyes wobbled around in their sockets. They couldn't fix on anything, like a compass at the North Pole. He opened his mouth, but at that moment, the receptionist cleared her throat. It sounded like someone whetting a knife. "I have to get back to my post."

I left.

I needed insect traps. Thanks to the guard, I knew where to put them—but I'd have to be sneaky about it. I tried to envision Melodía's look of surprise when I brought her a live, adult specimen of the bug she'd been trying to hatch. It would be the perfect present to get her to forgive me.

CHAPTER ELEVEN

arrived home at midmorning. My apartment smelled like beer bottles and dust. Even though the temperature outside was only pushing forty degrees, I opened a few windows. I turned a fan on low to get the air circulating. Ralph didn't appreciate any of it. He was trying to sleep the day away, as was his God-given right as a nocturnal creature. Normally, he slept in a nest he'd built in a corner of the terrarium nearest the wall, where the heater was. When I started letting all sorts of noise, light, and wind into the room, he scuttled into his plastic shelter.

I decided to clean my apartment and hope that maybe my life would follow suit. I dusted the furniture. I wiped down the door and windowsills, the baseboards, the light switch guards, all the kitchen fixtures, and the top of every surface in my bedroom and bathroom. I carried the rugs outside and beat hell out of them. I swept my wooden floors and replaced the rugs. I wrapped my hands in plastic bags—no kitchen glove made for humans would fit me—and did some serious scrubbing of sink, tub, and toilet. I rubbed my kitchen sink until it shone like sterling silver. I attacked my stovetop with a wire brush. Finally, I took the trash out. Only when I'd brought the trashcan back inside, did I realize that I'd cleaned the place in hopes that Melodía would drop by later that evening. We'd only been fighting for a day, and I already missed her.

Once my cleaning was done, I had practically the whole day to myself. I decided to spend it making horsefly traps.

The first step in creating a homemade flytrap is preparing the bait. Normally, a sugary solution works best for horseflies. Only the females drink blood; both females and males eat all sorts of other things like pollen, fruit, and vegetable matter. I could have prepared a sugary bait and taken my chances. But the guard, the crane, and the Captain had all been bitten by blood-hungry females. When a female seeks blood, it is a sure sign she's mating and laying eggs. I wanted to catch a female, so the first step in creating the particular trap I needed was acquiring blood. I made a few calls and found a butcher that could sell me pig's blood. The shop was located in the old neighborhood, not too far from my dad's house. I drove there, purchased a gallon of fresh blood, and was back on the road to my place by noon.

The weather turned. A savage wind swept down from the mountains and raked its claws across the city. I drove home, blasting the heater the whole way as the gusts swatted my truck around. They wanted to wrestle me off the road and throw me into the tumbleweeds. The trees in my neighborhood twisted their craggy, bare limbs in agony. Dirt around the arroyo manifested as a dust devil before shattering against a chain link fence. It was one of those crystal blue days with icy gales that cut the skin from your ears and sliced through whatever layers you draped over your sad mortal coil. New Mexican wind was invisible and cruel: you looked out your window at the pretty sunshine, and when you opened your door, it leapt on you like a starved wildcat.

I parked my truck and rushed for the front door. I had it unlocked, opened, and closed again before I noticed the shortish middle-aged Chicano man at my bar. He sat with his back to the wall and his left elbow on the bar top. His feet dangled two feet above the floor. He wore a fedora, trench coat, dusty brown wingtips, droopy dark green socks, and a cheap dark green suit. He had a trimmed beard and sunglasses on his face, and he held a little revolver in his right hand.

It was the man who'd been following me. The Newspaper Man.

"You the plumber?" I asked.

"Far from it." The pitch of his voice was a little high, with that slight Spanish vowel twist that English-fluent New Mexicans often have—even some Anglos. "You might say I'm here to fix something—but it ain't pipes."

"Can I get you a spider?" I gave him my cruel giant sneer. "Or maybe you'd like me to carry you outside and toss you into the arroyo?"

"You're big, for sure." He hefted the gun. "Lots of target to poke holes in."

I set my brown grocery bag of blood on the end of the bar closest to me. I folded my arms and leaned against the wall by the door. I'd seen my share of guns. During our teen and twenty-something years, Rex and I had shot up quite a few bottles, cans, and old cars. That had been one aspect of our early adulthood that was typically New Mexican.

Newspaper Man smirked. "You think you're something special. Biggest, strongest lug in the whole state—hell, the whole damn country maybe. These days, big and strong don't matter. Iron." He hefted his little gun. "That's what matters."

"You're confused," I said. "This isn't a Humphrey Bogart movie. This is my apartment."

He made a show of looking around. "Nice place. Must get plenty of black mold and millipedes. You own?"

I showed him some teeth.

"Don't answer. I already know. I've talked to your landlady. She smells like rosewater and chicken fat. She thinks I'm a city employee taking a survey of citizen satisfaction with the new tree-planting initiative. I've seen your voting record—you're not even registered. Never voted in your life. I know your employment history. I've seen your university transcripts. I have a copy of your driver's license in my wallet. Hell, I even know what library books you checked out as a kid."

I didn't like people mentioning my childhood. "If you know everything, then what do we have to talk about?"

"I'm here to tell you. You think you're special. You think just because you rent a leaky basement and have a job cleaning turtle droppings, you can walk all over the city talking to whoever you want. Poking around in business you don't understand." He wagged a finger of his free hand at me. "I'm here to tell you."

"So, tell me."

"There's a war on," he said.

"Are we talking about the war on Christmas?" I asked. "Because I hear that one's not going so well."

"I'm talking about a real war. In this city. We got a Guantanamo Bay for undocumented Latinos buried in the ground just the other side of the Sandías. We got secret weapons. We got puppet-masters pulling strings. We got brother versus brother, sister versus sister. We got cops and robbers, cowboys and Indians, spy-versus-spy."

"Don't forget about predator and prey."

"We got a man with his eye on this whole city," Newspaper Man said. "A man with his eye on you, zookeeper. His name's John White, head of Typhon Industries. Ever heard of him?"

"Name's pretty generic," I said. "I probably heard it and forgot it."

He gave me a sour smile. "Sure. You can be cute. You can go on and be cute until you find yourself buried in a metal box two stories underground. Pale as a fish. Living on a slice of bologna every breakfast and one again for dinner—and whatever cockroach wanders between your fingers."

"Sounds great," I said. "Sign me up. Better yet, get the hell out before I call the cops."

"Call 'em," he said. "They love to laugh."

"Who doesn't? The idea that you break into my house on my day off and hold a gun on me and tell me about some secret war. Funny."

"It's not ha-ha funny," he said. "It's got a dark streak you can appreciate, though. Funnier part is that you don't even know what's cooking. All the smells are wafting right in your face and you sniff 'em real deep. And you say, yum. Steak. When actually what's cooking are your shoes. Somebody's lit your feet on fire. They've piled charcoal under you and stuck pine needles in your socks and sprayed you up to the shins with lighter fluid. They struck a match and you didn't even hear it. They lit you up and you're burning and you say, yum. Dinner."

My little visitor loved his analogies. "All I smell is ten-dollar cologne."

"Point is, you're on fire." He tilted his hat back on his head. "Ever since you stuck your nose in that bird business."

"That was somebody else's nose I poked. It was a proxy nose. And, trust me, I regret it."

"Doesn't matter that you regret it," he said. "What matters is, now you're in, you get out. A cheap guy like you, no friends, no property, no family—hell, you don't have much to lose. You have to cling to the little you've got."

"Obviously, you're not doing a very good job of following me. Lately, it seems like all I've got are friends. They call me in the middle of the night. They show up at my place of employment. They try to get me mixed up in all sorts of plots and plans that aren't any of my business. I don't like business of any kind. I just want to sit quietly alone in a dim room and count the bugs on the ceiling."

His cheeks turned a little red and his mouth tilted up at the edges. "You knew I was tailing you?"

"In this state, it's not hard to catch a guy following you. Some stretches of road, you don't see another car for miles."

Newspaper Man took off his sunglasses and put them in his inside pocket. His eyes were chestnut with pleasant wrinkles at the corners. He looked like he knew how to smile—it stood at odds with his tough guy act. As he set his hat on the bar and mussed his hair, he rested the butt of the gun on his thigh, the barrel straying to one side. "I'm embarrassed. I didn't think you knew."

"I had a guy follow *you*," I said.

He cocked his head. "Really?"

"You like visiting the river." I leaned back and let him chew on it.

He made a show of shrugging it off. "So you followed me. So what?"

"So nothing." I said. "You like to have secret meetings in the woods in the middle of the night. Good for you. You like to meet people in vans with the license number—" I fished the Wendy's receipt from my pocket and read it to him.

"Fine. Tit for tat. I follow you; you follow me. So what?"

"So, you can tell me what this is about or I can have the Minutemen track down that van."

He sighed and thumped his fist on this thigh. "It's about the birds."

"The birds died," I said. "End of story. It's sad and all, but at the end of the day, that's what nature is."

He shook his head. "Those birds did not die a natural death. We know this."

"How?" I asked. "Did you ask your Ouija board?"

"We know it because *they* know it." He gave me a conspiratorial wink.

"And who're they?"

He laughed. "You really are in the dark, aren't you?"

I walked into the kitchen and opened the fridge. Three Tecates kept my vegetables company. I took two out and showed one to him. He gave me a half-hearted nod, so I opened them and threw the bottle caps out. I walked around the bar and handed him one of the bottles. "Mind if I put my groceries in the fridge?"

He shrugged his non-gun side. "Sure. You don't want your milk to spoil."

"This isn't milk." I lifted one of the half-gallon containers of blood out of the bag. "It's blood."

I put it about six inches in front of his face. His eyes ballooned. I had my grip around his pistol hand before he even knew I was going for it. I squeezed until he dropped the beer bottle and his mouth cranked open. The bottle rolled across the bar, spewing foam and beer, and shattered on the kitchen tile. An involuntary sing-song whistled out of his talk-box. I squeezed harder. He clawed at my fingers with his free hand. It was like a baby trying to open a walnut.

When I let him go, the gun fell to the floor. He didn't make a move for it. I picked it up, flicked the safety, and stashed it in my freezer. Then I put the blood in the fridge.

He sat at the bar, red-faced, kneading his hand. I let myself stand there a little while, calming down. I never got into altercations—not anymore. Those days were behind me. I was a calm, gentle, patient caregiver. The burst of adrenaline my body delivered when I seized the little man's gun made my vision shimmer around the edges. I grabbed for my beer too hard. I drank too fast. When I opened the third beer, I almost broke the neck off the bottle.

I set the new one in front of him. "Let's get back to those birds."

His face had taken on a droop. The skin around his lips was pale. He let some air stream out of his body and then seemed to come to a decision. His mouth and eyes relaxed and he sucked the foam from the top of the bottle. "What do you want to know?"

"Everything. I'm still not convinced you actually know much about it."

He smiled and it looked right on him, even if it was one of those patronizing expressions people wear when a kid says something cute. "We know more than you."

"How about you start with this 'we' you keep talking about," I said.

He got a cagey look. "I can't give you this stuff for free."

"How about you tell me the name of your Pan-Chicano militant group?" I wasn't sure if I'd gotten Tanis' words quite right, but I figured it'd be close enough to get him talking.

"You've been listening to some mouths. Lemme guess. That Jane you chewed it up with in the zoo parking lot. Tanis Rivera."

"I've heard it all over town," I lied.

He leaned over the bar and shook a finger at me. "Don't believe a wag of it. She's playing every angle. No one even knows what kind of meat she's got in this thing. She could be a fed, or she could be straight goofy."

"So, who're you with?" I asked.

His face went tight again and he looked at his watch. "I'll tell you: My name's Tony Chavez. I'm a gumshoe. I have a client and I'm looking into this thing for said client."

"You're a private detective? I didn't know your type lived past the fifties."

"Oh, we're still around," Tony Chavez said. "My client is a nature lover rolling in gold Krugerrands. Every time a butterfly dies, he sheds a single tear. Naturally, he's taken an interest in the birds."

"Sounds like my type of guy," I said. "You should introduce us."

"Would if I could," he said. "Confidentiality and all."

I was getting tired of trying to come up with clever rejoinders. I wanted to get to my trap making, and I was beginning to doubt how much I'd be able to learn from my visitor. "Simon Marchette. Know him?"

He wiped a thoughtful expression across his face. "Doesn't ring a bell."

"Then you're of no use to me." I got my broom and made a show of sweeping the broken glass clear of the pool of beer spread across my kitchen tile. Luckily, I'd caulked every seam of cabinet, bar, and refrigerator to keep Ralph's prey from squirming to safety, so the beer wouldn't be hard to clean up.

"If I did know him," the little man piped up, "I wouldn't tell you. Not without some sort of equitable swap."

I emptied the dustpan into the garbage. "How about information on Marchette for your peashooter?"

"That's a .38 special. It's a classic."

"I hear the cops have a program." I filled a bucket with water and a splash of bleach and set it next to the puddle of beer. "They collect firearms and melt them down to make license plates. It keeps the peace and gives felons something to do with their time."

"I'll give you this," he said, "but I can't tell you anything more."

I stopped swooshing my mop around. "Shoot."

He leaned forward until his chest was against the bar, his pupils as big as acorns. He held his finger out and let his mouth hang open for a few seconds, as if he were looking for words. When he spoke, his voice was just above a whisper. "You've been seeing beasties."

I stared at him.

He sat back in his chair, grinning and nodding. "I knew it. They're out there, Mr. Stick. They're real."

"Oh yeah?" I tried to get control of my composure by doing some mopping. "I did see something weird when I was down by Elephant Butte Lake. Could have been the Loch Ness Monster. Everybody's relocating to the Southwest these days."

"Joke around," he said. "Go ahead."

I put my mop in the bucket and leaned the handle against the fridge. "I have not seen any beasties. I have seen some strange dead bodies, but nothing beyond that."

"Let me guess. Odd teeth marks. Insect bites that don't make sense. Blood loss. That kind of thing?"

I gave him my most non-committal look. "You saying Albuquerque has vampires on top of everything else?"

"Ha. This is America. We don't need to import monsters from Europe. We have our own."

"You gonna tell me what they are so I can laugh you out my front door, up my stairs, into your car, and out of my life?"

"I didn't come here to give you the dope," he said. "I came to tell you: steer clear. This is not your business. Stay away from the dead birds. Stay away from the Minutemen. You work with them, and you become the enemy of my client."

"Your client, the tree-hugger?"

"My client, whoever or whatever they may be, is powerful. My client represents a lot of people interested in this bird business. You get on the wrong side—you get on any side—and you'll be in Dutch so deep even you won't be able to see out." His face became grave. "My client is Mary Poppins compared to the people you're mixing it up with—Typhon Industries and their muscle, The Minutemen. They'll use you, and when they've gotten everything they can out of you, they'll toss you in the trash. Or worse, they'll find you a nice dark cell where *habeas corpus* don't apply. Rubbing elbows with them is bad enough. But join 'em at your peril." He got up and walked to the door. "Consider this a friendly warning." He held out his hand.

I retrieved the gun from the freezer, dumped the bullets in the trash, and hovered the gun above his palm. "Which side is Marchette on?"

"He a friend of yours?" Newspaper Man asked.

"What if he is?" I said.

He gave me a sad smile. "He's on the wrong one."

I dropped the gun in his hand and locked the door behind him.

Making flytraps took up the rest of my afternoon. I started by cutting the tops from a few two-liter plastic cola bottles. Figuring they'd need the camouflage if I was going to hide them around the Typhon Industries complex, I painted each bottle brown. Then, I boiled some sugar and water, filled each bottle a quarter of the way full, and stuck the tops inside each bottle, nozzle down. This would make it easy for flies—or whatever mysterious mutant fly-wasps happened by—to crawl into the trap, but once they fell into the mixture within, it would be difficult to escape. I put the traps on my patio to cool, wedged against the side of the house with bricks so the wind wouldn't blow them around. An hour later, I brought them in, added an equal measure of pig's blood, and lined them up in my fridge.

I had a plan: catch a few horseflies in the mountains. But hearing what Tony had to say, it seemed small-time, like a guy watering his flowers as a tidal wave looms over him.

CHAPTER TWELVE

The next day, I drove out to the East Mountains before work. I put a couple traps in the northern part of Las Huertas Canyon, near bends in the creek where the water stood still and brackish. I saved the last two for the Typhon Industries facility. A clump of protesters chanted at the main security entrance. Their collective breath hung like thought bubbles in the winter air. They held handmade placards with peace signs and catchy phrases and exclamation points. They were attractive young activists in hipster clothing with curly hair and sunglasses. I stayed the hell away from them.

I drove around the perimeter of the facility, looking for a dumpster outside the secure area. I didn't find one. However, I did find a stream that ran downhill from the mountains, under a razor-wire fence through a channel cut into the ground, and directly into the uppermost building—the one with the domed roof that could open. From what I could tell, the architects had gone out of their way to erect the structure precisely in the path of the water. The stream wasn't big, but during the monsoon season, it would swell with runoff. The architects must have either had a good reason to put the building there or been drunk on creative power.

I put the last two traps along the banks a few yards outside of the security fence that spanned the stream. I masked them with some brush. It was worth a shot.

The University sat between the mountains and the zoo. I hadn't heard from Melodía since our most recent fight. I figured I'd drop in on my way through the city and try to make things right. Throw myself on the floor and grovel a little. It was the way our friendship worked.

Her lab was locked, but a line of light gleamed under the door. When I knocked, something banged within, like a cabinet door slamming shut. Then the room went quiet. I knocked again with authority. More silence. I pictured her sitting in her white lab coat, quietly waiting for me to leave. I wondered if Melodía did this whenever anyone knocked on her door. The thought made me want to apologize even more.

"Hernandez!" I bellowed. "It's Stick. Open up."

I could almost feel her hesitation, as if it were a quality of the chill basement air.

"Stick?" she asked finally. Her voice broke. She sounded miserable. I felt guilty for forcing myself on her and glad that I'd dropped back into her lonely existence.

"It's me," I said.

Her feet tapped across the lab, and she opened the door. She wore a white lab coat with her long curly hair splayed across the shoulders. The fingers of both hands twisted themselves into a clump in front of her stomach. The side of her face that could hold an expression looked anxious. Her lips were thin and gray. "What are you doing here?"

"Can't a friend stop by to check on a friend?"

"Of course." She stood, her body stiff, blocking the entrance to the lab.

"How are you doing?" It was a question strangers asked each other.

"I'm fine." Her eyes kept running away from my face.

"I'm sorry about our argument. The things I said."

"I don't even remember them." She spoke to the middle button of my shirt.

"Well, I'm still sorry. I hope you'll forgive me."

She shook her head. "There's nothing to forgive. I'm sorry too."

This was usually the point where she'd invite me in and we'd waste a few hours yapping away like a couple of normals. Instead, she gave our shoes a close inspection.

"So, any revelations about the birds?" I asked just to make conversation.

She shrugged her slender shoulders. "I've hit a dead end."

"Too bad about those specimens disappearing."

She stood there.

"They might have led you somewhere."

"Yeah." She closed the door a few inches. "Well, thanks for stopping by."

"You're still mad at me."

She sighed. "I'm not. All is forgiven. I'm tired, I have a lot of paperwork to do, and I just want to go home and take a bath."

"Do the paperwork in the bath," I said.

She forced her mouth into a smile and showed that to me for a second or two. It looked like hard work. "Goodbye Stick."

"Alright," I said.

She shut the door in my face.

I walked away. Something had changed. Melodía and I were the kind of friends who laughed or shouted or argued or quipped—but we were never cold and distant.

When I was almost to the stairwell, the lab door opened down the hall.

"Stick!" I turned. Melodía had taken two steps through the doorway. I waited. She took a few more steps. It looked as if her feet had been cast in cement. "I wanted to tell you—" She moved her mouth, but no words came out.

"Tell me," I said.

She shut her mouth and took a deep breath. "We need a change. We can't keep living life the same way, year after year."

I hated change. She knew that.

"You can't keep working the same job forever. Doing the same things every day."

"In fact, I can."

"I'm looking to change my life," she said.

"Good for you. I can't wait to see the new you." She opened her mouth but, again, no words came out of it. I thought maybe I'd been too gruff. "I like Melodía the way she is. She's been the same since we were in college. I've devoted my life to that person. I'm happy with her. I'm happy with my own life. Why change?"

She breathed heavily and some angles creased her brow. "I'm done with the way things were. Nothing has gotten better in my life. Everything has stayed the same, only I'm older. They tell you that as you get older, your life gets better. I'm tired of living in the basement of the Biology building. I'm tired of eating microwaved meals alone. Stick, I'm tired of you and me. Our friendship. It hasn't evolved."

Evolution was overrated. I was pals with beings that hadn't evolved in millions of years. They were fine the way they were. "Just to be clear, what are you saying?"

"I'm saying, take that job."

It took me a minute to figure out what job she was talking about. When I did, my face swelled with blood.

"With the Minutemen," she said. "For the change. It'll get you outdoors. You'll meet new people. It'll break up that stupid routine you love so much."

"They're a gang of vigilante racists," I said. "You've got more Chicano ancestry than I do. What the hell is wrong with you?"

"They're not after Chicanos—or Mexicans either. They're after lawbreakers. And I think working with them could open up a whole new side of you."

I wondered if she and Rex, who had never gotten along, had secretly started dating and pouring stupidity into each other's heads. "I'm leaving now. I'm going to assume that you've been drinking too much formaldehyde and it's gone to your brain."

"Take the job!" Melodía yelled at my back as I walked away. "It's the best thing for you!"

I held up my hand in a backward wave without turning around.

The next day, Thursday, I tried to work like nothing strange had taken possession of my life. I put a handful of crickets in the terrarium of the African spur tortoise hatchlings. They were herbivores. I worried for five long minutes that my python had escaped before I recalled she'd been sent to Colorado. I left a delivery of frozen minnows on a delivery pallet for six hours. By the time I remembered them, the whole back room smelled like the beach on a hot day.

After work, I drove to my father's house. I found him standing over the stove as usual, but the place smelled like chicken, mole sauce, and homemade corn tortillas.

"Son," he said without looking up. "Have a cold beer."

I helped myself.

He pointed his wooden spoon at a small bowl of lime wedges. "Squeeze one of those down the neck."

I opened the beer and pushed a lime into the bottle. The sharp scent that misted up smelled like spring. "Chicken. What's the special occasion?"

My father blinked up at me. He smiled. The flesh of his neck and cheeks tightened and his old man skin gleamed from a fresh afternoon shave. I liked seeing it. We didn't go around grinning all the time in my family. "Happy birthday, son."

I hit my head on the ceiling. "God damn," I growled. I'd missed my own birthday. That meant I'd signed the wrong date on every form that had passed over my desk that day.

"Don't cuss," he said. "It's a happy day. You're a year older."

"Nothing too happy about that." I rubbed my skull.

"It means you're wiser, and it means that you've given one more year of your life to the world. Each year on my birthday, I think about every good thing I've done in my life. I do it until I fall asleep. I never get through the whole list."

My father could nod off in the middle of writing a grocery list. He had a talent for it.

"I haven't done that much," I said.

"Think about every animal you've fed over your whole life. That's a lot of animals."

"Yeah. And every animal I feed eats something else. It's a regular smorgasbord of death." I swigged beer zinged with lime. I swigged again, and the beer was gone.

My father eyed the empty bottle. He turned back to the chicken simmering in thick brown sauce. "Something's bothering you."

"My birthday's bothering me. Why'd you remind me?"

He folded the mole with his spoon. "Little Rex would have let you know. He never forgets birthdays."

The old man was right. Rex celebrated birthdays like he was fighting battles. He attacked them furiously. The previous year, that of my 37th birthday, he'd arrived at my house before I left for work in the morning. He made pancakes. I didn't eat pancakes often. They were an Anglo thing that had never really become part of my personal culture. But I ate them that day, and they were fine. We washed them down with Irish coffee. In years previous, during my crazy twenties, we'd spend birthdays drinking some of the cheapest tequila the city had to offer in some of the rankest dive bars in America. We'd rambled through the streets and scared the traffic. We'd slurred words at any woman who would listen. We'd woken the day after and prayed for the reprieve of death from hangovers that felt like they'd last forever.

My dad held a bottle dimpled with sweat. I took it. "Wait a little while before you drive."

"Don't worry," I said.

"Supper will be ready in ten minutes," he said.

I went into the living room and turned on the radio. It was set, as always, to my father's Mexican polka music station. I came back to the kitchen, leaned against the wall, and drank my beer. We stood while he cooked. Men in the radio pumped their accordions like they meant business. My father doled the chicken mole out on piles of tortillas, which we carried them to the living room and ate. It was a routine birthday dinner with my father. He was asleep before I'd even set my plate down.

A strand of spider silk hung in a far corner of the room, undulating in a current of air too gentle for human senses. Curves traveled up and down its length in a rhythm neither chaotic nor patterned, graceful and ghostly. It stirred with the spirit of this world incarnate.

I took off my father's glasses, folded them, and put them on the side table. Once I'd done the dishes and finished my beer, I locked the door behind me and drove to my apartment.

With the lights off, I sat in the soft nighttime shadows with Ralph on my knee. The starlight sifted through the flora in my garden. Eventually, the moon emerged and hung its light in white drapes from the branches of the fruit trees, cottonwoods, and oaks. I didn't move from that place for some time. My spider and I were alone, pursued by strange adversaries. Our childhood friends were damaged, destitute, and distant. The world teemed with predators, and life had no purpose. My spider and I inhabited in a world where ten thousand birds could drop dead in a heartbeat, with no cause, for no reason.

It was my birthday. I spent birthdays with my best friend.

Half an hour and a short drive later, I knocked on Rex's door, a six-pack of Chama River beer under my arm. He lived in a run-down apartment complex. I stood outside his unit, bent at the shoulders to avoid brushing my hair in the cobwebs latticed in the beams of the catwalk overhead. I knocked again. I cupped my hand against the window. The front room of his apartment was bare. A disconnected cable lay on the stained shag carpet. The door of the refrigerator stood ajar, revealing a dark interior. Before I turned away, I spotted a tiny triangle of paper taped to the door. Some notice had been posted there and torn off, leaving a corner behind.

I drove home and called Leon Flowers.

"Hallo?" He greeted me around a mouthful of crunching corn chips.

"Flowers," I said.

"Sticky!" He took another bite and munched away.

I tried to keep the meanness out of my voice. "Hey, Flowers. How is everything?"

"Oh, pretty great, and all. Eating some guacamole. Wrestling match is on."

"Sounds fun."

"Come over!" he yelled. "We'll do Tequila shots."

Getting drunk and watching sports was actually one of the few fun things one could do with Flowers. "Is Rex over?"

"Nah," Flowers said. "He's depressed."

This was news to me. "More depressed than usual?"

Flowers crunched chips. "Yah. Can'tcha tell?"

Rex never exactly bubbled with joy. "What's wrong with him?"

"You didn't hear?"

"No," I said.

"Hmm," Flowers said. "Told me right away."

"Told you what?"

"Guess it's no surprise, on account of you being so distant, and all," Flowers said. "Maybe if you weren't always sitting down in that cave feeling sorry for yourself—"

"He's been evicted from his apartment." I gleaned that the corner of paper taped to his door was an eviction notice. "I've figured it out. Enjoy your tequila shots."

"C'mon over!" Flowers hollered.

I almost hung up, but realized I needed a little more out of him. "Where is he staying?"

"Beats me," Flowers said. "Some friend's house, he says. I offered him to stay here. I got the spare bedroom. I even offered him to drive my ice cream truck. Good money in ice cream. He bought me a beer and punched my arm, which is his way of saying no thanks. I bought him back, too. I got no money problems."

"Any idea which friend?" None of us had many friends, much less those who would let us crash at their houses after an eviction.

"Who the hell knows?" Flowers said. "He keeps his mouth shut almost as much as you do. You two need to loosen up and realize when a guy is on your side."

I smiled. "You're probably right, old buddy." Flowers had the uncanny ability to infuriate you one minute and charm you the next.

"Yep. Come on over. It's the Undertaker versus Triple H!"

I assumed those were the names of wrestlers. "I'll get back to you."

"Suit yourself." Flowers hung up.

I wracked my brain for friends Rex could be staying with. His father was dead. His mother had moved to the East Coast to live with family. His little brother Lucas had taken his own life when Rex and I were in our early twenties. His sister had been missing since their teens. That left friends. I wouldn't have been surprised if Rex had moved in with my father. However, I'd just been there—no mention of Rex. He had a couple of ex-army buddies, but none very close and all married. Wives didn't generally appreciate Rex. He had a few shady business associates. I didn't know them very well.

Except one: the Captain. His card still lay on my bar.

He answered after two rings. "Mr. Stick."

I hated cell phones. It meant that everyone always knew you were calling. It ruined the element of surprise. "Hello."

"You've thought about it, and you want the job."

"No," I said.

"You'll be paid well," he said. "You'll find, after a few weekends of duty, that you hate working at the zoo. That you loathe government work. Private industry. It's the American Way."

"I'm looking for Rex," I said.

"Give me a one weekend commitment and I'll tell you."

"I'll work at the zoo until the day I die," I said.

The captain blew a couple of nostrils' worth of air into the receiver. "I'm afraid I don't know where Rex is. No idea."

"He's your employee. If you don't know, you're not a very thorough boss."

"He's not my employee. His hire was contingent on your recruitment."

I hadn't known that. I felt a stab of guilt—maybe if Rex had been able to work for the Minutemen, he'd have been able to pay his rent. "You still know where he's staying."

"I suggest you check his residence," the Captain said.

"He's not there."

"How mysterious."

"You just admitted a second ago that you knew."

The Captain paused. Across the room, Ralph stood at full attention. He didn't like it when I got agitated. "He's staying at Enchantment Campgrounds. They're located—"

"I know where they are." I leveled out my voice to sooth Ralph.

"Consider my employer's offer, Mr. Stick. It's not going away."

I hung up.

I drove to the Enchantment Campgrounds, off I-40, west of the city, over the Rio Grande and past the volcanoes. The neon of the Dancing Eagle Casino bathed the turnoff in red light. I spun my truck around the curves and down the lanes of the site. There wasn't much action, it being winter. I found Rex's truck tucked away in the depths of the grounds. He'd pitched a dark green tent that he'd probably pilfered from the army. He sat by a smoldering fire, draped in a wool blanket, grasping a tin cup. His mustache hadn't seen a comb in a few days.

I parked my truck beside his and sat on a log beside the fire. It took effort. The result was barely better than sitting in the dirt for all it elevated me off the ground. I had to extend a leg on either side of the fire pit to avoid burning my shoes.

"Hooch?" Rex asked.

I nodded.

He splashed something rust colored from a half-gallon bottle into a tin cup and handed it to me. I drank. It scorched a swath of flesh from the roof of my mouth.

"I'll throw another log on the fire," Rex muttered. He heaved a few chopped-up two-by-fours into the pit and poked at the heap with a broom handle until it lit. I held my hands up to the tongues of flame.

"So," I said.

He grunted. I gave him a few seconds to mention my birthday—not because I needed the validation, but because it should have been the norm. He didn't.

I had planned on telling him my problems. Spilling about my fight with Melodía. Telling him about Tanis, Marchette's burglary, and revealing the Captain's connection with it all. I hadn't realized it until that moment, but I had an ulterior motive: I wanted to convince Rex to give up working with the Minutemen. Now that I saw him crouching in the dirt next to a fire made of scavenged construction lumber, I didn't have the heart. He needed whatever leg-up he could get.

Instead, I took another swig of whiskey. It carved a tunnel of heat into my middle. Rex drank too. We sat and looked at the fire. All around us, the world was still, apart from the occasional distant rush of a car passing on the freeway. I tilted my head back. Even just a few miles from the city lights, the Milky Way stood out in a dense stripe of sparkling white and silver in the sky.

"Flowers is throwing a party tonight," I said, still looking up.

"Yeah?"

"Wrestling. Tequila shots. Guacamole."

"Sounds like a real fiesta," Rex said. "I'm sure lots of people will show up."

"If you and I stop by, it'll triple the guest list."

Rex barked one short laugh. "Sad bastard." He sipped from his camping cup. I sipped from mine.

Rex sighed through his mustache. "You found me out here."

I nodded.

"How'd you do that, I wonder."

"Asked your pal the Captain."

Rex looked up. The flames glimmered in his eye sockets. They smoldered like two old coals. "You taking the job?"

I put my gaze on the smoke twining upward in gray vines.

"You're not," Rex said.

"I'm Chicano."

"I guess I never thought of you that way."

Nobody did. They all thought of me as a giant. At least Rex was blind to my ethnicity because he thought of me as a friend.

"I can't work for someone who goes around imprisoning Mexicans, Central Americans, or anyone else. It'd be like betraying my own blood."

"The Minutemen go after lawbreakers. It's only coincidence that they're Mexicans." Rex rustled the fire with his broom handle.

It was the same logic Melodía had used earlier that day, and the Captain before her. I didn't point out that the Minutemen were all white and everyone they persecuted was brown, which inherently made it racial. I hadn't come to argue with my friend.

"Anyway," Rex said, "The Captain told me that you wouldn't even be working with the Minutemen. You'd be with the company that develops the surveillance technology they're using."

"Same thing."

"Maybe it is. I don't think it's so bad. Fewer immigrants, more jobs for us citizens." He tossed a splinter of wood into the fire and a few limp sparks leapt out and died in the dirt. "Besides, when has blood ever meant anything to you?"

Blood didn't mean much, but it wasn't nothing either. "Why does he want me, anyway?" I knew the answer was more complex than met the eye, but I wanted to know what The Captain had told Rex.

Rex shrugged beneath the blanket. "Says they need an animal expert. Says his boss noticed you and wanted you to work for him."

"Who's the boss?"

"Man named John White. Don't know much about him."

John White. I'd heard the name from Tony. I'd seen no sign of any surveillance technology development facilities at the Typhon Industries campus. Unless they were engineering clairvoyant goldfish, then they must have had facilities elsewhere as well. "I wish I could take the job, buddy."

Rex nodded and some of the air deflated from his shoulders.

I didn't tell him that I knew it was ruining his shot at work. We liked to pretend that each of us still had his pride. "Wanna go to Flowers'? Watch some wrestling? Toss back some liquor? Laugh at the clown?"

Rex chuckled. "You know what he did the other day?"

I sipped my hooch and waited for him to tell me.

"He bought nunchucks." Rex's face split into a grin, revealing his stained and crooked teeth.

I chuckled despite myself.

"He starts whipping 'em around right outside the store." Rex's shoulders bounced up and down. "Hits himself on every elbow and knee he had on his body. Finally, whacks himself right in the forehead. He falls down on his butt in the middle of the parking lot. Cars are stopping. And he just sits there, big red mark on his forehead, big fat grin on his face." Rex could barely get the words out. His laughed in near-silent spasms of wind through his graying mustache.

I could see the whole thing as clear as a memory. I had to put my head between my knees to catch my breath from laughing so hard. "Flowers," I gasped.

Rex poked a finger in his eye. "That guy knows how to live."

"Yeah."

Our laughter stopped and we heaved a couple of sighs. We smiled into the fire pit. Later, we'd talk about driving to Flowers' house, but we wouldn't actually go. I'd offer to let Rex move in with me until he got back on his feet—he'd turn me down. Right then, it was enough just to sit together in the quiet desert night and enjoy the burning boards of an old fence.

I left Rex's campsite after midnight. I'd stopped drinking an hour or so before and was sober enough to drive back to my apartment without worrying about killing anyone or getting pulled over by the cops—it took a lot of alcohol to intoxicate my body. My neighborhood sat dark and silent. Few lamps lit the streets and motion sensor porch lights, dark and vigilant, guarded the houses. The families and old folks who lived there had all gone to bed. With no one else driving and few other lights to notice, my tail had become exceeding obvious.

I hadn't caught sight of it earlier, so I had no idea how long I'd been followed. I wondered if it were Tanis, the Newspaper Man, or someone new. Then I pulled up outside my house and found Tanis waiting for me. My tail eased on by and disappeared into the night.

Tanis wore a high-collared black coat over a black dress, leggings and knee-high boots. A rimmed black felt hat covered her head and sunglasses screened her eyes. She leaned against a big white van that read *Lavadería Blanca*—Spanish for some sort of cleaning service.

"You have a new job," I said, once I'd gotten out of my truck. "I'm so proud. Maybe now you'll leave me alone."

"Oh this? It's a fake decal. I have a dozen of them. I can switch them anytime I want."

"How nice." The back of the van exploded with the deep baying of some animal. It sounded like a mix between a basset hound and Cerberus. "I see you brought a monster with you."

"Oh, it's just a little pooch I'm hauling from one place to another," she said with a casual toss of her shoulders.

"I didn't know you kept pets."

"I don't believe in pets." Her face was smooth and expressionless, her eyes invisible behind the dark lenses. "A pet and a master: it's a sick relationship."

"I have a pet spider."

"You should free it."

"So it can die a noble death in the desert?"

Tanis nodded. "That's the way of the world. People keep pets for what reason? Because they get lonely? If you're lonely, shouldn't you go out and find a lover or a friend or reconnect with a long-lost family member? Pet owners are just using their animals as salves on an unhealthy lifestyle."

"What can I do for you, Tanis?" I asked. "Or are you waiting outside my house just by coincidence?"

Tanis giggled and smacked me on the belt buckle. "I'm here for our second date, stupid. You men are so forgetful."

"Did we have a first date?"

She applied a hurt expression to her face. "Why, I should slap you for being so insensitive. How could you forget our sexy beach barbecue date?"

"I forgot it because it wasn't on a beach, it wasn't sexy, and it wasn't a date." I leaned a hand on the van. The beast within clawed at the wall on the other side of my palm, shaking the vehicle from the tumult.

"Big dog. What is it, a timber wolf?"

"It's a mutt," she said.

The mutt howled. I wondered if it could tell that the moon was full.

"I will forgive you for insulting our first date if you invite me in and make me a cocktail. I'll give you a few minutes to put on some nice clothes."

"How about I give you five dollars and you can go buy yourself a malt liquor at the gas station?"

She hit me in the stomach and let her hand linger there one second longer than necessary. It made me feel something. Nerve endings lit up in neon and the rush of hormones overrode my good sense.

"Come in. I'll make you a Michelada."

She scrunched up her nose. "What's that?"

"It's beer, Tabasco, and Worcestershire sauce."

She put a hand over her mouth. Her eyes took on a horrified roundness.

"I also have wine."

She grabbed my arm and I escorted her down the stairs. Her dog sent a cascade of protest tumbling after us.

"Your animal is going to wake up the neighborhood."

"It isn't mine. Besides, I suspect it'll shut up as soon as it senses we've left."

"Most people refer to their dog as 'she' or 'he,' out of respect. You know, to show them that they're more than an object to you."

She smiled up at me and fluttered her lashes. "It's a hermaphrodite."

I let that one go.

I sat her at my bar. She removed her hat and sunglasses and craned her neck around, taking it all in. Her eyes settled on Ralph. He looked back at her. His eight eyes gleamed like polished obsidian.

"That is a big spider," she said.

"He's as tame as a puppy dog." I took a bottle of Muscat from the cupboard above my fridge and uncorked it. "You wanna hold him?"

Tanis stared at the wine. "I've never seen that wine before."

It was from Tierra Encantada, a local winery. "It's from the city."

"I didn't know New Mexico made wine."

"New Mexico makes just about anything worth wanting." I set a glass in front of her and poured.

She swirled, sniffed, and held the glass up to the light. "I suppose you know you were followed here."

"I was aware of that, yes."

"It was that same man."

"The member of the militant Pan-Chicano nationalist junta?"

She tilted her face away from the wine. "Don't make fun. They're serious."

"Well, I hope they know that I am not serious. About anything."

"Except your job," she said. "You take that very seriously, don't you?"

I didn't say anything.

"And your friend." She grinned, as if at something particularly delightful. "Dr. Melodía Hernandez."

A rumble rose in the back of my throat.

She leaned across the bar and grabbed my wrist. "I can tell that gets to you. You don't even like me to say her name."

I pulled my wrist away and took a swig of red, viscous sweet with a hard, tart punch.

"You are also serious about your friend Spartacus Rex."

"Enough about me," I said.

"He is a difficult one, that Spartacus Rex." Tanis' eyes were big and hungry. She looked as if she wanted to dig my friendships out of me so she could eat them. "He's your oldest and most loyal friend, but also your most criminal and racist one. What a conundrum!"

"Drink your wine."

"It's rude to interrupt a course of conversation before it's naturally exhausted itself," Tanis said. "Especially with a guest."

"It's rude to put your nose into my personal life."

"Not on a date. How else am I supposed to get to know such a stoic man, unless I force him to talk about himself?"

"This isn't a date."

"Then how do you explain the lingerie I'm wearing under this overcoat, dress, hat, boots, stockings, and thermal underwear?"

I groaned at her.

"Your father."

"What about the old man?"

"Your father, your job, your two friends, and probably your spider. Those are the things you care for."

"Should I be writing this down?" I dosed myself with another mouthful of wine.

"It's such a short list, a child could memorize it. Obviously, your ideology of life revolves around minimalism."

"No conversation with you is ever light, is it? What about your life ideology? It obviously includes harassing good, hard-working Americans. What else?"

She sipped the wine and her face split into a smile. "This is quite delicious!"

"New Mexico doesn't disappoint." I stole a glance at Ralph while she took another sip. He had crawled his front four legs up the glass wall of his terrarium, exposing the stiff, khaki-colored hairs of his abdomen. He wanted out for his nightly romp. "Mind if I let my spider out?"

She shrank back in her chair. "You mean to walk around the house?"

"That's what I mean." I lifted him from his terrarium and set him on the floor. A couple millipedes still roamed around for him to hunt. He stood there for a few seconds, angling his body minutely back and forth so that he could take in Tanis' image with his eyes. She stared back at him.

"He'll probably examine you for a half hour or so to make sure you're not a threat. Don't pay him any mind."

Tanis lifted both feet off the floor and tucked them onto the seat beneath her. I poured her more wine.

"So. Why exactly is everybody following me?"

Tanis smiled. "Because you're the tallest, darkest, and handsomest man in the city?"

"Wrong."

Tanis unzipped her coat and held it out to me. Beneath, she wore a red silk scarf over her bare brown shoulders. Her bust line scooped modestly, but enough to make me uncomfortable. It didn't take much. I took the coat and hung it on my hat tree.

"Seriously." I returned to my position in the kitchen with the bar between us. "Why?"

Her face settled from the smile she'd been affecting and she looked ten years older. Now that she wore the expression of a serious person, her eyelids and lips were heavy and expressive. Her voice dove deeper than the usual girlish giggle. "You are a lead. Every person with any stake in reality must discover why, in a single stroke, thousands of beings passed from life. It is a scientific, theological, sociological, ecological, and existential dilemma. It should be keeping every single person awake at night."

"It happens all the time. Things die. That's the way the universe works."

"Yes, but not all at once. Things die and breed in a staggered pattern." She sipped her wine and hummed with pleasure. "If everything died all at once with any frequency, life would cease to exist. Archeologically, when a big mass death occurs, it is a precursor to extinction. Theologically, it indicates an act of God—or Satan."

"You're saying that God is sick of birds?" I said.

"I'm saying that we, as humans, are pattern-seeking beings. We want to know that there's a purpose, or at least a trend, to events. Big events like this one, we want to believe, indicate something. God is angry. The Devil is loose and causing bad things to happen. Our ecological system is breaking down. The government or an evil corporation is running tests with massive and terrible side-effects."

"The birds just died. Maybe it's as simple as that."

She took a long, slow drink from her glass. Her dark eyes twinkled over the rim.

"Things die. There doesn't have to be a reason."

"You atheists are so cute," she said.

"I'm not an atheist."

She set the glass down. "To answer your question, people are following you, trying to hire you, and seducing you because you are making headway on solving the mystery."

"Untrue."

"Whenever competing parties simultaneously explore the same mystery, they don't just hire people to look at the clues. They also try to steal the insights of the other parties involved."

"That's what you're here to do."

She grinned and the fake Tanis sprung back into her face. "No, I am here because I am romantically interested in you. It's just a coincidence that the universe has delegated me to investigate the same mystery."

"I'm not investigating, and you're a liar."

She fluttered her eyelashes and crinkled up her nose. It was cute. I wasn't big on cuteness.

"How do I get everybody to stop following me and leave me alone? I've stopped investigating. I never really started."

She shook her head. "It doesn't matter what you do. From here on out, anyone who approaches you is probably working for one party or another. No one will ever leave you alone."

That much was proving to be true.

"You are cosmically inherent to the mystery."

"That sounds stupid."

"Are you calling gravity stupid?" She swatted at my hand. "How dare you!"

I wondered what the hell she was talking about. I told her so.

"The cosmos is held together by gravity. When I say you are cosmically involved, I am using gravity as a metaphor. But it isn't a metaphor, exactly. Ever since that moment when those thousands of beings suddenly ended, events have taken orbit around you. You are pulling everything toward you—in ways you don't even comprehend. There must be a reason for this. That is what everyone is trying to understand."

"I have a friend. She asked me to drive down—"

"I've heard all that before. However, many things have happened, very few of which you are aware, that center on you as a person. The few events you do know about, you have very little understanding of their consequence. You're in the dark."

"Well, illuminate me."

"No. Instead, I will kiss you." She knelt atop the stool, put her hands on the bar, and leaned across it. She lowered her eyelids and puckered up. I could have snapped a picture of her and sold it to a modeling agency.

I considered picking up Ralph and substituting his lips for mine. Instead, I waited.

She opened her eyes. She raised her eyebrows. Finally, she un-puckered her lips and spoke. "This is our second date. If you don't kiss me, I'll think I'm too ugly for you."

"It's the other way around."

"I'll develop a complex. I'll think you only like pretty blondes. I'll begin to loathe myself for not being white."

"I hate pretty blondes," I said, which wasn't far from the truth.

"Then kiss me."

"Absolutely not."

"You're shy." She lunged, grabbed me by the collar, and pulled herself up. She was strong, but she had a long way to climb. Eventually, she got her feet beneath her. Standing on the bar, she was a foot taller than me. She tilted my head back, my collar still clutched in her fist.

I had been kissed a handful of times, by only a handful of women, usually scavenged by Rex, most of whom I'd never seen again. That had been back in my late high school and early college days. I had also kissed a few women at bars, in Rex's various slummy apartments, and in my car during my lost twenty-something years. Alcohol and desperation were always involved on both sides. Since then, I hadn't kissed a woman.

Tanis' breath, sweet and dark with wine, nuzzled my face. A nimbus of cherry blossom hung from her hair. Her black eyes looked straight into mine, flicking back and forth minutely. I hadn't experienced anything so intimate in a long time. It made me fall in love, just a little, and only because I was, beneath my gruffness, a vulnerable person.

The dog in Tanis' van chose that moment to let out a long, morose howl.

We both turned our heads toward the street.

The howl transformed into a series of desperate yelps. The beast scrabbled its claws against the inside of the van.

"Should you check on your animal?" I asked.

The look on her face suggested that this incident was curious, but not entirely unexpected. She always wore that same half-smile, except when she was faking something else. "Hmmm. I suppose so. Will you step out with me?"

"Yes." I said but didn't move.

We stood nose to nose for a few seconds more before she broke away. She straightened her clothing and smoothed her hair, as if such actions were perfectly normal while standing in high-heeled boots atop a bar. I helped her with her coat. While I donned mine, she leapt from the bar and landed like a gymnast.

When we walked out into the night, my patio felt strange. The hound's wild barking was louder outside. I felt eyes on my skin. A scent I couldn't identify hung in the air. Hair. Heavy musk, like a badger or wolverine. A metallic tinge, the same scent I'd smelled at the Bosque as I passed the gutted van with Meat Shoulders and his loose-skinned friend.

I scanned the bushes that surrounded us on three sides. They seemed empty. The roofline two stories above showed nothing but the soft touch of the moon. The boughs of the trees trembled in the slight breeze.

Tanis had frozen too.

Something creaked and rustled to my right. I turned. The sound had come from the deep foliage of my garden, and it might have been a rogue wind.

It rustled again. The noise marked the unmistakable movement of an autonomous being. The full moon hung low and to the west, shining behind the wall of bushes and branches. I examined the outlines of shadow against the pale ivory light. Tanis stood stiff beside me, peering in the same direction.

I found it: A silhouette about the size and shape of a bulldog squatting on the limb of a pine tree. I stared at that blot against the moonlight. It stared back at me.

Nearby, Tanis' dog continued to freak out. Somebody was bound to call the cops. My landlady's light flashed in the upstairs window, flooding the patio with brightness. I blinked involuntarily. When I opened my eyes, I caught a glimpse of a dark shape leaping from the tree toward the street. A flapping sound beat against the tirade of dog noise. Even after it had gone, the heavy metallic scent still hung in the air.

Tanis stepped away from me, tapping her finger on the face of her cell phone. When she finished, she slipped the device in her coat pocket and gave me a business-like smile. "Lynxes. They really rile up my dog."

"I thought you said it wasn't your dog."

"I meant the dog that is temporarily in my custody."

"That was no lynx. There are no lynxes within the city limits."

"Coyotes, bears, rattlesnakes. They're always wandering into Albuquerque. Why not a lynx?"

"That wasn't a lynx." I didn't tell her I had heard the flapping of what sounded like leathery wings. I didn't know if I believed it myself.

Tanis smiled up at me. "You're sweet." She grabbed my coat lapels in her fists and bent me over. Hopping into the air, she managed to smear her mouth on the underside of my jaw. Her lips felt like a cashmere sweater. "I have to go."

I nodded. Somehow, I had the feeling this was all part of some bigger game she was playing. What that was, I couldn't fathom.

Halfway up the stairs, she turned. "Call me in three days or I'll think you don't like me. That's dating protocol."

I shook my head at her, the only thing I could think to do.

She gave me a little wave, and a moment later, the door of her van slammed. The roar of the engine and the mad howling of the beast faded into the night.

In the morning, I climbed atop a stepladder and examined the stout branch where I'd seen the silhouette. Claw marks from two broad and stubby feet cut into the bark. I stood on the ladder and pondered them. I knew them from somewhere, but I couldn't say where. I didn't know my mammals well enough.

Back inside, I sat at my bar and ate breakfast. When I'd finished, I put my face on my fist and leaned. It didn't get me anywhere. At work, my body droned around on autopilot. My fingers doled out crickets and cleaned up little dots of waste. My hands fished one sad, dead tadpole from the African dwarf frog tank. My body sat at my desk while my eyes gazed at my microscope without looking through the lens. After work, a coupe followed me home. Being followed was part of my routine now. I made dinner and ate at my bar, where I leaned my face on my fist some more. At ten minutes to nine, I was on the verge of a breakthrough when the phone rang.

The white noise on the line indicated that the call came from far away.

"John Stick?" a voice asked.

"Who is this?" I demanded.

The voice kept quiet.

"Hello?"

"*Verdad o consecuencias. Tengo su propriedad alla.*" The voice belonged to a white man speaking Spanish.

"Speak English," I said to a dial tone.

I returned to thinking, but had lost my place. I brushed my teeth and flossed. I lay down on my extra-long bed. My day joints creaked with delight. My night joints sighed at the hours ahead. A mobile of flapping wings, mysterious voices, and worry about my best friends spun in my head until I fell into a troubled sleep.

CHAPTER THIRTEEN

I **arrived to work on time the next morning. That was becoming a** rarity. I circulated around the back doors of the enclosures and terrariums, opening panels, inspecting animals. The western rattlesnake was molting and the sheath of mottled skin was stuck halfway down her body, like a ballerina in a tutu. I helped her shed it the rest of the way. I went into my room and checked the mail. I'd received a postcard with a lot of emoticons telling me that my python was thriving in Denver, as well as a few intra-zoo memoranda. I read them and threw them away.

I worked my day. It was pretty uneventful, or in other words, very pleasant. At the end of it, I made a run to the Tropical America building, a simulated rainforest environment, to check on a couple of green vine snakes housed there. I returned to my office and started to wind things up when something caught the corner of my eye. The leathery leg of the box turtle protruded from her shell. The rest of her limbs were retracted. The visible leg looked grayer than usual. I got up. I opened the top of her terrarium and poked her leg.

Esposita was dead.

I slipped my fingers beneath her shell. As I lifted her from the terrarium, her limbs and neck slid from the shell and hung. Her face wore a twisted expression. Her black tongue swelled with bloat. A wound punctured her neck. My magnifying glass showed a swollen protrusion with a deep pit in the center, surrounded by several mandibular gashes.

A serial killer was on the loose. It was the size of a hummingbird, wielded the sting of a wasp, and bore the mandibles of a horsefly. It had a thirst for blood. I walked a trail littered with the corpses of murdered animals.

I scrutinized every inch of Esposita's home. I armed myself with an industrial strength fly swatter and combed my lab. I stalked my prey into the next room, where I found the red-headed batgirl Abbey. She stood on a stool, rummaging through the high cabinets.

"Hi John," she said.

I held my finger up to my lips. "Have you seen a wasp?"

"No," she whispered. "Why are we whispering?"

I couldn't answer that. "We're not," I said at a normal volume. "A wasp killed my friend Esposita and I'm out for revenge."

Abbey looked me up and down. "Well, that wasp is a dead man. He doesn't stand a chance."

I didn't bother to tell her that the wasp was a woman. Instead, I scanned the walls, seeking out sticky spots and paying attention to the edges of window frames.

"Want an assistant?" she asked.

"Thank you. I've got this one covered. But if you see any animals with sting wounds, tell me."

The next thing I knew, Abbey had armed herself with a butterfly net and was poking around the room with me. I decided to let her. We found nothing. We searched the third room and even checked the back area of the bat cave and the adjoining nocturnal mammal rooms. All of the slow lorises, naked mole rats, brown kiwis, and huge-eyed bush babies seemed fine. When we'd finished, we ended up back in my lab drinking cans of Dr. Pepper from the vending machine.

"So," she said. "Explain."

"Esposita was my friend. No one kills my friends and gets to buzz around free to kill again."

"Can a wasp kill a turtle?" she asked.

"It was a tarantula hawk wasp. Their sting isn't fatal. It only stuns. But it's one of the most painful insect stings in the world. Esposita was pretty old. The pain was too much for her." I left out the details of the wasp potentially being a mutated monster.

"I'm sorry," she said.

"Me too. She's been with us for decades."

Abbey whistled. A strand of loose red hair that had fallen free of her ponytail vibrated. "That's a long time. So, you suspect that somehow a tarantula hawk wasp—which I understand are quite large?"

I nodded.

"One of those somehow made its way in here, broke into Esposita's cage—was it sealed?"

"The lid was on," I said. "It does have air holes."

"Big enough for a tarantula hawk wasp to crawl through?"

I hadn't stopped to ponder that, but she was on the right track. "Not that big."

"Hmm. So, a wasp broke into Esposita's home, murdered her in cold blood, and left again, covering up her point of entry and escape."

"When you say it like that, I sound crazy."

"John"—Abbey crumpled up her Dr. Pepper can between her palms—"the world is a crazy place." She tossed the can, sinking a basket from across the room. "But your corner of it seems particularly strange as of late." On her way back to the bat cave, she gave me a friendly smack on the knee.

Abbey was right. The wasp couldn't have penetrated the terrarium on its own. Judging by the multiple bites, it had been hungry. It had also been angry or frightened enough to use its stinger. I guessed that someone had brought in one of the wasp-fly creatures, stirred it up, and released it into my turtle's home. That person had given the wasp time to feed on her multiple times—or brought more than one wasp. Marchette came to mind. He could have hatched the wasp implanted on Jones the tarantula and used it to kill Esposita. The big question that remained was: Why?

The words of a conversation I'd had a couple weeks earlier came back to me. Words that I'd said to a certain militia leader about the identity of my favorite animal at the zoo.

I knew there was a link between the Captain and Marchette. That link was Typhon Industries. Now I had another link: Marchette had access to a mutant tarantula hawk-horsefly, if such a thing actually existed. The Captain had been bitten by one—and a population of them lived near his place of employment. He could have caught one, probably as readily as Marchette could have hatched one from Jones' body. Or the two men could have been in cahoots.

It didn't add up in my mind. Marchette was a good man. The Captain was not. If they were working for the same employer, which they undoubtedly had been, that could explain it. But I couldn't imagine the scientist helping the militiamen even if they were working for the same corporation. And I couldn't imagine him killing an innocent turtle—even if he was an insect man at heart.

I was sitting in my chair pondering it all when Abbey poked her head in.

"You're here late," she said.

I looked at the clock: 7:15 p.m. Another symptom of my crumbling routine. "I guess I got to thinking too hard."

"I have something for you."

No one ever had anything for me. I wondered if she'd found out about my recently passed birthday somehow.

She presented her index finger to me. It was slender and that orangish-pink color of fair-skinned Anglo people. The pad of the fingertip bore a deeper orange dust.

"Is that what I think it is?" I asked.

She nodded.

"More orange dust," I said. "Where did you find that?"

"Three inches from the base of the door leading from the back rooms to the main hall of the Reptile House. On the outer edge."

"By outer edge, you mean where the door meets the frame, on the side opposite the hinges."

"Right," she said. "The edge with the knob."

"How the hell did you find a finger's worth of orange dust at the bottom of a door?"

"I stood in the middle of the room and let myself find something out of place." She positioned herself in the center of my lab and stretched her arms out to either side, as if she were getting ready for a hug. "It jumped out at me."

"Is your last name Holmes?" I asked.

She giggled. A red flush rose in her cheeks. She looked even cuter than usual. "I suspect that someone waited for the exhibit room outside of the door to empty. Then they slipped through the door. We never lock it. We assume that nobody will come back here, and if they did, we'd see them. This person must have been staking the place out. They waited for you to leave. When you did, they slipped back here and put a tarantula hawk in Esposita's terrarium. They waited for it to kill her. They captured it again and went back to the door. They opened it a crack and peeped out, waiting until no one was around so that they could slip out without being noticed. When they were peeking out, they rose up on their toes, like this." She modeled the pose. "The top of their shoe rested against the door."

"Perfect," I said.

"That's the same dust I saw on Simon's shoelaces."

I nodded and sighed.

"Is he our man?"

"I have trouble believing that. It doesn't seem in his nature."

"He stole your western albino rattlesnake, allegedly. Is it such a big leap to think that he might have murdered your friend the turtle?"

"I guess not."

She sat on my desk and swung her feet. "He does seem like a good guy. Besides, who assassinates a turtle in cold blood? What's the motive? Maybe the wasp got in through some crack we haven't noticed. Insects can squeeze themselves pretty small. It escaped through the same route. Maybe it flew out of the Reptile House before we were even looking for it—when we opened a door or something."

"That doesn't explain the orange dust." Nor would it explain the coincidence of my telling the Captain that I had special feelings for Esposita.

"That's a tiny detail. It could be coincidental. Or it could be from another day when Simon was working here."

"Could be."

Abbey jumped down from my desk. "I guess I should get back to my babies. Do you want me to tell security about all this?"

I waved my hand. "I'll handle it."

She didn't leave. Instead, she did some fiddling around with the zipper of her zoo jacket, pursed her lips, and did an inspection of the corners of my ceiling. "So... you really don't know where Simon went?"

I shook my head. "I have a few theories, but nothing substantial."

"Wanna talk about them over dinner?"

I'd never been invited to dinner before. My face probably showed it.

"Did I say something wrong?" Abbey asked.

"I'm not used to people being friendly, I guess. It's giving me an identity crisis."

"We're colleagues. Let's go have a brewski and talk shop!"

I ran the scenario in my head. Happy hour and my eight-feet of awkwardness didn't sound like a good plan. Plus, I had fly traps to check.

"Sorry. Another time. Too much work to do."

"I know the feeling." Abbey fluttered some fingers at me. "Good night, John."

I had a date with the East Mountains and four fly traps that night, which I hoped might hold answers to at least a few of the questions that had been buzzing around since the day of the mass bird death. If I could find, intact and alive, a specimen of the wasp that had bitten the whooping crane, the captain, the security guard at Typhon Industries, and Esposita, I'd know for certain if it was merely a wasp or if something new really had come into being beneath our tired sun.

I stopped home for a brief cold meal before I drove to the Typhon Industries site. I arrived past eight and protesters still ringed the entrance. I didn't get close enough to read their signs, so I couldn't tell whether they were animal rights activists, immigrant rights activists, or Native American rights activists. My mind conjured up an image of an eight-foot tall John Stick in a zookeeper uniform among them holding a sign with a picture of Esposita the box turtle. I'd never been part of a protest, march, or parade in my life. You had to share solidarity with more than one or two people to do so.

Instead of entering the Typhon Industries parking lot, I pulled my car to the side of the road that led there and hiked the few dozen paces beneath the conifer boughs and through the brush and blanket of pine needles to the small stream that trickled down the mountainside. Dozens of them spanned the breadth of the Sandía Mountain range, many of which dried out during the winter and sprang back to life come the March thaw. This winter had been mild, which might have explained the persistence of a stream in February. When I squatted down to pick up one of my traps, however, I sensed something about the water. I dipped my fingers into it. Winter runoff is freezing. It turns your skin numb and freezes your guts if you drink it. This water felt like a freshly drawn bath. It was somewhere around 90 degrees.

It came from a hot spring: a well of water that ran deep into the earth's crust, where either hot rock in the earth's mantle or magma heated it. New Mexico was peppered with hot springs. Tourists flocked to them and said things about how magical and healing they were. I didn't like tourists.

The gibbous moon washed my path in ivory light as I walked up the course of the stream. I poked my fingers into spots where the water eddied deep and dark. The water became hotter, in some places painfully so. It pulsed gently up against my fingertips. The sources of the hot springs probably went down thousands of feet, drawing up water from the vast basins that had accumulated in the earth's crust over millions of years.

Typhon Industries used this water, but their purpose was unclear. They'd constructed a building directly in its path. If they used it for geothermal purposes, they would have simply run pipes uphill to siphon off the water. As soon as it came above ground, the water lost heat. I imagined that by the time the open-air channel actually reached the building, the water would have fallen to a temperature that would render it essentially useless.

I wanted inside that building. I wasn't much for hatching schemes or orchestrating complex plots to infiltrate buildings. The next best thing to getting into the building was to talk to someone who had—one more reason to find Simon Marchette, a task I had yet to begin.

I trekked downstream and checked the rest of my traps. I found a few blood soaked pine needles, a dozen gnats, and a thin layer of orange dust floating in them. It wasn't insect season, especially in the mountains. In the summer, the traps would have been thick with the writhing bodies of creatures glutting and drowning themselves slowly in delicious blood. In the winter, I was lucky to catch pine needles.

As I knelt peering into the fourth trap, something whirred past my left ear. It buzzed like a small helicopter. I froze. The moonlight poured down around me. The protesters made their distant clamor. The stream trickled by like a tumble of loose change.

A flying insect landed on the back of my left hand. It was slightly bigger than a well-fed humming bird. It had the tapered abdomen and torso of a tarantula hawk wasp and the bulbous eyes of a horsefly. It washed one hand over the other like a horsefly and sported a proboscis and mandibles of gargantuan proportions. Its stinger could have punctured the skin of a rhinoceros. Its wings were long, elliptical in shape, and shined like stained glass.

I knelt next to a stream whose water had emerged from thousands of feet below the Earth's surface. It had flowed for eons of geological history. The mountains cradling this stream had arisen over millions of years. Every being that buzzed or bit, stung or sang in this desert was as old as humanity itself. But this being was brand new.

The creature sporadically rustled its wings, fanning my wrist and fingers, but didn't fly away. Its weight was marvelous. Each foot pressed individually against my skin. It turned a half circle across my hand, stopped, and rubbed its forelegs one over the other while rotating its head in quick jerks. This was not the behavior of a fly looking to feed or a wasp looking to sting. This was resting behavior.

I'd discovered a chimera. In science, a chimera is an organism with traits from two or more distinct gene pools. Genetic researchers had spliced together mice, for example, from four parents instead of two. These mice featured genetic pieces of each set of parents. Their fur often looked like patchwork quilts. Science had taken the term from Greek mythology: the Chimera was a monstrous fusion of lion, goat, and snake that Bellerophon slew from atop the Pegasus—also a chimera. One chimera was white and feathery and beautiful; the other was scaled and fanged and ugly. The latter, of course, was an abomination that had to be destroyed.

The being on my hand was the most wonderful abomination I'd ever beheld. I had no idea whether it was a natural mutation or the product of science gone awry, but I instinctively wanted to protect it. Had a Bellerophon emerged from the forest at that moment, sword in hand, I would have thrown two liters of pig's blood in his eyes and shooed the wasp off toward safety.

A second wasp landed on my elbow. It was slightly bigger than the first and made itself equally at home. It whirred its wings, shuffled its feet, and rubbed its forelegs together. Both of the insects ignored the blood trap right in front of them. It would have driven a normal hematophage mad—unless it preferred to feed on a particular species' blood. They'd bitten two humans that I knew of. They'd bitten a whooping crane and Esposita the turtle, the latter under duress. But they did not seem at all interested in drinking my blood, even with the veins and arteries in my hand pumping away right beneath one of them. It didn't add up.

Two more wasps landed on my arm. Another took a seat on my knee. Neither horseflies nor tarantula hawk wasps were social animals. Horseflies might swarm to feed on the same food source, but they didn't group themselves together intentionally. Tarantula hawk wasps lived solitary existences. It didn't make sense for a chimera of two solitary species to gather. Either these insects amounted to more than fly and wasp combined, or I was a very likable guy. Or, as Tanis had once said, chaos was at play. One and one didn't equal two; they equaled anarchy. I didn't like carrying her around in my brain.

I knelt there for a while. No more wasps came and none left. They ceased their stirrings and sat still. The night had no wind. My knees ached. The arches of my feet hurt. Every joint of my left arm cooked in my skin from the strain of holding it still. I could have stood there in pain for hours.

Feet crunched in the dirt behind me, almost blending into the other noises of the night. Whoever they belonged to tried to be stealthy. I rose slowly and turned. The insects perched on me, even the one on my knee, stayed where they were.

"I can hear you," I said to the shadows between the aspens and pines.

A flashlight clicked on and paved a circled of ground with yellow light. "A la verga," a man's voice whispered, "you found yourself some beasties."

It was the gumshoe, Tony, who'd invaded my house. He wore a fedora, trench coat, off-the-rack suit, and loafers, as usual. "Actually, they found me."

"Are they biting you?" Tony asked.

"They're using me for a lounge. What the hell are you doing out here?"

"You look like Cinderella. I used to watch that movie with my girl. Cinderella would sing to the birds. They'd perch on her hands and tweet. It was cute." He walked toward me, lifting the flashlight toward the sky and shining a cone of light in the space between us. "This ain't nearly as cute."

"I'll take these over cartoon tweeters any day," I said.

"I guess you would." His eyes fixed on my arm. "I've never seen one before. Half a dozen at once—I guess the rumors are true."

"What rumors?" I took some steps toward him, careful to avoid getting the light directly on any of my guests.

"There's some chatter," he said. "I wrote it off. It sounded hocus-pocus to me."

I felt like giving him a mutant-wasp-armed bear-hug. "Spit it out."

"The chin is that they like you," he said.

"Who likes me?"

"The beasties." His dark eyes gleamed beyond the cone of light between us. "We have eyes and ears in the enemy's network. We've been hearing it for a while now. That they're sweet on you."

"Insects cannot like or dislike. That's human baggage. Insects eat, rest, procreate, metamorphose, and die."

"What about bees?" he asked. "Bees sure do swoon over their queen."

"That's different. That's genetic memory, not affection."

Tony's grin spread his mustache wide, exposing teeth as white as the moon. "Maybe they think you're the queen bee."

"What do you want?" I growled.

"You were gone awhile," he said. "My job is to watch you."

The wind kicked up from the west. It threaded down through the forests above us and threw the scent of pine needles and water in our faces. The ruckus spooked the wasps, which all buzzed off into the darkness. I worked my arm around in my shoulder socket to ease its stiffness.

Above our heads, stars shone through a perfectly clear sky. I could pick out every constellation. But in half an hour, they'd would vanish behind a screen of black and a downpour would tear through the forest.

"I guess you're free to waste your time any way you want," I said.

"You and I both know it ain't a waste. The more we look at you, the more we learn."

"If you're getting so much from watching me," I said, "how about some payback? What do you know about these wasps? Where do they come from?"

Tony shook his head. His pupils caught the moon. "They're a plague sent from Old Testament God, some say. Others say they're escaped lab rats. More than that, I'm not at liberty."

"You're not much of a detective. Those were my first two guesses."

"I'm not saying I'm in the dark. I'm saying we're keeping *you* there—unless you cooperate with us."

"I'm not a cooperator," I said.

"You agree to give us what you know, and I'll get clearance to enlighten you."

"Tell me what Typhon Industries has to do with this, at least."

Tony laughed. "Far as I'm concerned, you're their stooge. No way I'd give up what we know to a turncoat like you. You're poor. You're brown. And you're working for John White. Makes me sick to my stomach." He spat in the pine needles. "You and that Tanis Rivera."

"She works for John White?" I asked.

"She does their moral heavy-lifting for them, and that's all I'm saying." He squinted. "I just called you a traitor to your own people, and you didn't blink."

"The only people offended by being called names are people who're afraid they're true. I'm not a traitor because I've never been part of any group to betray."

He pondered it. "Fair enough. But you still gotta do the right thing."

"For me, doing the right thing is looking out for myself, a couple of humans, and a zoo full of animals. For you, doing the right thing is following me around. Whatever will get you into heaven. But don't think you've got me pegged just because my childhood friend is confused and unemployed. I'm no Minuteman."

Tony pursed his lips and stared intently at my face as I spoke. "Okay. I believe you. You seem like a straight-shooter. Hell, maybe before this is all done, you and me will be chums."

"Only if your employer pays you to be," I said.

"My employer is a group of people I have a lot of common ground with. I'm no mercenary. I make scratch and do good at the same time."

We walked back to our cars. By the time we arrived, the first fat drops plopped into the matted pine needles and burst on our windshields. The air had that heavy smell that would turn the hardest man nostalgic.

Tony turned as he opened his door. "Say."

I raised my eyebrows at him.

"How'd you know I was following you? You know, in the first place. How'd you make me?"

"The newspaper. No one reads them anymore."

He banged his fist against his forehead and chuckled. "I thought it made me look nonchalant. That's what the snoops do in all the old detective movies."

"It was a dead give-away."

He smiled, got in his car, and drove off into the rain.

I parked my truck outside my house a few minutes shy of midnight and sat there, treasuring the quiet. The rain had come and gone. Around me, the trees and rooftops dripped in a gentle and organic rhythm. The gutters shone in the moonlight. Nothing living stirred.

My back ached. I wanted to go to bed and rest my creaking limbs. Instead, I found myself holding the Captain's business card in my hand. He'd killed my turtle. Whatever conflict I was wrapped up in was between people, and like so many conflicts, the bodies piling up were innocent. Albino rattlesnakes, whooping cranes, bullfrogs, and now my dear friend Esposita the painted box turtle. I was also innocent. I was beginning to understand that the Captain wasn't after me just for my expertise with animals, as he claimed. He was, as were many other parties involved and for reasons unknown, chattering about me. I didn't even like people looking in my direction, much less gabbing about me behind my back.

I looked the Captain up in the phonebook. He lived in the Heights, in a middle-class neighborhood between two major streets called Comanche and Montgomery. They ran all the way west to where I lived, only in my neighborhood we called them Griegos and Montaño. I plodded out to my truck, and half an hour later, parked along the curb outside of his address, in the cul-de-sac of a gently curling street. The surrounding houses were painted pastel green and blue—the hues of three decades ago. Their yards were the victims of do-it-yourself xeriscaping, odd patchworks of red, teal, and gray gravel punctuated by clutches of lone desert plants or an old, sickly tree. Neighborhoods like this had once been the hallmark of a thriving class of people with good middle-income jobs, healthy pensions, and leisure time to spend with their kids. Now, they were rotting away, signs that good middle class living was going the way of the whooping crane.

The Captain's doorbell played "Oh Susanna!" It had probably been installed by the members of the Greatest Generation who sold the Captain his house. When the tune finished playing, its echo bounced around the neighborhood before scattering into nothingness. I wondered what the neighbors would think if they happened to wake up and glance out the window. It isn't every day you see a visitor who bumps his head on your neighbor's rain gutter.

After the third ring, footsteps thumped within the house. Someone inside flicked a switch and the porch light sprang to life one foot from my eyeballs. The door opened on a squat, dark form with chicken legs and a round middle. I knew enough about the Captain to recognize his shape.

"Get the hell inside," the Captain said. "My neighbors are going to think they've woken up in Wonderland."

I bent through his doorway and managed not to hit my head on anything. I hated visiting other people's houses, for the simple reason that I hadn't memorized when to duck.

"Christ," he said. "It's past midnight."

"What can I say? I've been staying up nights thinking about you."

"That's sweet." He took two mugs down from a peg rack on a floral-papered kitchen wall. "Coffee?"

"Sure."

He doled a couple spoons of instant crystals in each mug, filled them with water from the tap, and put them in the microwave. While he was busy, I scanned the small foyer for shoes with suspicious looking laces. There were none in sight, and he wore slippers.

"Classy."

"Nothing but the best for men who show up uninvited in the middle of the night. My wife would have come out and cooked you a meatloaf, but she's too busy cowering under the sheets with an automatic in her nightgown pocket."

"I hope she's got the safety on."

The microwave dinged. The Captain handed me a mug. The coffee tasted like the inside of my mouth after a long sleep.

"So to what do I owe?"

"I've been thinking about your offer," I said.

"Oh yeah?"

"Yeah." I sipped the coffee.

"Reconsidering?" he asked.

"I wouldn't use that word. I've been mulling it over."

"Good." He nodded. "I hope you're mulling in the right direction. If you need help, we can talk incentives."

"Like giving my friend a job?"

"Rex is a great volunteer. He'd make an okay paid escort. But, without you signing up with him?" He shrugged.

"Let's talk other incentives."

"Name 'em," he said. "Good paycheck. I can tell you that."

"I'm thinking information."

His gaze wandered the room. "Sure. You want to hear about the Minutemen? It's a long, rich history. Starts about 250 years ago."

"I want to find someone."

"Like a girlfriend? I can set up you with my niece. She's a bookworm, like you, and not too hard on the eyes."

"I'm overstocked with girlfriends right now, actually." It wasn't even a lie, exactly. "I'm up to my neck in them."

"Good for you. May they never meet."

I clinked his glass. It was tough—misogyny didn't come to me naturally. I had to put on a show. "No, I'm looking for that scientist friend of mine. He's still missing."

The Captain relaxed his eyebrows. His retinas drooped. "Too bad."

"He's been gone for two weeks or so. Skinny, coke bottle glasses, bald. Talks like a tweed-wearing English professor. Name's Simon Marchette."

"I remember you mentioning such a fellow the other day. Sounds like you need to talk to the cops."

"I'm worried about him because I think he might have mental issues."

The Captain's eyes sharpened. "That's sad news."

"You see, I think that he may be guilty of murder," I said.

The Captain's head jerked back on his neck just a hair.

"—ing a turtle." I tacked it on to gauge his reaction.

His whole body relaxed. His shoulders fell forward, his chin went down, and he rambled across the room to a cabinet above the kitchen sink. He pulled a half-full bottle of scotch down, sloshed some into his coffee and held it out toward me. I let him pour a finger into my mug. He took a big sip and made a sympathetic smile out of his mouth. "This a zoo turtle, I assume?"

"Remember that one I told you about? My favorite?"

He wrinkled his forehead. "I seem to recall something like that. A colored turtle, was it?"

"Painted," I said through my teeth.

He snapped his fingers. "Gotcha. Very old. Unique."

I nodded.

"I'm sorry for your loss. Why do you say it was murdered?"

"Certain details. It gets a little technical for the layperson. But the details are irrefutable. The turtle was killed. And I assume only a disturbed mind would break into a zoo and kill an animal."

"You want my take? It sounds personal. That scientist—he wasn't after the turtle. He was after you. 'Watch it,' is what that turtle says to me. Objective third party, you understand. He kills your favorite turtle. You've got a nut after you. I'd tell the cops—of course, they're probably too busy dealing with human murders."

I took a mouthful from my mug and let the whisky burn me before I swallowed.

The Captain snapped his fingers. "Tell you what. You sign up with us for one weekend—just try it out. We pay you a very healthy consideration. We also put a man on your Reptile House. He watches out for this scientist. We put a man on your house." The Captain shrugged. "You're safe, your animals are safe. It's a win-win."

I'd gotten all the answer I needed out of him. I held up the mug. "That was some delicious beverage."

"It'll make a man out of you."

I wasn't a fan of men. They killed turtles. I poured the rest of my drink down my throat and set the mug in the Captain's sink. I could feel the hair growing inside of my esophagus all the way down to my tailbone.

"I'm telling you," the Captain said. "You come work for my employer. You're looked after—and we can drink one of these together every night."

I smiled at him for a few seconds longer than either of us felt comfortable with. Then I walked out of his house. He followed me to the doorway and stood watching me walk to my car. As I put my key in the lock, he yelled after me. "Is that a no?"

I stopped what I was doing and gave him a good hard stare. I'd learned how from watching the African wild dogs at the zoo intimidate each other.

He walked down his driveway in his slippers. "That's a bad answer. Looks like I'll have to find some better incentives."

"I can help you brainstorm if you come up short."

He stood on the asphalt in front of my truck and hollered at me. "I get it. You're not the kind who goes for money. You're one of those high and mighty types. You think you're incorruptible. You think you're a loner. I'll tell you something: you're neither. You've never been tested, John Stick. You've lived a clean, quiet life because you've never seen the outside of the shoebox you live in. You're like one of your zoo animals. You keep your cage nice and tidy. My type is the type that breaks open cages. I set animals loose. They don't like it at first. But if they don't want to come out, you just have to turn the cage upside down and give it a shake. Sometimes, you have to douse the cage with gas and throw a match. The animal makes a real fuss at first. Then it runs wild and free and is loyal for life."

The porches of neighboring houses lit up. Dogs yowled and barked. Behind every portal, some normal lurked, peering out through the peephole of their shabby American dream.

"Go back inside, Captain. You'll catch your death out here without your socks."

He stayed put long enough to show me that he wasn't following orders and then turned around and walked up his driveway. As I got into my car, he tossed a final malevolent look over his shoulder.

There is something about having an enemy. It makes you feel alive. I felt so alive that I drove with the windows down. Some stray raindrops hit me in the face. The wind slapped me around a little. I needed it. I felt like I was waking up.

CHAPTER FOURTEEN

Albuquerque sat in a heavy stasis the next morning. The wind had stolen off to a hideout beyond the horizon, and the sun shined so brightly that every detail of the world looked freshly carved from whatever template God had used to create it. As I walked from my apartment to my truck, I felt like a turtle in a terrarium that looked pretty on the surface but had gone far afoul of its original design.

I sat in my truck when I should have been turning the key and driving to work. I stared at my hand as it gripped the steering wheel. Yesterday, my new friends had perched on that same hand. They were the relatives of Esposita the turtle's killer. Usually when I met a species I'd never seen before, I wanted to put them in a cage and feed them vittles for the rest of their lives. I treated them the way I treated myself. Thinking about these new wasps—these mystery beings that were either a leap in evolution or a medical lab abomination, buzzing free through the lush eastern forests of the Sandía Mountains—a smile spread across my face.

I drove to work. I had a turtle terrarium to clean.

My back-corridor way to the Reptile House took me past the staff lounge. An unusual amount of hubbub bubbled out the open door. I ignored it, but found Abbey lurking in the portal to her bat cave, waiting for me.

"Did you hear?" Abbey's green eyes were open wide, like a kid who's just seen Santa. Her long eyelashes were moist and rumpled. The light flew through them in pretty prisms.

"I did not."

"The Tasmanian devils are pregnant."

"Good for them. And us. Everybody loves zoo-babies."

"You don't understand. The tazzies are female."

"No wonder there's a riot in the break room. Pregnant females. It's preposterous."

She smacked her palms on the inner sides of the doorframe. "There are no males! All three females are pregnant, and the zoo houses no males! Remember how Zappy died last year?"

"False pregnancies. Happens all the time."

Abbey slapped her forehead with the palm of her hand. "Duh! Why didn't anybody else think of that?"

"Alright. Take it easy."

"Of course, everybody thought that," she said, "until this morning when we gave one of them an ultrasound. There are twenty-three little embryos in her. She's pregnant. They're checking the other two now."

"Did we mess up the gender on one of the others?"

Abbey rolled her eyes.

"One of them could be a hermaphrodite. Humans can go through their whole lives with organs of both sexes. It's not that uncommon."

"Stop raining on my parade!" Abbey yelled. "I want to believe in miracles."

"Believe!" I said. "Don't let me stop you."

"I'm sure," she said, "that they'll figure out the rational scientific explanation for it and then the world can go back to being normal and boring. But today it's magical."

"Maybe Jesus is coming back as several score of marsupial embryos, and the Rio Grande Zoo Australia Exhibit has been chosen to house three furry, bad-tempered Marys."

"Thank you." Abbey stopped gripping the doorframe and folded her arms across her chest. "Did you ever find Simon?"

I shook my head.

"Any leads on Esposita's killer?"

"Maybe," I said. "It's complicated."

Abbey smiled and infectious glee poured out of her. She had one of those faces. Maybe it had to do with all those wonderful freckles. "Miracles, John!" she yelled as I walked away. "They do happen!"

I did my rounds. Everyone seemed in good health. I fed the creatures that needed to be fed. I cleaned some terrariums. It occupied my morning peacefully until I came to the task I'd been putting off. No animal needed to be transferred to another cage or shooed into a corner while I did my work. There was just a sad circular imprint in the wood chips marking where a red and blue-swirled shell with white flecks had come to rest. I thought about leaving it that way as a means to honor and remember. Then I realized I hadn't lost a child in a tragic playground accident. I emptied the cage, scrubbed it down, and set it on a shelf with dozens of other empty terrariums.

As I bent into the day's paperwork, my mind hovered over Esposita's death. The Captain had obviously been involved, whether he'd done the deed personally or delegated it to some sneaky underling. It was meant to put pressure on me to come work for him. At first, the Captain's motive for recruiting me had been a mystery. I could still only guess, but it seemed he wanted to hire me because the wasps—how did Tony put it? They liked me. They hadn't landed on me to sting me or feed from me. They'd landed on me to rest. They'd been enjoying me, like old men in a smoking lounge. Tony had said his mysterious chatter told him the "beasties" liked me, which meant that the other parties involved already knew it. The trouble was I had no idea how they knew it. I'd never been in the presence of one of the wasps before yesterday. No one could have observed their behavior around me.

I needed to find Simon Marchette. He had answers.

After deciding to put some effort into it, I realized I had no idea how to find a missing person. Looking him up in the phone book and calling his home phone yielded a fun conversation with a voicemail system. Googling him revealed a little about where he'd gone to school and where he'd published articles on the medical potential of funnel web spider venom a dozen or so years ago. An online bio told me he was from Las Cruces originally and that he'd interned with a lab that mapped scorpion genomes in the late 1990s. After 1998, all references to his work disappeared. It was as if he'd given up a promising career and vanished.

I found few pictures of Marchette. Most were head-and-shoulders shots posted with articles he'd written. One showed him in front of a classroom giving a lecture somewhere. That man was the same person I knew, only younger. His head sprouted a fringe of corn colored hair. He wore a white button up tucked into khakis. He held a piece of chalk in one hand and gripped the other to his stomach as he doubled over with laughter. All the kids at their desks laughed, too. The picture made me miss him.

The final picture I found showed a young Marchette, again smiling, with his arm draped around the shoulders of another man. This one had an average Anglo face, with brown hair, brown eyes, and forgettable features. He looked to be about medium build and height. I almost passed it by, but then noticed the caption: "Dr. Simon Marchette and Dr. Jacob Charon at Las Huertas Hot Spring, 1998." I went to the image's webpage, but found the article it had accompanied had been deleted. All that remained was a picture of the two men floating in cyberspace. I recognized the other man by his name: I'd met him on the day I'd first gone to the Bosque to gather dead birds. His face was so bland that it'd slipped from my memory altogether.

Three things lined up: the date, Las Huertas Hot Springs where I'd made a few stinger-wielding friends the night before, and the fact that Typhon Industries was located in that spot. It didn't take a detective to figure out that 1998 must have been the year Marchette had gone to work at Typhon Industries and that this Dr. Charon was also employed there. It confirmed what I'd already suspected: if I wanted to find Marchette, grab him by the vest, and ask him what the hell was going on, the Typhon Industries Complex was the place to start. I'd tried the direct approach; I occupied my afternoon developing a more subtle plan. I ended up sitting around realizing how little I knew about anything besides the slimy, scaly, and skulking things of the world.

My mind eventually turned to Melodía. All this was about her.

I tried her lab number, her cell, and her house. All three played generic voice messages. After work, I went home, showered, and stepped into fresh clothes. I brushed my teeth and combed my hair. I tried to stare at my face objectively enough to decide whether I liked my stubble or should shave it off. My few days' growth of dark beard was sparse across the low cheeks, but grew heavy along the jaw line, chin, and upper lip. The hollows below my cheekbones were deep and bare. It was not part of my routine to think about my looks. In my twenties, I used to stand in front of this same mirror and hate myself. It had been my hobby. I'd stand there and behold the gaunt, brown, bony face staring back and wonder why the universe spun out abominations. I'd look until I broke down and thumped my face with my fists or wept terrible giant tears into the sink. My face looked worse wet. At some point in my early thirties, I'd stopped looking in the mirror. I used it to shave and comb my hair. But I didn't really look at myself. That shimmering square could lead a person back into dangerous territory.

I walked away from the mirror without shaving and drove to the university. Melodía's lab was locked and dark. I drove across the city to her house, far out on the West Side. In the spare desert neighborhoods, my tail was exceedingly obvious. A blue van, much like the one Rex had described to me over the phone, followed me to Melodía's house, where it hovered by the curb a block distant.

I rang the doorbell and banged on the wood. Nothing stirred except the west wind sweeping in from the desert. It had nothing good to say.

The van fell in behind me again as soon as I started driving home. I drove all the way there, not really knowing what to do about it. I just wanted to miss my best friend in peace without it becoming a spectator sport. Lava built up in my stomach. I drove past my house and headed toward the river, following the directions Rex had given me when he'd tailed Tony to the Rio Grande. I found the dirt road he'd described and traced it to the riverbank. The waters were black in the night sky. I killed my truck's lights before I'd even come to a stop, parked it behind some scraggly winter trees, and jumped out.

The van had killed its lights, too. It sidled down the dirt road, crunching rocks under its tires and growling each time the driver gave it a little gas.

I moved among the trees, matching their tall winter skeletons. I made more noise than I would have liked to, but stayed invisible in the long angular shadows. The van eased to a halt a few yards from the riverbank. The passenger window rolled downward with the halting motion of a hand-cranked mechanism. No one moved inside. The forest was silent. The river made no sound as it funneled water toward the dark ocean far away.

The passenger window cranked back up, and the door opened, emitting a blue-jeaned leg atop a cowboy boot. The leg led a body into the night, a holstered bowie knife at the waist. A leather jacket gleamed in the moonlight, and a Stetson cast a deep shadow over the woman's face. Long straw colored hair trailed down the woman's back. I held still as she crept toward the riverbank, peering left and right. All else was still and quiet. Her gaze lingered on the spot where my truck sat behind the screen of trees. Figuring the person would spot me, I stepped out of my hiding place and put myself between her and her van.

She spun. Her hand went to her knife but quickly dropped to her side. "It's you." Her voice was rasping and tough, like a cowboy's.

"Yeah? And who the hell am I?"

"You're the archaeopteryx," she said.

The word stunned me. My childhood leapt into my throat and wouldn't allow me to breathe. Before I knew it, I had her leather jacket in my fists and was sputtering curses into her face. Her Stetson fell off, revealing hard coils of whipcord hair. I knew no words. I knew only thirty years of pent up rage, loss, and frustration.

The van shed other occupants. They leapt on me, pried at my wrists, and levered my arms. A fist beat on my oaken back. I was stronger than a dozen normals put together. No mortal could budge me. The tough woman gripped my wrists and stared her own lifetime of hate back at me. We were like two mirrors trying to burn each other alive by reflecting the high noon sun.

The standoff continued until a hard foot stamped on the back of my leg. I fell down on one knee. Arms constricted my neck and head in a chokehold. A different pair of fists rattled my right kidney. Leather Woman snaked free of my fists and planted the point of a boot in my solar plexus. Fault lines crackled through my skeleton. I swiped my arms behind me at whoever was in love with my neck, but it was like a windmill pawing at a still day.

As I continued to struggle, a dark form swooped from the tree line and collided with Leather Woman. The black-furred animal was the size of a bulldog, with a heavy tail and stout body. It's wings spanned a normal's height. The two staggered in a tangle of wings and arms and fell toward the river. The thing detached right before they hit the water. It cracked its leather wings against the air as it gained altitude, then flapped across the river in the manic way bats do. It traced the far shoreline for a few yards and disappeared into the forest. From the depths of the trees, a shriek like a lamb being tortured echoed across the river.

I recognized that shriek. A little kid named Daniel had described it pretty well when I'd removed a dead snake from his lawn.

The water by the riverbank wasn't deep. The woman thrashed around some, but when she stood, it only came to her knees. Her hair was a stringy mess. She wiped mud from her face with both hands and yanked them away from a rake down her right cheek. Blood leaked from the wounds onto her soaked white shirtfront.

I rose, shrugging off my assailants, and reached my arm out over the water. "Gimme your hand."

She stuck out the arm she wasn't using to hold her face together. I pulled her up the riverbank gently, and her comrades pitched in. Mud booted her jeans up to the calves. Her hat was probably nestled in the mud of the river bottom. Microorganisms would move into it. They'd raise babies. It'd become a nice little habitat.

Leather Woman took her hand away from her face while a young guy in skinny jeans and a floppy haircut examined her. The scratches were about two inches long, jagged, but not very deep. She'd need some butterfly bandages, a gauze dressing, and whatever shots you give someone who'd been attacked by a gargoyle.

"I have a first aid kit in my truck," I said to a young woman with copper hair and Doc Martin boots. I could still feel the tread of one of those boots on the back of my knee.

"We have our own. What in the good Lord's name was that?" The Leather Woman spoke with a good rural twang.

"Devil," I said. "It lives in a tree outside my apartment."

"You must be a real savory character with devils watching your back."

"I'm a saint. You can tell because I don't stalk people around the city and then ambush them in the forest."

Leather Woman turned to me as Floppy Hair came back with a first aid kit. "We weren't fixing to bushwhack you. We have a message for you, but we had to wait for seclusion to deliver it."

"Why not just have Tony Chavez do it? He's your man, right?"

Floppy Hair pressed gauze to the woman's wounds. She waved him away and held it there herself.

"Tony has other duties. There's a lot of pieces to this puzzle."

"What's your message?" I asked.

"Stop looking for Simon Marchette." Her eyes were hard and gray. "He's safe and secure. We'll keep him that way."

"Who says I'm looking for him?" I asked.

She snorted. "You ain't subtle. Everybody knows what you're doing whenever you're doing it."

"He's my friend. He goes missing, I look for him. Plus, he stole something from me."

"We know what he stole from you and your lady friend—"

I stuck my finger in her face. "Unless you want another fight, don't mention her to me."

"Don't take offense," she said. "I'm not trying to upset you. I'm telling you: he took what he did for your own good. Now it's gone and so is he. Best to let sleeping dogs lie."

I felt exhausted. Whether it was the adrenaline rush of the fight ebbing or simply my life catching up with me, all I wanted was to go home and find a prone position. "Thanks for the message. It was real considerate."

"It's for your own good," she said. "Keep clear of this thing and let Simon go."

"If I'm supposed to listen to your advice, you should probably tell me your name."

"They call me Crazy Patty," she said.

"Figures," I said.

As I walked toward my truck, she yelled at my back. "Any idea what that varmint was? It wasn't a bat and it wasn't a bird."

"It wasn't a plane," I said without turning around.

Nobody laughed.

"This city's going to hell," she said.

"Hell on Earth has always been a New Mexican specialty." I slammed my door.

CHAPTER FIFTEEN

At the zoo the next day, the word buzzed so loud even I heard it: all three of our female Tasmanian devils were pregnant. Ultrasounds had confirmed it, and thorough exams had ruled out hidden sex organs. All three were strictly female, and we hadn't had a male around in more than a year. I listened to a few people gush about it in the mailroom, where I stopped to pick up my pay stub. I'd also received a promotional flyer for the Gamut Circus and Freak Show. I tore that in half right through the face of an oily-mustached ringmaster and retreated to my corner of the zoo.

I quickly became preoccupied with the tiger salamanders. They weren't eating enough. We had two of them and I was trying to figure out which one of their appetites was lagging behind. The three of us sat still for half an hour. A handful of crickets bounced around the vegetation in the bottom of the terrarium. They were the only ones having a decent day.

Just before noon, I gave up and went to the bat cave. Abbey sat at her desk amidst a catastrophe of paperwork. She wore the usual green zoo polo, lace up boots, khaki shorts, and spot of guano in her red hair, which she'd tied up in a charmingly sloppy ponytail.

"Thank God," she said when she saw me. "I'm dying in here."

It was the end of the fiscal quarter, when our receipts were due to accounting. I did mine on a daily basis. Other zookeepers experienced minor crises every three months.

Abbey pushed the mass of paper away from her like a meal she'd finished with. She shoved a chair at me with her foot. "Take a load off."

I sat, feeling like a yeti cramming himself into a child's car seat. Once I was as comfortable as I could get, I sighed and mussed a hand through my hair. "I need you to tell me I'm crazy."

She stabbed a finger at me. "You're crazy!"

"Thank you. That comes as a great relief."

"Any time," she said. "Would you like a fruit punch?"

"Sure."

She opened a mini fridge under her desk, took out two Capri Sun drink pouches, and tossed one to me. I hadn't seen a Capri Sun since the white kids brought them to elementary school in their lunch boxes. It took me an eternity to get the plastic off the tiny straw and jam it into the heart of the bag. It took me two sucks to empty it.

"We're all crazy." Abbey sipped her pouch. "We're humans."

I liked Abbey.

"What in particular makes you crazy, John Stick? I imagine you didn't come over here to talk about the general depravity of our species."

I crumpled the pouch in my fist and tossed it in the trash. The motion hurt my ribs, still sore from Crazy Patty's kick. "I know why the Tasmanian devils are pregnant."

"You must be a genius. Everyone else around here is stumped."

"Before I tell you, I want you to settle something else for me. I saw a bat near the river last night. I'm going to describe it, and I want you to tell me what kind it was."

"No prob. There are under a dozen that it could have been. Let's see how quickly I can figure it out." She rubbed her hands together and slapped her thighs. "Go!"

I focused on the few seconds I'd seen the thing and found myself wishing I had Abbey's photographic memory. I opened my mouth, but no words wanted to emerge.

Abbey fidgeted with her drink pouch until she couldn't wait anymore. "Was it a Mexican free-tail? They're common. Was its tail connected to the wing tissue?"

"I know what those look like. That wasn't it. The tail was free, but it was big."

"The tail or the bat?" she asked.

"Both. The tail was long and heavy. The bat was—well, it was big."

"How big?"

"It was night. I might not have seen it perfectly, but I'd say the wingspan was at least four feet." The actual wingspan had been at least six feet, maybe seven. I understated it. I wanted to ease Abbey into the warped reality I lived in.

"Did it have golden fur?"

I shook my head. "Black."

She tapped her chin with her fingertips. "Describe the ears."

"Round," I said. "Very pink inside."

"Not pointy?"

I shook my head.

Abbey folded her arms across her chest. Her cheeks welled red. "You're a liar. There's no such bat."

"Maybe I saw it wrong. It moved pretty fast."

She crunched her brow and the pupils of her eyes shrunk into angry pits.

"I said something wrong. Tell me what."

She pursed her lips. "Sometimes guys make fun of me." Her voice was tight and hard.

That took me by surprise.

"Bat lady. That's what they call me. In high school, it was bat girl. It wasn't a compliment. They thought I was weird."

"Normal people are the ones I call names. We weird people have things figured out."

Her eyes relaxed and the edges of her mouth tugged upward. "What names do you call them?"

"Normals," I said.

She looked disappointed.

"The point is, I'm not making fun of you. I'm serious. I saw some flying creature last night, and I need to figure out what it was."

She leaned back in her chair and swung her feet back and forth. "Let's start from the top. Let's pretend we're scientists. No assumptions. Let's gather evidence and come to an objective conclusion."

I liked Abbey's style. "Lead the way."

"Round ears with pink insides. Black fur. Large wingspan. Nocturnal. Long tail."

"Heavy too," I said.

"Long, heavy tail. Did it look fat?"

"The tail?" I asked. "Yes."

"Describe the legs."

"I didn't get a good look. Short, I think." I envisioned the claw marks in

Crazy Patty's sun-worn skin. "Four toes."

She cocked her head. "You didn't get a good look at the legs, but you counted the toes? That's curious."

I opened my mouth, but once again didn't have any words to shoot through it.

She grinned big. Her teeth were just a little crooked. "You're hiding something. How fun. Did you see any markings on the coat?"

"Not on the back," I said.

"Did you see the front?"

I shook my head.

She kept smiling. "Bats fly. I know you think you're very tall, but even you probably see flying beings from below. You're telling me you saw the side of the bat that usually faces the sky, but not the side that faces the earth."

I nodded. I'd seen the back because it had swooped along the ground and then planted its feet on Crazy Patty's face, with its back to me.

"Was it sunbathing?"

I smiled at her.

"Sometimes, in detective novels, the protagonist comes up against a witness who's only telling part of the truth. It's fun to be the protagonist."

"That makes me the lying witness," I said.

She nodded, grinning like an excited kid. Her green eyes bloomed big and her eyelashes reached all the way up to her eyebrows. "Any vocalization?"

"It screamed. Sounded kind of like a lamb from hell."

"What you're describing isn't a bat." She laced her fingers together, crossed her legs, and set her hands on her knee. "It is a Tasmanian devil. They're black, have round ears with pink interiors, thick tails where they store their fat, and distinctive vocalization. However, they don't have wingspans. They have forelegs."

"Now you know why I'm crazy," I said. "Call the men in white coats."

"What else do you want to know?" she asked.

"Anything would be helpful. When it comes to mammals, I'm in the dark."

"Well, they're marsupials." She bounced up to her knees in the chair. "I love marsupials! Have you ever seen a little baby marsupial crawl from the womb to the pouch? It's like watching a living jelly bean."

"Sounds like a good snack for my pet tarantula."

"You're bad. So," she said, regaining her professional demeanor, "that's why you're here. You're here because you saw a Tasmanian devil with wings last night and you think it's the same one that impregnated our females. Their cage is open-air. You think it swooped in and ravished them."

"In a nutshell."

"Why are you talking to me? You should be telling the Australia exhibit people about it. They'll be happy to hear you've solved their mystery."

"Yeah. I'll walk right over and do that."

"Ha! I can't wait to see their faces."

"I have more questions before I go make their day," I said.

"Shoot."

"What do Tasmanian devils eat?"

"They like carrion, but will eat just about anything they can get."

"Do they drink blood?" I thought about the albino rattlesnake I'd recovered from the lawn of the skinny boy.

She stared at me levelly for a few seconds. "What is up with you, John?"

"I already told you."

"Oh yeah. You're crazy. Okay. First you're talking flying marsupials and now you've moved on to vampires."

I decided to level with her. "Last week I got a call to handle a dead snake in the North Valley. It had been drained of blood, but not otherwise predated."

"The one that Simon stole from your lab," she said. "Continue."

"Also last week, I saw a big bat-like creature outside of my house. Then last night I saw it again near the river. I believe that creature might have also killed the rattlesnake."

"Things always look bigger at night, you know. They also look bigger when they surprise you. When people get scared or attacked by an animal, they consistently exaggerate its size. Villagers in Thailand describe hundred-foot-long serpents. Sailors see squids the size of whales. Fear hormones enhance the senses. Perception gets distorted."

"Maybe that's it." I felt exhausted. The notion that maybe I'd been chasing the phantoms of my own warped perception made me want to go to bed for a week.

"Some idiot probably kept a flying fox as a pet and it got loose," Abbey said. "The flying fox has a five-foot wingspan. They're huge. Some of the other details don't match up, but that could be your answer. It was *not* a vampire bat. They're tiny."

I nodded. I fought the voice in my head that said if a wasp and a horsefly could blend into a super blood-sucking chimera, why not a Tasmanian devil and a vampire bat?

"Just out of curiosity, when you saw the bat outside of your house, what was it doing?"

"Sitting in a tree watching me."

Abbey leapt up from her chair, donned her green zoo cap, threaded her orange ponytail through the closure, and picked up a black canvas bag.

"Sudden urge for lunch?" I asked.

"No. We're going to your house so that you can show me the exact spot in the tree where your visitor was perched."

"What's in the bag?" I asked.

"A low frame rate digital video camera. We're going to catch your bat on tape and prove it's within the parameters of the normal animal kingdom. Let's go."

"You're just trying to avoid doing your paperwork."

I drove since Abbey owned a Volkswagen Beetle and there was no way I'd fit into it. My neighborhood was quiet, as always. The sun was so strong you could feel it pressing you into the earth. I led Abbey down the stairs into the shade of my patio where winter temperatures still crouched in the shadows.

"This is beautiful." She bent over and pinched the soil in one of my planters. "This must be insect central in the spring. I bet you have all kinds of bat visitors."

"Probably." I wondered if Ralph could take on a bat. A South American spider, the Bird-Eater Goliath, predated on small birds and bats, but it had the advantage of a web.

"So, where's the spot?"

I positioned my stepladder under the tree and pointed out the branch. Abbey climbed up with a flashlight between her teeth and a magnifying glass in the back pocket of her shorts. She spent several minutes scrutinizing the claw marks on the branch and the surrounding limbs, twigs, needle clusters, and trunk. Then she descended the ladder and rummaged through the foliage below.

"Bingo," she said.

I leaned over to see what she'd found. Puddles of black, tarry spoor lay amidst the stalks of flora.

"This is the guano of a very large bat. Most bat guano is off-white or brown and pill-shaped." She put a finger in the center of one of the puddles and sniffed at the dark stool that clung to her fingertip. She made an appropriate face. "Yuck."

"What does it smell like?" I asked.

"Ammonia."

"Give me a sniff." She held her finger up and I snorted a little air across it. I regretted it. "Should I bother to guess what kind of bat makes stool this disgusting?"

"You already did. Vampires. Their urine is just as bad."

"The urine around the dead snake was pretty damn strong," I said.

"You found urine around the snake?" she asked.

I nodded

"Vampire bats have to drink so much during a feed that they urinate while they're still in the act." Abbey shut her eyes and stood very still. The birds of early spring chirped around us. A half block away, some kids shouted at each other in the careless way that kids do before they're aware of how foolish their human noise sounds.

"This is no time for meditation," I said.

Her eyes stayed shut. "When I'm dreaming, sometimes if I close my eyes in the dream and squeeze them really tight, when I open them up again, I wake up." She squeezed her whole face and gave me several seconds to scrutinize her nose crinkles. Her eyes popped open, and her pupils contracted into small dark orbs.

"You're not dreaming," I said.

"It was worth a try." She sprung to her feet and started bustling around my patio, peering into bushes and pawing at patches of soil. Her work produced a few plastic bags of guano and a few more of hair. I enjoyed watching another professional at work. "How far is the river from here?"

"The spot wasn't far. A mile or so."

She stood and whacked her palms against the thighs of her shorts. "You have a stalker. It comes here often, judging from the amount of spoor. It must have followed you to the river."

I shook my head. "Not possible. I drove there."

"Insectivorous bats use echolocation to hunt. Vampire bats are highly macrosmatic—they use smell."

"I know the lingo. Just because some of my people smell through their tongues doesn't mean I'm a novice."

Abbey grinned. "Sorry. I talk to a lot of 'normals.' " She put air quotes around the word with her fingers. "Anyway, a vampire bat can smell its prey from miles away, just like any good smeller. So can another creature that we've been talking about today, only it likes to smell carrion."

"The Tasmanian devil. Horseflies also have excellent smell." My brain was making connections—finally.

Abbey pulled a video camera out of her bag. "So, if this animal wanted to, it could have followed its nose and found you at the river. Bats are excellent flyers. It might have simply followed your truck from your home." She fiddled around with some settings on the camera.

"Fancy gear," I said.

"This is a motion activated digital camera," she said. "The kind you use to capture rare animals in remote locations. This kind of camera caught the famous video of wolverines in Montana. I've been using it to figure out what Ferdinand gets up to at night."

"Ferdinand?" The name seemed vaguely familiar.

"My little problem bat. I come to work in the morning and he's wet. Just soaking wet. I can't figure out what he does to himself. Anyway, this project seems slightly more urgent."

"You're saying," I said as she moved the ladder to a nearby tree, "that this vampire bat or Tasmanian devil could have the ability to smell me from a mile away. Fine. But what motive could it possibly have? Does it want my blood?"

Abbey climbed the rungs, positioned the camera in a crook of branches, and lashed it there with duct tape. "That's a mystery." Once she'd come back down, a light sheen of sweat stood on her forehead, a stray pine needle hung in her orange hair, sap clung to her hands, and bat droppings stained her index finger.

"Wanna wash up?" I asked.

"That'd be great. And maybe I could ask you for a glass of water."

Inside, the light on my answering machine blinked. I pointed Abbey toward the bathroom and prepared a couple of ice waters. She splashed around for a minute or two, walked back into the living room, jumped on one of my bar stools, and took the huge glass I offered her with both hands. She looked like a kid drinking out of a flower vase.

"You have a message." She hit the play button on my answering machine.

The same man's voice from the other day spoke cryptic Spanish in a gringo accent and the usual panicky pitch.

"It's just a prank caller. His passion in life is leaving me nonsense messages."

Abbey had frozen mid drink, staring at me wide-eyed. Her mouth hung open. Her bottom lip was huge through the distortion of the water glass.

"Don't worry about it."

"You don't speak Spanish, do you?"

"Never learned," I said. "Do you?"

"Of course. We live in New Mexico. How can you not speak Spanish? You can learn it just from walking around Old Town."

I didn't tell her that strolling around the historic district chatting up bilingual strangers was outside my comfort zone. "Fine. I'm a bad New

Mexican. What did he say?"

A flush rose in her forehead and cheeks. "It was Simon."

It took me a second. "Marchette?" I wanted to smack myself for not recognizing his voice.

"Yes. He's in Truth or Consequences. He says he's hiding out there."

"Did he say from what?"

Abbey nodded again, slowly.

"Well, spit it out!" I almost yelled.

"*El hombre quien maté los pajaros*," she said. "The man who killed the birds."

CHAPTER SIXTEEN

made Abbey translate the entire message word for word and write it down. While she worked, I spent some time kicking myself. When she'd finished, it read like this:

Mr. Stick. I have left you several urgent messages. I hope you are safe. I am hiding in Truth or Consequences, New Mexico. My hope is that using Spanish slows down anyone listening in. I am in the inn named for an intelligent rhinoceros. Come see me. The white man I am hiding from is powerful and he'll silence anyone who exposes his operation for what it is. He is the man who killed the birds.

"There's an inn called the intelligent rhinoceros?" I asked.

Abbey shrugged. "That's what he said."

"The words 'white man...' what were they exactly?"

"*Señor blanco,*" she said.

"Could that mean Mr. White instead of white man?"

She shrugged. "It could. Listen, I want to come with you to T or C. Simon's my friend. If he's having some sort of paranoid breakdown, I want to help him."

"He's not paranoid."

"Well, then I want to come even more."

"Let me figure out what's going on first. When I do, I'll let you know."

Abbey's eyes got steely. "Don't go without me."

"I won't," I lied.

Once I'd dropped Abbey off at the zoo, I drove south. Truth or Consequences was half an hour beyond the Bosque Del Apache. I figured if I got going right away and found the inn without trouble, I could interrogate

Marchette and be back by bedtime.

It was one of those New Mexican afternoons. The sun beat through the turquoise sky and hammered the world with gold. Tan winds swept in from the west, kicking up dirt devils and scouring the right side of my truck with sand. While the sun hung high, I drove with the windows down. When it settled closer to the horizon, bathing my cab in light and heat, I switched to AC. In this mile-high desert, the sun ruled everything. Seasons were relative.

Truth or Consequences had earned its name from a game show contest back in the fifties. The winning city had the honor of naming itself after the TV show. Hence, "Truth or Consequences" wasn't a sardonic reference to the history of lies, war, and ethnic conflict the state suffered from; it was a fun game to distract us from the realities of our impoverished lives. The name also made a lot of East Coast tourists swoon from the quaintness of it all.

The town nestled in the river valley between the slate gray Magdalena Mountains to the west and the brown peaks of the Turtle Mountains to the east. It lay a few miles from Elephant Butte dam and its resultant lake, where people sped their boats around during the summer, water-skiing, jet-skiing, and generally pretending they lived in a different biosphere. T or C itself was a tourist town, with plenty of cheap motels, distinctively cute little inns with funky decor schemes and ancient furniture that people deemed "retro," and that therefore didn't need to be replaced when worn out. T or C also boasted a robust hot springs that provided geothermal energy for the town and healing waters channeled into spas and inns for the tourists to soak themselves in and swear by the wisdom of the noble savages who had discovered them a millennium before and from whom they'd been forcibly appropriated after that.

I got off the interstate and rolled into town around four. The slanting afternoon light painted the west sides of the buildings in pale gold, rendering their cracks and stains in minute detail, like really tender portraits of old people. The main road led through strips of auto repair shops, a couple of diners, and a seafood joint at least a thousand miles from any salt water. The road turned west and took a sharp drop downhill, a waterfall spilling traffic into the flow pool of downtown. It consisted of a central square block around which four one-way streets eddied. On the edges of the square lay the library, civic buildings, and charming inns that had hand-painted signs proclaiming unique rooms, free breakfasts, and private hot springs. I trolled around, turning down the off-jutting parks and places and courts. Finding no leads, I explored the outlying vestiges of the southern edge of the town and found a scattering of gas stations and derelict motels. Nothing I'd seen so far had been named after a rhinoceros, or any other beast remnant of the Pleistocene age.

I drove back to the town center and parked in front of the tourist information building, which doubled as a café. I ducked through the low 1950s doorframe, and when I straightened up again, found a little old Anglo man wearing glasses, a white apron, cowboy boots, and a bolo tie. His eyes were as wide as his glasses and he wielded a pink feather duster in one hand. The room featured a few tables along the east side, a cluster of spinning racks showing off clever greeting cards and scenic postcards, and a sales counter with a refrigerated case of pastries and an espresso machine.

"I was just dusting," the little old man said.

"Lookin' good."

"The place gets real dirty real quick." He hadn't moved since my entrance. He brandished the duster in the air over one of the display racks as if my presence had turned him to stone. "You know, what with the desert and all. Tourists don't understand what it's like living in the desert. Wind. Dust. Old buildings. It all adds up."

"You don't have to tell me. I'm local."

"I've never seen you before." He blinked once and when I didn't disappear, he blinked harder.

"Down from Albuquerque. Looking for a particular inn."

"Oh." He dropped his arm, and his body relaxed, as if the return to his job routine had transmuted him from stone back into human flesh. "Well, I sure can help you there. Which one you looking for?"

"The Intelligent Rhinoceros," I said.

He squinted at me. "None by that name here. You must be thinking of a different town."

"You're sure?" I asked.

He beamed proudly. His face was round and the smile suited it well. "I know every inn, motel, hotel, and every other business in the city limits. Been living here my whole life." He circled behind the sales counter. He lifted the apron over his head, revealing a white cowboy shirt printed with blue milkweed blossom and with peaked stitching on the pockets and epaulettes. He hung the feather duster on a hook on the wall beside a sign that said NO CHECKS.

That he didn't recognize it confirmed what I'd suspected since Abbey'd told me the name to start with. "The buddy that I'm meeting is tricky. I think he gave me the name in the form of a riddle."

The old man scratched his gray head and smiled. "What goes round the house and in the house but never touches the house?"

"What?" I asked.

"It's a riddle."

I tried to force myself to think about it, but all I could think about was that I was wasting time. "I give up."

He shook his head sadly, took off his glasses, and polished them with his shirttails. "Now, a riddle is all about the person telling it. What does that person know? What do they care about? Do they do a lot of crossword puzzles? It may be a play on words. Do they like to make lewd jokes? It may be something crass about the fairer sex. You have to figure out your teller, then you figure out the riddle." He put his specs back on. They gleamed. "So, what about this buddy of yours who told you to meet him at this Intelligent Rhino?"

I'd never been good at riddles, probably because no one ever told me any. I wasn't from a riddling family. Rex wasn't a riddler. My snakes, lizards, and frogs told no riddles. If any animal were a riddler, it would probably have been Esposita, my painted turtle. And she was gone.

"Well?" the old man said.

"He's a little guy. Early forties. Anglo. Bald and skinny."

"But what's he interested in?" the old man asked. "What knowledge does he have to draw from to write his riddle?"

"He's an entomologist. He studies insects."

"Ahh. Do you also know something about them?"

I gave him a half-hearted nod.

The man leaned across the counter and pulled a sheet of paper from a plastic display sheath attached to the front of the counter. "Let's take a look at this. It lists the names of all the inns in the area."

I scanned the list of a score or so names. I recognized most of them from my tour through the town. None of them did anything special for me.

"Say the words out loud," the little old man said. He leaned both his elbows on the counter and put his chin in his hands. He mooned up at me over the tops of his glasses.

I ran down the list again. It was hard to concentrate. I wasn't used to doing anything difficult with another human being watching me.

"In-tell-i-gent Rhi-no," the old man pronounced slowly. "You can say it in your mind, if you prefer. Intelligent Rhino."

The words didn't help me. "I'll take the list and look it over," I said. "I'm sure the answer will come to me."

As I started to pick up the sheet, the old man put his palm on it. "Hold on, now. It's always harder on your own. Two minds are better than one. Let's take a few more minutes and see if we can't figure this out."

"I don't want to waste your time."

The man straightened up and put his hands on his hips. "You kiddin' me? This is fun!"

I was beginning to like the old man. "Alright. What's the next step?"

"Well, most riddles, they're old. They're made up long ago. But new ones, first you ask yourself what do I know about the person who wrote it. We've done that. Now, if it's a personal riddle, written from me to you, you don't just ask what you know about me. You ask what you and me have in common. A good riddle between two people draws from what they share. If he wrote this for you, and he's your buddy, he's drawing on something particular to your friendship. So you ask yourself, what do you share?"

"We both know insects."

"We already covered that. What about your friendship? What have you shared there?"

I could have told him that we were both embroiled in a conspiracy that involved dead birds, a biogenic experiment and immigrant detainment facility, The Minutemen, and mysterious nocturnal chimeras that sucked blood. He probably could have used a good laugh.

"Say the words out loud while you think," the old man said. "Intelligent Rhino."

The wheels in my head stuck on the last word I'd thought of. Blood. I had a vision in my mind of a particular bloodsucker, the brown dog tick. Marchette always used Latin names. The Latin for the tick was *rhipicephalus sanguineus*. It was a play on words: rhinoceros was close to *rhipicephalus*; intelligent was a synonym for sanguine, which played on *sanguineus*, Latin for bloody. Intelligent Rhino was a pun for the brown dog tick—Marchette *would* deliver important information in a pun.

I pointed to a name on the list: The Brown Labrador Spa and Inn. "Where's this one?"

The old man lit up. "You figured it out! How?"

I explained the logic to him.

He shook his head in admiration. "What an intimate riddle! You must be close friends indeed." He took a sheet with a map of the downtown on it from another plastic sleeve, and marked an X over the location of the inn. "It's this one. Walking distance, if you'd like to enjoy a stroll through town."

"Thanks. I'll let you get back to your dusting."

"Just one more thing." He held up a finger and made a swirling motion. "What goes round the house and in the house but never touches the house?"

I thought about it. "Mosquitoes."

He laughed. "Nope. The sun."

The Brown Dog Inn, which enjoyed a spot right on the downtown square, was an enclave of several structures gathered together by a high adobe wall. The courtyard featured a tidy gazebo of white latticework, red brick paths, and planters of wispy Greene's beargrass that would bloom lilac in the spring, spiny-leafed amole grasses, and yucca stumps with their saber-length green fronds. Each building wore a jacket of vibrant paint—canary, lime, fuchsia, teal—probably meant to inspire the place with a cheery atmosphere.

A willowy woman with a long brown face, long gray hair, and long patchwork skirts emerged from the central structure. Her face drooped with worry lines, some old, some new as the day. "Can I help you sir?"

"I'm looking for someone."

"Are you with the police?"

"He's small, skinny, pale, and bald. He wears big glasses. Whatever name he gave you probably sounds fake."

Her eyes sharpened and her mouth tightened up. She definitely knew who I was talking about. "I can't reveal any information about our guests unless you have a warrant."

"Lady, I'm not the police. I'm a friend. The guy I'm looking for has been trying to get through to me for a week. He'll be happy I'm here."

"No man like that comes to mind, but if you wait I'll just make the rounds and let the guests know that a stranger is here. What name shall I give them?"

"Just tell him Stick's here."

A lifetime of worrying about other people's problems had carved deep lines in her face. I could almost see them deepening as I watched her. "Please stay in the courtyard." Her voice was as hard and brittle as shale.

I wandered around under the bare limbs of the trees while she was gone. I guessed that an Arizona oak and weeping willow might be among them but it was hard to tell without leaves. The winter stripped trees of their identity. I had a brief vision of people walking around all winter without their skins and was glad when the woman interrupted it by emerging from the blue-walled office.

She'd restructured her lines into an etching of a smile. "He didn't tell me about you."

"Shame on him," I said. "Where is he?"

"I've hidden him in the orange wing. It's behind the other buildings, out of the way of prying eyes." She motioned for me to follow her and walked back into the door she'd come through. The office was a study of idiosyncrasy. It had an old-fashioned cash register next to a credit card swiper, a rack of pamphlets promoting local attractions, a placard with a Wi-Fi password, a topographical map of the outlying area, and a whole wall of Polaroids depicting smiling guests. Each snapshot was signed. Many of the guests wore outdated wedding garb; there were also a few newer photos with same-sex couples, also in wedding garb. It looked like a jolly scene for newlyweds.

We entered a side door of the office and walked down a hall punctuated regularly by doors. Each door opened onto a large stone tub with a heavy spigot above it. The walls had hooks for robes and benches with stacks of towels on them. The gray-haired woman saw me looking.

"That's where guests can take the cure," she said.

"The cure?" I said.

Her smile got that twirl at the edges people get who think they know something you don't. "Healing waters."

A lot of hot springs people talked like that. They swore that sitting in a tub and letting geothermally enhanced water turn your skin red was the magic touch for everything from cancer to depression to the common cold. They might have been right. Personally, I imagined that it probably just relaxed a person, which could cure all sorts of things.

She led me out a back door, which let into a parking lot. We crossed it, penetrated a gap in a wooden fence, and found ourselves in a small dirt lot with a few skeletal-looking scrub oaks and globular juniper bushes. The orange wing and apparently the magenta wing lay across the vacant lot. The one-story buildings were side by side and looked like they might have once been cheap apartments. Each one had several doors labeled with room numbers and flanked by lawn chairs. Curtains dressed the windows in the color of their corresponding wing. The inn was one of those shabby-chic affairs, where rustic charm went a long way.

"It's room 56," the gray-haired woman said. "Knock two fast, two long, and three very fast."

"A code knock. Very cloak and dagger."

"There's a back door he can use if someone gives the wrong knock."

"So, you know about the trouble he's in?"

She touched her nose. "I'm a Good Friend."

I touched my nose. "I guess I'm his friend too."

She shook her head back and forth in a grave display of negation. One of her long gray strands came loose from the bundle behind her head and snaked in the wind. "Good Friends. We're a movement. I shouldn't say anything else. I've known Simon a long time. He's very dear." Her big gray eyes hovered sadly in her face. The bottom of each socket hung low, revealing the red flesh within. She was one of those women on the verge of old age, who'd endured tough times and come out a little crazy but a little wise, too.

"He's alright. I've worked with him for years, but I'm really just getting to know him."

"Go on." She lifted one of her loose-sleeved arms. "He's waiting for you."

I walked across the field toward the orange wing. A whiptail lizard scuttled among the brambles. A few big desert grasshoppers buzzed at me before taking flight. A crow ripping apart a white fast food bag grudgingly flapped up to a low-hanging power line and waited for me to pass. Unit 56 had a heavy oak door, ornately carved, one of those old things crafted when people used to care.

I gave the secret knock. The door flew open on Simon Marchette. He wore white tennis shoes, a khaki wind jacket, and red trousers. He looked paler and moister than usual. His glasses were dirty. His stoop was a little more pronounced. But he grinned so broadly I thought his head might break in half.

He grabbed me by the hand and pulled me through the doorway. I had the presence of mind to duck. He slammed the door all while pumping away at my arm.

"Hail Zookeeper Stick!" he trumpeted. "You have arrived, if not in a timely manner, then at least not too late—or so may we hope!"

"Marchette." I pumped his arm a little, too. It felt good. I fought the impulse to pick him up under the armpits and toss him in the air. I hadn't realized how much I liked having him around until he'd vanished.

We let each other go. He swept his arm across the small spare outer room. "Please sit. I regret that I have little hospitality to share, but that which I do enjoy, I gladly offer you."

The room was decorated with an orange corduroy couch, a pair of rust-colored recliners, and a wooden coffee table spread with an orange runner and a vase of plastic tiger lilies. An alcove with a small sink, mini fridge, and microwave punctuated the wall. A door led into a bedroom with a predictably gaudy orange bedspread and framed paintings of orange houses. I sat on the couch and tried to pretend I was comfortable.

Simon perched himself on the front edge of a recliner. His cornflower blue eyes danced in their sockets. "You received my messages and deciphered my code. I knew you would."

"Yeah. Sorry it took me so long. I had to find a translator."

He tilted his head like a puzzled cockatiel. "I presume you mean a Spanish translator? I assumed you spoke the language, given that your father is Hispanic."

"Never learned. My father is very stubborn about denying that part of his identity."

"Well," Marchette said, "I'm embarrassed. I used Spanish because I conjectured it might slow our enemies."

"Hold on." Something occurred to me. I never talked about myself. I never saw Marchette outside of work. We didn't have any friends in common. "How did you know about my father?"

Simon's smile vanished, and he let out a deep breath. His face hung limp, and he slumped back in his chair. "The answer to that question is mired in other questions."

"No riddles. You said the white man who killed the birds was after you. You meant John White, the head of Typhon Industries. Why is he after you?"

"He is after me because I have mutinied. I have fled the reservation, so to speak, and he cannot abide insubordination."

"It's a free county. He can't make you work for him if you don't want to."

"Work. How casually you put it. When one works for John White, it's closer to a pledge of fealty. He's arranged the entire compound in a hierarchy of security clearances. As one moves up through that hierarchy, one sees things—secrets that John White wishes to keep hidden as long as possible."

"What kinds of secrets?"

"His identity, for one. No one knows who John White is. There are no records of him attending school or being born. There are no pictures, tax documents, or voting records. I'm surprised you've even heard his name."

"A guy in a cheap suit told me. A gumshoe."

"You're speaking of Tony Chavez. Tony's a Good Friend."

"These Good Friends," I said. "They need a new name."

"Why, I rather like the name. They're a movement of people who believe in goodness, kindness, and generosity."

"Are they communists?" I said.

Marchette's ears turned red.

"You have to admit, doc, those aren't exactly American values."

"They are the most noble values of humanity."

"How can you expect us to suddenly be good friends with everybody after all we've been through? Our blood is too bitter. It's full of bile. Hell, after only half a lifetime in this world, I'm ready to write off every other human being except for a handful."

Marchette leaned forward and stabbed a yellow finger at me. "Then you are part of the problem." But he held up his palm when I started to retort. "And so am I. We're both bitter men, contaminated and twisted by a bad world."

"This coming from the guy who whistles while he brushes the tarantulas' belly hair and polishes the centipede chitin. You smile all day, Doc."

"That smile, like so much else, is window dressing on a very bleak house. I'm a parasite. I spent years burrowing into the neck of a monster, sucking life from it, and only realized later what tainted blood I was drinking."

"You're going to have to be less metaphorical."

Marchette's eyes were small and hard in sockets ringed with red. His mouth hung in a slack slash across the bottom half of his face. He was a man mangled by guilt and misuse. "It's never easy to admit one's crimes."

"I'm not asking to hear them. I came down here for my snake. And my friend's egg. And Jones the spider."

"I released that dear arachnid in the desert east of the San Andreas Mountains. He will bear out the remainder of his life with at least a sporting chance at survival."

"And the egg?"

"That infernal spawn?" He smacked a fist into his palm. "I crushed it beneath my heel, doused it with gasoline siphoned from my vehicle, and burned it."

"Doesn't that seem a little over the top?"

"No act of defiance is too strong, Zookeeper Stick." Marchette whacked his fist into his palm again. "These monstrosities must be destroyed wherever they flourish. I'm sorry. I know you found it, but that egg and the beast inside would only have brought you ill fortune should you have hatched it."

"It was just a bug egg. What's gotten into you?"

"Wrong," he said. "It was a *chupacabra*."

I stared at him. "You mean the Mexican monster that sucks blood?"

"That is the nomenclature Typhon Industries has given the beast within that egg. I destroyed it because these chupacabras in all their forms are evil. I'm sorry I robbed Dr. Hernandez. Though I've never met her in person, I can only imagine she was quite upset. And I'm ever so penitent toward you, as well." He bowed his head. "I hope you can forgive me."

"You can make it up to me. You left a message for me that said John White killed those birds. Tell me how."

Marchette's mouth softened and his eyes lost their glint. "I don't know."

"Then what the hell am I doing here, doc?" I regretted saying it. I wanted him to know that I was as worried about him as I was anxious to solve the mystery of the dead birds. But I wasn't equipped to spill my warm gooey center out in public.

Gravity dragged his shoulders a hair closer to the center of the Earth and his face aged a year or two. "My deep apologies. I know I have betrayed your trust, and dragged you scores of miles downriver. And—" He hesitated, lingering over words that didn't want to form.

I jumped in. "No apologies. I enjoyed the scenery. I've just been running low on sleep lately. It's given me the temperament of a zebra."

"Ah-ha!" Marchette's face remained a dangling mess of lips and eye sockets.

"Listen. Tell me what you know. If you don't know how this mystery man killed all those birds, can you at least give me a motive?"

"It may not have been intentional." Marchette straightened his spine, adjusted his cap, and tugged his shirt into place. "I shall tell you what I know. Then I have one more truth to tell you. Something that must be said."

"One step at a time."

He nodded. "I've always admired your bearing. You never rush, you never skip ahead, you always take care. These are the qualities of a hero."

"Enough," I said.

"Right! No more compliments! Let us to business."

He crossed his skinny legs and braided his fingers together. The packet was nearly as big as his head. When he spoke, his voice was crisp and precise. "Every year on exactly the same day, the roof opens up over Mount Olympus and the sun shines inside. It remains like that for approximately one hour until the sun passes over the crest of the Sandía Mountains and shade falls over the compound. Then the roof closes."

"What the hell is Mount Olympus?"

"Why, it is the home of the Greek gods! But in this instance, I refer to the heart of the Typhon Industries compound, a modestly sized, but intricately crafted structure that sits at the northernmost position of the campus. John White named it Olympus."

"A creek flows into it."

"Correct," he said.

"Why would anyone plan a building right in the path of a creek?"

"No one knows."

"What does he do with the water?"

Marchette lifted his shoulders and spread his hands.

"What is the purpose of the building?" I asked.

Marchette wagged his head back and forth and shrugged even bigger.

I figured I'd better stop asking questions before he strained himself.

"Apart from John White himself, no one knows what happens in that building—save for one man. His name is Dr. Charon. He's the chief scientist of the entire facility and the only member of the staff allowed access."

Charon, the average man I'd met the day after the birds died and the man I'd seen in the picture with Marchette. "No one else goes in? No janitors, secretaries, lab assistants, electricians, delivery men, security guys—no one? C'mon, Doc. Somebody else must have access. Every building in the world needs peons."

"This one doesn't." Marchette leaned back in his chair and folded his arms. "I've tried. I've sounded out every member of staff and security. No one enters. No one leaves. Unless John White has a secret entrance—which he very well might—he lives in Mount Olympus."

"Except Charon. He comes and goes."

"Yes," Marchette said. "He's the only one. And he's a trained dog, a bland man with no vision."

"You're jealous of him."

Marchette's ears turned red again. He got up and paced the room. "John White made me promises." He slashed an arm through a phantasm only he could perceive. "I was an up and comer. I was to be part of the biggest discoveries. My brother was an astrophysicist. He was discovering planets. I wanted to find my own planets, as it were. Arachnologists were unearthing new species every year, mainly in the rain forests of South America, but also in farther flung locales such as Papua New Guinea, Thailand, and Sri Lanka. I specialized in venom. I believed—as many do—that study of new arachnids and their venoms might lead to medical innovations."

I didn't like humans who studied animals only to benefit other humans. I didn't buy the Bible line that the animal kingdom was our own personal farm.

"Typhon Industries was interested in venom," Marchette continued. "But their primary field is genetics. They wanted to genetically modify spiders to produce custom venoms—or so they claimed in their call for researchers. I was working at Cornell University at the time—I had a post-doctorate fellowship with strong possibilities for future tenure—but I abandoned my post for an opportunity to work with Typhon Industries."

"You got the job," I said, trying to speed him along. I hadn't come for his life story.

"I did." He stopped pacing and gazed into a far corner of the room where the orange floral wallpaper met the ochre baseboard.

"And?" I said.

He took a deep breath and fidgeted his fingers against the change in his pants pocket, which jingled in the closeness and quiet of the room. "This is the hard part to tell you." He angled his eyes toward me.

"Just spill it."

"John White lost interest in venom almost immediately," he said. "He shut down that section of his lab and assigned me to the zoo."

"Typhon Industries has nothing to do with the zoo," I said.

"On the contrary, John White is the chairman of the board of trustees. He's obsessed with the zoo. He's an animal fanatic—for all the wrong reasons."

"How do you know all this if you've never met the guy? And what does any of this have to do with me?"

"I know because he issues directives. I've never met him, but I've read thousands of pages of his writing. They read like manifestos as much as memoranda. He blends instructions and polemics into a mélange that can barely be described as sane." He held up his hand to keep me from interrupting him. "And as far as you are concerned, over the past six months, one of my primary duties at the zoo was to spy on you."

Gravity swelled into my skull and red flowers bloomed in my peripheral vision. My fingertips went numb. A trapeze act did some flips in my stomach.

"John White is obsessed with the zoo—and its most accomplished keeper." Marchette dropped his eyes. "I've been writing regular reports on you."

I didn't have any words, so I kept my mouth shut.

"That's not all—I've also been collecting samples." His voice was raspy, as if he needed water. "Snapshots. Vocal recordings. Fingerprints. I pilfered a zoo polo that you neglected to take home one day."

"Those cost a lot of money. The zoo has to get my uniform custom made."

His huge mouth bent up in the center and down at the ends, like a cartoon version of sadness. "That's not the worst of it."

I waited. Far off, a dog bayed.

"I collected strands of your hair." His face twisted around the words as if he were eating a wedge of lemon. "Flakes of skin. I invested hours in your office at night with a headlamp and magnifying glass. He's even given you a code name: Archaeopteryx."

I tried to take it in. I felt numb. The distant dog barked. A couple others joined it. I pushed a word out my throat. "Why?"

"He's a geneticist."

"That makes no sense." My voice was louder than I meant it to be. "My—condition. It isn't genetic. It's glandular."

"But your mother had the same affliction, did she not?"

If he mentioned my mother again, I thought it might be reasonable to ram his head through the cheap plaster ceiling. I stood up. A carousel wheeled around in my head, and the room staggered in dizzy turns. Marchette gushed words all over the place. He got his tiny body between me and the door. I tossed him out of the way. I stepped out into the sun, the wind, and the howling choir of dogs. Marchette poked his bald head through the crack in the door and whispered at me.

I turned. "I came here for one thing." My voice rumbled the windows of Marchette's crummy room. "What happened to the birds?"

"Come back in and I'll tell you." He clung to the door, the fingers of both hands wrapped around the edge.

"Tell me now or I'll stuff you in a duffel bag and deliver you to the steps of Mount Olympus."

"I don't know." His voice was tinny with shame and desperation. "What I do know is that on the same day every year, the roof of Mount Olympus opens. On that day, during that hour, something bad happens."

I snapped my fingers in his face. "Specifics."

"The first year, a new strain of hanta virus broke out. No one linked it to White's work, of course. Some people died on pueblos, there was a little panic, people bought mousetraps, and they never asked where it came from. The next year, on the same day, a string of tornadoes did a dance down the Rio Grande valley."

"We get one every now and then."

"Not like that year."

I remembered those tornadoes. Every resident in the city had hidden in their pantries and garages. No one dug basements in Albuquerque—the soil was too dense. My home below the earth was a rarity. It'd been untouched, but dozens of other houses had been chewed up by the funnels of furious air.

"Next year it was a drought. Then a mass beaching of silvery minnows.

Then a pox that wiped out half the state's roadrunner population. Can you guess the date upon which all these disasters transpired?"

"The same date my life went down the toilet."

"The birds were the worst yet," Marchette said. "I can only imagine what sort of catastrophes will occur when Mount Olympus opens again next year."

"I'm leaving. I'm going to go listen to some pop songs about true love on my truck stereo. They make a hell of a lot more sense than you do right now."

"You must listen!" he yelled after me. "Every time John White opens the roof of that room, calamity strikes! He's channeling an evil power through it!"

I stalked back to my truck, trying to stay mad enough at Marchette so as not to take his blather seriously. Around me, every dog in the town howled at the moon that hung in the afternoon sky. It was white and fragile, like the skull of an ancient god watching over a world lost to him. The dogs weren't actually barking at the moon—of course. I'd heard that racket before. Tanis' white van sat behind my truck. A dark car with government plates edged it in from the front. She leaned against the white van. Inside, the maniacal beast she rode around with bayed, scratched, and whined.

"We placed a tracking device on your car," Tanis said by way of greeting. She wore jeans, a tan trench coat, a blue blazer, a white blouse, and cowboy boots. A toothpick hung from the corner of her mouth. She examined her fingernails. This time her decal read White's Express Delivery Service. "I'm surprised you didn't look for one."

"You forget that I'm a simple zookeeper. I'm not trained, nor do I have intent to evade you or anyone else."

Two big men flanked me. They'd been lurking on either side of the entrance to the motel. Their suits, sunglasses, and practical shoes gave them away as low-level feds, and they hung their arms like gorillas do when they're trying to prove something.

"These things belong to you?" I asked Tanis.

"They're my pawns." She flashed each of them a big grin. "Aren't you boys?"

The gorillas' brows crunched up and their mouths collapsed toward the shelter beneath their massive nostrils. Their bodies could have been overfed twin brothers, but their faces exemplified opposite extremes of brutality: one was gaunt and steel eyed; the other had a jaw like a semi cab and huge, purple lips.

"They're cute. Like Nazis only in cheaper suits."

Tanis ran her laugh up and down a scale. She smiled merrily. "John Stick, you're under arrest."

"You get funnier every single time you show up uninvited into my life. This one was a real hoot. Next time, you'll tell me you're my doctor and I have only one month to live."

Tanis lifted the right lower corner of her blazer. A gold badge hung from the waist of her jeans. It told me she was a Chief Patrol Agent of the Department of Homeland Security. She spat her toothpick into the gutter. "Cuff 'im, boys."

Her boys edged up on me from either side. I wondered what sound their heads would make when I knocked them together.

"Come over here and cuff me yourself," I yelled. But she was already ambling around the front of her van toward the driver's side door. Her goons pinned my arms behind me and pressed my wrists together. "Careful. I've got ten thousand year-old bones."

"Shut up," Purple Lips said.

The handcuffs pinched my skin and wrenched my wrist joints. "I'd like to see a warrant. Preferably with my name on it. You guys are probably mixing me up with another person. I wouldn't blame you. People get confused about my identity all the time."

Purple Lips blew some flecks of spit between his teeth. "We got a comedian here. Zip it, funny man."

"Shouldn't you be encouraging me to speak? I might reveal some key detail of my entirely legal and boring life of hard work and on-time tax payment."

"My partner brought a staple gun," Purple Lips said. "You can seal your lips or he can do it for you. You're under arrest."

"For what, I wonder?"

"Harboring a fugitive from justice," Steel Eyes snarled.

"Who? My spider? He's from El Paso."

Purple Lips turned me around and Steel Eyes tried to stick his face up in mine. He didn't have an easy time doing it. His cheekbones were so sharp he was in danger of being mistaken for a man with three noses. He spread his lips savagely. His teeth were jagged at the edges and brutally white, as if he bleached them every morning before he did his pushups. His breath smelled like fresh meat.

"Antonio Vicarollo Reyes DeRosa," Steel Eyes said.

"Never heard of him."

His grin stretched to crocodilian proportions. "You've never heard of your own father?"

"My dad's name is Tom. Tomás, if you want to get technical. You've got the wrong guy."

Purple Lips kicked me in the heel. "It don't matter if we have the wrong guy. We can chain up the Pope for twenty-four hours if we want. It's the law."

They marched me to their car, one man holding me by the shackles, the other leading the way. My face burned from some awful internal heat building inside my body. Stars danced in my peripheral vision, and I didn't know whether they were a result of the sun blazing above, the rage burning below my skin, or some latent magic searing the earth at the farthest reaches of human perception. The gray-haired woman stood in the doorway of the motel, running prayer beads through her old dry fingers. Our eyes met. She laid her finger against her nose, just as she'd done earlier. I suppose she thought it'd give me comfort to know that I was part of something bigger. She was another rube, looking for meaning and connection where there was none.

Tanis' van pulled away from the curb and kicked dust into my eyes. I blinked and grinned, and my eyes produced some water. I wanted to laugh and laugh. And I did. I leaned my head back and let the moon see how big and crooked my teeth were. My captors had to go through some exercises to get me loaded into the back of their sedan. My legs were a couple feet too long and everything above my chest was a real pain in the neck. I didn't make it any easier on them. In the end, they crammed me in, and it was hilarious and traumatizing and absurd—and then I saw another couple of gorillas in dark suits leading little Marchette in cuffs to another car. I'd led them right to him.

I stopped laughing. I didn't think I'd ever start again.

CHAPTER SEVENTEEN

I **sat in a chair in an abandoned warehouse south of Central Avenue.**
The neighborhood had once been an industrial zone, but as the ever-expanding belt of Albuquerque widened and property taxes edged upward, the industry died or fled and the whole area fell to waste. Outside the warehouse windows, the stars cast their yellow eyes over streets lined with liquor stores, quick loan offices, dilapidated casitas, and apartment complexes like terrariums for human beings stacked one upon the other. Around here, murder and meth came easy, and fresh lettuce was as rare as gold.

My hands were still shackled. The joints of my upper body felt as if they'd been slow cooked on a rotisserie. I had to urinate, but I felt too tired to get up and do it even if I'd been able to. I'd been sitting for hours alone in the long dark room, once the beer-hall of America's industrial success, now twitching with rats. Finally, as the belt of Orion floated toward its zenith, Tanis Rivera walked in.

She wore the same trench coat, jeans, white open-throated blouse, and cowboy boots. Her hair was up. The gold homeland security badge hung from her belt.

"You never called," she said.

I didn't reply. Her steps kicked up the desert grit that had built up over the years of the warehouse's abandonment. I fought back a sneeze. I didn't want to give her any sign that she was getting to me.

"A girl throws herself at you, and you hang her out to dry." She pulled a chair opposite me, lifted a boot atop it, put her elbow on the raised knee, and set her chin thoughtfully in her hand. Her trench coat opened just enough to flash the gun hanging under her armpit. "How heartless."

"There's another woman," I rasped. My throat was lined with sandpaper. I hadn't had a sip of water since the drive to T or C.

"Is she prettier than me?"

"Let's say she's sane, honest, and good."

"I have other qualities."

I sat there and ached.

She stamped her raised foot to the floor. The rafters sloughed a rain of dust down on us. "I am, in fact, sane, honest, and good, but you shouldn't think so. My sanity, honesty, and goodness are much larger than our pitiful human struggles. I serve the universal truth."

"And the government," I said.

She flicked at the badge with a forefinger. "What, this? This is just one of the little costumes I wear."

"Did you steal it off another man you've been lying to?"

"No, it's mine. I'm a senior officer of the United States Border Patrol but only in the most superficial way."

Something happened in my brain, deep down. It felt like several gears that had been spinning madly in isolation—the chupacabras, the dead birds, the various agents chasing me—were all pressed together. They clicked and spun in synchronous motion for a split second and everything almost made sense. Then the works got jammed up and I enjoyed only a headache to show for a moment of clarity that happened too fast for me to follow. It did leave me with a question.

"Where's my father?" I harbored a sick dread that I already knew the answer.

Tanis smiled girlishly and tapped her lip. "Hmmm. What's his name again? Oh, that's right, you don't know your own father's name."

"My father's name is Tomás."

"Wrong. Tomás Ramón García died in 1970. We found the death certificate in a dusty filing cabinet in a tiny village near the Colorado border. His death hasn't dulled his American work ethic, however. He's been logging hours for forty years—paying taxes, contributing to Social Security, opening a couple bank accounts, earning himself a nice city employee pension."

"There are ten thousand Garcías in this state. You've been researching the wrong one."

"Let me ask you this question, John Stick," Tanis said. "Why is your father's name García, while yours is Stick?"

My head was full of helium. "Stick was my mother's last name."

"And why wouldn't your father want to give you his name? After all, it's the tradition. Children get their father's last name. Now, you were conceived in the seventies, so I might believe it if your name was hyphenated. Stick-García. García-Stick. But for a man—a Chicano man, who are stereotypically pretty traditional, especially in areas where feminism has made inroads in the Anglo community—to name his son after his wife's ancestry and not his own—it's surprising. A person more skeptical than me might even say unbelievable."

I'd never questioned it. In fact, I'd never thought of my father by any name, whatsoever. He was my father. We hadn't, as a pair, done a whole lot of identity probing since my mother died. We didn't think of ourselves as part of anything. We weren't The Sticks, a family that sent out a mass Christmas card every year or invited people over for cocktails. We didn't think of ourselves as part of a race, a class, or even an extended family. I'd heard other people proclaim their Irish decent, Northern New Mexicans talk with pride about their Spanish heritage, First Nation folk talk about how their pueblos were older than any American city. I came from one man and one woman. Our names and their significance had never mattered.

"So I'm wondering," Tanis said, "did your father love his wife so much that he let her do anything she wanted? Did she 'wear the pants,' as they say? Or was he hiding something? Was he worried that if he passed on a stolen name, his son might suffer? Or did he simply not have enough attachment to the name to care? Did he feel more attached to his wife than to this stolen name?" She paced the floor and threw her hands around as she spoke. "My mind has been running non-stop. These are the questions you should have been asking yourself all these years. That you haven't is"—she rolled her eyes into the corners of her sockets and gazed up at the ceiling, as if searching for the right word—"perplexing."

My brain wanted to hibernate for a year and then emerge into a world where all of the recent tumult had expired. I inhaled a deep breath and spoke. It took effort. "So, you're saying that my father stole a name. What is he, a criminal? Did he forget to pay his parking tickets? Because that's the worst thing he's capable of."

Tanis whacked the seat of the empty chair with her hand. The dust billowed directly into my face. I choked on it a little despite my best efforts. She sat and crossed her legs. She wiggled a foot up and down. "Your father is guilty of a much larger crime. He's an illegal immigrant."

I blinked. The room did a couple of twirls. My arms and legs throbbed, as if a surge of blood were trying to bring them back to life. My mind felt like it was floating in ether somewhere high above any connection to reality.

She nodded at me. "Yes. It is surprising." She opened a folder that she had tucked under her arm. "From what we could gather, your father paid a coyote—that's the modern word for it—to smuggle him across the border of Mexico and get him an identity in the States. Back in the seventies when he did it, coyotes were more honorable. They kept their end of the deal. These days, an illegal alien's coyote is as likely to steal their money, rape them, or abandon them to die in the desert as they are to get them across."

"The preferred term," I rasped, "is undocumented person."

Tanis smiled. She was pure sunshine. Nothing got to her. "Words. How meaningless they are."

I didn't disagree with her.

"In any case, your father stole Tomás Ramón García's identity and became a good American, working his fingers to the bone for very little money. Now that we've caught him, we've thrown him in a detainment facility, and the American government gets to keep all of the taxes he's paid into the system. It's a good deal for us. We'll use it to buy some fun stuff like smart bombs or hip replacements for senior citizens. As one of us, you should be happy."

I showed her my happy face. It had been known to scare the wigs off old ladies.

Tanis didn't even blink. "Would you like to know your father's real name?"

I sighed. I took my time with it, burying the air as deep in my torso as it would go. My lungs floated like two balloons in my chest. When they couldn't handle it anymore, they let loose and my breath gusted out to mingle with the stale warehouse air. Once my chest was empty, my body felt like an old snakeskin shed from the being that had given it life.

"Your goons already told me down in T or C." My voice sounded like it belonged to an old man.

"They ruined my coup de grace." She clenched her fist. "They will be punished."

"Do two things for me," I said in my new voice.

She snapped the folder shut. "I can't promise you anything."

"First, take these handcuffs off. My hands haven't felt their own calluses for five hours."

She shook her head. "Second?"

"Tell me what you've done with Marchette."

Her eyes glimmered. "The turncoat? Something poetic. If you had security clearance, I'd tell you so we could share an evil snicker." She stood and whacked me good-heartedly on the chest with my father's rap sheet.

Tanis left me in the dark. The warehouse was quiet at first, but as the night seeped into the seams of the place, mice started to scuttle behind the walls. The old wood clicked and squeaked as gravity slowly crushed the building into the earth. Periodically, a car cruised by on the street below, the subwoofers of its stereo system beating at the trunk like an animal trying to escape. The entire building convulsed to the rhythm. It was anybody's guess whether forces of man or nature would eventually deliver the last blow to the building's old, rickety body. The warehouse was dying, like all things in our world.

The two goons came for me some number of hours after dawn. I heard their car doors slam and their stomping feet from a mile away. It was something I did: sit in the dark and listen to approaching footsteps. I excelled at it. The men blundered in through one of the doors still on its hinges and shined flashlights in my fragile pupils. Steel Eyes went around behind me and released my handcuffs from the chair, but not from my wrists.

"Get up," Purple Lips commanded.

I closed my eyes against his flashlight. "Show me your badge first."

He kicked me in the foot.

"Easy on the shoes. Each one cost a month's salary."

He kicked my other foot. "Up."

I didn't open my eyes. "Give me another five minutes, Dad."

He kicked me in the ankle. "I can keep moving up the chain, pal."

"I'm wearing a cup," I said.

He kicked me in the shin. A red flower bloomed in my shin bone and pain radiated up and down my leg. "I'm up, I'm up," I said through my teeth. It took me a few tries. I felt like the Tin Man after a few seasons without oil. Once I was up, I got a push in the back for my trouble.

They took me downstairs and put me in a white van, like the one Tanis had shown up in at my house a million years ago. This one had a decal that said "Ivory's Chimney Sweeping." The interior had a couple of benches with steel rings attached at intervals. Once I'd made myself at home, Purple Lips attached my manacles to one of the rings and sat across from me.

I flashed him a great big smile. "This van smells funny."

He sat with his hands folded in his lap, feet set far apart, knees splayed wide, and chest stuck out as far as he could get it. He was too busy trying to eradicate all trace of humanity from his face to answer me.

I took a deep sniff. The air smelled like a wet dog had been dipped in ancient molten iron and then let run around a while. It reminded me of a smell I'd recently come across, but my head was too loopy to do simple math. I loosed the air through my nose and did it all again. "You must use some special soap to wash up after you work a guy over."

"No talking." He tried not to move his face as he said it. He was probably training to be a ventriloquist in his free time.

They deposited me on Central Avenue. They pried the shackles off and gave me a spirited shove in the lumbar. I staggered onto the asphalt and fell to one knee. By the time I'd pushed myself upright, the van had sped away. My arms were weightless, and I was dried up like the shell of a cicada. My truck was God knew where. My body felt like it had aged ten years overnight. An armada of clouds advanced from the west to cover half the sky. Electric current ran through the air, and every human felt it. Bums hunched their bodies over their grocery carts. Hipsters with their big sunglasses and tote bags squinted up at the overcast sky. Shopkeepers hauled their sidewalk displays beneath the shelter of their storefront awnings, and waiters bustled around opening umbrellas over the sidewalk cafes. Everyone was readying for the first spring monsoon to unleash hell across the desert.

I bought an umbrella from a souvenir shop that sold made-in-China bric-a-brac and naughty greeting cards. The cashier, a blond girl with braces and baby fat on her cheeks, gave me too much change, and I didn't correct her. She moved her mouth at me like a fish trying to learn vowels. Back on the sidewalk, a shapeless man in a motorized wheelchair rammed into my shins. The dozen plastic bags hanging from the handles and affixed to the undercarriage jolted, spilling clanging cascades of plastic and aluminum treasures. I cursed and dropped my coins. They jingled amidst the fat raindrops plopping dark on the sidewalk. The man sprawled forward onto his hands and knees. He scraped the coppers and silvers into a pile and covered them with his palms and cackled as if the city had taken possession of him and spilled its manic fever through his old, sick lungs. This was Albuquerque, this mad scramble for pocket change beneath the shadow of a deluge.

I moved on. The sky opened its throat and screamed at the earth. A wrath of water hammered down on humanity's petty works. I unfurled my new umbrella and tangled its spokes in the cords of an awning. I yanked it free, ripping a hole in the cheap canvas. A triangle of rain gnawed at my shoulder as I stalked west. The downpour escalated until it eclipsed the visible world. I stood in a collapsing cylinder of shelter amidst the furious gray sheets. People fled the streets. Cars pulled to the curb and drivers gaped up through their windshields at the heavens. Lightning stabbed the earth in blue lances and shockwaves of thunder undulated across the city.

I kept moving. The storm wouldn't last long, but the floods would clog the streets for hours. Already, the gutters brimmed and water stood on the blacktop. Low pockets in the asphalt cupped dark pools shimmering with oil. The cuffs of my trousers were sodden. My shoes sloshed with every step. The right side of my body was soaked and the water quickly bled through to the left.

After a few minutes, the rain eased. The drops struck feet apart. But the world still sat in darkness. A shiver convulsed the air. I knew what was in store for me even before the first crystalline globe skittered to a stop atop a newspaper machine. The next popped against my umbrella. I ran against a stoplight and found sanctuary beneath the drive-through of a bank just as a battalion of mad angels opened up with Gatling guns upon the mortal world. Salvos of ivory bullets pelted the sidewalks, streets, buildings, and cars. The clatter occluded all sound. It lasted only moments and when it was done, the sun burned through the diminished clouds and cast a golden net over the drifts of alabaster hail.

I closed my umbrella and dropped it into a trashcan. I continued west on Central toward a double rainbow that stood akimbo over the volcanoes. Everything's beautiful, the rainbow told us, a cheap lie dressed in six colors. I arrived at Melodía's building as people began to poke their heads outside again. Once within the quiet halls of the university's basement, I wrung out my sleeves and pant legs. I stamped the water from my shoes. The air was chilly. The florescent lights blinked, buzzed, and shed their ghoulish luminance.

I could have called Rex or Flowers for a ride. I could have hailed a cab. Instead, without thinking, I'd walked straight to Melodía's lab. It must have meant I missed her. I was numb from a night without sleep and hours upon hours chained to a chair. I was numb from Marchette's betrayal, allegations my father was not the man I'd always thought he was, and racist militias recruiting my childhood friends. I was numb from Tasmanian vampire bats and blood sucking tarantula hawk wasps. My world had gone mad. I wanted to see my friend with her copious curly dark hair and her willowy frame and her familiar face, beautiful and stricken. I wanted to quip about scientific jargon and I wanted to laugh at small, harmless jokes.

So I knocked on her door. A kid opened it. He had acne, glasses, and ears.

He wore a white coat with blue ink stains on the sleeve.

I checked the room number. It claimed to be the right one.

"C-can I help you?" The kid had one of those voices that hovered just between adolescence and adulthood. It sounded like a badly played violin.

I didn't know if anyone could help me. Maybe my life was beyond help. "I'm looking for my friend. What have they done with her?"

The kid blinked brown eyes magnified by his glasses. "Who's your friend?"

"I lost my truck. It's hailing out there. The whole city's underwater."

The kid took my elbow, guiding me into the lab—Melodía's lab. All of her instruments stood arrayed as they always had been. The air reeked of formaldehyde underscored with the subtle lavender shampoo she'd been using for twenty years. The kid sat me on a stool. He got me a paper cup of water. I sat there and held it, a vessel as fragile and tiny as anything in life had ever been.

"Sir, can I make you some tea?" The kid poised a kettle above a Bunsen burner. He had a motherly quality despite his tragic adolescence.

Tea. It was too much. I couldn't handle the choices involved in drinking tea. It came in infinite varieties and one could take it in at least three different ways. I shook my head.

He settled himself on a stool opposite me. "You're shaken up."

I nodded, clinging to my water.

"You're looking for your friend. Who's your friend?"

He was attacking this problem like a scientist. I liked his style. "My friend is Melodía."

"Dr. Hernandez?"

I nodded again.

He sat with his feet on a rung of the stool, arms crossed over his narrow chest, bobbing a knee. "She's taken a leave of absence. I shouldn't have told you that, but—" He shrugged. "If she's your friend, it seems like you have a right to know."

"Absence?" I said. "Why?"

"Medical reasons. I'm a graduate student. It's my job to watch over her lab while she's gone. Easy job. Nothing to do really except my own experiments."

"What medical reasons?" My mind was beginning to wake up. If Melodía was in trouble, I should have been the first person to know.

He shrugged. "I'd tell you if I knew. I can tell you that she planned it in advance. It wasn't an emergency or anything. She gave the Biology Department notice. She'll be back for fall term, from what I hear."

Fall was months away. I didn't go months without seeing Melodía. I rarely went more than a few days without talking to her, seeing her, or smelling her hair. These past two weeks had caught up to me. A pocket of air was stuck high in my chest. I couldn't exhale or swallow. It cramped my lungs and oppressed my heart.

"You're turning white," the kid said. "You want me to call someone?"

There was no one to call. I handed the kid my cup of untouched water. I patted him on the head and left.

I hailed a cab across the street from the university in front of the Frontier Cafe, a popular spot for cinnamon rolls and early morning knifings. I gave the cabbie my father's address and endured his eyes in the rearview mirror. He must have been driving by braille because he stared at me the whole way. I tipped him in pennies and his cab snarled as it sped off toward richer neighborhoods. My father's street was quiet, as always. Smoldering hailstones clogged the gutters. The windows of the houses watched me. My skin crawled beneath the invisible gazes of a community used to witnessing atrocities and hiding from them. In the poor neighborhoods of Albuquerque, people were as afraid of the police as they were of criminals. Police entered neighborhoods with battering rams and riot gear. They hit hard and left quickly.

Police tape hung across my father's bashed-in front door. I broke through it. I walked just far enough in to see the boot prints on the living room carpet, the cold plate of half-eaten beans and rice on the table, the dirty pan on the stovetop. They'd taken him during dinner, the bastards. They'd dragged my tiny father from the home he'd been living in for forty years, the home where his boy had grown too much and his wife had died too early.

I tore the police tape from the doorframe and closed the front door. It swung open again. The muzzle of a battering ram had scarred the wood beside the doorknob. The frame around the latch and deadbolt hung in splinters. I tied the police tape around the knob, pulled the door shut, and secured the other end to the little fence that enclosed the flowerbed my father planted every April. I walked out into the middle of Spring Street. I looked up and down the block and knew a dozen cowards were watching. I cursed them. I let the deepest voice in the state of New Mexico bellow out thirty-eight years of bitterness. I started with my early life and moved forward. I gave them a dose of what I'd been getting from them for nearly four decades. I told every one of them about the ugly heart of the human race and related in detail how they'd succumbed to it. I lifted my arm high in the air, extended my finger toward heaven, and preached. My reach was higher than the rooftops. I was a mighty being from another world and I was passing judgment. When my voice was hoarse and my arm sore, I sank to one knee and clutched a handful of hail from the gutter. I held the ball of ice high aloft and let it trickle through my fingers.

I vowed never to set foot on the street where I grew up again.

CHAPTER EIGHTEEN

No cabs trolled my old neighborhood. I had to walk a mile north into downtown Albuquerque. I strode along crumbling streets with no sidewalks that ran between old shacks that had been on the verge of collapse for decades. I cut through dirt alleys and more than once had to shoo a chicken out of my path. Once past the rail yard, I emerged into a downtown district of public utility buildings, courthouses, and law firms during the day, and thumping nightclubs after sundown. I towered over every living thing. I could have plucked birds from the air and crushed them in my fists. Traffic halted in tribute to my passing. I stood taller than the cops on horseback who danced their steeds in circles to gawk at me. Upon reaching Central Avenue, I looked up and down the street for a cab. Instead, I found a small man in a trench coat and a fedora sat on a bench reading a computerized tablet. It was Tony, the Good Friend gumshoe.

"You dropped off the map," he said, without looking up. "We thought maybe they'd taken you to Hades along with your dad."

"Who says they didn't?" I said.

He took his eyes off his tablet and scanned me up and down. "You look like hell. You need a new dry cleaner."

"What I need is a taxi."

"I'll give you a ride," he said.

"That'll make it easier for you to follow me."

He gave me a tight smile. "I do my job. That's all any of us do."

"Maybe that's the problem. Everybody does what they're paid to do. We're all slaves to a picture of Washington."

Tony stood and tucked the tablet into a cloth case, which he stuck under his arm. "You're cranky. Let me take you to my house and pour a cup of coffee down your throat."

He led me toward a parking garage.

"I hope I'm not interrupting a stakeout. I know you probably have cheating husbands to photograph and fallen daughters to rescue."

"I was out here looking for you." We jogged through a yellow light, framed on four sides by windshields of open mouths and gaping eye sockets. I was giving everybody a story to tell their kids.

"You just happened to be in the right place at the right time?" I asked. "I haven't been downtown in ten years."

"You were spotted. We have a safe house in your neighborhood. It's part of our underground railroad. Ever since you were hauled away from T or C yesterday, we've had every eye looking for you." He smiled up at me. "We've already brought your truck back for you, as a gesture of good faith. You'll find it in the usual spot in front of your house."

"Thanks. What's with the computer tablet anyway?"

"It's the newspaper of the modern age. Look around. Everybody uses them. I blend right in."

He'd taken my comment about his newspaper to heart. I chuckled all the way to the car.

Tony's house was an average home for Albuquerque, a little poor by regular American standards. It had sound gray siding, a peaked roof, a sheltered driveway, and a decent paint job. He'd xeriscaped his yard with white gravel and plenty of prickly pear and several desert candle yucca that crouched in globes of spikes on the earth. In the spring, they would each project a tall yellow blossom several feet into the air. No plant more beautiful existed on the planet.

His house was clean, plain, and cozy. The furniture was earth-toned and old but in good shape. The morning's newspaper sat on the dining room table, and a girl's socks lay strewn across the living room floor. Tony went into the kitchen, which emitted the quick and quiet sounds of a man practiced in brewing a pot of coffee. I made one of the chairs around the dining room table work for me. My bones felt like they might just crumble to dust on the spot. As the coffee maker sputtered and steamed, Tony walked out of the kitchen.

"They picked up your dad. I suppose you're already wise to that."

I nodded. My rage had melted away. I felt too heavy to even speak, but I forced myself to open my mouth anyway. "Tony, I've been kidnapped, chained to a chair, and pummeled by a storm from hell. What do you want?"

Tony smiled. It happened on his exterior, and like every other exterior human expression, there was no telling what secrets it masked. "We want to help you. We have access to lawyers. We can apply enough pressure to get them inside to help your father. Undocumented immigrants aren't guaranteed legal representation. We can arrange that for you."

"And why would you do that?"

"Because we want you on our side. We believe you could be key to this whole thing. Hell, you might even be a good man."

I sighed and let my head hang down on my chest. I put my elbows on my thighs and dangled my hands. When I lifted my head up again, it felt as dense and heavy as an anvil. "Tony, you obviously don't know me. I'm not a good man. I'm a simple human with simple needs. You keep using this word: 'We.' I don't know who that word refers to, and I don't want to know. Every person I've met over the past three weeks has been an extension of some mysterious 'we.' I'm tired of it. I'm a person. Singular. I don't want to have anything to do with anyone who refers to themselves as 'we.' I'm developing a plan to help my father. It's still in the early phases, but at least it involves someone I trust: myself. So, unless you're going to spill some truth in my direction, call me a cab so I can go home and sleep for a month or two."

He hooked his thumbs in his belt loops and leaned against the wall. "Fair enough. I'm a Good Friend. You met another of our order at the Brown Dog Inn."

"Yep. She was as weird as any of you."

"You could be one of us, too."

"I have one good friend, and she's abandoned me." I regretted saying it before my mouth even closed.

"You could have thousands of Good Friends." Tony said.

"No thanks," I groaned, stretching my spine. "Every new friend I make wants something from me."

"We help people. Let us help you."

"And who, besides me, do you help?"

"Primarily undocumented immigrants. Good men, women, and children. People like your father."

"What do immigrants have to do with any of this?" I asked. "You've been after me long before my dad was taken."

"It's got something to do with the birds. I got a call from a Good Friend the day the birds died. I'd worked for them before, so I wasn't surprised to get the call. But I admit I was a little surprised he had me scoping the Bosque."

"Hold on. You said you got a call the day the birds died. What time?"

"I don't know. Two in the afternoon. No—make it half past one."

"The birds died at noon, almost exactly. How did a Good Friend find out about the birds and call you so quick?"

Tony took his chin in his fingertips and massaged his beard.

"Who's your employer? Who exactly called you?"

Tony shook his head. "I can't disclose that. I'm a snoop. I don't rat out my client."

"I already know the organization. What does the individual matter?"

He kept shaking his head. "My client has asked not to be named. The Good Friends are a loose affiliation. We have a common goal, but no central leadership. We're like the underground railroad. This particular member is in a vulnerable position. He or she wants to remain hidden."

"Doesn't it seem strange to you that this mystery person found out about the bird deaths so quickly and thought to call you up to check into it?"

"You're saying that this person knew those birds were going to die?"

"I'm saying that the more I look into this thing, the less I see nature and the more I see the face of a man."

"We both know the name you're thinking of."

"John White," I said. "I have reason to believe that he knew something was going to happen—something bad."

Tony got up. He rubbed his hand over his beard and stared out the window at the quiet midday street. "You're saying my client is John White."

"Am I?"

"You're wrong, but not by much. My client is a defector within Typhon Industries. My client feeds me information from time to time—the location of field operations, anti-protester actions, details about the surveillance and tracking products Typhon Industries is working on. You know him. His name is Simon Marchette."

The preceding day had become somewhat of a blur in my mind. My body was mush and I had an adrenaline hangover from finding my childhood home burglarized by the Man and my father kidnapped. But at that moment, a word Marchette had used came out of my mouth. "Chupacabras."

Tony twitched.

"You've heard of them."

"That word is under wraps, but it's what Typhon Industries calls their beasties. We don't know a whole lot about the chupacabras. As a gesture of good faith, I'll tell you what I know. The name comes from Spanish. Means goat-sucker. It's an animal from modern Chicano folklore. It sprung up around the time NAFTA passed. Some say it was a creature created by the American government to terrorize Mexican farmers. Others say it was a story made up to distract the population while the Dole Fruit Company and Monsanto moved across the border and started industrial farming outfits that put every small Mexican farmer out of work. Other people say it's a monster born from the evil ways of our contemporary world."

"That chupacabra is a myth. Tell me about the real ones."

Tony leaned against the wall and crossed his arms. "You might have to face the fact that they're one and the same. The chupacabra that you call a myth is a being that is part lizard, part coyote, part bat, and part alien, depending on who you talk to. It's a hybrid beastie. You and I ran into a half dozen insects part wasp, part horsefly the other day. We know Typhon Industries runs genetic experiments. Is it such a stretch to believe that the wasps we saw the other night were manmade?"

I kept my mouth shut about the Tasmanian devil-vampire bat I was trying to videotape outside my house. "You're saying that the chupacabras are real and that a genetic industrialist created them. For what purpose?"

"I have a proposition for you about that," Tony said.

"Great."

"We know the beasties are linked to Typhon Industries, a company that is both invested in genetic engineering and incarcerates undocumented people. It's a subcontractor for Border Patrol and Immigration. Beyond that, we're fuzzy. We have to figure out the link between the science side of the company and the prison. We need a man on the inside. The Minutemen have offered you a job. I propose you take it."

"And what do I get in return?"

"We build a fortress of lawyers around your father. We get you regular visits. We make sure he receives due process. We wrap the deportation process up in miles of red tape. We mummify it. Meanwhile, we file documents to put him on the road to citizenship based on his marriage to your mother."

Infiltrating a chimera-breeding complex sounded as crazy as anything else I'd become involved in. "How about that cup of coffee?"

"Is that a no?"

"It's not a yes. I'm not joining any revolutionary underground organizations until I've had a decent night's sleep."

He grinned. "Lemme get you that cup of coffee, Good Friend."

"Don't call me that!" I hollered at the doorway he'd gone through.

We sat around and sipped coffee and I filled him in on what had happened to me over the past twenty-four hours. He ended up cooking some eggs, refried beans, and *huevos rancheros* sauce. We rolled it all up in flour tortillas and chewed while we drank more coffee. My body throbbed in gratitude. I'd been running on anger for a day. It wasn't good nutrition.

Tony dropped me back at my house, where I found my truck waiting for me. My plan was to sleep for sixteen hours and then go to the zoo. I made a call to one of the other keepers who looked after the Reptile House on my days off and asked her to check on the animals. She said something sarcastic about how everything managed to survive on my days off. I hung up, fell down on my mattress, and closed my eyelids. They kept snapping back open, like those dolls that you tilt and they roll their eyes as if they're possessed.

CHAPTER NINETEEN

The next morning, I roused my battered body late and took it to work. By the time I walked into my room at the zoo the clock read almost nine. A memo waited for me. It addressed me by name and instructed me to report to the director's office. I hadn't seen the director in a year. I did my work. I stayed in my corner of the world, and the director sat behind his big mahogany desk and shot rubber bands at the moon for all I knew.

But I was a dutiful employee. I reported to the director's office. Behind his desk sat a slim woman in a pants suit with short salt and pepper hair and a big friendly smile.

"You"—she let her eyes goggle as she looked me up and down—"must be John Stick."

"I guess I must." I sighed.

"My most notable and talented employee," she said. "At least, so I have heard."

"Not to be rude, but whose employee am I?"

"Georgia Tameed Schultz," she said. "I'm the new director."

"What happened to Jim?"

"He retired. I'm shocked you didn't hear about it."

"When did he retire?" Jim had been the director since my teenage years. I'd assumed he'd sit in his office collecting dust until zoos were outlawed as socialist institutions.

Georgia cocked her head. "Last week. It was sudden. The board of directors decided we needed new blood." She spread her arms. "I am the new blood."

"Well, consider me the old."

She pushed a jovial laugh out of her lungs. "That's charming." She gestured at the chair opposite her desk.

"I don't tend to use chairs unless I'm going to be in one place for a while."

"Your choice. Every day we make choices. You just made one. Congratulations." She leaned back in her chair and put her wingtip shoes up on the polished ruddy wood. The desk was perfectly empty save for a fancy looking gold pen in a stand-up holder. She laced her fingers behind her head and showed me some teeth.

I waited.

She smiled a little bigger. She looked very happy with her new job.

I waited some more. One of the zebras, which lived in a pen right behind the director's office, whinnied. Zebras were pretty on the outside but had unpleasant personalities.

"You're late for work this morning." The director smiled as if it were the greatest thing in the world.

"You can take it out of my flex time," I said. "I must have over a thousand hours racked up by now."

She laughed and slapped her knee. "You are a delight. Just like everyone said you'd be."

"No one has ever used that word to describe me."

"I didn't call you in because of how popular you are. I called you in because you've been very remiss in your duties of late." She took her feet down, removed the gold pen from the holder, and scrawled across a pad of paper she removed from one of her drawers. When she finished, she returned the pen to the holder, slid the pad across the desk, and put her feet back up.

I stood there.

"Go ahead. I've written a special message just for you."

I picked up the pad. It was blank. "Your pen's out of ink." I tossed the pad at her shoes.

"Surfaces, Mr. Stick. That's all you can see."

"That's true. Human eyes, and all that. I'm not an x-ray machine."

"I have video tape of you. Hours and hours and days of it. I've been sitting and eating popcorn and watching it in fast-forward. You spend a lot of time chatting with people, making non-work related phone calls, and destroying zoo property. You bring strange dead creatures from somewhere beyond the zoo campus and spend your time examining their corpses instead of feeding the living ones I pay you to maintain. You flirt a lot. You skip a lot of days. And you steal cameras." She punched a button on a remote control and the TV mounted to her wall sprang to life. It displayed Abbey and I in her bat cave. The picture had a low frame rate. We moved as if the camera were a strobe light flashing out moments of our lives and stringing them together into a video flipbook. I watched as Abbey stuffed the camera into her bag in halting motions and we both left the room. Georgia Tameed-Schultz pressed another button and a camera over the parking lot displayed us getting into my truck.

She twined her fingers behind her head and stuck her elbows in the air. "You're a thief who doesn't come to work unless it pleases you." She made a clicking sound with her tongue. "Very naughty zookeeper."

"I'll consider myself chastened. Go ahead and watch all of the footage from those cameras—which, when I tell the other keepers they exist, will cause a riot—and you'll see me working fifty hours a week for the past fifteen years. And the camera's coming back. We're using it to track an animal involved with official zoo business."

She flashed her eyebrows at me. "This is fun. I'll make you a bet. I'll bet that you can't guess what I wrote on that pad. If you do, I won't call the police and report your little ginger girlfriend for theft. If you don't, well, she'll be a delicious treat for the women in county lock-up." She kicked the pad back in my direction.

"Are you going to try writing your message down again? That'll be fun."

"I've already written it," she said.

"Did you write it with an infrared pen? Most humans can't see that wavelength."

"Ha! Very good."

I left the pad where it lay.

She took her feet down, leaned forward, and beat a little rhythm on the desk with her fingertips. She gazed at me with her big blue eyes. "Or better yet, let's bet your job. If you can guess what I wrote, you may keep your job. If not, I'll find another snake-handler."

I picked up the pad to verify that it was blank. "Does the board of directors know you have a gambling problem?"

"I admire your irreverence. Especially toward someone who holds so much power over you."

"You won't fire me. I'm a model employee. I only embezzle crickets."

She came around the desk and poked me in the chest. Her finger bones must have been reinforced with titanium. "You think this zoo is yours." Her expression had gone from playful to ruthless in one move. "It isn't. You work here—or, you used to." She picked up the pad and held it up in my face. Ghostly green ink read *You're fired*. "Appearing ink. I bought it at a magic shop. It's one of my favorite things. You write with it and nothing happens at first. Then a chemical agent in the ink, as it interacts with oxygen, slowly turns green. Very dramatic. It's the cousin of disappearing ink, which you write in and then it slowly vanishes. Just like you will do by the end of the day today."

"You can't fire me," I said.

"It's already done. Approved by the board of directors. And as a bonus—" She opened a drawer and brought out a thick sheet of stationary with a court's stamp and judge's signature. "As of 5 p.m. today, a restraining order will be in effect. You are not to come within a hundred feet of zoo premises."

I stood there. My body wouldn't move.

"Get out. Go back to your snake house, pack your cardboard box, and leave."

The old Stick would have shuffled back to the Reptile House, packed his things, and faded quietly into oblivion. The new Stick at least had the guts to stick up for his friend. "Leave Abbey alone. The camera will come back. We're using it to track a bat. That's zoo business."

"You're in no position to make demands, but don't worry. We'll keep the bat girl right where she is. In the dark."

I trudged back to my Reptile House. I spent an hour or so with the king cobra. He flared his neck at me and looped his body around my arm. I fed him a rat. After he'd swallowed it, he coiled up in my lap and went to sleep. He was a real puppy dog.

After I returned the king cobra to his home, I packed up my things. My hands felt like they belonged to someone else as I added personal effects and papers to my cardboard box. Plaques of recognition and certificates of service. My favorite photos of zoo animals. Zoo jackets, uniform pants, and polo shirts with the zoo logo insignia that would fit no other human on the earth. It amounted to several boxes that I carted out to my truck. Lastly, I dragged my old, punched-in locker through the public section of the zoo. The metal scraped on the cobblestone and rumbled across the concrete. People stared. I wanted them to notice. I wanted people to see the man cast out from the place that he'd devoted his life to. I wanted my co-workers to see me leaving and feel the keen injustice of it all.

Instead, they probably just saw a sad giant hugging a broken locker.

No one followed me home. No one waited for me in the shadows of my patio. No one had broken into my apartment and put their feet up on my bar. No creatures skulked in the shadows of my trees, seeking out my company for obscure reasons. It was my old normal life, returned, only with no purpose.

I stood inside the door of my house in the permanent twilight that crouched there. I was at the center of a web. Each strand connected me to somebody pulling—the Good Friends, the Minutemen, John White, Tanis Rivera, ten thousand dead birds, mutant hybrid chupacabras. The structure of the web remained a mystery to me. I couldn't figure out the motives of anybody doing the pulling, but I was beginning to understand every strand was connected. A smarter man than me could have tracked down answers, traced each tendril back to its source, and divined the deeper meaning of it all. I wasn't a detective. I was a zookeeper.

I knew one thing about a web: if the creature caught in the middle thrashed around enough, the entire structure would collapse. I was a big creature. It was time to start thrashing.

CHAPTER TWENTY

sat at my bar. The light flashed on my answering machine. Outside, dusk clutched its fingers around the air and choked the light out of it. I lifted the receiver in the darkness and dialed. I decided to tangle myself up with Tony first.

"Call me Good Friend," I said to Tony when he answered.

"Don't use those words on the phone."

"I've gone through purgatory and I've seen the light. I have a proposition for you that'll make you and me pals forever."

"Swell. Better to talk about it in person. Hyder Park. Tomorrow morning at eight."

After we hung up, I listened to my answering machine. Abbey's voice filled my apartment.

"John. I heard. I'm coming over. I can't believe—those bastards! I'm coming over right now."

Five minutes later, her feet cantered down my front steps and she hammered on my door. I opened up. Her orange hair had half fallen out of its ponytail and her face was beet red. She puffed through her nostrils like an angry racehorse.

"I tried to lodge a formal complaint with the union, but they told me it had to be in writing. And they told me you have to do it."

"I'll get right on that," I said, even though I suspected that my firing was beyond the remedy of any union action.

She slammed a fistful of crumpled papers on my bar. "I printed the forms out for you, but I got them all crumpled up because I couldn't believe—damn those bastards!"

"Relax. You're going to blow an artery."

"Let's look at the footage," she yelled. "I bet we caught something."

Abbey retrieved the camera and hooked it up to my television. It took her several minutes of grumbling and fussing behind the big gray monitor. She emerged with spider webs in her hair and even redder cheeks than when she'd arrived. The camera was motion activated, but we still had to skip through several hours of tree branches bobbing in the wind. I was ready to declare the whole thing a bust. Abbey sat on the edge of my couch, hunched over the camera, her thumb on the fast forward button, a look of grim determination crimping her features.

The frame of view shifted downward.

"Dammit!" Abbey said.

The camera had slipped in a particularly strong gust of wind. It hadn't fallen from where she'd secured it to the tree, but now it shot the upper bare branches of my butterfly bushes and the truck of the pine tree several feet below the beast's perch.

Abbey was still holding the fast forward button, but looking at me. "Well, I guess we failed."

"Stop!" I said.

She dropped the camera.

The image froze. It captured a figure dressed all in black picking the lock on my front door. Abbey picked up the camera and pressed play. The figure disappeared inside my house. We waited in the silence of the night. Ghostly shadows dragged their fingers across the cobblestones. A quarter hour or so passed and the figure re-emerged. It flitted up the stairs and vanished.

"You got burglarized," Abbey said. "What are the chances?"

The figure hadn't carried anything substantial out of the house, and I didn't own anything small of value that it could have stuffed in its pockets. Whoever it was hadn't come to steal. And it was no coincidence that this person had broken in while I was shackled to a chair.

Abbey was watching me. "You're hiding something."

I sighed.

"Don't deny it!" She whacked me on the knee. "I can tell!"

"I'm not hiding anything. I simply don't have the words."

"Find them."

I tried. All I found was more air in my lungs that wanted loose.

Her face softened. "Should we go through your stuff? See if anything's missing?"

I made my mouth into a crescent. It was the closest I could come to smiling at her. "I'll do that myself. You take the camera and go on home."

She ejected the memory card and shook it in the air. "I'll copy this and get you the footage. So you can show the police."

I had no plans to call the police. But I nodded anyway. When she was gone, I rummaged through my house. Nothing discernible was missing, nor did anything appear to have been tampered with. I racked my brain for places to hide a clandestine listening device. I checked the ceiling tiles, but none of them had been disturbed. I went through some cupboards, scrutinized dusty corners and out of the way nooks. I knew my house backwards and forwards. All was as it should have been. By midnight, I was stumped.

I tossed myself on a barstool. I'd forgotten to liberate Ralph from his terrarium for his nightly romp. Normally, he would have been standing up and tickling the glass with his forelegs. Instead, he crouched in the shadows of his plastic castle, his eyes gleaming like polished obsidian.

He was alarmed. It could have been all the activity of me turning over my apartment, but he'd been hiding there all night. Something had scared him before I'd even come home. I thought about it and smacked my forehead.

I found the bug—no bigger than a thumbnail—buried in the cedar chips in a corner of Ralph's terrarium. I tried to think up some clever words to say to whoever sat at the other end, but my brain was too tired for witticisms. I considered feeding it to a boa constrictor back at the zoo and letting its owners listen to a month or so of reptilian digestion, but realized that for the first time in twenty years I no longer had access to such an animal. Instead, I took the thing outside, put it on the cement and gave it a single rap with a hammer. It melted into metallic dust.

I met Tony the next morning in Hyder Park, a hilly irregularly shaped patch of grass near the university notorious for drug deals. Tony was already there when I arrived. He sat on a bench in his trench coat, fedora, and sunglasses reading his computer tablet. A trashcan separated his bench from another one, where I sat. We didn't look at each other.

"You followed?" he asked of no one in particular.

"How the hell should I know? I don't think so, but I'm no secret agent. I'm just a normal guy—who got fired yesterday, by the way."

"We thought that might happen," Tony said to his tablet.

"And why, if you already knew, didn't you tell me?"

"We didn't want you to panic. You're in this pretty deep, Mr. Stick. Some might call your position inextricable."

"As of yesterday, I'm no longer in denial about that," I said.

"You've got to choose a side."

"Done," I said.

A smile tickled the corners of his mustache. "Glad to hear it. Now you've just got to prove it to us."

"I'll take the job with the Minutemen. I'll be your guy on the inside. I'll get in with whatever operations they have. I'll feed intelligence to you and your friends—"

"Good Friends," he said.

"—and you use that information to wreck John White's plans, whatever the hell they might be."

Tony spared me a glance from the corner of his eye. "Always suspect someone who offers something without wanting anything in return. What's in it for you?"

"Revenge."

He shook his head. "Not good enough. And don't try using any other purple words with me. Justice. Truth. Freedom. This is America. Altruism is dead. We can get some lawyers on your father's case."

"Fine. And one more thing. You're a sleuth. I need a person found. If I give you information that can take down White Industries, or at least give them a black eye or two, you find my friend."

"Sounds like a bargain. You better feed us good info."

"Count on it. I've got a lot of free time on my hands."

"What's this friend's name?"

"Dr. Melodía Hernandez," I said. "She's been missing for a week."

He stood and tucked the tablet under his arm. "We'll get on it. In the meantime, surprise us with something we don't already know."

I made sure to think about how much I hated the Captain as I drove to his house. There was no way he would believe sweetness and light. I thought about losing my job and my turtle, spending a night in handcuffs in the slums, being forced to wander all over town in the middle of the day. I thought about cops battering in the door of my childhood home and surrounding my father where he sat in his olive green recliner, the confused look in his old, moist eyes.

I parked and strode across the Captain's brown yard. I banged my fist against his kitchen window until his bald head appeared behind the glass. A frightened woman hovered behind him.

"What do you want?" he asked, his voice muffled.

"I want to track down Mexicans," I yelled through the glass. "I want to lock them in cages. I want to put them on rafts and float them down the Rio Grande until they drift into the Gulf of Mexico. I want to put them to work in copper mines. I want to feed them to lobos."

The Captain emerged through his front door. "Would you keep your voice down."

"Hire me," I said. "I want to be John White's right hand man."

The Captain made a downward gesture with his hands like he was trying to stuff my voice into a barrel. "Come inside. Let me fix you a drink."

"I'm done drinking," I said. "I'll be at Typhon Industries tomorrow morning."

"Calm down, would you? It doesn't work that way. These things have to be arranged."

I grabbed him by his lapels. I raised him to the tips of his toes and let him understand how I felt about him. I held him there until he understood my power. Then I dropped him on his heels, returned to my truck, and drove away.

The Captain called me the next morning. "It's all arranged." His voice was tight.

"When do I meet him?"

"You'll start in two days. We'll give you a trial run. See if you're as useful as everybody seems to think."

"I'll be as surprised as anyone. I've never claimed to be useful."

The Captain grunted. He gave me directions to a location in the desert a hundred miles to the south. When we hung up, I was left with a couple of days to kill and no routine to kill them with. My house was quiet and my brain kept insisting on filling the silence with thoughts of my father. If I hadn't gotten myself mixed up in this business, he'd be at his elementary school changing light bulbs and oiling door hinges. The teeming hordes of children would throng around him and fill him with that quiet certitude that life has meaning. Both of us had found good work; now we'd both lost it. And it was all because of the birds. I wished they'd had the good graces to fly north and pelt Colorado with their bodies instead of New Mexico.

I got in my truck. My street was quiet. I drove a couple of circles through my neighborhood. I kept my speed under the limit and my truck's engine noise to a minimum so as not to disturb the delicate harmony of the morning when most adults were at work and children were at school. Neither Tanis nor Tony stalked me. I felt strangely abandoned.

I drove to Melodía's place.

She lived in a newly built home on the West Side in a patch of barren desert called Anasazi Ridge, one of many new developments clawing their way out into the unclaimed emptiness that stretched west of the city for a hundred miles. For a modest sum, any aspiring professional could purchase a quarter-acre of their very own dirt, clone a house on it, and spend the rest of their days in commuter-land splendor. Melodía's place was the farthest of the far flung. Anasazi Ridge was a few loops of street beyond Splendid Vista, Paradise Hills, and other such neighborhoods that developers must have named while looking at pictures of wonderful places far away. West of her house, the desert was unending.

I coasted up her driveway. A ridge of dust had gathered in front of her garage door. Her mailbox was stuffed beyond capacity. I got out of my truck and peered through a couple of windows anyway—which was hard because all her shades were, predictably, drawn. The place was dark. Emptiness sat on her living room sofa in a jacket and hat made of shadows. Her kitchen wasn't the kind of cheery spic-and-span you see when someone's using it day in and day out. It was the kind of clean you leave behind when you're skipping town. It all confirmed the account the graduate student had given me: she'd gone somewhere premeditatedly.

It made no sense. She would have told me. Sure, after the birds died, we'd had a few arguments, but that was normal. Since I was the only person she consorted with, she regularly treated me as her scratching post. I got to be the object of the joy, the rage, the frustration, the hope that every person experiences from day to day. It had been a privilege. We fought, we reconciled, a healthy and pleasant cycle. Something hidden from my view had broken that cycle.

I circled her house. Deadbolts sealed her front and back doors. I lifted some rocks that looked suspiciously perfect, but none turned out to be hide-a-keys. She wouldn't lose her keys anyway. I considered lifting her garage door and if it didn't budge at first, cranking it open against its gears. That might draw unnecessary attention, so I checked her windows. The first few sat flush with the walls and didn't move when I shoved them. But the fifth or sixth one I pushed on swung open. The frame splintered inward where someone had forced it—apparently, someone else had the bright idea of breaking in, too. Eyeing the size of the window, I wished I'd come during the night instead of in the broad sunlight of an early spring. I could only hope that since her house backed up onto the barren desert, no one saw me cram my long body through the aperture and land in an awkward tangle on her laundry room floor.

All of her counters and side tables stood empty. The place stank of stale disinfectant. Rummaging through the drawers in her kitchen, the nightstand in her bedroom, and the papers in the stand-up file in her home office revealed nothing. Her answering machine harbored no messages. Her garbage cans held fresh bags. I went to the front window, watched the street until certain no one was around, then went out and got her mail. Her junk mail revealed nothing about where she'd gone. At a loss, I opened up her bedroom closet. It had sliding doors and spanned the entire wall. Inside, her clothes hung: dresses, button-up sweaters, jackets and coats, blouses and slacks, a half-dozen white lab coats. A few ingenious collapsible shelving units hung from the clothes bar as well. Made of cloth and wooden dowels, they probably had some clever Swedish name. Inside the shelf spaces nestled her socks, underwear, bras, leggings. A wooden shoe shelf sat beneath them. It held her sneakers, sandals, flats, boots, and a pair of plain black half-inch heels.

The closet housed the things that, after Melodía woke every morning, she hung, draped, zipped, buttoned, or laced around her body. They smelled like her and each one cupped her ghost within it. I'd seen her wear them all. Her empty clothes hit me harder than Rex burning two-by-fours in a campsite, my father's door battered in, or toting my punched-in locker through the zoo grounds from which I'd been banished. I ran my hand down one of her lab coats, pinched the soft material of a sock between my fingertips, and held it. I knelt by her shoe rack and silently thanked the items that helped my friend walk back and forth across the short spans of the earth that she'd come to occupy.

A pair of black, dusty flats caught my eye. I took them out and held them beneath the light fixture of her bedroom. Orange dust powdered the soles and sides—the same dust I'd been tracking since the bird fiasco began. It shouldn't have surprised me. If Typhon Industries was so deeply interested in me, an errand boy who'd gone to pick up the birds, it made even more sense for them to have gotten their hooks into Melodía, the actual scientist investigating the case. I'd agreed to work with them; maybe she had too. Maybe she had moved temporarily into an apartment in the East Mountains or within the Typhon Industries complex itself, where she could get quickly to and from a lab they'd assigned her. It would probably be an ideal life for her. She'd never have to leave the building. She'd never have to interact with an unscheduled human being.

The words she'd said at our last encounter came back to me: *Take the job,* she'd said. *The change will do you good.* She hadn't been talking to me. She'd been justifying a choice she'd already made.

CHAPTER TWENTY - ONE

I **drove south. Rex sat in the passenger seat wearing camouflage** pants and jacket, cheap mirror sunglasses and a billed cap. He hugged his rifle, the butt between his boots and the muzzle resting against his shoulder. An ammo box jingled at his feet. We were on our first Minutemen mission.

After around an hour, I pulled off the minor state highway at an exit that appeared to serve empty desert. It was a windless, cloudless day. I drove east on a dirt track. We wound through boulders, stands of shrub, pitfalls of prickly pear cacti squatting low in the terrain. We dipped through a small gorge where a nameless and forgotten stream had once run. Mesquite, yucca, and clutches of elm lined the shady bank, yearning for the past when water had trickled. I blazed up the far side of the gorge, my truck roaring like a warthog as we crested the edge. The world teemed with hardy plants digging their fingers into the earth, the sun scorched the earth from its perch on high, and the profile of the mountains loomed ahead. Civilization had vanished. The only link between us and the human world was the line of kicked-up dust that hung in the air between my back tires and the highway.

After half an hour of bumping along, we rumbled over a high crest of land. The desert flatland below spread all the way to the foothills of the San Andres Mountains. A few hundred yards down the gentle slope huddled several off-road trucks jacked up on huge tires with spotlights mounted above the beds and a couple of white vans like the one Tanis had pulled in front of my house. Several of the trucks either had ATVs strapped in the beds or to trailers. Anglo men in fatigues, mustaches, and aviator glasses hung around drinking coffee and grinning at each other. They leaned on military rifles and thirty-ought-sixes. Hunting knives and pistols dangled in sheathes at their waists.

I parked the truck and Rex got out. A few of the men glanced casually in his direction. I emerged and one of them nearly dropped his AR-15. They muttered and stared, and no one said anything nice. The closest van erupted in a cacophony of barking and howling. I knew that racket. It was the theme music of my new life. The Captain emerged from a group near the van and swaggered over in army boots, camouflage clothes, reflective sunglasses, and a nine-millimeter pistol next to his crotch. He bellowed my name so everybody could hear it.

"John Stick." He forced his mouth into a big fat smile, but the tension around his eyes told me he was still sore that I'd shown up at his house and scared the devil out of his wife a few days before. "Glad to have you on board."

I took his hand and squeezed, yanking him close. "I told you I want to meet the man," I hissed. "Not come to a Timothy McVeigh lookalike contest in the desert."

"Take it easy," he said under his breath. "Play the game and you'll make some serious scratch. You'll earn a place for your pal. There are steps you have to go through."

"I'm not here to go through steps. I meet John White soon, or I'm gone."

The Captain spoke through gritted teeth. His breath smelled like donuts and spearmint gum. "I haven't even met him. He's not a socialite. Come for a ride with us this morning. We'll test you out. See how you fit. Then maybe in a week or two—who knows? Maybe we'll get you in to see your dad."

I let his hand go and worked hard to keep from re-clasping my grip around his neck.

"Want a cup of coffee? Donut?" he asked.

"Let's just get on with it."

The Captain nodded. "Whatever you say." He turned to two men standing by the closest white van. One held a rope that went through the front passenger window connecting, I could only assume, to the animal losing its marbles inside. The man had his feet planted in the earth and was trying really hard to look like he wasn't straining to keep from having his arms yanked off. It was Meat Shoulders, the kid I'd run into at Typhon Industries and the Bosque Del Apache. He looked less friendly in his militiaman getup. Beside where he dug his heels in the dirt, the whole van rocked back and forth. The dog's barking sent spirals of birds twisting up from the surrounding desert, eager for quieter pastures.

"Boys," the Captain said to the two men. "Mr. Stick here wants to get on with it."

"Whatever he says," said the one not holding the rope. His voice was like sandpaper on granite. He was a wiry guy with a lot of wrinkles and loose-hanging skin. He could have been forty-one or fifty-nine. He tugged at a chain around his neck until a key came out of his shirt and unlocked the back door of the van. A few other men edged up behind me. They nudged and coaxed me forward until I was face to face with the door. Sandpaper Voice looked all eight feet of me up and down. "You're going to have to dive in there. Try not to hit your head."

Words came out of my mouth, but no one listened and they didn't mean anything anyway. Half a dozen men pressed down on my shoulders and pushed the backs of my knees until I bent in half. Sandpaper Voice opened the door, and they crammed me through and slammed it behind me.

I came face to face with a soggy monster the size and shape of a big dog with floppy, fleshy ears and eight eyes. Clusters of wiry hairs sprouted from its black, rubbery skin. It ran in place, its claws scrabbling at the plastic floor of the van, held back by the length of rope fastened to its collar and extending into a hole that led to the front of the van, through the window, and into Meat Shoulders' firm grip. I prayed for the surety of his footing. The beast's face was droopy, jowly, and devoid of hair. It opened up its round mouth and sucked at the air between us, revealing three interior jaws and dozens of saw-blade teeth.

"Keep your goddamn hold on that rope," I yelled, getting to my knees and pressing my back against the doors.

A key ground into the van behind me.

"Don't worry, Mr. Stick," the Captain said from outside. "He's very friendly." A chorus of man guffaws punched at the flanks of the van.

"Let me out of here. I quit."

"This is what you signed up for," the Captain said. "You're our new Cerberus handler."

The van stunk like wet dog and old metal. The beast snuffled at the ground between us like a mop, lapping up my scent. It had huge slits for nostrils and compound eyes like an invertebrate's that hung in drooping sockets. It lunged at me a couple more times, raising its sucker-like mouth to gulp at the air between each lunge. After a few tries, it sat back on its haunches and wagged its wide, flat posterior back and forth across the floor. Its loose, rubbery skin hung in folds around its neck and shoulders. The beast whined at me, and when I didn't move, leaned its head back and emitted a long, aching howl.

I was looking at a chupacabra, based on the rubbery skin, the drooping ears, the tripartite jaws, and the anterior and posterior suckers, a chimera of bloodhound and leech. I guessed *hirodu medicinalis*, or the European medicinal leech. Which, scientifically speaking, was absolutely impossible.

"Scratch him behind the ears," Sandpaper Voice rasped from outside the van. "He won't hurt ya. He might just take a sip or two of your blood, is all." The psychos all chuckled.

Cerberus howled again. I clicked my tongue at him. He made a panting motion with his mouth, ruined by the fact that he had no tongue. He wagged his posterior suction cup playfully. I reached out my hand, and he put his paw in it and lolled his head to one side. I gently kneaded his paw with my fingers, discovering doglike pads and hard claws. His skin felt warm and tough like industrial rubber left out in the sun. He seemed content to sit there with his paw in my hand like a regular dog. I wondered if he wanted me to rub his belly while he suckled one of my arteries.

"We're letting go the rope," the Captain yelled. "You heard me," he said more quietly. "Let it go."

The rope went slack. I dropped the beast's paw. He sat there for a few seconds slapping at the air, trying to get me to shake with him again. When I didn't, he threw himself at my knees, stuck his legs up in the air, and showed me his underbelly. He was a lot like a dog down there, except for one detail: he wasn't a he. He was a very pronounced hermaphrodite. All leeches were. They were mutual inseminators. My new pal had the ability to give and receive genetic material.

I rubbed his—or hers, or its, or whatever—rubbery belly. He groaned and hung his sucker mouth open in blissful appreciation.

"How you two getting along in there?" the Captain asked.

"Come on in," I said. "I'll show you."

"I'll stay out here. Just make sure you two bond real good. You're his new best friend." His voice moved away from the van. "Alrighty boys, saddle up!"

Boots stomped through the dirt in all directions. Truck doors opened and slammed. Feet leapt up into truck beds. Men climbed into either side of the van's cab and Sandpaper Voice stuck his face up to the square window where the loose rope dangled through.

"He likes you. Just like they said he would."

"He probably likes everybody," I said.

"Nope. Hates most of us. Gave me this." Sandpaper voice pulled his face from the window and stuck his forearm into the aperture. It bore a scar that looked like three sharks had bitten him at once. The hound snarled at it. I rubbed his chest until he smiled again.

All around us, the trucks growled their guttural songs. Tires spun out in the dirt, and we bounced along the bumpy terrain. There were no windows. I soon lost my bearings and couldn't tell where we were headed. My new friend was unaware of anything other than my knees under his back and my hand rubbing his chest and scratching his sides. The two of us rattled around for an hour or so. After a few minutes, I sat with my back against the cab and my legs extended toward the doors. The beast flopped down along my leg and rested his head on my thigh. I ruffled the folds of his neck for him. Thin grayish drool leaked from his anterior sucker-mouth into my trousers. By the time the van lurched to a halt, he was snoring like a kid after Christmas dinner.

They let us out. I held my new friend's rope even though he tagged right along with me. The sunlight gleamed on his dark skin, and loping along through the dust, he looked as out of this world as anything I'd ever imagined. The men stayed pretty well clear of us, apart from doing some involuntary gawking. Our convoy had stopped at the base of a natural trail that wound up through the foothills toward San Andreas peak. The men unbuckled the straps holding their four-wheelers in place on trailers and in the beds of their huge pickups. They arranged themselves two to an ATV, a driver and a gunman. I wondered what sort of terrorism I was about to participate in.

The Captain gathered everyone together. "We have a tip that some illegals are coming over these mountains. Coyotes dropped them off a day's walk south of here to avoid the border patrol roadblocks near White Sands. They're hoofing it through the foothills, thinking they can skirt around the main roads and get picked up north, past border patrol." The Captain cast his eyes over my new shadow and I. "Looks like you're living up to the legend."

I didn't say anything to him.

"This little pooch is going to pick up their scent." He removed a gallon zip-lock baggie from his satchel. It held a woman's blouse, soiled with dried sweat and dirt. My friend went nuts. He strained at his rope, and when I held him tight, he leapt straight up into the air and banged his otherworldly baying against the sky.

"Atta boy." The Captain held the garment out to Cerberus, who took it in his jaws, dropped it in the dirt, and snuffled its creases and folds. "Get a good whiff."

The men revved up their ATVs. Others piled into the beds of pickups with wheels as tall as a normal. Rex stood in the truck bed among them, his head reaching the height of their shoulders, a thin arm shoved through the press of torsos to hold onto the bar that ran along the back of the cab beneath the floodlights. He looked like a lost puppy. It was the same expression he'd worn most of his life when he forgot his tough guy act.

Sandpaper Voice pulled his ATV up next to me. "You're with me."

It was everything I could do to hold the hound's leash. He'd been sweet napping in the back of the van, but after catching that scent, he'd become pure muscle. His haunches bunched with power and legs stocky and dark like polished tungsten powered him forward. A voice like an artillery battery crashed from his barrel chest. Like any carnivore, despite his sweetness to his master, he was a weapon.

"Let him go," Gravel Voice said.

"We'll lose him," I said.

"Not if you do your job. Slip him loose and get on." He revved the engine. "We're driving fast, so if you have a problem, yell Ned. That's my name."

I got my hands down to his collar and unhooked the leash. He tore off across the dirt and through a prickly pear cactus that should have turned him into a porcupine. He didn't seem to notice. In seconds, he'd disappeared around the shoulder of a hill.

A dozen motors roared, and we were after him. Our ATV led the pack. I hugged Ned as if I were in love with him. He was one hell of a driver, bouncing at the knees for every bump we hit, dodging the pitfalls hidden by crackling elm and mesquite, tracing the natural contours of the earth carved out by the eons of wind, runoff, and gravity. For all his skill, it was still slow going. We sporadically lost sight of Cerberus. Then we'd see him again, standing atop a hill and raising his triple-jawed face to howl at the sun.

"That's for you," Ned shouted over his shoulder. "He's waiting for you. He doesn't normally do that."

"I'm honored," I said.

"Love at first sight."

"Drive."

He did. We chased the hound for what seemed like an eternity to my battered groin, my knee joints, and my shoulder sockets, but was probably only an hour or two. As the sun hovered at a halfway point toward its zenith, spilling spring heat across the glittering rock and spines of the desert, we crested a ridge between the last of the foothills and the sheer mountain surge toward the heavens.

A small ecosystem harbored in the valley there, where water flowed and the sun beat down for fewer hours of the day. Chihuahua pine, gray oak, and fir clustered at the low points. In a clearing bristled with brown and olive wild grasses, a dozen or so men and women stood atop boulders. Some of them shrieked. Some of them sent up pleas to God in the language of my ancestors. One woman hadn't treed herself. She faced off with Cerberus. She wore dusty slacks, a denim jacket, and tennis shoes that looked like they'd trekked all the way from Mexico City. She held a stick in each hand. Cerberus crouched, leapt, and bayed. Each time he lunged too close, she lanced him in the face with one of her sticks. It was a standoff.

Our cavalcade rumbled up in a cloud of billowing dust and men leaping from ATVs, bellowing phrases they'd heard on cop shows. They aimed their assault rifles from the hip like Rambo and brandished pistols in two-handed grips. The people they accosted cowered in ragged clothes and broken shoes, the whites of their eyes huge against their sunburned skin. What must we have looked like, a fleet of men riding four wheelers and armed with guns of war, a giant with a face like a bare cliff, and an eight-eyed hound from hell? What must these people have thought of America?

I leashed Cerberus as quickly as I could. He alternately licked my hands and sprung toward the men and women, whom the militiamen rounded up and made kneel in the dirt with their fingers laced behind their heads. A couple of the militiamen made a pile of grungy backpacks. The Captain silenced any of the immigrants who spoke. The woman who'd fended off the hound with sticks stared straight at me while the others looked at the ground, stared straight ahead, or clamped their eyes shut. She had hard, high cheekbones, skin the color of the most fertile earth, a straight mouth, and eyes like foundry fires. She could have won a staring contest with continental drift. She looked like an actress hired to play a persecuted and resilient heroine in a Hollywood Western. And I was the brutish henchman of the arch-villain, sent to kidnap her people.

Back at the base camp, the Minutemen unloaded the prisoners from the back of the pickup truck and made them sit in the dirt near the second white van. A woman in blue scrubs who must have been a nurse stood outside of it fending off the militiamen who tried to hit on her. I did my best to keep the hound calm. Our prisoners must have thought he wanted to eat them. I wished I could have explained he was a tracker. They were quarry. A deep-seated genetic urge drove him, not a desire to consume their flesh. But I didn't speak Spanish. One small reason to hate myself among many large ones.

I called to Ned. "You want me to put him back in the van?"

He shook his head. Two men flanked him. Each held a long pole with a loop of wire at the end, the tool that dogcatchers use to secure dangerous animals.

"It'll calm him down. Block out the scent. At least get him out of view so that maybe these people all don't die of fright."

"We're not done with him." Ned snapped his fingers. The two men slipped their nooses around Cerberus' neck and stood on either side of him, pulling the nooses taut. "Let the leash go. Your work is done. You and the little guy should leave now."

I dropped the leash. My new friend whimpered as they led him a few paces away. "You didn't need me here today." I said. "All you need is a GPS tracker or a strong retractable leash."

"Tell me something I don't know," Ned said.

"So what the hell am I doing here?"

"The boss speaks. I obey. He wants the zookeeper. I use the zookeeper."

"You're a real independent thinker. That's what I like about you."

He blew a kiss at me. "What I love about you is your way of holding a guy so tender-like. I've never been hugged as sweetly."

That round went to Ned.

Rex stood alone nearby with his rifle in his hands. He stared at the circle of people seated in the dirt. His mouth and eyes were numb.

"What about them?" I asked Ned, gesturing toward the cluster of petrified men and women. "Off to jail?"

He fake grinned. "You did good today."

"You gonna give them some water at least?" I asked.

"What do you care? You're our monster handler. You've done your job. Drive back to Albuquerque and let us do ours. In this operation, you know what you need to know and feel thankful. Ignorance is bliss."

As Rex and I climbed into my truck, Ned pulled one of the prisoners, a short dark man wearing rags and with bangs that hung in his eyes, to his feet and marched him into the white van near the woman in medical scrubs. The woman with the hard and beautiful face tried to rise and they pushed her back down. I drove away. In my rear view mirror, the two men drew the beast toward the same white van. Then my tires kicked up a cloud of dust and I could see nothing more.

I stared at the winding dirt road before us. I had a sick feeling in my guts. I'd learned some stuff to feed Tony, but recounting it wouldn't be any fun.

"Those people," Rex said. "Coming hundreds of miles across the border, filthy and poor. And for what?"

"Work."

"What work? If there was work up here, I wouldn't be living in the campgrounds." His face twisted with bitterness, a comfortable mask for him. His wrinkles were exactly where they'd grown accustomed to. "They must have it rough back home if they're willing to go through all this just to come to a country where they won't do any better. Suckers of the world hoofing it to America."

"They're just people," I said. "Trying to make it whatever way they can. Give them a break."

"You don't get it. What I'm trying to say. Those Mexicans are just like me."

CHAPTER TWENTY - TWO

After I'd dumped Rex back in the dirt circle he now called home—and reissued an offer for him to crash at my place—I ended up sitting at my bar. I slid the phone toward me, despite how much I loathed that machine. But I had news for Tony that would wind a strand or two of web around his neck. I planned on yanking the strands until all the spiders ended up in a ball biting each other. Then maybe I could sneak off in the tumult.

I sat in the darkness of my apartment, lining up my thoughts. I treasured that space, where I could predict and order everything and living beings followed natural laws. I held Ralph in my hands and let his coarse belly hairs prick my palms. He twitched with every sound, vibration, or alteration of light in his tiny sphere of the world. He was a furry handful of intuition wrapped up in a primordial package of sensors and muscle. He behaved according to the laws of neither good nor evil, and was too inconsequential to get ensnared in the wrangling affairs of humans.

I put some pieces together. I'd met three chupacabras: the wasp, the bat, and the hound. All three were chimeras of hematophages and another animal. I knew that John White had genetically engineered them somehow, and that he also ran a prison for undocumented people. I'd learned that morning that he used at least one of his chupacabras to hunt down these same people. That marked the first connection I'd made since the day the birds died. It also made sense: John White's company built animals as border patrol devices. That explained why two such disparate enterprises as a genetics lab and a prison would be housed under the same banner; it also explained why he'd recruited the Minutemen. They knew the area, carried their own armaments, and had plenty of motivation.

The rest made no sense at all. No scientist, no matter how mad, could combine Tasmanian devils and vampire bats, much less leeches and bloodhounds. And none of it had any logical connection at all to the birds—or to me—unless I could take Marchette's crazy theories seriously.

Ralph jolted particularly hard. Outside, the crickets played their seesaw harmonies and the trees quaked their craggy limbs in the desert wind. Ralph spun his body clockwise, toward the window overlooking my front patio. Like a compass, he pointed toward danger instead of north. He hunkered his cephalothorax low and raised one of his back legs. The stiff hairs on his abdomen prickled like the finest cactus needles. He could kick a cloud of them into the air. They'd get into your eyes and embed themselves in your skin, and God help you if they made their way into your mouth. It was his first line of defense. His posture told me that a potential threat lurked in the night.

I considered retrieving my gun from its safe and felt pleasantly surprised I'd only now had that instinct since the birds fell from the sky. I'd considered it a means of self-annihilation for so long that I'd never pondered it for any other purpose, until now.

Leaving it in the safe, I dropped Ralph in his terrarium. Without bothering with any lights, I eased open the inner door and pushed the screen ajar several inches with my toe. The scent of aroused musk glands and rusty metal shouldered their way into the crack and punched up my nose. Whatever exuded that scent was either in high gear for mating season or very territorial. I stood quietly, breathed through my mouth, and listened. I roved my gaze across the shadows and got a practical lesson in how useless human eyes are in darkness. Our cones are short and shoddy. We really are one of the worst animals in the world. We'd abandoned all of our useful muscles and senses and teeth and claws, all in the name of tools. We could make a killing machine out of a stick and a shard of rock, but at night, we'd stumble over a saber toothed tiger and not even know it until we had two swords sunk into our guts.

The shadows of my pine tree fluttered. Claws clicked on bark. I stood there with my eyes wide, seeing nothing. The hidden creature licked its chops.

The bat had returned. It made sense for a beast that had impregnated three females and attacked Crazy Patty to exude strong musk. I put two and two together and figured out that it didn't smell like metal. The monster probably toted a quart of blood in its belly. The hound stunk like blood too, though I didn't want to guess what kind they were feeding it. Vampiric animals also explained the stench in the backs of all the Typhon Industries vans.

I hung out in the crack of my door. The animal didn't make any more noises, but I could feel him lurking in the creaking night shadows. I considered giving the Captain a call, luring him onto my patio, and coaxing the bat into attacking him. I bet he tasted like cheap hamburger and Diet Coke. Instead, I crept back into my home and dialed Abbey's number.

"Hello?" she said around something crunchy.

"I need you to come over here."

"Why are you whispering?" she whispered.

"I have a visitor."

"Are you talking about who I think you are?" she asked.

"Come on over and find out. Park your car a block or two away and approach on your tiptoes. He's sitting in the same tree as before."

"Keep 'im there." She hung up before I could ask how one kept a bat from flying away.

I snuck back to the door and listened. The patio was quiet, but the creature's smell was still strong. Eventually, my mind calmed and I acclimated to the soft noises of the night. Amidst the other soft night sounds, a pair of lungs pumped in my pine tree. The creature breathed deeply and slowly, emitting a slight rasp on each exhale. I fixed my eyes on the dark space where that breath hovered above the earth. I waited for my vision to adjust to the darkness, but even when it did, I couldn't pick out any variance in the dark boughs and needle clusters that might have been the outline of my visitor.

I pondered how life must have been for him. No others of his kind roamed the earth. Bats usually lived in colonies, though Tasmanian devils were solitary. Maybe he was lucky and he'd inherited the Tasmanian side of his ancestry. A bat living alone with no others like it would be a lonely being. Maybe that was why he sought me out and perched outside my door. Maybe he sensed a kindred spirit, someone else who carried a genetic code suited to living in a society but whose body didn't make it very easy.

I stood in my doorway and duped myself with these kinds of thoughts for a while. The beast didn't move. For a half hour or so, we perched and stood together in the same proximity, much like my father and I had over the years, though with only the music of the night breezes, crickets, and distant traffic to listen to instead of my father's Mexican polka music.

A hellish bleating knocked me out of dreamland. The spot I was staring at in the pine boughs exploded. A dark hairy form burst from it, showering my patio with pine needles and twigs. I ducked back through my screen door. The beast hurtled into my cheap plastic patio table, breaking off two of the legs. The thing was a furious ball of wings and black fur, and it shrieked like a tortured lamb. I flicked on my porch light so I could get a look at it. As man and monster blinked in the glare, Abbey leapt down the steps with the butt of a rifle in her armpit. A feathered quill blossomed from the bat's shoulder. It screamed and scuttled across my patio on its wingtips and hind legs, tried to climb another tree, fell on its back, and passed out.

I stepped past my screen door and waited for the beast to spring back to life and lunge for the nearest jugular. Abbey stood at the foot of the steps, rifle aimed, breathing heavily. A tip of the bat's right wing twitched, but it didn't otherwise stir.

"I think I got him," she said.

I spotted another dart in the bat's rump. "You're Annie Oakley."

"He better not die. Posterity would judge me."

I pulled the darts out and examined them. "He should be alright. This dosage should knock him out for a while, though."

Abbey was still panting. "He ran like a vampire bat. Most bats don't run on the ground. They hop into the air and fly as soon as possible. Vampire bats have adapted to be able to run on their wingtips. They land on the ground near their prey, then run up and attach to feed. It's easier to sneak up on a cow or a capybara that way."

"So, our hypothesis was right. This thing is half devil, half vampire."

"Yeah." Abbey squeezed her eyes closed and held them that way.

"You're still not dreaming," I said.

She popped them open and stared at the bat. She squeezed them closed again.

"It moved!"

She opened her eyes and aimed the rifle.

"Just kidding."

"Not funny." Abbey balanced the butt of the gun on her hip and crept toward the bat. She ran her fingertips along the long slender lines of muscle and bone in the wings. "These evolved from fingers. Bats essentially flap through the air with webbed hands. Isn't that amazing?"

"It is," I said.

"He has perfect vampire bat wings, which is impossible. If this were some sort of mutant or genetically bred hybrid, it would be a mess. This combination of Tazzie and vampire bat—it shouldn't look this good."

Once again she was right. None of it was possible.

Abbey stood up straight. "So, we bagged a brand new species of animal that by all rights shouldn't exist. What do we do now, other than try to wake up from the dream whichever one of us is dreaming?"

"The first order of business is a paternity test."

She nodded. "We'll draw some blood. If your theory about our pregnant Tazzies is right, then this is the discovery of a lifetime. We'll have zoo babies that will be the hit of the century—if they're carried to term."

I bet they would. A resilient energy inhabited these chupacabras, as if they were imbued with a particularly potent dose of life.

Abbey stared at me. "You're hiding something from me—again."

I sighed.

"Don't even think about lying. I see all."

"You might want to turn off those powers of detection for a little while. I'm standing in quicksand and it goes pretty deep."

"Share. I deserve it."

"I'm not saying a word."

"Not with your mouth. Your face says it all."

"Stop reading my mind and help me find a cage for this thing."

"We're caging it? For the zoo?"

"I haven't decided yet. I know who it belongs to, but I'm not sure if I should give it to them."

"Why not?" she asked.

"Because they're evil."

"Well I shot our little friend here with a zoo tranquilizer dart. As far as I'm concerned, it belongs to the city."

"It may not be that simple." I thought of the new director, Georgia Tameed Schultz. "The zoo may be compromised."

She pursed her lips and stared at the sleeping monster. "Should we set him free?" She posed the question like I would have—with the reluctance of a person conditioned to lock the things they cared about in little rooms so that they could watch over them with great diligence.

"We could drive him out into the desert and let him go."

"He would starve. If you remove an animal from its habitat and insert it into a radically new one, it doesn't adapt. It can't find food. It dies a slow and awful death. We might as well just put him out of his misery."

"We could drop him near the river. There are lots of little critters for him to suck on."

"Look at him! He doesn't eat little critters. He sucks the blood out of big fat housecats. He attacks horses in their sleep. He needs lots of blood every day. A vampire bat feeds on mammals twenty times its size. This thing should be biting the arteries of killer whales. Field mice and turtles won't cut it."

I poked the bat with my toe. His body was firm with healthy muscle. He looked much smaller in the light with his wings limp. He probably weighed twenty pounds. His body was the size of a large cat, only with a stockier build. "Seems like he's doing just fine in Albuquerque. Maybe this is the perfect ecosystem for him. Should we just set him loose in the city?"

"Eventually, somebody credible is going to see him. They'll get a picture. Then animal control will hunt him down."

"Or people will just point their guns at the sky and open up. More guns live in this city than people. I'd put the chances of a pistol taking the first shots over a camera."

Abbey put her finger on her lip. "We're in a pickle, aren't we?"

"You could get a travel kennel from the zoo, just for the time being."

"So we can cage him for a few hours? A day at most? He'll need blood."

"We'll need a cage whatever we decide, unless you want to stuff him in your Volkswagen and take him on a driving tour. When he wakes up on the Interstate, you'll have a problem."

"I'll go get the cage." She held the rifle out to me.

I waved it away. "I'll bring him into my apartment. That way if he wakes up, he won't fly off into the night."

"You're taking him inside?" She looked at me as if I were a crazy person. "Have you ever seen a Tasmanian devil when it's threatened? It has a mouth like a crocodile and a temper like a toddler possessed by Satan. Those Bugs Bunny cartoons weren't lying. He'll turn into a tornado. With wings. He'll tear your apartment to shreds. You'll never get the smell out."

"Then you better get going before he wakes up."

She hesitated halfway up the steps. "Stick?"

I looked at her.

"This is the weirdest night of my life."

I wished I could have said the same.

I was on the road ten minutes after Abbey left. I wrapped the Bat in a blue camping tarp and rope. I tied him up like a special Christmas present you'd leave on the doorstep of your worst enemy. I folded his wings up around his body and secured his back feet in a bundle of claws that stuck out the bottom of the package. His face hung from the other. He purred gently in his stupor. With his bat face, pink ears, and slight overbite, he was pretty cute.

I buckled him into the passenger seat of my truck and drove north through the cloudless night. A stripe of cold white stars pricked holes in the eternal darkness of space. Space looked dark, but it wasn't. It was simply nothing. An absence of light, heat, matter, or energy. As I drove north, the city lights faded and the fainter stars peeked down. These vast suns, some of them bigger than ours, succumbed to the petty street and porch lights of my dingy city. Just like the parade of people who had been waving their hands in my face so I couldn't see the greater machinations doing their work. Putting my father behind bars. Stealing my best friend. Corrupting the other and using him as a cheap ploy to get me to play ball. Extricating me from the work I'd devoted my life to.

No more. I hurtled toward that big star pulling me ever inward. I had to square with it before it sucked me too close and obliterated me altogether. Abbey's timing in shooting the bat couldn't have been better. He'd buy my way in.

At Paseo Del Norte, a thoroughfare like a headband across the northern part of the city, I nearly turned west. The wrong way. Melodía lived on the west side. Her disappearance without a word sat in my lower bowel like a cramp I couldn't shake. Maybe that's all love was: a stomach ache.

I wanted a drink.

Beside me, the bat snored like an old woman with bronchitis. He oozed pheromones. The cab of my truck filled with his stench, making my nostrils sting and the back of my throat fill with phlegm. I drove as smoothly as I could and took the less worn streets. When I reached a span of smooth asphalt, I sped. I stuck in the left hand lane and flicked my lights at anyone in my path. I rode a few bumpers. I figured if the cops pulled me over, they'd go blind from the animal musk as soon as they stuck their faces in my window. Either that, or I could show them a real live vampire and watch them faint like Victorian ladies with their corsets stretched too tight.

When I'd pulled off the Interstate and was making my way through the village of Placitas, a glint flashed in the seat beside me. I spared a glance at my passenger. A dark, shiny slice of eye shined through the black fur on his face. His lips twitched. I jogged my attention back and forth between the road and the bat. His eye remained open and his breathing quickened. He showed me his sharp front teeth and pink tongue. The blue tarp I'd straight jacketed him with rustled as he breathed harder. With each exhale, he let out a wheeze. His breathing became harder and heavier. The wheezes became groans. His long mouth hung open and his voice cracked out of him in a half-bleat, half growl. He wasn't struggling. He didn't move. He just lay there swaddled in my tarp, shrieking at me.

He was happy. I'd seen the female Tazzies at the zoo posture their mouths in that way and emit the same cry when their keepers rubbed their bellies. I lay my palm on his flank. He groaned louder. I rubbed him through the tarp. He loved it.

I felt a pang of guilt about using him as a tool to infiltrate Typhon Industries.

The complex was quiet when I arrived. Floodlights cast their cones of white light up the flanks of the buildings. Razor wire glinted in the starlight. A couple of security Humvees trolled the perimeter of the fence that held the place together. Mount Olympus, the crown jewel, was the only building not lit up. It sat invisible at the top of the campus.

I rolled up to the security shack and leaned back so the guard could see my passenger.

"Is that what I think it is?" the guard asked.

"Move your mouth a little more and we'll find out. He's waking up."

The guard flapped his hand at me. He hit the button to raise the gate and babbled into his walkie-talkie. As I drove through, he yelled after me.

"Hades, Hades!"

I hit the brake and stuck my head out the window. "Hell?"

"The building," he hollered and pointed at the building with the long rectangular structure attached. "That building. Take it there!"

"You named a building after Hell?" I asked.

He made a frantic gesture with his arm and went back to pouring words into the radio.

The building wasn't far. I drove at a crawl, brewing up a con to get myself inside. The curbside crowd at Hades looked equipped to handle a Sasquatch. A handful of guys in coveralls with tranquilizer rifles and catchpoles stood with itchy pants. A few gorillas decked out in armaments and armor hung to the sides. A single Anglo man in a white lab coat stood at the center of it all, with thinning brown hair, average build, average height—average everything. Before I got out, I checked on my little friend. His eyes were open and drizzled reddish fluid at the corners. He cracked his mouth again and moaned. He sounded like a sheep that craved meat.

"Sorry pal." I scooped him up like a baby and stepped out of the truck. The coverall guys drew a bead on the beast against my chest and more than a small part of me hoped they'd pump my heart full of sweet numbness. The handlers with catchpoles looked like they didn't know whether to put a ring around my neck or the bat's. Only the scientist seemed able to hold himself together. He walked up without ceremony and stabbed the bat in the neck with a needle. In no more than a few seconds, the creature's eyes fluttered shut and his body went limp in my arms.

The man in the lab coat was Jacob Charon, the man I'd met at the Bosque a thousand days ago. "This night is pure evil."

"It's a good night to catch devils."

He angled his face up at the stars, which this far from the city, were polychromatic and infinite. "Every star is a tear in the fabric of space-time."

"That, or a fistful of dying fire."

"Either way, the gods' creation is slowly coming apart at the seams. It's only a matter of time."

"I'm beginning to see why you call this place Hades," I said.

He barked out a laugh. He put his arms out and flapped his fingers. "Give him to me."

I passed the bat over. My body felt a little colder when he was gone.

Charon passed him off to the posse of coveralls, one of which stuffed him in a steel cage. They put the cage on a cart and wheeled it off through the doors of Hades before I could open my mouth. The guards faded into the shadows, leaving me alone with Charon.

"Your name is John Stick, and you don't remember me."

"I do actually. We met at the Bosque Del Apache."

"I am the everyman. No one ever remembers me."

"Must be nice," I said.

"It has its advantages. Well, my master would throw me in Tartarus if I didn't lure you inside and interrogate you."

"Let's say I come quietly. Would something stiff in a glass be part of my torture regimen? Maybe on ice?"

"I'll pour you an elixir even Zeus wouldn't sneeze at."

"I guess if it's good enough for the god of thunder, it'll have to do."

"Come in out of the moon"—he turned toward the entrance—"before it sucks you into space." He trudged through the automatic doors before I could think of a rejoinder. I followed him into a quiet lobby. Guards cocooned in Kevlar and guns sat on stools behind the counter. Their heads traced our journey across the tiled floor to a narrow door with no sign or knob. Charon swiped a card, and it opened with a hiss of balmy air. I followed him into an ecosphere of swelter and the sour musk of lusty animals. He led me down some featureless halls, swiped his card again, pressed his thumb against a pad, and spoke into a small microphone.

"Jacob Charon."

The door clicked open on a dumpy, windowless room. A stained brown couch sat against one wall; a mini-fridge and microwave sat in a shelving unit huddled against another. A card table and a few fold up chairs occupied the middle. Against the farthest wall clung a shallow counter with a hotplate, coffeemaker, and sink with a dead teabag in it. It looked like any break room in any workplace in America.

"That's some serious security for a few square feet of cheap furniture and appliances from last century," I said.

"This is my Zen space. It's full of spiritual energy. The material aspects of it don't matter." He threw his body into a chair and ran fingers through his frail hair. His slight baldness was unremarkable, like everything else about him. "Choose a seat."

I stood. The ceiling was just high enough.

"Or don't. Good idea. You choose a seat, you could inadvertently change the fate of the world. Butterfly effect. You never know. I like your style." He folded his hands across his belly and settled into a slouch. He fixed his sepia gaze on me, and for a second I felt like I was face-to-face with the Sphinx. The moment passed, and he smiled mildly. "Thanks for returning our lost demon."

"No problem. He just kind of fell into my lap."

"Whatever they're paying you, you deserve a raise. We've been hunting Dracula for weeks."

"Dracula," I said. "Cute."

"Nicknames." He shrugged. "They're one of the small pleasures the master allows."

"I've been calling him O-negative. He smells like my favorite blood type."

He shook his head. "That's disappointing. Only weak men choose the universal donor. I had higher expectations of you."

"You barely know me."

"Everyone knows you. You're the Pied Piper."

"What does that mean?" I asked.

"You already know the answer to that," Dr. Charon said. He placed a hand behind his ear. "Listen."

I did. Coolant trickled inside the refrigerator's compressor unit. Air huffed through the ductwork. Some machine in a neighboring room whined. Then I caught it: a burbling swell below the derma of commonplace sound. I couldn't pinpoint its nature or origin. It sounded as if someone was boiling the call of a dozen animals together into a sonic broth.

"That"—he held up his finger—"is for you."

I tilted my head this way and that, trying to angle the sound more directly into my ear.

"You've been here once before," he said.

I didn't say anything.

"You caused an uproar then, and you're causing one now."

He was talking about the only other time I'd tried to get into Typhon Industries. An alarm had gone off while I'd been there. Now I knew what that meant. It meant a room somewhere in this building packed full of cages. Those cages teemed with beasties. And those beasties, for some mysterious reason, liked me.

"Where's that drink you promised me?"

"It does not yet exist; however, I have power to create it." He lurched up from his chair and bustled around the room. "So, you work for us now. *Auribus tenere lupum.*"

"Excuse me?" The words were Latin, of which I'd only caught a form of the word wolf.

"Nothing. Just words. The Romans and Greeks understood the world perfectly and designed sayings for every situation. Our progress over the millennia has simply been a process of forgetfulness."

"Didn't they own slaves and rape women?" I asked.

"What's so wrong with that? People were born to exploit, humiliate, and destroy each other. It's the gods' plan. We're an awful race. The fern is the only noble being left on the planet." He took two tall glasses from the cabinet and filled them with ice. After removing a bottle of champagne and two cans of synthetic energy drink from the mini-fridge, he popped the cork from the bottle, poured champagne over the ice, and added a can to each. Passing me a glass, he bobbed his head at me. "Chin, chin."

I tossed a mouthful back. It tasted like candy, gasoline, and helium.

"Five of these between dusk and dawn, and you'll never need a bed. I drink them all night. Then in the day, I switch to coffee. Around eleven in the morning, I fall asleep on the job and travel to a distant dimension, where humans created God and he's forced to live on some slummy planet while we enjoy milk and ambrosia."

"Sounds just great. You're going to live a long and happy life."

"*Sine labore nihil.* Now that I have my vampire bat back, I have a thousand hours of tests to perform." He lifted his glass, chugged down half of it, and swelled his cheeks with a close-mouthed belch. "How'd you catch him?"

"I shot him with a tranq rifle," I said.

"Neat. Where'd you get one of those?"

"Contraband. I embezzled it from the zoo, along with my collection of emu eggs and polar bear teeth."

"Ha. Humor. Where'd you find him?"

"He took a liking to my pine tree. He liked to sit there in the evening when he wasn't out making bedroom eyes at the Tasmanian girls in the zoo."

"Heard about that. We have people on it. Can't let these species fall into the wrong hands. Might have to napalm the whole zoo. Kidding."

"What are 'these species'?" I asked.

"Classified."

"Listen doc, I brought your bat back because I'm a nice guy. I could have blasted him out of my tree with a shotgun or turned him over to animal control. I figure that earns me something in return."

"*Quid pro quo.*"

"Exactly."

"It's quaint that you think so. We already have the bat. If you plan to use a bargaining chip, you don't hand it over first and then try to haggle about its value."

I started to respond, but he cut me off with a wave of his hand.

"The truth is, I don't care. I watch over the animals. I study them. I care for them. Whatever schemes John White has incubating in connection with you—and I'm sure he has plenty—don't concern me in the slightest. What do you want?"

"Answers."

"Ask away," he said.

Put on the spot, I didn't know exactly what to ask. I should have had a lot of questions, but they were tangled together in my head like rodent bones in an owl pellet. "Do you know Simon Marchette?"

A veiled expression passed over his face. He nodded once.

"Where is he?"

Dr. Charon sat still for a moment. "Gone."

"As in dead?" I asked. "Imprisoned? Escaped?"

"As in deep." Dr. Charon's lips tightened and his eyes narrowed. "Below ground."

"Are you saying he's buried?" I asked.

"You might say so." Charon's voice was as thin as a disposable razor. "He was a traitor."

"And exactly what did he do?"

"He stole company secrets." Dr. Charon shook his head back and forth very slowly. "That's a no-no."

"I have trouble believing that. What did he steal?"

"Genetic material."

"Spit it out, doc. Which genetic material?"

"Which do you think? Dracula's genetic information, for one—and every other unique animal we've got here."

"And what sorts of animals do you have here, exactly?"

"Hybrids. Your liger on steroids."

A liger was the offspring of a lion and a tiger. "Ligers occur naturally. Lions and tigers are the same genus. They can mate. A Tasmanian devil can't impregnate a vampire bat."

Charon snapped out of it. A half-smile sprung to his face and his body relaxed back into a slouch. "Of course not." He sipped his drink and smacked his lips. "Genes don't match up. We have special techniques. Surprised you haven't been briefed."

"I'm new."

"Ahh. They didn't want to tell you. Security clearances and all. Secrecy is a waste of energy. The truth will get out."

"Suppose we give it some air right now."

He downed the last of his drink and emitted an "Ahh!" of appreciation. "What with the big operation coming up, the more you know, the better."

"Big operation?" I asked.

"Operation Velvet Ant." He leapt up and slapped his thighs. "You haven't heard of that either. Guess I'm doing everything I can to get fired tonight. Come on. I'll take you across the River Styx."

Dr. Charon trotted out the door without further ado. I guzzled the pale yellow concoction left in my glass. My stomach felt like one of those volcanoes kids make for science projects in elementary school. He led me down deserted halls that hummed with fluorescent light on white tile. The place felt more like a hospital in the dead of night than a genetic research facility. As we stalked the corridors, the scent of life grew stronger and so did the cacophony of animals losing their marbles.

"I'm the lead biologist around here," Charon said as he jogged along. "I keep the animals healthy and study their growth and physiology. For every one of them we—for lack of a better word—breed, there are hundreds of years of research and study to be done. Full of surprises. Who knew, for instance, that when you combined a tarantula hawk wasp and a horsefly, you'd end up with a species that secretes anticoagulants from its stinger?"

That was news to me, but explained why the bites and stings I'd seen sometimes overlapped.

"Or," he said, "that so many of our animals would have genetic predispositions for social behavior. Based on their parent species, they should want to remain solitary. Yet, time and again, they seem to enjoy grouping themselves socially. Which is why you're a part of the team, I suppose."

"I suppose so."

He gave me a sidelong look. "They do seek you out, after all."

I didn't say anything.

He faced forward again for several quiet strides. "Quite curious."

"Tell me about this big operation you mentioned," I said.

"It's why we're rushing with you. Normally, we wouldn't shove a new employee into the back of a van with Cerberus until we knew he could be trusted. Or until we'd obtained appropriate collateral for his silence. Put certain safeguards in place, as it were. With you, there's no time. The master needs you now, and he's taking a big risk that you won't betray him."

"Why is that, exactly? So, your"—I almost said beasties, but caught myself. It was a word Tony used—"your creatures like me. So what?"

"You're like a magnet," he said. "They're drawn irresistibly to you. That's how Dracula escaped—did you know that? The first time you showed up at the Bosque. We had Dracula in a van. As soon as he smelled you, he became absolutely manic. Bit two fingers off a handler. Tore the inside of the van to shreds and sprayed the entire thing with musk—you can still smell it. We had to burn the handlers' coveralls. The handlers, being cowards, fled. They had to open the doors to do so. Before you could say 'broken arrow,' Dracula was flapping off into the woods."

"Any idea why I have that effect on them?"

"At first, we thought they wanted to eat you." He laughed. It echoed down the short span of hallway still before us. "Now, we're stumped. John White has his theory, which like everything else, we mortals will never know. But you should know they don't act that way around any other human."

"They... How many of these things do you have?"

"Over the years, we've made seven from scratch." He swiped his ID card and opened the lone door. "But now we have quite a few more." He grinned widely, showing me a lot of not too crooked but not too straight teeth. "They have voracious sexual appetites." We entered another small room with a security booth of one-way glass, through which I assumed a team of guards gave us a thorough inspection. A red light above the final set of double doors turned green and Charon led me into a cauldron of hissing, screeching madness.

The stench of animal musk, blood, and urine hit me as hard as the sound. It smelled like an indoor zoo with no windows, one where the animals were sexually supercharged and drank blood by the gallon. Dr. Charon led me up a few flights of stairs and through a door that opened on a chamber the size of a football field. It sunk a story into the earth and had upper walls and slanted ceilings made of greenhouse plastic. Fenced enclosures with a few hundred square feet of floor space lined the walls. Periodically, a wall rose between the enclosures to screen them from one another. The walls were only two stories tall at most; the chamber itself was four stories high. From my vantage point on the balcony overlooking the place, only the closest enclosures, cubed with mesh netting, were visible. The one on the east side had a cement floor, contained small simulated bogs of shallow water and river grasses, and seemed otherwise empty. The western enclosure was a desert-scape, bristling with cacti and scraggly milkweed. It buzzed with hundreds of finger-length wasps.

"Welcome to the zoo of the future," Dr. Charon yelled over the din.

I stood at the railing and had some fun trying not to faint from the stink. I let my brain sort the cacophony. A choir of birds screeched and chirped. A single warbling growl occupied the middle range. A deep thrum underlay the other sounds, like a sawing orchestra of tiny chitinous instruments. Above it all, Cerberus' howl rose and fell like a virtuoso dying for a solo.

"You're telling me," I yelled, "that they're never this enthusiastic?"

"Never," he yelled back. "They get half this excited at feeding time."

"It's just for me."

He nodded.

"How do they feel about you?"

He smiled without separating his lips. "I'm a doorknob."

"What did I do to deserve this?" I asked of no one in particular.

Charon let me linger there, probably worried about what would happen if I got any closer. There might be a prison riot. As I bathed in adulation and raw stink, I pondered my life. I'd never been liked—or even known—by more than a couple of people. I usually talked to one person at a time in a secluded place if possible. No one had ever cheered when I walked into a room. No one had ever dissolved into ecstatic screams upon seeing me. Having that happen, there in that zoo from another world, set all sorts of chemicals loose in my bloodstream. My head felt light. My body ached less than usual. It felt—what was the word? Good.

After a few minutes, things calmed down. As the hound had relaxed with me in the back of the truck, the creatures in the chamber settled down and their din became the usual animal chatter.

"Shall we descend?" Charon asked.

I nodded.

He walked down the stairs. "You'll notice that we use greenhouse siding to concentrate solar energy for the plant life in our animals' habitats. But it also holds out prying eyes."

"That's what puzzles me, doc. It seems like you're trying to keep these things secret, yet you take one out for a morning stroll in plain daylight. You let it scare the devil out of a bunch of immigrants. What gives?"

"We do that because it is the animals' purpose," the doctor said.

"Nothing has a purpose. Things just live."

"Every manmade thing has a purpose. We made these animals for a reason. Those trips into the desert are their sole purpose for existence."

We stopped in front of the first enclosure. I peered through the netting. The air was rank with stagnant water. I picked out a spindly form only inches from my nose. It was the size of a fingernail, with long appendages, bluish ovular wings, red eyes, an amber body, and a long proboscis. After I found the first one, I saw a dozen more, and soon, the entire enclosure resolved into tiny insects. Clusters of them covered the surfaces of the pools, patched the netting, colored the leaves of the tropical trees. Thousands of them.

"These are drosophila flies," I said, "combined with mosquitoes."

"We call them lamiae, after the bloodthirsty Greek monster. You know your insects."

"A seventh grade biology student can pick out a drosophila."

"Yes. I also imagine Simon Marchette told you. What else did you learn from him?"

"Your goons showed up pretty quick. He didn't tell me anything. But I'm not an idiot either. I've figured out your recipe: you're combining bloodsuckers with other species."

"You're half-right about the recipe. You're wrong about Dr. Marchette. Those agents were not ours. They were border patrol."

"Border patrol doesn't arrest citizens, or lock us in abandoned warehouses."

A curtain dropped over his face and he turned back to the flies. "The interesting thing about these animals is that they have formed clans. We've been breeding them for years—eight to be exact. At first, we only hatched one single organism, which normally would have been foolish, since drosophila flies, like any insect, have a tremendous mortality rate. However, we only had the capacity to produce one. It thrived. We bred it with a mosquito. Their offspring were the hybrid, every time."

"Wait. You somehow coerced this monster drosophila-mosquito to get romantic with a regular mosquito. They mated. And the fly-side genetics of their larvae weren't diluted?"

"They should have been. The offspring should have been much more mosquito than fly. This was not the case. It took close study of the genome to discover why."

I waited for it.

"Every gene of the hybrid is dominant. That has held true for each species we've created."

"That's impossible," I said.

He shrugged.

"How the hell do you make these things?"

"Only John White himself knows how it is done. As I was saying, these flies have formed themselves into clans. We've tracked them. They always associate with the same individuals. They feed together. They mate only with each other. They rest and socialize together. And they go to war together."

"You're joking," I said.

"The different clans periodically do battle. It's unlike anything I've seen in animals before, save chimpanzees, which are almost as brutal as humans."

"Are they fighting over territory?" I asked. "Food?"

The doctor shook his head. "There is no clear reason. However, they commit terrible atrocities. Butchery of egg clusters. Sucking nymphs dry. Isolating individuals and tormenting them to death." He wore a thin smile on his face. "It is as if, having been made by man, they are stained with our evil spirit."

"What do they eat?" I asked.

"Why, blood of course. We have vast... stocks of it." His smile brightened. "Shall we move on?"

He turned and walked to the facing enclosure before I could respond. I wasn't sure if I wanted to see the rest. I'd come here with the intention of piercing the skin of Typhon Industries; now that I was in, I wondered if I could stomach it. The flies were robust and healthy. They were perfect. If I'd encountered one, I would have been fascinated. Confronted with thousands of mutated, bloodthirsty, warlike hybrids, I felt sick.

"These you know," Dr. Charon said, as we faced the opposite enclosure, also draped with netting to keep the insects in captivity. Hundreds of the tarantula hawk wasp-horsefly hybrids carpeted the netting, all edging and shuffling to get as near to me as possible. However, like the flies, they clustered in defined groups, buzzing and gnashing at other groups that strayed too close.

"I've seen these in the outside world. You have an escapee problem."

"We're aware of it," he said. "We call them harpies for their fleet nature."

"Were you aware that one of those escapees flew all the way to the Bosque Del Apache and laid its egg in a whooping crane—one of the ones that died?"

"Indeed. This species is quite difficult to keep in captivity. They covet freedom. I suppose it's only a matter of time until they're just another denizen of the New Mexican desert."

I wanted to confront him about Melodía, but I held back. I was there to gather intelligence, not exact revenge on one of John White's peons.

Dr. Charon led me past the next pair of enclosures. The one on the right was divided into smaller cubes that housed families of hairless black rats with six legs, flat chitinous torsos, long pink tails, and red eyes—assassin bug-rat hybrids. John White had named them gremlins. Their flesh was charcoal black and their insect shells gleamed like polished evil. They grumbled and squeaked and shuffled in their cages. One of them unfurled its long proboscis at me as I passed. The organ snaked from its face like a party favor. The cage opposite was a warbling madhouse of flying beaked snakes, which Charon called hydras. They wound their feathered tails through the mesh of their cage and chirped their twisted song while licking the air with forked tongues. After these two cages, we visited the empty enclosure of Dracula and Cerberus' cage, who I let snuffle at my hand for a little while. He—or she—was so overjoyed to see me that he couldn't choose between slurping my palm with his face sucker and flopping on his belly to show off his double genitalia.

Finally, we stopped in front of a cage where a young bear pranced around a generous habitat with a small, simulated creek, several smooth rocks to lie on, and plenty of toys to bat with his massive paws. His body was burly, hairless, and gray. He swished the water with his long slimy tail, and when he yawned, displayed a pink circular mouth with spirals of barbed teeth. He was a playful lamprey-bear, as happy as could be. His name was Goliath.

"Have you deduced the pattern yet?" Dr. Charon asked.

"Fly-mosquitoes. Wasp-horseflies. Rat-assassin bugs. A bloodhound-leech, a Tasmanian devil-vampire bat, and a lamprey-bear. All regular animals bred with hematophages. I can't quite figure out the python-bird."

"The vampire finch, a denizen of the Galapagos Islands. In the wild, they peck wounds into other birds and drink the blood that spills out."

I remembered him mentioning the vampire finch during our first conversation at the Bosque. "So, you've combined all of the world's famous blood-eaters with your favorite animals. I'm sure you'll win some prizes."

"Hematophages are slightly less than half of the pattern, and stop saying 'you.' I'm an employee."

I thought about it while the bear cub with the wet rubbery lamprey skin and hundreds of teeth bounced his burly forelimbs on a big plastic buoy in his play pool. He gave me sidelong glances to make sure I was admiring him. "The other species are all exceptional smellers."

"Bullseye," Charon said.

"So, you're breeding macrosmatic hematophages. A smarter man than me wouldn't ask why."

"They're weapons. The new face of border patrol. The government needed to be able to locate people across vast distances. Thus, we've developed animals that can follow scents for miles."

"And that are thirsty for blood. The mind that came up with that scheme must be a pearl."

"The challenge was incentive," Charon said. "We could use regular bloodhounds to do our tracking, but they can only track humans whose scent they already have. We needed a tracker who would see their quarry as prey. We also needed a tracker who wouldn't chase down just any animal. We needed them to hunger for human blood and more particularly the blood of illegal immigrants."

"How the hell do you teach an animal to like only the blood of illegal immigrants? That sounds like a fascist fantasy."

Dr. Charon's eyes sparkled as they followed the bear around his cage. "You're not far off, really. We teach them to be racist." He swiveled his head slowly until he was staring at me. The casual half-mast eyelids that he usually wore were high and taut. His mouth tightened until his teeth showed. "John

White spliced a nugget of human DNA into each chupacabra. Scientists have been mapping every double helix of the human code. Not just for the sequence of proteins but also for function. Other scientists look for criminal behavior or genetically inherited diseases. All well and good. But John White is the true visionary: he isolated the alleles that code humans for prejudice. Those that bond us to people who we perceive as similar and that repel us from people who are different. That instinct to notice the distinctions between your clan and the other guy's, and to treat his as the enemy. Humans excel at prejudice. It's one of our great evolutionary advantages. John White perceived this trait, located it, and extracted it. He spliced it into these animals. We train each one to focus that prejudice on Latino people. We train them to thirst for Latino blood above all else. We've bred an army of animal tracking devices that search only for people of a particular race."

"That's the stupidest thing I've ever heard. It's impossible. You can't train animals to perceive race. We're all human. There's no genetic difference. How is an animal going to differentiate between a Hispanic American and a Mexican who both look the same and have the same ancestry?"

Dr. Charon pursed his lips. "Maybe I've said too much."

"I would say I wouldn't want to get you into trouble with your boss, but the truth is I don't give a damn."

His face tightened. "And here I thought I was making a new friend."

"I'm just like Cerberus over there. I have no choice in any of this."

Dr. Charon glanced at the bloodhound wiggling his posterior sucker and staring at me, his eight compound eyes full of longing. Charon's pupils slowly expanded until they filled his irises. He was seeing something far away. "None of us does. Our courses are set long before the first smirk shared between our parents. Our world is a dictatorship. God is Hitler."

"God hasn't dictated any of this. He's probably sitting on a fluffy white cloud somewhere scratching his head and wondering whether he should toss a couple thunderbolts down here and pound this whole enterprise to dust."

Charon smiled mildly and didn't say anything.

We spent some minutes sitting side by side on a bench in a zoo from the far side. The songs of birds never heard anywhere else surrounded us. Animals that should not have existed, but that did, seeming happy and normal, made their quiet animal sounds. Claws clicked on rock. Tongues lolled or lapped. Wings fluttered and fur rustled. They were the sounds of any normal zoo. I felt right at home.

CHAPTER TWENTY - THREE

At five in the morning, I parked my truck and dragged my body down the stairs to my front door. I found Abbey asleep in a patio chair. A medium-sized dog kennel sat on the ground beside her, and the tranquilizer rifle leaned against it. Her arms hugged her chest, and her head lay toppled onto her shoulder. She'd propped her feet on another chair, and crossed her short, plump legs at the ankles. Her pale, freckly face was smooth and still, her mouth slightly open. A strand of orange hair had fallen over her lips. It twitched in time to her breathing. She was cute and tough, and I wondered how a person like her could ever feel lonely. The world was terrible. It was getting worse and worse.

Whatever Abbey avatar was wandering around dreamland must have noticed the giant watching. Her eyelids fluttered open. Lines creased her forehead. "You lied to me."

"I misled you," I said.

She propped up in the chair. Her eyes held an early morning squint. "You're just like all the others." Her voice was thick and low.

"Which others?"

"Men are liars. They're butterscotch to your face and poison as soon as you leave the room."

"I'm not a man," I said. "I'm just a male. And I'm sorry I lied to you. Whatever's going on has hurt me and I don't want it to hurt you."

Her green eyes studied me from beneath her rumpled eyelids. "I don't like you anymore."

"You should go home. You'll like me again after you've spent a few hours in your bed."

"I won't go," she said, "until we have a plan for getting your job back."

"I have a new job and I'm holding onto it for the time being."

She shook her head vigorously. "You have to tell me what's going on. I hate being in the dark."

I opened my mouth to make a joke, but she cut me off.

"Tell me!" she yelled. "I've done you so many favors. You owe me!" She got up and kicked me in the foot. "Start with the orange dust on your shoes. Then tell me why you smell so funny."

I couldn't. I lacked the powers of narration to lay it all out for her. I could describe individual strands of something larger, but couldn't see how they connected. The pieces of a big, strange creature lay in my lap, but I couldn't puzzle them together into a whole. I knew Typhon Industries was producing monsters that thirsted for human blood. I knew that these monsters were being trained to hunt humans. I knew that two of my close friends had disappeared and Typhon Industries' fingerprints were all over it. I knew tribes of poor people were wandering through the desert and that my countrymen were warring over whether to give them safe harbor. And I knew that somehow, as Marchette had put it, John White was ultimately responsible for killing the birds all those long days ago. They were irregular chunks of a jigsawed whole—that whole was a Frankenstein that I couldn't perceive.

Abbey gazed at me with her head tilted to one side. "You look incredibly sad."

"My world is collapsing. All I've got left is a spider and a very forgiving ex-work colleague."

"I haven't forgiven you yet. Tell me one true thing and I'll go home."

"Simon Marchette is a good man. He was misguided for a while, but he came out on the right side of things."

She raised her thin ginger eyebrows. The gray light of dawn fell over her tired features, and she looked worn and mishandled. She belonged, if only for the few moments before the sunbeams hit her fully, in my world. "I've been worried about him. He's a cutie."

"I'm worried about him, too. For now, go to bed. And know that you helped me tonight more than I can express in words."

"Try," she said.

"I can do an interpretive dance. It will involve me collapsing on the ground and sleeping for three weeks. You'll be moved."

She fixed her eyes on mine. The city was silent around us in that big deep breath the world takes between night and day. With each heartbeat, the sky

flushed a shade brighter. An arch of orange light bloomed over the Sandía
Mountains where the sun flexed its muscles beyond the horizon. "Okay. I'll
leave, but just so I can go home in the sunrise. It's the most magical time to
drive." She collected her rifle and her cage and walked up my stairs into the
land of the normal.

I tried to remember what I was doing before the bat showed up on my
porch. It involved piecing everything together, but I didn't have the mental
wattage to recall my train of thought. Instead, I went to bed, where I passed
from my waking life into something so deep it could barely be called sleep.

After what could have been minutes, hours, or a day, the lights in my brain
flickered on. My body was a collection of bones and aching muscle that didn't
feel like they were associated with one another in any meaningful way and
that I didn't trust to cooperate if I put any sort of demands on them. I took a
risk and opened my eyelids. Nothing important broke. I raised my head and
got an eye full of Tony sitting in a chair in the corner of my bedroom.

"For your own sake, you'd better have brought your gun," I growled.

"Sorry. Had to enter on the down-low. This place is being snooped from
every angle, including from below. Satan has a special interest in you, little
brother."

"I'm bigger than you. In three days, when I'm ready to move, I'll prove it to
you. And Satan is nothing compared to what I've seen up on Earth lately."

"Glad to see you're getting some perspective," he said.

My arm seemed like it would hold together despite the ache in my joints,
so I used it to pull the blanket over my head.

"You went there." My comforter muffled his voice. I pretended I couldn't
hear it. "C'mon. Dish."

"There was a chupacabra in my pine tree," I said to my sheets. "I thought
I'd put it back in its cage before it bit any children."

"You caught one of their beasties and you didn't even think to make us
wise to it? I thought we were working together."

"I improvised," I said. "I'm not the type who makes quick choices. I need a
dozen or two years to get my ducks in a row."

"You chose wrong. My people are not happy."

I peeled the blanket from my head. "I've never been happy. After seeing
what I saw last night, I'm less happy than ever."

He snapped his fingers. "Describe."

I did. I started with the scene in the desert. I recounted it for him, detail
by detail. I left as little out as I could. I sat up and propped myself with a few

pillows. By the end of it, I needed a cup of coffee. I told Tony as much.

"I need something stronger than that," he said. He was a tiny man in an old chair. The creases in his face ran deep. The gray hairs in his goatee stood out.

"Let's start with coffee. That way, we have something to look forward to."

He went into my kitchen and started a pot. I got dressed. Neither of my feet turned to dust and neither of my femurs split apart like old spaghetti noodles. My arms didn't fall from the sockets and my vertebrae didn't crumble. I brushed the badger out of my teeth and ran my fingers through my hair until it did something sensible. I moved away from my reflection before it scared me into a crisis and plodded to the kitchen. It smelled like sunbeams, Dracula musk, hot coffee, and shoe polish.

I sat at the bar. Tony slid a cup of coffee at me and leaned on the bar top.

"You got any food?" he asked.

"Oodles."

"You look like you could use breakfast." He hitched up his pants and opened the fridge.

"I'll take eggs," I said. "Scrambled. Toast. Butter. You could give me an orange with that if you felt like it."

"Coming up." He started banging stuff around. "You did real well with that thing out in the desert. But I have to say." He wagged his head. "It was hard for me to hear. Those are my people." He stopped working to look at me. "They're yours too."

A month ago, I would have told him that I didn't have any people. But I thought about my father. Long ago, he'd been one of those migrants.

"Now." He tapped the eggs on the edge of a bowl, grasped each side of the shell, carefully broke each one in half, and spilled its slime into the bowl. "What about inside the facility? How far did you get?"

"Far." I opened my mouth to say more but something stuck in my jaw. Some mechanism inside my body didn't want to talk.

He stopped beating the eggs to focus on me. "Well? What did you see?"

It was the beasties. I didn't want to rat them out. They liked me. They flocked to me as no one else ever had. I tried to put my reservations away and think about my father. "I saw quite a bit. Probably you already know most of it. You have people on the inside, right?"

"I'll tell you what we know," Tony said. "*Nada.*"

"That means nothing."

"You need to learn your language."

"Spanish is not my language."

"It's your heritage."

"It's not my heritage," I said.

"It doesn't even matter if it's your heritage or not. It's your father's native tongue. That's not heritage. That's birthright. You should be bilingual. The fact that you're not is an outrage. It's oppression."

"My people don't speak a language. They talk with scent glands and mating calls."

"I'm going to start giving you Spanish lessons right now, whether you want them or not." He held up the frying pan. "*Sartén.*"

I sat there.

"*¡Sartén!*"

"Alright," I said. "Frying pan. *Sar-ten.*"

"Your pronunciation is terrible," he muttered, flicking a pad of butter into the pan and turning on the stove. "Back to Typhon Industries. Which part did you see? Offices? Labs? Did you question anyone?"

"I talked to one guy," I said.

"Who?"

"A man named Charon," I said.

Tony almost dropped the spatula. Then he put it in my face and yelled, "*Espátula.*"

"That one's easy," I said.

"*¡Repite!*"

I gave him a blank look.

"*Espátula. Repite, por favor.*"

I caught on and gave the word my best shot. It limped across my tongue.

"*Muy bien.* You met Dr. Charon? He's in charge of the daily operation of the lab. He's one of John White's top people. What did you get out of him?"

"That he never sleeps," I said. "Listen, before I give away all my bargaining chips, what have you done about finding my friend?"

Tony gave me a hurt look between scraping the eggs around the pan. "Is that really how this is? Bargaining chips? We're part of the same struggle now. We're Good Friends. *Amigos.* You can trust us. We're doing everything we can to find your girlfriend."

"She's just a friend," I said. "And I still don't really know who 'you' are."

"We help people get around," he said. "We help them escape *la migra* and find life-saving work. We reunite families. If a chick from America and a cat from El Salvador fall in love, we hook them up with papers—even marriage if they're crazy enough to want it."

"Isn't marriage an automatic thing?" I asked. "Get married, become a citizen."

"It's not that easy anymore. There's a huge waiting period, interviews—all sorts of bureaucratic blood has to be let. It takes years, and during those years, the spouse has to stay abroad—unless they have Good Friends like us. We know a lot of sympathetic lawyers."

Tony shoved a plate at me. "*Buen provecho.* Eat. And tell me what you got out of Charon."

I ate a few bites. There is something special about scrambled eggs. Every human on Earth has a slightly different way of cooking them. Every person's eggs hold a hint to their human mystery. Tony's eggs had a crisp exterior and contained a gooey gift inside.

"I saw his zoo," I said.

Tony's eyes got wide.

"That's exactly the expression you should be wearing."

"What was in it?"

"Animals. Lots of animals with beaks, claws, fur, scales—the whole gamut."

"What was he doing to them? Did you see any beasties?"

"I did, in that they were all beasties."

"How many did you see?" he asked.

I made a quick count. "Seven."

Tony's eyes narrowed. "Seven is a low number. How come you had to count?"

"Seven types, dozens or hundreds of each type," I said. "In the cases of the bigger ones—the hound, the bear, the bat—there was only one. But the littler ones had obviously reproduced."

"Tell me what the little ones were like."

"Rats mixed with assassin bugs. Pythons and vampire finches. The wasp-horseflies you saw. And mosquito-drosophila flies."

"You realize that what you're telling me changes everything. This is the moment that I will look back on and realize, yep, that's when the world was totally damned to hell. It's like suspecting that aliens have visited and then seeing their spaceship land in New York."

"That's exactly what it was like, but it wasn't really how I felt. It had felt more like going home. The association leapt into my head and lingered.

"The mystery is how they reproduce, since we know John White can only make one being at a time. You need two."

"For animals that reproduce sexually, yeah, which all of these do. But I think the more important question is how does he make these things? You can't just make an animal. Even if you can splice a bunch of DNA together, all you have is some DNA. An animal needs a parent, usually two. You need a mother, at least, to carry it to term. How does a thing get born without a parent?"

"That is another of the mysteries we're trying to solve," Tony said. "We suspect that he places a fertilized embryo in the mother of the larger species.

"That wouldn't work. Especially in mammals. You need some compatibility between mother and offspring. You don't see surrogate pigs giving birth to human babies. A walrus can't give birth to a rhino."

"We have heard something, but it sounds—made up."

"Have you been listening to me at all?" I asked. "I'm living a fairytale, one of the old German ones where Red Riding Hood actually gets eaten and Cinderella's sisters chop off their toes to make the slipper fit."

"What I've heard sounds stupid," he said.

"I've been talking stupid all morning," I said. "Spill it."

Tony shrugged expansively. "We've heard chatter about a hot springs. Magic waters and what not."

I waited.

When he saw I wasn't talking, he went on. "You know how people are always chinning about hot springs with special properties, medicinal and so on. Been the wag for centuries. Well, John White captured one. He built his headquarters around it. The thing has a few apertures high on the slope of the mountain. They form a creek that flows down into a channel he's built. But the main springs is smack in the middle of his floor plan. I've seen blueprints—obtained with considerable criminal infractions. It bubbles up in a big chamber—he calls it Mount Olympus. Word is, he's doing experiments in the pool. Not only that, but the room is designed to open. It's rigged with a huge hydraulic system. If you show up at the exact right time on the exact right day, you can see the whole room split down the middle to let the sun shine in. It only happens on one day a year, or so we think."

I sat there and stared at him.

He gave me a cagey smile. "Do you want to know what day?"

I already knew.

"I'll give you a hint," he said. "It rained at the Bosque Del Apache that day."

"You're saying that there's a connection between that room, the chupacabras, and the dead birds. I've heard it. I'm not buying it."

"It's as plausible as anything. Whatever happens when that room opens up is connected to all of this: the chupacabras, the Minutemen, the migrants in

John White's prison, and the dead birds. Everything is connected. That room has been there for seven-plus years, and there are seven chupacabras. In police work, we call that a pattern."

"Yep," I said, "which doesn't add up. If it's been there for seven full years, there should be eight chupacabras."

Tony cocked an eyebrow at me. "Have you seen a beastie that was only a couple weeks old?"

I hadn't.

"Then there's a new one," he said. "God only knows what monstrosity John White is swaddling up there. It's part of a pattern, and the pattern's only going to get worse."

I didn't care about patterns. Every damn thing could be connected to every other damn thing, and I would have lived out my happy life below ground and behind walls. But the few people and hundreds of animals I cared about had been swallowed up by the world's messes. Like a fog descending, images of my scaly, slimy, forked tongued and whip-tailed friends filled my mind. I wouldn't see them again. It hadn't hit me until that moment. I was dizzy. I had to close my eyes and hold onto the bar with both hands. It felt like I'd lost custody of my children.

It took me a few minutes to get a grip on myself. When I did, I opened my eyes, found Tony floating out there in the bobbing world, and tried to breathe. After I managed to stuff some air into my lungs, I found myself thinking not about any of that, but about a tall dark-haired woman scientist who I missed more than my own father.

Tony's brow was furrowed. He looked at me like you do an old person when you think they're about to have a heart attack and you wonder what you should do about it.

"My friend, Dr. Hernandez. Have you found her?"

"Working on it," Tony said. "We're busy."

"I'm letting hell hounds sniff my finger tips and you're too busy to find my friend. What am I doing any of this for?"

Tony gave me a cautious look. I might have erupted a little louder than I meant to. "We'll get more people on her. For the time being, you've got to hold yourself together. Keep playing their game. Go off into the desert and use your charms on their beasties. Persecute some more innocent families."

"Oh yeah," I said. "My new pal Dr. Charon mentioned that a big operation is in the pipeline. Operation Velvet Ant."

"What's that?"

"No idea. He was hush-hush."

"Make that your number one priority. If they've got a big operation in the works, we've got to throw a wrench into it."

"I'll open my ears," I said.

He walked into my bedroom, where he scrambled up through the window and out into the day. I finished my eggs and tried to figure out what to do with myself. A couple of empty eggshells sat in the kitchen sink. They looked exactly like my life.

CHAPTER TWENTY - FOUR

spent some hours straightening up my house and my headspace.
The house was quick and easy. Once I finished, I groomed and dressed,
fixed myself a weak whiskey and water, and set myself up at the bar.

My headspace was tougher. A myriad of problems danced around in there.
I tried to focus my shaky brain on conniving machinations that would smash
the Good Friends into the Minutemen, hopefully obliterating both. But
Melodía wouldn't leave me alone. I sat, sipped booze, and saw her dark hair,
her blood shot eye, her long slender limbs. I could smell her as if she were
standing beside me. I'd spent most of my best moments over the past twenty
years looming over her with the scent of her lavender shampoo wafting into
my nose. I called her house and listened to her voice on the answering
machine. I thought about going to her lab even though I knew she wouldn't
be there. With no leads—except the orange dust—I didn't know what else
to do.

In the end, I called the Captain. I considered driving to his house instead,
but I didn't want him to get the mistaken impression we were becoming
friends. He answered from a place whirring with white noise. Either he was
driving on the freeway, or he was in one of those contraptions where you
skydive indoors.

"We don't need you today, Mr. Stick," he said as a way of greeting. I
appreciated that he cut right to the chase.

"I met your roomful of monsters last night. I met Dr. Charon too. Pretty
interesting guy if you're into club drinks and Latin."

"He's a good puppet when all his strings are attached correctly," the Captain said. "He gives the puppies their chow, and that's all we really need out of him. He most definitely was not supposed to take you into Hades."

"It's too late for regrets, Captain. He told me about Operation Velvet Ant, too. Now that I've met your brood of vampires, I think you should let me in on your big plan. I know your monsters' natural behavior backwards and forwards. I've been studying their genetic forefathers for my entire life—or at least half of them."

"You think you know what you're talking about," The Captain said, "but you don't."

"I know that there's a little genetic sprig of human in each one. I know you're training them to be racist."

"Cultural discernment is what we call it, because we're politically correct and all. And if you think we don't have biologists who specialize in each one of our creatures' gene pools, then you haven't been thinking hard enough." A car horn beeped on his side of the line. A few other horns followed. "I'll be in contact when we have instructions for you. Until then, sit in your room and keep your mouth shut."

"I'm getting in my car as soon as I've eaten my breakfast. I'll be popping by your little enclave in an hour or so."

"You won't be admitted. Listen, I'll send you a babysitter if you're lonely. Just stay away until you're told to come. You frazzle the animals. You rile them up. It interferes with their training."

"You don't get it. I'm in. I'm a Minuteman. I know about Operation Velvet Ant. I can help you plan it."

"We have it under control. Your only job is to sit on a bench and look pretty."

The line went dead.

I hung out at my bar some more. My brain jogged in place. It didn't get anywhere. Quiet as a shadow, Ralph crept from beneath the fridge. He climbed the handles of the drawers beside my sink as if they were a ladder designed especially for eight-legged beings. He crawled across the narrow ledge of counter in front of the sink and leapt to the bar top. I showed him my palm. He crept into the basket of my fingers and ticked his feet up and down against my calluses. His belly hair brushed my skin in a sensation just shy of a tickle. Ralph was sneaky. He knew how to get what he wanted.

I picked up the phone and dialed Tanis Rivera's number.

"John Stick. What an unexpected delight."

"Skip it," I said. "I want you to do something for me."

"Is it something exciting?" I could envision her dark eyes getting big on the other side of the line, like they did when she got manic about tormenting me.

"Yes," I said. "Very exciting."

"And why should I do this exciting something for you?" she asked.

"Because you owe me. You chained me to a chair for a night. You imprisoned two of the only human beings I like." My voice boomed as the anger washed back through me.

"That was just a ruse. They would have been snatched up with or without me. I insinuated myself into those operations as a precautionary measure. You should be thanking me. I'm your guardian angel."

I gritted my teeth. "Are you going to help me or not?"

"Yes," she said, "not because you asked me to—you didn't even ask nicely—but because it'll balance the scales."

I didn't want to ask what she meant, but I did anyway.

"Think of our world, in which men do things to each other, as two sides of a math equation. Each man wants to destabilize the equation. They want to have more value, more power than the person on the other side of the equal sign. I'm like a natural phenomenon whose job it is to balance the equation."

"You're saying that you're math."

"I'm correct math. Men will always try to imbalance the world in their own favor. I will always be around to correct that imbalance. At least, until I die."

"Well, you're doing a bang-up job," I said. "We are living in a world of total peace and harmony. You can tell by the number of fatal car accidents on the freeway each morning. Or the number of kids who shoot their moms. Or you can just take a drive through the shacks of the lower west side showing people pictures of the mansions in the foothills—they'll let you know how balanced the math is."

"I didn't say it was an easy job," she said. "Men are terrible people."

"I've met a woman or two who aren't so wonderful."

"Those women are confused."

I sighed. Tanis inspired me to loose a lot of frustrated air. "Are you going to help me or not?"

"Of course." Her smile blazed through the phone. "After all, I owe you."

I drove out to Typhon Industries the next morning, early, where I'd arranged to meet Tanis. I weaved my way through the scattered dozen or two protesters holding signs of bunnies with electrodes fastened to their eyes, pictures of Latino men and women with the word missing beneath them, and slogans condemning the theft of land and heritage. The man at the guard post took one look at me and waved me through.

A figure in a white coat, dark slacks, and a teal blouse stood in front of Hades. She had dark hair and brown skin. I parked far away, and she hung in my sightline for nearly a minute as I walked. She was too short, too dark, and her hair was straight, but I was still disappointed to discover that she was Tanis and not Melodía—even though I knew which of them would be waiting for me.

"You do not look happy to see me. My feelings," Tanis said, "hurt."

"Do we actually have feelings, or are they just an illusion in a meaningless universe?"

"You are making fun of your own atheism."

"Should we get on with it? I don't want to keep you from your day job of kidnapping grandmothers and confiscating their retirement money."

Tanis smiled. "By all means. Let's get on with it."

"I was thinking that you could show me—" I didn't have time to finish. Tanis grabbed me by the arm and hauled me through the outer and inner doors of the building. She waved at the gorillas on duty, who all tried to pretend their chests were made out of cement. She led me to a door in the side of the antechamber and into a tangle of featureless corridors. We walked over tile, under florescent lights, and past doors that led into rooms that would forever remain mysterious. Tanis bounded along on rubber-soled sneakers and didn't waste time with chitchat. It was a refreshing change and a little unnerving.

As we penetrated deeper into the building, the din of animal noise rose from the joints of the place, the song of my people calling out to me.

Eventually, we burst through a door that opened on a stairway leading down. Tanis leapt down the first flight before I could even duck the doorjamb. I took them three at a time and barely kept up with her. I was a giraffe chasing a jaguar. We descended three stories below the Earth's surface. No one in New Mexico dug so deep. The desert earth was hard. Eons of pressure had packed the clay and rock into an impenetrable crust. Besides, the desert offered limitless space to sprawl above ground.

Tanis didn't give me a chance to voice my grievances against the engineers who'd defied geologic common sense. The staircase led to three corridors, each barreling off in a different direction. She power-walked down the rightmost corridor like a secretary on her lunch break.

"Hey!" I yelled after her, just to see what would happen.

"This way, please." She didn't even turn around.

I had no choice. I caught up to her without much trouble. The cacophony of the chupacabras faded away and we walked in that careful silence of space carved out beneath tons of earth above. I guessed that the corridors connected the buildings of the campus so that employees wouldn't have to leave their respective buildings to travel from one to another. This also made no sense. The air was perfectly fine in New Mexico. It never became dangerously hot or cold. There were no wild animals waiting outside your door to bite your head off—or at least not until recently.

The tunnel ended in a freight elevator on one side and a pair of double doors on the other. Tanis spun on me in front of the doors and wrapped her fingers into the front of my jacket. She pushed me into the corner where the two walls met and pressed her body against mine. It would have felt good if I hadn't been worried that all this cuddling was a precursor to a cold blade between the ribs.

She cranked her head back, locked her big dark eyes with mine, and pointed straight up. A camera hung still and lifeless overhead. After a few seconds, a green light blinked on, and the camera began to calmly scan the hall we'd just come through. We occupied one of the few blind spots on the campus.

"It doesn't record sound," she said.

"That's too bad. Now no one can hear me scream for help."

She slapped my chest. "Be serious. I sabotaged the cameras just before you showed up."

"I would ask why, but you'd only lie to me."

"That's correct, but the truth is mostly relative anyway."

"Now that you've given me your daily dose of wisdom, I don't suppose you'd like to tell me what we're doing down here, other than hiding from a camera."

"I'm taking you somewhere I'm not supposed to. You wanted information about this place. I'm going to show you things that nobody wants you to see."

"Why?" I asked. "Because you owe me? Or am I just part of your math equation?"

"I'm doing it because you're so handsome." She gave me a flash of her Cheshire cat smile. "And because I want to."

Something snapped in my brain, and I found that I'd picked Tanis up by her lab coat. She weighed as much as a winter sweater. I held her nose three inches from mine. Her shoes dangled three feet off the ground. I gave her a few blasts of air from the deepest hell of my lungs. "I'm done with games. Since they abducted my dad, I've been taking life more seriously."

Her smile vanished, replaced with an impassive mask, but her eyes held that same distant amusement they always did. "And what do you want, John Stick?"

"I want my animals back," I said. "I want my best friend and my father back. I want my platonic but flirty friendship with a female. I want my quiet home and peaceful, endless desert. You've ruined all that. And I'm mad."

"What if I told you all those things were delusions?"

"I'd say that compared to what I've got now, those delusions seemed pretty real."

"Nothing in your life was what it seemed," Tanis said. "It was a bunch of childhood perceptions you clung to or people masquerading behind lies."

"And you're a truth-teller?"

"I'm a trickster. I'm a woman who sheds her skins, but who ultimately unveils great truths."

"Did you read that on a napkin at a Pueblo casino?"

"You're getting closer to your life-truth. You're getting closer to becoming a man."

"I hope that doesn't involve another growth spurt, because I can't afford new outfits."

"You're on a vision quest. It's not easy, but in the long run, you'll find out who you are. You've been malingering in adolescence for thirty years. It's time you figured out how to move on to the next phase of existence."

"I find it hard to listen to the advice of a woman who coerces me into helping sic a vampiric dog on a band of helpless migrants."

Her expression became more earnest. "I'm bringing you down here for the greater good. You have to trust me."

"It would take a minor miracle for me to believe that you're helping me now after everything else you've done. I'm just another man in your power equation."

Tanis sighed. Her body rose in my hands and then fell. I realized that I'd been holding her aloft for our entire conversation. I felt kind of bad about it.

"Can't you see? I'm helping you exactly because you're not part of my equation. I'll put it to you in a new analogy. I serve the universe. I'm a facilitator. When the natural order of things becomes clogged up, it has to be loosened. Think of me as a plumber. When the pipes of the universe get clogged, I shoot some liquid plumber down into the works to get things moving again. You're the liquid plumber. The pipes have been static for a while. As soon as you stepped into the equation, things started to move. That's all I'm trying to do: get you where you need to be."

"So, I'm liquid plumber."

"Yes. And the universe is poopy. There's a chance you'll clear it out. There's also a chance you'll only make it worse."

"What will you do then?" I asked.

"I'll try something else. There are many tricks a woman like me knows."

"At least you've said one true thing to me today."

"Truth." She sighed. "People should stop using that word."

"Want me to put you down now?"

"I like it up here." She smiled, put her palms on my cheeks, and wrinkled her nose. "Your face is scratchy."

I lowered her to the floor. She landed noiselessly on her rubber shoes, and her hands slipped from my cheeks.

"Put your game face on." She straightened her lab coat and ran her fingertips through her hair. "We're not supposed to be down here. If anyone challenges us, give them that look you wear when you're mad."

I showed her the look I thought she meant.

"That's the one! The security guards have obviously turned all the cameras back on, so it's only a matter of time before the eyes of this place notice that we're in an area we're not supposed to be and send their lackeys after us."

"And where exactly are we going?" I asked.

"Toward a lower level of Hades. They call it Sisyphus."

She barged through the double doors and set off down the hall before I could ask why. I followed. It wasn't a choice I made. It happened. My body was connected to strings and everybody held the end of a strand or two except me.

We wound through a series of hallways and doors until we emerged into a room featuring a large window that ran the span of the far wall. It went from waist height to the ceiling, reinforced with wire mesh. The glass revealed a large windowless chamber with a vaulted ceiling. Several vents were positioned at the highest span of the ceiling. Roughly a dozen capstans spanned across the floor of the room. Each one consisted of a central hub with several regularly spaced spokes projecting out horizontally three feet from the floor. They looked like giant steering wheels of old pirate ships turned on their sides. The cement beneath the spokes was scuffed and worn by the passage of many feet.

We waited only a few moments before several doors opened along the walls of the chamber. A parade of men and women plodded into the room. They all looked like Latino immigrants. They were dressed in clothes dark with stains. Their hair was matted and dirty. Their shoes had seen miles of dirt, rock, river and cactus. A handful of armed guards herded them to positions behind the arms of the capstans. When everyone was in place, a guard blew a whistle and the men and women plodded forward, pushing the capstan arms. They walked in circles, turning and turning the central hubs. It looked like a medieval regimen designed to break the spirits of heretics. The people walked and sweated. The heat of the room radiated through the big picture window—which I hoped was made of one-way glass.

The people treaded in quiet circles. They didn't protest, speak, or even look up. It took me only a few minutes to pick out the face of the woman with the high strong cheekbones and the piercing gaze I'd seen out on the desert. She pushed her arm of the capstan along with everyone else, only instead of looking down, she fixed her gaze directly ahead. She was fierce and beautiful.

"What is this?" I asked.

Tanis stood quietly.

After fifteen minutes or so, all of the people turning the capstans dripped with sweat. Their clothes were dark in the armpits and lower backs. Their foreheads glistened. After half an hour, the guards called a break and allowed the prisoners to drink for a few minutes. Then they were back, turning the great wooden wheels.

I turned to Tanis. "What is going on here?"

Tanis gestured through the window at the large vents in the ceiling. "Those vents don't blow air in. They suck it out."

"Thanks. That clears up everything."

She tipped her head to one side. "Now, why would anyone install such vents in a room where people toil and sweat? Wouldn't you want to circulate fresh air in, not export the smell of people working to another place?" She let me chew on that question. It took me some time.

"The animals in Hades are all good smellers."

She nodded.

I recalled the many vents in the floor of the main chamber. "This room is designed to drain the scent out of people and send it upward into the animal enclosures." My head was making connections. It felt good, but before I could get too far with it, human screams rung through the corridors.

Tanis took my hand. "I may be able to smuggle you into one more room."

"If it's the cafeteria, don't bother. Watching a bunch of innocent people power the wheel of pain has dampened my appetite."

Tanis grimaced. "In a way, it *is* the cafeteria."

We moved even faster this time. Around a few corners and down a hall or two, we found another door with a keypad. Tanis swiped a card and punched some numbers. The picture on the card showed the face of a middle-aged man with black hair and deep jowl lines. She'd obviously stolen someone else's security badge.

This observation room was smaller, but followed the same formula: a couple lines of chairs in a blank room with a window for the fourth wall. Beyond was a small chamber, this one with a dozen chairs outfitted with wrist and ankle restraints bolted to the floor. Guards buckled in several women and men. They fit the people's faces with masks and chinstraps to hold them in place. The people were young, their hands were knotted with callous, their skin dark and lined. They'd spent their lives working.

Once the guards had buckled the people in, they left. Above our heads, the quixotic din of raving animals rained down. There were no vents in the ceiling of the room, but the outline of a square trapdoor showed in its center. The trapdoor slowly slid open. As it did, hundreds of buzzing insects—the drosophila-mosquito hybrids that I'd seen in Hades—spilled through. They traveled in separate swarms, and each swarm settled on the body of a different person. The eyes above each body were wide and white, the faces obscured by the masks, but the horror showed through fine. I was too far away to see, but I imagined a thousand abdomens, each the size of a pea, swelling with blood. After a few minutes, the insects buzzed around the chairs in lazy clouds where their prey sat helpless, or simply rested above the puncture wounds from which they had fed. A few swarms drifted to the glass in front of me and settled there. Eventually, air swept up from the vents in the floor and the clouds of insects floated upward and back through the ceiling. Men in yellow hazmat suits entered and shooed at the few hundred netted over the window in front of me. They swirled around a little bit and were gradually shepherded up, up, and away.

At that point, the door behind us opened and some men who'd been fed too much beef thundered in on black boots. The Captain stood at their center.

"You know," he said lazily, regarding Tanis through half-mast lids, "if you weren't the boss' favorite pet, I'd drive you out onto the mesa, chain you to a cactus, and leave you for the coyotes."

Tanis fluttered her eyelashes and splashed a vapid look across her features. "This is Mr. Stick. He's the new supervisor of feed training. Isn't he?"

The Captain shifted his gaze to me. His face was studiously bored. "He is not in charge of anything. Nor does he have clearance for anything."

"But Dr. Charon let him into—"

"Charon is a glorified zookeeper. We should build him his own cage next to Goliath's." The Captain stood with his meaty arms crossed over his meaty chest and shot me a look. "I guess you've figured a few things out."

"Give me one and one and I'll make two," I said.

Several dozen flies had evaded the men in hazmat suits and persisted in batting themselves at the glass between me and the chamber with the people still strapped to their torture chairs.

The Captain sighed. "We've got to get you out of here. You're turning this place upside down."

"Suits me," I said.

The Captain turned to one of his overfed lackeys. "Take Ms. Rivera to the cafeteria and buy her an ice cream cone."

Tanis gave the lackey a dose of her perfect white teeth and took his elbow. "I like strawberry."

Arm in arm with Tanis, he wobbled out on weak knees.

The Captain's eyes remained fixed on the door after she'd gone. "That woman is either the emptiest skirt I've ever met, or she's Machiavelli reborn. Either way, it would be in everybody's best interest to expel her from the state of New Mexico."

"I used to think that expelling people was your answer to everything. Now it seems you have other uses for people you don't like."

"Let's talk in Delphi," the Captain said. "That should be far enough away."

"You love your Greek mythology around here."

"Everything in this place gets named by one man."

"This Zeus," I said. "Am I about to meet him?"

"Neither you nor I, will ever meet him. He doesn't see people. He communicates by directive. I've seen his signature. That's as close as I've ever come."

"Sounds like a guy with issues," I said.

"No mortal climbs to the top of Mount Olympus. That place is reserved for the gods."

"I see the blood suckers aren't the only ones drinking crazy juice."

The Captain glared at me. "You don't know anything."

We drove to Delphi in a black security Humvee topped with spotlights and a 50-caliber machine gun turret. I told the driver that black wasn't a camouflage color in the desert. He waved a hand at his ear as if a gnat were troubling him.

Delphi's interior was black marble and velvet couches. Picture windows lined the walls all the way around the circumference of the circular building. It had an open floor plan, partitioned into wedge-shaped conference areas and lounges by ten-foot tall screens decorated with frescos of Greek monsters. The Captain and I ended up between the Hydra with its dozen necks and Scylla the sea monster. Delphi was named for the city at the center of the ancient Greek world. A few thousand years ago, the real Delphi had housed an oracle that revealed truths. Now it was a pile of dust and old rocks, like every truth. This Delphi looked more like one of those exclusive clubs where rich people sat around drinking martinis and lying to each other.

The Captain and I sunk our bodies into overstuffed leather seats and faced each other across a low marble table paved in panes of polished steel and glass. It probably weighed as much as a small car. A man in a tuxedo served us coffee. It tasted like pure exploitation. Finger sandwiches with cucumber and raw salmon sat nearby, looking like the trappings of a different reality than I'd ever been let in on.

"Let me begin with this." The Captain handed me a white envelope printed with my name and bearing a double helix on its upper left hand corner. It gave the unmistakable impression of housing a check.

I opened it. There was a number with some zeroes after it. It made my zoo checks look like suckers. It also made them look honest.

"A reward for a job well done and in anticipation of many more," he said.

I slid the check back into the envelope and tossed them both on the table. "I'm not here for the finger sandwiches."

"The value of a man is dollars and cents. That check expresses your value."

"I feel special. Now, where's my father? And how many pints of blood is he missing?"

The Captain snorted some air through his nostrils like a frustrated warthog. "You weren't ready to see Sisyphus yet."

"On the contrary, it reminded me of my favorite historical period. The Dark Ages, when torture and humiliation were embraced as good clean fun."

"It looks barbaric to the casual observer. I admit that. But it's all part of a regimen for the animals. It has nothing to do with the inmates—who are lawbreakers, after all."

"Is there an article in the Constitution about bloodletting as part of a reasonable penal code? I must have missed it."

"Illegals aren't subject to the protections of the Constitution."

"Oh well, if a piece of paper doesn't say you have to treat people like human beings, then why do it? So much easier to put them in the equivalent of hamster wheels and use them to generate power. Or are you running a grist mill as a side enterprise?"

"That is all for the chupacabras. It's part of their training."

"I would ask what you're training them to do," I said, "but I've already been briefed."

The Captain popped a lox sandwich into his mouth and licked every finger of his right hand as he chewed. When he'd swallowed most of it, he spoke, still inspecting his fingers. "They're hunters. We're training them to focus their predator instincts."

"At last, a little honesty. It's like honey in my ears."

He shrugged. "Might as well be honest at this point in the game. Homeland Security hired Typhon Industries to breed animals that can sniff down an illegal immigrant. We tried dogs and rats. Even worked with pigeons. A dog will track down any human in the desert. No problem. But, they won't chase after a person say with a specific ethnicity or who speaks a particular language. The illegals we're after are mostly from the parts of Mexico where farming has gone bankrupt since NAFTA allowed big US agribusiness to move in. So, we needed animals that would single out Mexicans of a few distinct ethnic groups. Not New Mexican Hispanics, who've been living in the state for three hundred years and trace their ancestry to Spain. So, we can't just breed and train an animal that'll discriminate based on skin color. They need to pinpoint a specific culture of Hispanic person. That's tough to do. Animals aren't naturally like that."

"So you feed them the blood of the migrants you pick up in the desert." I said it like it was the most natural and logical thing in the world. I'd put together that Sandpaper Voice had made Rex and I scram so that Cerberus could sip blood from the prisoners. "Wouldn't work. Blood all tastes the same, regardless of ethnicity. You can't condition an animal to like a certain type of person's blood if there's no way to distinguish the taste."

"You haven't let me finish," he said. "We pick them up and put the poorest ones—the ones who the Mexican government could care less about, the ones with no significant family—in a place the boss dubbed Tartarus. We feed them their traditional foods. We let them use all of the cosmetics they would use back home. We transfer them to Sisyphus, where we make them move the capstans, and we funnel the scents of them working up into the enclosures. We do this for an hour before we feed the chupacabras."

"And then you feed them blood."

"Fresh blood," he said. "Straight from the spigot."

"I'm trying not pick up my chair and use it to crush you into the carpet right now. I want you to know that it takes a lot of effort."

"Relax. Your father's in Elysium. It's nice. He has sheets and eats shrimp cocktail. Somebody does his laundry for him."

"If there's any justice, your vampire finch snakes will escape one day and tear your liver out, night after night, for eternity."

"They don't go after white people unless they're starving."

"That's where that bite on your arm came from," I said. "Escaped hydras, starving in the wild."

"Hydras have proven very adept at escape. They do not like being cooped up together."

"They're solitary animals. Putting them in the same cage is a form of abuse."

"They're not purely solitary." The Captain wore a smug smile on his ham of a face.

"Horseflies are indifferent to each other," I said.

"I'm not talking about horseflies."

"You're talking about the human part. I've heard that tripe. It's impossible. You can't take a handful of genes and toss them into an organism and expect your zebra to grow wings. It doesn't work like that."

"We have top secret methods, known only to the Man himself. You can't deny that Cerberus led us straight to that pack of migrants we picked up last week."

"I can't deny it," I said. "But you give any bloodhound a woman's shirt and he'll chase her down. That's how the breed works."

The Captain smiled even more smugly. "It wasn't *her* shirt. We took it from one of the wetbacks after a good day's work in Sisyphus. Cerberus wasn't looking for a specific wetback; he was looking for any wetback."

I picked up the check that lay on the table in front of me. I held it between my fingers, poised to rip it up and stuff the shreds into the Captain's eye sockets.

"Of course, in doing so, we also bred them with the instincts to notice that they're different. That they don't fit in. That they're freaks. And we failed to calculate that they'd fall for other, unique individuals that don't fit. Other freaks." He grinned at me. "You can rip up that check. Go ahead. We'll print you a new one. You're part of our family now. You've got a few thousand little brothers and sisters in Hades just dying to see you again."

I almost did it. I almost turned it into a pile of confetti. But I got a grip on myself. I folded the envelope and slid it into my back pocket.

"That's more like it."

"I'm in a transition period," I made myself say. "You'll have to pardon my humanity getting the better of me. I've signed on. I'm a Minuteman."

He shook his head. "You're more than that. You're key to our next operation. If you can get a hold of yourself."

"What do I care about humans anyway?" I said. "What have they ever done for me?" I was playing a part, but the words came out pretty honestly.

"John White's the only human you need. He values you above anyone else."

"That's sweet," I said. "He sounds like a real swell guy."

"That mission with Cerberus." The Captain brushed it off his sleeve. "It was minuscule. It was a trial run. And unfortunately, circumstances have forced us to push forward the big show. I hope you're ready."

"Operation Velvet Ant."

The Captain grunted. "I don't think you're ready for it, but the boss has issued instructions. So, I'm gonna talk."

"No one's holding your lips shut."

"You've seen too much, too fast," he said. "You're not in a position to understand all the angles. You've got too much of the wrong meat in the fire. Our people—I'll tell you straight—are Anglos. You let Hispanics see Sisyphus, and they take it wrong. You have to be eased into it. First, you see Elysium, where we keep good folks—working guys like your father. It's nice. Two men to a cell. Decent food. Rec rooms. Exercise in a yard. TVs and whatnot. We don't have to treat anyone nice, not if they're illegal. They don't have rights. But we treat 'em nice anyway. We give 'em the red carpet."

The Captain had a restless way of talking. His eyes roved away from my eyes as he spoke. His meaty, callused hands would lift from his thighs and flex during key points he made. It was as if he searched for something to strangle and was frustrated that all he had to express himself with were words.

"You happened to see Sisyphus, a lower level. That's for the bad guys: drug mules, petty criminals, fraudsters. They're here costing us dollars to find, catch, and detain. We're talking billions. Our logic is: you're costing the American taxpayer. You should give a little something back. Typhon Industries, with our genius leader at the helm, is developing technology to track down illegals on the cheap. We're at a crossroads: we can either invest in drones that cost a hundred million apiece, run on jet fuel, and take a network of operators, satellites, and mechanical crews to run. Or we can train a dog to sniff them down. The dog eats for next to nothing. He lives in a pen. He mates with other dogs and they have puppies that can carry on in their father's footsteps. All for cheap. But we need a little sacrifice from these lawbreakers. Hell, you can't even call it a sacrifice. They owe us."

"So, you let your devils suck juice out of them."

"It doesn't damage them," he said. "Not permanently."

"Fine. You've been straight with me. Let me be straight with you."

He nodded. His big bald head crinkled at the brow where his eyebrows met. His meaty palms lay half-clenched on his big thighs.

"First," I said, ticking off a finger, "I'm not interested in any of your angles. That's fancy talk for lying to yourself. Anyone who has to go through a lot of contortions to rationalize what they're doing is fooling themselves. You don't do good by doing evil. You do good by doing good."

His face went a shade darker. I could tell he wanted to interrupt me so he could play some more ethical Twister with himself. I held up a palm.

"Second. I don't care. I don't have any meat in any fire but my own. I'm not part of a race, class, or gender. I'm John Stick. I care about my father. I care about my spider. I care about myself."

That should have made him smile—all these border patrol fanatics were libertarians at heart, where self-interest was king—but he held the same stern expression as if he were posing for an old-timey photograph where everyone tries to look as miserable as possible.

"Third and lastly," I said, "don't ever imprison me again. If you do, I'll pick you up by your head and shake until your neck has an identity crisis. I've signed up to do a job. When I say I'll do something, I do it."

"Fair enough. You're a free man. You'll keep your lips together. You'll come when we call."

"I don't talk to people unless they force me to." I gave him an angry-giant glare.

He glared right back. I had a height advantage, but he had the arrogance of white privilege behind his. In the end, it was a standoff.

"Deal," he said.

We shook hands. I planned on dipping mine in acid later to get it clean.

The Captain filled me in on the twisted details of Operation Velvet Ant. Apparently, White Industries was part of a network of government surveillance operatives, transnational spies, coyote informants, and immigrant turncoats, all who indicated that a big influx of immigrants was nigh. It was the beginning of spring, when planting would begin, to be followed by months of picking and harvesting on farms and orchards across the country. Construction boomed in the spring after a lagging demand over the grim winter months. Tourist season was starting, which meant hotel rooms to clean and dishes to wash. According to the various chatter networks the Captain had access to, the coyotes had a plan to blitz the border with thousands of migrants on the same day. The logic was that border patrol might catch a few, but couldn't possibly intercept them all.

John White had deemed it the best opportunity to roll out his new tracking equipment at full force for a field test.

"And you're the key to it all," the Captain said.

"If migrants are really pouring across the border, how will I do any good?" It was stupid. Even if I were a magnet for the animals, they'd have to stay within a mile of me.

"They're all outfitted with tracking devices. Even the wasps. Microchips. State of the art. We drive a route along the border, releasing them—harpies and hydras over the desert, gremlins in the forest—at regular intervals. They fly all over the place looking for food. They hunt down illegals. Wherever they cluster on the map, we send an intercept team."

"Sounds like you've got it figured out," I said. "I don't fit into the equation at all. I could just stay home. I have a few weeks of sleep to catch up on."

"The problem isn't getting them to the aliens. The problem is picking them back up. The wasps are impossible to catch. They can fly for prolonged periods of time, covering miles. And you can't shoot them with a tranquilizer rifle. You can bring them down with poison or maybe even birdshot, but otherwise, they're just gone. Dracula—he escaped weeks ago. It took you to get him back.

"You're our magnet. We let these things loose all across the desert. We drag you back across the route and all the little monsters flock to you. We net 'em. We bring them back here. A week-long operation at most, depending on how far they disperse."

"Doesn't that seem risky?" I asked. "Dribbling out your mutants across a couple hundred square miles of land? They're going to spread all over the place. They'll cross into Mexico. They'll get eaten by predators. They'll wander into caves. They'll fall into the river and get washed into the Gulf of Mexico. You're going to have ranchers posting YouTube videos of dead chupacabras by the dozen. It'll be a disaster."

"The boss believes in you," the Captain said.

I opened my mouth to tell him how idiotic that sounded.

The Captain held up both hands. "He believes in you. This whole operation is in your hands. I hope you're ready."

"I don't have to be ready," I said. "All I have to do is be myself. Right?

The Captain leaned back in his chair. He stretched his heavy ex-weightlifter arms. "I bet that's a good feeling."

I didn't want to admit it, but it was.

CHAPTER TWENTY - FIVE

Less than ten minutes into the drive home, I pulled over to a gas station in a little mountain town called Cedar Crest. It smelled like pine trees and spilled motor oil. I went inside, bought the biggest cup of gas station coffee they had, and loaded it with French vanilla creamer packets. The huge cup fit my hand perfectly. I set it on the counter in front of the clerk, who'd been giving me the eye, but who when we were face to face, managed to act pretty casual.

"Anything else?" she asked.

"Just the coffee," I said.

"Any gas?" Her voice held a hint of a Native accent. The slightly clipped words stepped out of her mouth at a cadence more compact than your average Anglo or Chicano speaker. I liked it, but I didn't tell her because humans aren't supposed to be nice to each other.

"No gas."

She punched a couple buttons in the register.

"You know what? Give me some cigarettes."

"Sure," she said. "What kind?"

I hadn't smoked in a decade. I'd never been a regular smoker, but during my lost twenty-somethings, I'd swallow one or two on a particularly raucous or desperate night. I'd smoked a few packs over a span of seven or eight years and quit before I was thirty. "Camels." I couldn't think of any other brands.

"Lights? Filters?" She stood on her tiptoes, examining the packs in the rack that hung from the ceiling.

"Give me whatever's easiest for you to reach," I said.

She took a pack out, lay it on the counter, and punched her fingers at the register. "I wish I had your height advantage. It's hard being short."

"My height is a mixed blessing."

Outside, I walked to the edge of the forest behind the station and lit up. I indulged in some light coughing. Birds tweeted nearby and grey squirrels scampered among the twigs and pine cones and scrambled their clawed feet up the trees. I closed my eyes, held the smoke in my lungs, and felt the pocket of heat hover inside me. I pretended that the birds were not birds at all and that the squirrels were not squirrels at all. I pretended they were animals who by their very nature, by some unknown innate complexity woven into them, were my friends. I envisioned a forest full of them. When I opened my eyes and blew the smoke from between my lips, the world was still the world and the squirrels remained simple squirrels, but I felt different.

On my way back to my truck, pain stabbed me in the foot. I grabbed the pay phone to steady myself and looked at the bottom of my shoe. I pulled a goat head from my sole, the thorny nutlet of devil's weed, a European species that had infested the Southwest during colonial times. The nuts resembled goat's heads with two upturned thorns and sat on the ground like caltrops, ready to ambush any living thing that stepped on them. The one in my shoe was abnormally large and nasty.

A circus flyer clung to the side of the pay phone, the same outfit I'd been seeing signs for since the birds died. It read "Have a Galloping Good Time at the Gamut Circus," and featured a robust normal on a robust horse. This circus had some impressive poster hanging operation. In another age, I would've been consigned to a circus, a freak in a cage for every village bumpkin to pay a nickel to gawk at. I wondered if my new blood-sucking friends would get as sweet on circus abnormals as they had on me.

I ran the goat head thorn between my fingers and glowered at the circus poster. The route of Operation Velvet Ant glowed in my memory; it trailed right by where the circus would set up. A scheme was forming in my belly, in that deep place where evil breeds.

I plugged some silver into the machine and dialed Tony.

"*Digame*," he said. Spanish. I tried not to let it throw me off.

"We need to meet. I hit the jackpot."

"What kind of prize money are we talking?"

"The whole pot. I got exactly what you asked me to."

"That was fast." His voice tightened. "Too fast."

"I'm in up to my neck," I said. "John White has a special obsession for owning my life."

"You didn't meet him, did you?"

"I'm done gossiping on the phone. Where and when."

"1421 Bridge Street. It's a doctor's office. No bugs. Two hours." The phone went dead.

I swaddled the goat head in my wallet and went back into the gas station.

The girl turned from restocking candy bars. "You're back."

I pointed to a rack of prepaid phones. "Those work right away?"

"You give me nineteen ninety-five plus tax and you're good to go."

I paid her. She handed me the phone. I ripped it open right on the counter and pushed the power button. She showed me how to call a number and enter an activation code. She tossed my garbage in a bin and made sure I remembered my receipt on my way out. I wanted to high-five her. I had a plan.

I called the zoo and got through to Abbey.

"I want to get further into your personal debt," I said.

"Interest on my debt compounds daily. What do you need?"

"Something shady."

"Does it have to do with orange dust?"

"Assuredly," I said.

"Will it get me another meeting with that bat-devil?"

"It's related."

"I can't stop thinking about him. I want to be his best friend."

"Do this thing for me."

"Give me the details."

"I need you to follow a guy. Covertly. Tell me where he goes. I'll trail you by a few blocks. This is part of unraveling the web I'm tangled up in."

She let the line sit in silence for a few seconds. The birds chirped. The squirrels scrabbled and squeaked at each other. A new world sat lurking behind it all, ready to burst forth and obliterate the reality that we humans had become so comfortable with.

"I've never followed anyone. You want me to do this now?" she asked.

"I'll need you to meet me in about two hours," I said.

"I'll be there in an hour and forty-five."

I took it easy on the drive back to the city, following the route along the western foot of the mountains and then Alameda all the way to the river and across. I drove south on Coors Boulevard, past the interstate and into the winding old neighborhoods straddling the river where I'd grown up. The streets huddled with crumbling houses shouldering into each other for space.

Entire blocks of dirt lots lay overgrown with desert thorns and spawning the frames of rusted-out cars. I took the back streets to subject myself to poverty and hopelessness. I let the dilapidated neighborhoods tell me the story I wanted to hear of a world full of tragedy, waste, and despair.

The doctor's office told part of that story. It sat a quarter mile east of the river, couched between a bail bondsman's office and a check-cashing place, behind a McDonald's where the great white clown sat laughing over his piles of cash. I walked into the doctor's lobby and a dozen senior citizens looked at me like I was the angel of death come to herd them across the barrier between worlds. Most of them dangled tarnished crucifixes around their wrinkled brown necks, and a few of the men wore the *vaquero* hats from older, simpler times. I loomed over the plump receptionist in pink scrubs and a nametag that read Gabriela. She scurried around the counter and ushered me into a room with a stool on wheels, an examination bed, and jars of tongue depressors, cotton balls, and gauze. I sat on the bed. The paper crinkled under me. I tried not to think of all the visits I'd made to similar poor people doctors during my childhood. I tried not to remember the way my father would sit and stare at the floor as the doctor recorded my height, drew my blood, held his tape measure up to my lengthening bones. Instead, I focused on the poster of the cute white kitten and the adorable brown puppy dog getting along so well despite their racial differences.

I was on the verge of tearing the poster down and crushing it into a cosmic singularity between my palms when Tony opened the door and slipped silently into the room. He wore his usual gumshoe get up, but his pants held some creases and his shirt was damp and rumpled.

"You look like hell," I said.

"I haven't slept since Birdmageddon."

"Being a geriatrician and private dick must take it out of a guy."

"This is the practice of an ally." He fell atop the rolling stool with the posture of a stunted noodle and drooped his head. "We hold meetings here." He pointed to the ceiling and walls. "Nobody bugs a doctor's office." He laced his fingers together with his elbows on his knees and tilted his head up at me. "Now spill."

I'd been calculating how much to tell him, and in the end decided to open the floodgates. I told him about the wheels of pain, the torture chairs, the white-supremacist training the chupacabras were undergoing. I saved Operation Velvet Ant for last. When I was done, Tony looked like he'd been through a harrowing ordeal. I felt bad for him, but I tried not to let it cloud my judgment.

"This is—I don't have words. God help us."

"God's keeping out of this one. It's up to us humans."

He took his fedora off and held it in his hands. His hair was limp and tired. "Just to make sure I'm getting this: they're going to unleash their whole army of racist chupacabras on the southern border."

"They're like heat-seeking missiles, only they're alive and they want to suck your blood. I've seen them in action."

He ran his fingers through a few handfuls of hair and sweat before putting his hat back on. "I've gotta make some calls."

"This border crossing blitz, it's a real thing?"

Tony hesitated.

"What else do I have to do? You can trust me."

He shrugged. "I guess I can. It *was* a real thing. Looks like we better call it off unless we want the desert to turn into a horror movie."

"Don't call it off," I said.

"*Por dios*, why wouldn't we?"

"I have a plan."

"No plan can change this equation. The odds are stacked against us. The only thing we had on our side was surprise."

"That's exactly right," I said. "And you still have it. They don't know that you know about Operation Velvet Ant. I have a way to blow this whole thing up, but good."

"It can't hurt to hear you out, I suppose," he muttered.

"They're sending everything south in a huge convoy. I say, we ambush it."

"We're not a militia," Tony said. "They'd massacre us. Plus, most of the Good Friends are peace types."

"You don't ambush them with weapons." I pulled the thorn from my wallet and held it up between my fingers. "You attack them with this."

"A goat head."

"Make a bunch of these only ten times as big and forged in iron. I'll send you a signal when the convoy's ready to leave. You dump these in the road right in front of it, and you'll cripple the whole thing. Do it when they're moving fast, and you'll pile their parade into a junk heap. By the time they recover, the Good Friends should be able to get all the migrants safely into the hiding."

"That's a hell of a messy solution," he said. "In a pile up, some of those monsters will break loose."

"It'll get everything out in the open."

"You want to use a disaster to avert a disaster."

"You can have one big, concentrated disaster that takes these chupacabras from behind closed doors and shows them to the world, or you can continue to have a series of small disasters. And they'll only get worse."

"I'm beginning to see things your way."

I handed him a sketch I'd made of the route Velvet Ant's caravan would take through Albuquerque. I drew an X on I-25 in the southern fringes of the city. "That's the spot. Need me to draw up schematics for your metal workers?"

He waved his hand, still studying the caravan route. "No need. I get the idea." He straightened up and stuck out his hand. "We'll get started right away. I'll pass your plan on to my people; I'm guessing they'll go for it once they've heard about everything you've seen. I gotta say: you've surpassed my expectations."

I shook his hand as if we'd made a pact. It was another small lie.

I waited in my truck until he'd left the parking lot. He made a left turn and drove down Bridge Street. Abbey's little Volkswagen beetle pulled out behind him. I waited for them to vanish before I followed. I held the cell phone in one hand and steered with the other. The device was minuscule. When landlines ceased to exist, I'd be stuck in a world of instruments too tiny for my fingers to operate. Every step of progress moved the world further away from my touch.

The phone lit up after a block or two east.

"Take I-25 south," Abbey said once I'd answered.

"Gotcha," I said.

She hung up.

Once on I-25, I drove past the Gibson exit and the special ramps they'd made to connect the Albuquerque Sunport—the cute name someone had come up with to get tourists to swoon over our airport.

The phone rang again.

"Get off at Rio Bravo," she said.

I pulled off and found Abbey's car parked on the shoulder before the stoplight. I drove up behind her and got out. A driver saw me and got so distracted he had to slam on his brakes to keep from running the red light. Rubber screamed in agony.

"You lost him," I said.

She smiled. "You don't know it, but we're still following him."

I looked around. All I saw was New Mexican dirt, asphalt, and a few hayseeds with drooping jaws. "Did you put a tracking device on his car?"

She grinned bigger. "Better. I know where he's going."

"Educate me," I said.

"I looked over his car in the parking lot while you two were inside. His tire treads had feathers in them. A few loose ones were stuck up in his undercarriage."

"Great," I said. "More birds."

"These feathers were unusual." She held up a tuft of white and gray fluff. I inspected it and got nowhere. "Ostrich feathers."

"Where do you drive to get ostrich feathers in your tires?"

She held up a palm-sized machine that looked like a cross between a computer and a cell phone. "I ran it through my smart phone. There are five ostrich ranches in the state of New Mexico. Four are pretty far away. One is about twenty miles south of Albuquerque." She pushed the screen of her computer-phone up toward my face. It showed me a route highlighted in pink that led from Albuquerque to a patch of desert east of the river. "All you have to do is follow this map. Want to borrow it?"

I logged the thing into my knowledge of the cities, rivers, valleys, and mountains. "Got it."

"Are you going there now?"

"Yep," I said. "Alone."

"I didn't ask to go with you." Her face was a brick. I'd never seen it like that before.

"You're done with this. I'm glad—and jealous."

She touched me on the arm. "Be careful, friend."

I left my truck in the weeds. Barbed wire stretched between rough wooden posts spaced regularly as far as the eye could see, fencing in acres upon acres of wiry grasses, cacti, low trees, and tough shrub. I stepped over it and crept through the jagged desert terrain. Between watching for rattlesnakes and steering around prickly pear, I kept my eyes peeled for livestock. Finally, a herd appeared a few hundred feet to my left, seven feet tall and erect on two feet, marching, their knees high in the air. They snaked their long necks to nip at the soil and then sent them skyward to survey the horizon. Their bodies were puffs of black and dark brown with white tail feathers. It was an ostrich ranch, alright. They'd sprung up in New Mexico and West Texas to feed the baby boomers, who lusted for lean meat.

Eventually, I came upon the ranch house. I moved closer and crouched behind a squat cypress. The house was appropriately sprawling, with decks that spanned the entire west and south walls. Pens and barns stood to the south within a perimeter of corrals, some empty, others housing the birds with their puzzled faces and jerking necks. Crazy Patty rode a monstrous horse by the side of the road. She wore a Stetson weathered by sun and dust and wind, cowboy boots with steel-barbed stirrups, leather chaps shiny from wear, and a white button up shirt. Her wheat hair hung in coarse spirals around her shoulders and she squinted through crow's feet as hard and resolute as any gunslinger. She and Tony in his gumshoe suit and fedora looked like movie extras who'd ended up on the wrong set together.

I couldn't hear what they were saying. I had no lip reading skills. But Tony passed over the map I'd given him, and I could only assume he was relating my plan. Tony's mouth moved and his hands flapped around. The woman held the map and said nothing. Her face looked carved from bare rock.

A pickup appeared on a road that wound around the back of the ranch house. It jerked to a halt near Tony and the woman. A crew of half a dozen brown-skinned guys in vaquero hats and work boots leapt down from the bed, and another disembarked from driver's seat. A little white guy in a baseball cap and knock-off aviators emerged from the passenger's side door. It took me a minute to recognize that the clean-shaven face which had worn a mustache for twenty years belonged to Spartacus Rex, my best friend. The skin across his upper lip was pale and soft. He looked twice as handsome without it. He also looked ten years older.

The sun set behind me. A front of clouds eased in from the east. They'd block the stars and make it a good night for sneaking around. I backpedaled into the brush and leaned against the trunk of an elm that bore the black jag of a lightning strike. A tree was like a person. Its wounds never fully healed.

After dark, I made my way around the ranch house. An orchestra of crickets fell away under my feet and rose again behind me. I snapped twigs and crunched sand despite my best efforts to be silent. The earth dropped in a gentle slope to a bunkhouse that sat partially hidden in a grove of cottonwoods. I moved among them like a rogue trunk emancipated from roots and boughs. An outhouse stood a dozen paces down slope from the bunkhouse. I stood in the night shadows, prepared to ambush a man I'd once called brother. If I'd had a six-gun in each fist, we would have been reenacting the quintessential New Mexican bromance.

A few brown men emerged from the bunkhouse and made their delicate journeys to and from the outhouse. Rex came out after all the lights had vanished from the bunkhouse windows. Charcoal clouds hung across the sky from east to west, the moon a white blur behind their shroud.

Once he closed the outhouse door, I took long careful strides across the ground. He cleared his throat. His belt jangled and urine dribbled into the septic mush half a dozen feet below the earth. I lurked outside the door and listened to him zip up his fly.

He opened the door and almost fell backward into the toilet.

"Jesus man," he hissed. It was weird seeing him speak through lips instead of a mustache. "Crazy Patty'll shoot you if she sees you out here."

"Nobody'll know I'm here unless you keep yelling about it."

He looked over his shoulder and pushed me back toward the cottonwood grove. We found an obscure pocket of shadow to whisper in. "How did you find me?"

"By accident. My hobby is ostrich poaching."

"Get serious," he said.

"Is this your new gig? Spying on the enemy? Or are you just a simple cowhand now?"

He slipped his hands into his pockets. A little smile messed with the edges of his mouth. "I got a good thing out here, buddy. Maybe it's the answer to all life's woes."

"I thought you were a Minuteman hero, ready with a rifle and a four-by-four to defend Mother America."

"I'm done with that. This place—you gotta keep your mouth shut."

"I don't know why everyone thinks I walk around talking to people."

"Swear," he said. "Hold up your hand and swear."

I left my hand where it was. "I'm going to tell you something you already know: this ranch is part of a secret organization."

He didn't blink. "Why do you think I'm here?"

I thought back to the day I first met Cerberus the leech-dog and recalled Rex's words as we'd driven away: *Those Mexicans. They're just like me.*

"You've switched allegiances."

"How could I be a decent person and stick with the Minutemen after seeing those people get chased down by that fucking monster? Damn right I changed sides."

"So, what, you're a double agent now? You pretend to work for Typhon Industries, but really help their enemy?"

"I could disappear from Typhon Industries, and no one would give a damn. They care about you."

I was tired of being cared about.

Some of the tension drained from Rex's face. His lines went slack, and he looked sad instead of angry. "That was the old me—always out to get somebody else and scramble a few bucks for myself. This place—we help people. This is a station in an underground railroad. We get people where they need to be. We scoop people up from the desert and dribble water back into them. We find them a shitty job where they can scrape some change into a pile and ship it back to their grandmothers. It's a terrible world. We help people survive in it."

"Giving yourself a shave doesn't make you a new person. You're Rex. I'm Stick. People who pretend they can choose their identities are living in Candy Land."

"I'm tired of thinking about who I am. I've been thinking about myself for near forty years, and I've had a head full of bad thoughts for forty years. Maybe it's not about who I am. Maybe if I stop caring about Spartacus Rex, he'll become a decent guy to live with."

Wind rustled the limbs of the trees. Gray moonlight shifted across Rex's weathered face. Night had settled fully around us. I imagined a world where the sun never came up again, where the landscape grew dark and the silent chill winds chased the heat of day away for good, until the desert sat silent and dead like the surface of the moon. I wondered how long it would take for all life to fade to gray beneath the cold stars. I wondered if anything could adapt to such a planet, if life would go on with no prospects for warmth ever returning.

"What happened to our lives?" I asked.

"Nothing. That's the problem. We started out on the bottom and we've stuck it out down here, duking out an existence for who knows what goddamned reason. I'm a tin can. I've been kicked back and forth along the same street for forty years. I can't figure anything will ever get better."

"Neither of us are optimists," I said, "but I thought at least we'd find a comfortable place to wait out our lives."

Rex spoke softly. "Our lives are shot to hell. But maybe we can help someone else. If that's all the hope I can get, so be it. For the first time since I joined the army, my life's actually looking up. Helping others. It feels good. I should have tried it earlier." He laughed an easy, natural chuckle. It was the first time I'd ever heard Rex laugh at himself. He looked like a different man.

"I guess I should congratulate you."

"You'll keep your mouth shut about this."

"I don't even open my mouth for the dentist."

"Don't mess this up for me, old pal. It's my last chance to die content."

"There's nothing as content as a corpse."

He gave me a tight smile. "You say some dark shit, brother."

"It's a dark world."

"Promise me, nothing about seeing me to the Captain or any of his psycho cronies."

"I promise," I said, knowing that human promises are just bad breath.

CHAPTER TWENTY - SIX

got home to my answering machine flashing its light at me. I pressed the button and braced myself. The Captain's voice punched its way into my home.

"Got a present for you. You can go see your pops tomorrow. Call it a little reward for standing around doing nothing. If I had it my way, we'd send the man to a lower level of hell for every word that comes out of your mouth crosswise. But the boss has a soft spot for you. So, go get an eyeful of the geezer before we put him in an iron box and dump him in the Rio Grande."

I sat at the bar and felt mean for a little while. After about an hour or so, the hairy mound of my pet spider twitched inside his terrarium. I went out into the moonlight and tickled a couple small orb spiders into a drinking glass. Ounce-for-ounce, spiders were the most protein-rich beings on the planet. I dug into the dark soil of my garden, laced with worms as thin as angel hair pasta and the roots of shrubs, little weeds, and snake-thick tree roots. I unearthed a millipede and a couple of stubby desert sand cockroaches. I put them all in the drinking glass, gave it a shake to stun them, and—voilà—I had a salad fit for a tarantula. I dumped it on my living room floor, scooped Ralph up, and set him a few feet away.

I felt better.

The next morning after breakfast, I drove back to Typhon Industries. It was all I did anymore. Get manipulated by a stranger. Eat a meal. Drive somewhere I didn't want to be to talk to someone I didn't like about something I didn't care about. Drive home. Eat another meal. Have a couple of drinks with someone who showed up at my house uninvited. Drive somewhere else. Every now and then, I got to sleep a few hours or spend some time in chains. It wasn't the American Dream I'd been promised.

A cloud front moved in from the West. It wasn't fooling anyone. It was too fluffy and high to do anything for anybody. It'd stay up there, promising rain to any fool naïve enough to listen. Even after all these years of desert life, you'd overhear Albuquerque residents pinning their hopes on a cloud. Rain, they'd say. It's coming. It'll stomp the dust into the ground, turn my grass green, and give my rose bushes some relief. None of us with any sense bought into it. Those clouds were a pie in the sky.

Elysium, a bulky structure surrounded on all four sides by three stories of razor wire, squatted between the vaulted roof of Hades and circular Delphi. The only way in or out of Elysium was through a guardhouse separated from the main structure by a broad cement pathway bordered by more razor wire and a tall steel gate in the middle. Guards in a watchtower on the perimeter operated the gate remotely. To get in, I had to pass through a metal detector. I had to remove my shoes, belt, and pocket change. The guards took a copy of my ID. They told me I was lucky I hadn't worn jeans because all inmates wore them. It was the prison uniform. Before I was allowed onto the cement alley that led from the guardhouse to the prison, a guard stamped an invisible symbol on the back of my hand.

"What is this, appearing ink?" I asked, thinking back to Georgia Tameed Schultz and her unique method of firing people.

"Infrared," he said. "Only see it with a black light."

"You afraid someone's going to steal my pants and impersonate me?"

"Procedure is procedure," he said.

I could relate to that. It was comforting to know that no matter what happened or who walked in the door, you dealt with them in absolutely the same way. That was how I'd handled my days before the cursed birds rained from the sky and ruined everything in my life.

An escort walked me through the double set of doors that led from the entrance building onto the cement walkway, stretching all the way to the main prison facility, a distance that had looked small from outside. But walking down it, I felt tiny on that vast gray expanse. The razor wire fence towered over me on all sides. For a moment, my consciousness slipped, and I became a prisoner freshly interred. I felt tiny in the clench of that fortress of steel and cement. I slipped back into my identity quickly, but the vision left me sweating and my heart banging its fist against my ribcage.

We passed through more steel doors operated by someone unseen. My escort led me to a long room partitioned into alcoves along one side. Each alcove contained a stool, a counter where you could lean your elbows, and a phone receiver. Across the counter was a window crisscrossed with security wire. The window revealed a mirror world of identical stools, counters, and phones, but in a fundamentally different dimension of existence. A few people occupied the stools on either side of the glass. When I walked in, they all stopped their conversations and held their phone receivers beside their stupid, slack faces. They stared at me, and for a moment everyone in both dimensions of society banded together to treat me with ugliness, and I'm sure prisoner, visitor, and guard alike felt the better for it.

I packed myself into the alcove my escort led me to and managed to sit on the stool, my knees bent up around my shoulders. I plucked a receiver the size of my thumb from the wall and waited. The visitors around me got back to their conversations, most of them in Spanish and a few in what I guessed were tongues native to Mexico or Central America.

My father stepped into the frame of the window in front of me. He'd dressed neatly in a blue button down shirt and baggy jeans. His forehead shined with oil, and his eyes sunk into his face like caverns. He'd grown a black and gray beard, heavy at the chin and spare on his gaunt cheeks and upper lip. His hair was white, as it had been for years, but I'd never really noticed before. He looked like he'd been in prison for a couple of decades. Beside him stood another man in his middle fifties, his face clean-shaven, his hair curly and black. He had the solid body of a man who worked. He pulled up a second stool and the two men sat beside each other in the alcove. The other man picked up the receiver and held it to his ear.

"I am Manuel," the telephone said in time with the man's lips moving on the other side of the glass.

"Dad," I said at my father's face. I touched the window with my fingertips. The glass was a slab of ice. It was as thick as tank armor. "Are you okay?"

"He's okay," Manuel said. "He's doing fine."

I fixed my eyes on Manuel. "Put my father on the goddamned phone."

Manuel turned to my father and said some words in Spanish. My father said words back. Every single one of them was foreign to me. "Your dad says you look tired."

"If you don't hand him the phone right now, I'll punch a hole in this glass and give it to him myself."

"Calm yourself," Manuel said. "I'm a friend."

"I have no friends. I have a father. I want to talk to him."

"He can't speak to you," Manuel said.

"Why the hell not? Is it against regulations or something?"

"He's lost his English," Manuel said.

I opened my mouth and told him how stupid that sounded. But as I said it, I watched my father. He wore the expression of a lost person. His eyes flicked across my mouth as I spoke, and then he turned to Manuel with a pained look in the corners of his eyes. Manuel said some Spanish words to him. My father turned his face back to me and looked incredibly sad. He put his hand on the glass where my fingers had been and trailed some sentences out into the hazy ambient noise beyond the mouthpiece of the phone in the other dimension behind the glass.

"It happened when the police came for him." Manuel had an accent, but spoke English well. "They broke in the front door of his home. They pointed their guns at him. He was afraid. He had never been so afraid before. And when they yelled at him, he couldn't understand the words. He tried to reason with them, but he heard only the old language in his head. They brought him here. His English has not come back."

I sat there with the tiny receiver pressed against my cheek and my body cramped into a child-sized chair. My father's old palm, lined with the years of toil he'd spent cleaning the schools of little American kids—making sure their light bulbs worked and their chalkboards were clean and their toilets flushed—that palm pressed against the barrier between us. The face that he'd shaved twice a day since before I was born bristled with hair I'd never seen and formed words that I'd never comprehend.

I put my hand against his. It was cliché, but it was all I could do. "I'm getting you out."

My father spoke to Manuel through the side of his mouth, his eyes still on my face.

"You can't," said Manuel.

"Things are in motion," I said. "Tell him. I'm getting you out."

Manuel shook his head. "Your father's going back to Mexico. Lawyers have tried to see him. He's turned them away. He wants to leave. He has money saved. It will go a long way in Mexico. He'll be happy. He's returning to his home village."

I pointed a finger at Manuel. "Don't talk. Translate."

"I'm just telling you what I know about your father," Manuel said.

My fist tensed up, and I thought about belting the glass in front of his face to show him how I felt about what he knew. "Translate." My teeth gritted so tight they squeaked. "Don't say another word unless it comes from his mouth."

Manuel got my drift. Sweat broke out across his upper lip.

"I'm getting him out. Tell him."

Manuel translated as my father talked. It was a tumble of rolled r's and *las* and long *o*'s. He'd never spoken so easily or naturally to me in his life.

"I'm done with America," Manuel translated. "I have retirement they say I can keep. I have savings they say I can keep. I'm returning to Tula, my hometown in Mexico. I will visit the graves of my parents. I will tell my sisters that I'm still alive. I will be able to help the family with the money I've made here, and maybe they will forgive me for disappearing for so long. I should never have left my home. People belong where they're born."

My father's eyes clouded as he spoke. He touched the glass again with his fingertips as he spoke more Spanish.

"You should come with me, son," Manuel said. "Hidalgo looks much like New Mexico. Mountains, cacti, rivers. There are churches unlike any in America. And monuments left by our ancient ancestors." Manuel turned to face me. "He says some names of plants and trees that I don't know in English. He says the names of the mountains and the rivers. He talks about *avenidas* lined with trees and *plazas* where people gather in the evening to dance. He talks about the nieces and nephews he might have. He talks too fast about it all."

I waited for him to run down. My father hadn't spoken so many words in a row since I'd ruined his life by being born. This might have been the only time I'd ever seen him get excited about something. He had hope. It looked good on him. Behind the bags beneath his eyes, the beard, and the sallow skin from too much time indoors, he harbored that special glow that only people who face a bright future exude—or at least a future that they've duped themselves into believing.

"Sounds like his mind's made up," I said. I was talking to Manuel. The man beside him was barely recognizable as my father.

"*Sí*," Manuel said. "It's for the best, too. He's going back whether he wants to or not. The sooner the better."

I sat trying to figure out how to say goodbye to my father. I couldn't do it.

"Don't worry," Manuel said. "You'll come see him again. He'll be here for a few months at least. The process—mountains move faster."

"Alright," I said. I shifted my gaze to my father. "Bye dad. Anything I can do—or for you, Manuel—let me know."

Manuel translated. He said something extra at the end. Both men laughed. "Thanks." Manuel spread his hands and shrugged. "We're here. Nothing much to do. We wait. We go back to Mexico. That's it."

I rose from my chair and towered over the partitions between alcoves. Members of both the free and the enslaved worlds gave me a good stare. Apparently, the first time wasn't enough. I drank in the small man below that was once my father. He had a new friend. They chuckled and joked together in a language I'd never understand. He had a hometown I'd never seen and a family he missed. I wasn't part of that family. I'd always thought I didn't have a family—and I hadn't been wrong.

I drove home. My throat was a dam that wanted to let water, but I had no one left in my life to talk to. In my old life, I would have shared a six-pack with Melodía. I tried to summon the smell of her hair. I tried to hear her voice thick with sarcasm and the slight slur of her stretched left lip. I tried to picture the latticework of arteries in her left eye. It all flitted just outside the peripheries of my memory. All I felt was my heart beat a little more desperately. My blood was sluggish and thick. I had to pull over and take some deep breaths. I gripped the steering wheel and felt gravity reversing itself inside my guts. I thought I might rise up and float off into the abyss of deep space. Instead, I opened my door and barfed on the blacktop. Afterwards, I felt solid enough to make it home.

Tony was waiting in my foyer. "I have something for you."

"Is it a special hat?" I sighed. "Are we going to start dressing like twins?"

Tony lifted his hat from his head. He fingered the hatband and looked mildly hurt.

"If it's a visit to my dad, don't bother. I've seen what's left of him."

"Nope." Tony handed me a CD with a label that read *Spanish for Beginners.* Rubber-banded to it was a slip of paper with the name of a private hospital and a room number. "You're welcome." He slipped up the stairs.

The address led me to a hospital in the rich part of town on Tramway Boulevard, where small mansions tucked themselves into the crooks of the foothills and red speedsters purred alongside lumbering Humvees. The Sandía Mountains raced for the sky overhead; they didn't quite make it all the way, but you had to give them credit for trying. To the north, the Sandía tram station, for which the street tracing the foot of the mountain range was named, sent a car up the long drape of cable that stretched all the way to the peak.

During the drive, I popped the CD into my player and listened to the velvet voice of a woman pronouncing the vowels and consonants of my father's language. I couldn't even spit the first half of the alphabet between my clumsy lips. Rolling an r was like tying a cherry stem in a bow. My tongue was a big oaf. I broke every crisp, delicate sound the woman offered me. I pulled into the hospital parking lot with a pile of splintered words in my lap.

The hospital was so high into the foothills that the patients probably didn't even have to worry about cockroaches. The parking lot brimmed full of cars with sunroofs and paint jobs and clean windows and two working headlights. It was real classy. I edged my truck into a space among them and took a walk to the main building. The wind had calmed, and the sun baked the earth with happy springtime beams.

I walked past the front desk without making eye contact with anyone. I thought maybe they wouldn't notice me. I figured I'd just sidle by. It worked, in that no one questioned me. They were too busy cradling their jaws, busted from dropping so fast. I got on the elevator with a gurney presided over by a muscular orderly. A woman lay swaddled inside. Only her wide blue eyes and an oxygen mask protruded from the blankets. We acted out the mummy meets Frankenstein's monster. I dodged a few nurses in the halls of the third floor. The acrid stench of chemical cleaner and medicine hung over an undertone of suffering and disease.

A nurse or two stumbled up to me, but I waved them away and found the room without a catastrophic fuss. The door stood open. I poked my head in and found a woman sitting up in a hospital bed. Her body lay long and willowy beneath the blanket, and slender brown arms lay beside her with hands folded on top of her stomach. Between narrow shoulders, her clavicles stood out above the line of her hospital gown. Auburn highlights shot through her dark brown curly hair. She had wide-set chestnut eyes, high cheekbones, and slender lips. Clean white bandages traced her left jawline. A dark and muscular man with thick hair and a firm jaw sat on the bed next to her. He looked like he made his money modeling hospital scrubs.

The woman bloomed with happiness when she spotted me. "You found me!" Her voice could have belonged to any bubbly person on the face of the earth.

I knew her despite the symmetrical face and the voice that spoke without a slur. The pitch rung sonorous and clear, the vowels hitting all the right notes, the consonants breaking crisp between her lips. Nothing was right about her. I said her name, and didn't believe it even when her face lit up. A beautiful, happy Melodía spoke through a new face.

"Come in!" She flapped the hand not attached to an IV. The guy turned his head and zapped me with some twinkling eye beams. He had the facial structure of a Greek statue. "I can't believe you're here!" Melodía said.

I entered. "You—" She looked like a typical beautiful woman whose face happened to be swaddled in a few bandages. I didn't know what to do with this new woman wearing half the face of my old friend. I opened my mouth to talk and left it like that for a while. I finally got out a few words. "You're different." I tried to feel happy about it.

She beamed. "I look in the mirror, and I see the person I've always known I was."

"You look great." I'd heard people on TV say such words to each other. If you memorized enough of TV, you didn't ever have to say what you meant.

"Thank you," she cooed. "I feel so good. It's so good to hear you say that."

"She's ravishing, isn't she?" The man said. He had a voice like oiled leather. His forearms were made of grade A beef, and the left one rested next to Melodía's knee.

Melodía blushed. "This is my physical therapist, Bruce."

I didn't like Bruce. His five-o'clock shadow and straight white teeth made me angry.

"Bruce." She touched the hand connected to the forearm. "This is John Stick, my best friend."

"Great to meet you," he said, barely looking at me. He got up. He had excellent posture. He'd obviously never had to slouch around under the burden of a lifetime of self-doubt and evil eyes. He touched Melodía on the shoulder. "I'll leave you two alone." His cologne hung in the air after he left. It made me want to wash out my nostrils with roach spray.

"So," I said, "you've experienced a miracle."

Melodía spoke. I could barely follow the words. It was like knowing someone your whole life and then meeting their identical twin. She was familiar but utterly strange. "A week ago. It was a complicated procedure. Bruce has been monitoring the muscles in my face to make sure they're functioning properly. He's a miracle worker. I'll have some small scars around my jawline. Besides that, I'll be normal!"

"Your surgeon's the miracle worker," I said.

"My surgeon!" She spun sentences out of her face with all the enthusiasm of a teenage cheerleader who'd learned nothing about the miseries of life. "Dr. Hudson. He's English. They flew him in from the Mayo Clinic."

I already knew 'them.' The orange dust on her shoes had told me everything I needed to know. John White had systemically dismantled my life with the intention of replacing it with blood sucking Greek monsters. He'd soon send my father back to his happy homeland, and now he'd cured my best friend. If he made enough of the people close to me happy, I'd have no one left. I'd been too miserable too long to change. The world was a compost bin. Life lived and died, new life sprouted from the dead, and each living being's rotten core stunk more than the last.

I vomited up a smile from my stinking rotten guts. It made it through my teeth, but barely. "Are you going to tell me how this miracle occurred? I thought your tumors were inoperable."

"Apparently, a lot has happened over the past two decades." She looked exactly like a normal—no, she looked better. She was prettier than a normal. "Plastic surgery has made progress."

"Imagine that. Progress."

"Yeah." A little of the bitter, sardonic woman I knew sliced through. "I always thought progress was for normals."

I wanted to tell her that she wasn't allowed to use that word anymore. It was reserved for those us of still held in the thrall of abnormality. Instead, I apologized for not bringing her flowers.

"Don't worry. My benefactor sends me flowers every morning. I'm so lucky."

"Yes. You are lucky." I added some nods to convince everybody that I meant it. Half of me did. The other half pitied her for feeling so lucky with what every other human was born with. There's nothing more pathetic than a dog that gives you doe eyes simply for not kicking it.

She raised her eyebrows. "Aren't you going to ask me who my benefactor is?"

"I don't want to pry," I lied.

"His name is John White."

My guts rotted a little more.

"He's the president of Typhon Industries, and he set up the surgery in exchange for some information sharing." Her face sobered a touch. "He's studying the birds, Stick. I was at a dead end. I couldn't figure it out. I gave Typhon Industries my data and they gave me this." She framed her face in her hands as if she were showing off a particularly resplendent piece of jewelry.

"Sounds like a great deal," I said.

Her smile went stale. "You don't look happy for me."

"I'm happy for you," I murmured. "I'm also exhausted."

"Tell me about it. Long hours at the zoo?"

I could have told her everything. But we had nothing in common anymore. I couldn't talk to her about anything that mattered. I could barely look her in the eye. "Yeah, and a little worried about my best friend, who disappeared without telling me."

"That's sweet." She reached toward me with her free arm, as if to tenderly touch her fingertips to my cheek. I stood near the door of the room and impersonated an oak. When I didn't move toward her, she let her hand fall atop the blanket. "I'm sorry I didn't tell you. I didn't tell anyone. I couldn't. It was something I needed to do alone."

"I get it," I said. I knew what it felt like to do things alone.

We chatted a little bit more. She reviewed the nuts and bolts of the procedure with me, the hours of work her team of surgeons had logged in the OR to remove the tumors and restructure the system of arteries, muscles, and underlying tissue. How they'd peeled her face from the jaw line so that the incision would hide in the shadows beneath her jaw. How it had gone flawlessly and after only a week, the swelling was down, blood flowed, feeling was sharp, and the incision site was healing like magic.

"And now"—she smiled in a way I'd never seen before—"I can have a good life."

I said some more words about how happy I was for her, and as soon as I could, ducked back into the hallway, making my escape among the nurses padding back and forth on rubber soles and the moans of dying invalids and the cloying hospital stink. I took a lungful of that stink with me into the parking lot and released it. With that double fistful of breath, I saw a friendship vanish into the bright desert day.

I twisted the key into my truck's ignition. The Spanish-speaking woman poured her velvet voice into the cab. The sounds she made were beautiful. Every feature of every syllable adhered to a perfect form. I'd never make those sounds. I'd never live up to the templates that the normals crammed themselves into. I punched the eject button, rolled down my window, and hurled the gleaming silver disc at the sun.

CHAPTER TWENTY - SEVEN

I **went home and haunted my cave. No one called. No one came by. I**
kept company with my spider, and the rest of society forsook me. I lay on
my long sectional couch, the only piece of furniture that fit me. It was
freakish and modular, a Frankenstein. I lay on it for an absurd span,
unable to sleep. The sun stretched the shadows of the pines across my patio.
They looked like dark doppelgängers of trees, but really, they marked an
absence of light. The shadows morphed as day grew thin. They prickled with
spikes. They grew taller, thinner, and more monstrous until the sun set, and
then they vanished into universal darkness. I lay there as the stars irradiated
the patio with feeble light and as the life of night awoke, skittering amidst the
desiccated bramble of late winter, chirping in the corners of my escape-proof
room. I stayed up all night tracking the movements of the tiny lives of
nocturnal creatures. Even they thought their lives had purpose, and they went
about fulfilling it without question or self-consciousness.

The three humans in my life were like the shadows of the trees. They could
transform. Melodía had vanquished the part of herself that had made her my
kin. She could flit among the normals now without any hint that she'd once
been shunned by them. My father had chosen to give up our life together and
metamorphose into the man he'd once been. He could fold himself back into
the family and language he'd never shared with me. And Rex. He'd found
compassion and joined a movement, where he'd become just another ranch
hand. I lay on my couch laughing about it. I was a tree. I'd always be a tree. No
miracle could transform me. No country or movement would accept me.

When the sun rose, I still lay awake. I decided to stay that way across the span of the day, into the next night, to eventually witness another sunrise without shutting my eyes. It would be the same sun, and I'd be the same man watching it. By the time that second dawn arrived, I vowed never to sleep again. I vowed to sit and watch the sun fly through the air like a celestial yoyo until I was immortal.

I stood during the day after that second dawn. My legs worked by remote control. I hit my head on the doorframe of my bedroom. I switched on my bathroom light and found a man in that cramped cabin. Yellow stained the armpits of his undershirt beneath his stooped shoulders. His limbs, like the long and spare limbs of winter trees, clumped with muscle and bone at the joints. Thick brown hairs stippled his oaken skin. His eyes, like black stones thrown in a sandpit, gleamed from their deep places nestled in the harsh geology of bone. His teeth were big and crooked and his lips sloughed skin like a snake having trouble molting. I let myself look at this monster and hate him. I let myself be honest and thorough about it. I'd hated John Stick for a long time.

I went to the kitchen and removed a can of black paint from beneath the sink. Taking a brush, screwdriver, and stir stick, I returned to the bathroom. After setting the paint can on the toilet and prying the lid off, I dipped the brush in the can and painted the mirror in broad, careful strokes. The paint beaded and ran at first, but I smoothed and thickened it until no light gleamed through. The full-length mirror that had come mounted to the closet door held the paint a little better, as did the faces of the microwave and the oven. I saw faint specters of a giant hanging in the windows overlooking my patio and painted them. It was tough going and I nearly ran out of paint. It lasted just long enough to cover up the same phantom giant in the television screen.

After cleaning the brush with turpentine and placing it on a paper towel on the windowsill to dry, I retrieved the shoebox of photographs from beneath my bed and set it on my bar. Outside, I gathered twigs and pine needles from the litter layer under the skirts of the trees and fluffed them in a small pile in my kitchen sink. A wooden match set them ablaze. Once I'd removed the battery from my smoke detector and activated the extractor fan above my stove, I stood over the fire and added clusters of photos like I was folding hands of cards in a poker game, one after the other. Greasy smoke trailed up like the agonized appendages of a tortured creature. I breathed in the poison fumes of my life. Little Johnny Stick in a rusted red wagon with ragged bangs in his eyes. Little Johnny Stick standing in a dirt yard looking at a gray cat. Stick in his third grade photo as tall as his teacher. Stick cramped behind the wheel of his father's green Datsun in the snow, the trees in the background, spindly, brown, and as knobby as the boy's hands gripping the wheel. Stick's crooked mother holding his fingers in her twisted, broken hands just weeks before she died. Stick's father smoking a cigarette in the yard with thirteen-year-old Stick towering over him. Stick at his high school graduation, the robe sweeping at his knees, looking past the camera at something out of view, a frown on his long, brown face.

I fed the pictures in until they were black husks, like the skin shed by a snake made of despair. The ceiling above the sink rippled with the black stains of memories burned away. The fire slowly died. Through my black windows, I couldn't tell what time of day it was. My apartment had sunken into permanent night, and I'd transformed into a nocturnal monster that would never sleep again.

Someone came for me a few hours after the fifth dawn. I'd spent the past dozen or two hours pacing my carpet. The someone knocked on the door. Without thinking, I opened it. All the blood drained out of Tony's face. I must have looked even worse than I imagined, which meant that my gaze probably stopped just shy of turning him to stone on the spot.

"God man... What happened to you?"

"I've evolved," I said. "I no longer need food or water."

He surveyed me as if I were a shattered vase that he were somehow responsible for piecing back together into a functional whole. It would take a miracle. "We need to get a cup of coffee into you."

"Very sound. I'll get to growing the beans."

He herded me backwards into the apartment with some flapping of his hands and gestured at the barstool. "Sit. Don't move."

I obeyed. I wasn't sure whether this was the real Tony or whether he was a new and more advanced chupacabra, but I determined that it was best to listen to him—or it—until I had more information. What I could tell was that he had colors coming out of his ears. Or maybe my eyes just needed rest.

He gave me a glass of water. I waited until his back was turned before I poured it into one of my shoes. He started some coffee brewing. The water filtered through the shoe and spread across the floor in a dark gray octopus. The sputtering and steaming of the coffee machine made me tear up. My coffee maker sounded like it was in so much pain. I wanted to liberate my coffee machine. I wanted to find a nice marshy bend of the Rio Grande, and set it beneath the shade of some cottonwoods where it could be free to live out its natural life.

"Wow." Tony was looking at my empty glass. "You were thirsty."

I smiled at him. Real big.

He rolled back on his heels. "I don't think I've ever seen you smile. It's quite an experience."

"Thank you," I said. "I'm only now feeling happiness for the first time. It's a very special emotion. No wonder everyone's talking about it."

"You on something?" he asked. "Head-shrink dope?"

"I'm on life. It's what's hot right now."

Tony stuck his pointer finger in my face. "I need to tell you something. I want you to listen and not say anything batty."

I listened.

"Are you listening?"

I nodded and titled my ears toward him. I had the feeling I was about to hear the most important news of my life.

Tony hung his pointer there for a few more moments. Then he slapped me. His hand left a bright streak in the air. I blinked. The whole room flared red and then faded slowly back to the color of newspaper.

I blinked my eyes a few times. "Thanks. I needed that."

"You're welcome," he said.

I felt like he'd jerked all my gears together. "How about that coffee?"

"That's my boy," he said and loaded up a mug with sugar.

"Black."

"Today you're taking it the way I say you are."

I couldn't argue. I sipped the concoction. My body lit up like a Christmas tree.

"You're a good man."

"We're both good men, John Stick. That's all we can ever try to be."

This was the deepest day of my life. "You're right. All we can do is try to be good."

"It's simple."

I nodded a whole bunch. Even after I stopped, the room kept bobbing. "So, now that we know to be good, what's next?"

"We get you a shower. And donuts. And chorizo and eggs." He looked me over. "Then we pray."

"Why don't we hang around together for thirty-six or sixty-four hours first? If you stay up long enough, you can actually feel the planet wobble."

He squinted at me. "How long have you been awake, exactly?"

"I've been exactly awake never until five days ago, when I woke up and decided never to sleep again."

"Is that when you painted your windows black?" he asked.

"That happened while I was away. Atheists did it."

Tony flapped his hands at me. "Go take a shower. I'll drum up some food."

I took my time in the shower. The hot water was like maple syrup straight out of the microwave. It lingered in every pore. I shampooed my hair three times until it felt like human hair again. When I was out, dressed, and had brushed the five days of moss from my teeth, I felt as focused and sharp as an aluminum hunting arrow. After a few donuts, two more cups of coffee, and a plateful of animal protein and grease, I was the fiercest, most acute warrior to ever live in the desert. I slapped Tony on the back a few times on his way out the door, assuring him that I was dandy and that I would have a good nap when he was gone.

"You've got to be ship-shape for the big day. Operation Velvet Ant could happen any time."

"I'm okey-dokey," I said. "Hunky-dory."

"You remember the signal?"

"That's a trick question, you sneaker. There is no signal because you'll be watching. All I have to do is be myself and you'll take care of the rest."

He smiled proudly. "Your plan is in place. We're all set."

Once he'd driven away, I got the gun out my safe. I loaded it. I sat on my couch and made myself comfortable. I put the barrel in my mouth and released the safety catch. My mind was as clear as the turquoise New Mexican sky.

CHAPTER TWENTY - EIGHT

The cold gun barrel tasted like outer space. I could sense an entire lifetime of disappointment in the vast hollowness of the bore. Beyond that emptiness, a bullet crouched in a nest of dynamite, ready to lunge into my mouth and erase me from the universe forever.

I'd been thinking about this moment for a very long time. I'd resolved that I'd have to pull a trigger on myself when I was a teenager. I procrastinated for a while, pulled my death wand out of its safe a few times in my lost twenty-something years, then stored it in an out of the way corner of my mind during my thirties. This was the first time I'd cradled it with my tongue. The dull metal numbed my taste buds. The gun oil I used might even have been killing them slowly, as the world had been slowly gouging away at me.

With the weapon cocked and ready, I felt like pulling the trigger would be pretty easy. I'd been laboring mentally with this moment for twenty years, and completed all the heavy lifting. I was ready to go. I probably wouldn't even notice. I'd squeeze the trigger and then vanish. Some unlucky interloper would find my body with an extra hole near the top and the brains on the outside. Somebody would burn the mess up in an oven, and within a week or a month, no one would care except Ralph, who'd be crouching in a corner, trying to figure out exactly where his next meal would come from.

My one reason to live: a spider. He was a stalwart friend, but hardly an anchor with enough weight to hold me on the surface of a planet where I'd never belonged.

I didn't rush it. I wanted to take my time. I took the gun out of my mouth and examined the ring of moisture around the end of the barrel left by my lips. The trigger, handle, and hammer would hold oil imprints of my fingers. Those swirls of pattern in calloused skin had been forged over years of touching objects in my world. No other person left the same ones. I had a vision in my head of all of the reptiles, amphibians, and invertebrates in my zoo, patterned with my fingerprints. I'd touched them all. They all wore my unique signature on their bodies, and I couldn't even go peer at them through a pane of glass and feel depressed that we weren't together anymore. We left our prints on everything we touched. They washed off easily, and then we vanished.

I checked the chamber. Six rounds. Shiny and new. I snapped it shut. I put the barrel between my teeth again and angled it at about forty-five degrees so that the bullet would hit the part of my brain that counted. Maybe I'd get lucky and the bullet would knock the chunk out that stored memories of other people, leaving everything else intact. I'd pull the trigger, black out, and wake up with no memory of another living person. I'd experience a good couple hours of happiness until I set foot outside my house again and saw another human being. Then I'd have to go through forty more years of betrayal and humiliation before I shot another bullet into my memory.

I settled both hands around the grip, closed my eyes, and let out a deep breath.

A car door slammed. Feet tumbled down my stairs. The screen door whammed open and Dr. Charon exploded into my apartment. He wore his white lab coat, half glasses, jeans, and a white button up shirt. He looked as average as usual, except for his breath, which heaved exceptionally in his chest.

"*Scire mori sors prima viris, sed proxima cogi!*" he gasped.

I took the barrel out of my mouth. "Speak English. And be quick about it."

"You've obviously," he said, panting, "learned the first happiness: to know how to die. It's equally obvious that you haven't learned the second: to be forced to die. Only the impetuous are eager to cross the river Styx and forget all they know."

"That's exactly what I'm after," I said.

Charon took a step toward me and held out his hand. "Let me at least clean it for you. That instrument is probably covered with the blood of innocents."

"It's a virgin."

"Give it here. I've been looking for something to point at the animal rights nut jobs as I leave the parking lot."

"You can have it when I'm done with it. This won't take me a minute."

"Don't waste bullets. Imagine all the resources that go into a bullet. Consider the planet. And all that garbage."

"Quit trying to stall me." I put the barrel in my mouth, but took it back out. "How the hell did you know to come over here, anyway?" I put the barrel back in.

Charon pointed to a corner of the living room. At first, I didn't see anything. Then, after I squinted a bit, I spied a tiny tube half the diameter of a pencil protruding from a ceiling tile.

"Eye in the sky," Charon said.

I spat the barrel out. "I should have guessed."

"Yep," Charon said. "You should have."

"Lemme get this straight," I said. "You were enjoying a normal day at Typhon Industries, torturing women and breeding demon horseflies. You were sitting there, watching me sit here. You noticed that I was about to blow my head off, and you jumped in your car and sped across the city to save me."

"Nope. I got a call. I was at the Chucky Cheese watching the dancing animatronic mouse and eating a pepperoni pizza. My phone lit up. John White gave me the lowdown. I sped a few blocks. I nearly broke a hip rolling down your stairs."

"You're kidding."

"Only about Chucky Cheese. Let's just say I was in the neighborhood."

"John White is watching me? Doesn't he have better, more profitable things to do with his time?"

"You are the center of John White's attention. He watches you more than you might imagine. Besides, he's not much of a sleeper, so he has a lot of time to get things done."

"Is he watching now?" I asked.

Charon pointed a finger at the camera. "He's right there. He wants to make sure I do my job and save your life."

"My life is not something anyone can save," I said. "I'm a mortal."

Charon shook his head. "Most of us are mortal. But not you, Mr. Stick. You're a titan. You don't understand—which is no surprise. You've been living in a morass of mediocrity. You're up to your neck in the mud of human normalcy. You are extraordinary. You were destined for great things. What would you say if I told you that this entire sequence of events has been John White's doing?"

"I'd ask why he assassinated Esposita."

"Forget the turtle. I've heard all about her. This is bigger than a turtle."

Nothing humans did was ever bigger than a turtle. That we thought so was what made us so goddamned evil. The gun was getting heavy. I set it on my thigh, the hammer still cocked.

"John White has done everything for *you*, Mr. Stick," Charon said. "He's had his eye on you for a very long time. There is no person he cares about more."

"That's sweet," I said. "How come he didn't remember my birthday?"

"We toasted to it. You'll have to trust me."

"What does he want with me?" I asked.

"It's simple. John White wants to see you thrive."

"He's not doing a good job so far. My life barely exists. It's a fourth dimensional inch from vanishing altogether."

"Stretch that inch. Make it a foot. That's all John White asks. He needs you for Operation Velvet Ant. Everything will become clear after that. This whole city believes they know John White's motives. They think he's after money, justice, fame. They think he's motivated by racial prejudice or greed or philanthropic goodwill or ambition. Everyone is wrong. They're wrong because no one thinks on the scale John White does. He's doing something larger than a normal human imagination can match."

"Sounds okay, but can he resurrect my turtle?"

Charon's face twitched and a little corner of annoyance flashed. "Stay with us for one more day. If at the end of that day you want to swallow a couple of lead pills with your orange juice, go right ahead. He says he'll even come and pull the trigger for you."

"He said that?"

Charon nodded.

"He's intense, isn't he?"

Charon nodded again. "Being in the same room with him is like rubbing elbows with a super nova."

"When do I meet him?" I asked.

"Tomorrow." He smiled. "You'll be one of only a select few people that have met him in person."

"Why not today?"

Charon smiled. "Because today we execute Operation Velvet Ant."

"That's a dumb name."

He shrugged. "*Qui habet aures audiendi, audiat.*"

"Knock it off with the Pope talk, and tell me what John White has in store for me. I want to know what kind of a mess I'm getting into so I know whether to pack a lunch."

Charon grabbed my jacket from where it hung by the door. "I'll spell out all I know about him in the car. We'll have a half hour of silence to fill."

"That's fine," I said. "No tricks."

Standing felt like lifting a fallen redwood and balancing it on its severed roots. Five days without sleep hung around my shoulders like bags of sand. My knee joints were as brittle as archaeopteryx fossils. I thought for sure they'd crack from their moorings. But everything held together. Realizing I still held the revolver, I eased the hammer down, engaged the safety, and stuck the weapon in my pocket. I made my way out the door and up to the car, resolute in my mind that Charon would either tell me everything I wanted to know about John White or I'd grab the wheel and steer us into an embankment.

Thus resolved, I crammed myself into his vehicle, buckled my seat belt, and passed out.

I awoke in the middle of a military convoy. Charon's car was at sea in endless black asphalt. Vans, trucks, and Humvees painted in desert camouflage giraffe patterns surrounded us. Men bearing military death sticks, their torsos bulky with Kevlar, bustled around and barked orders at each other. Reality and the deep dream I'd been roused from blurred into a moment of stupefying disorientation. The remaining dream state hung like ether in my senses in a living nightmare of soldiers descending on me for malicious purposes. When I'd shaken it off, I realized I was one of those soldiers. I wished I'd stayed in the nightmare.

Charon turned to me from the driver's seat. "Here we are."

There was no debating it. We were here.

"This is the day we'll look back on and say, 'that's the day it all changed.' "

Charon's world was about to change more than he realized—if Tony's people were doing their job. "Are you coming along for Operation Velvet Ant?'

"No. I have duties here to attend to. But I look forward to seeing you upon your return. I'd like to think that we're friends. *E duobus, unum*. Or should I say, *de dos, uno.*"

"I'm tired of asking you to keep it in English, doc. My head can't handle any other language right now. I'm not entirely convinced I'm even awake."

"Just some Spanish to show you my intentions are pure."

"Intentions are like candles on a birthday cake. A strong gust of wind and all you're left with is wax in your frosting."

"I'll see you on the other side," he said.

"You enjoyed saying that."

He grinned. "I did, actually."

"You see? English does have a few sayings that can compete with Latin."

"Good bye, John."

I opened the door and got out of the car. It was a lot like an arthritic giraffe climbing out of a telephone booth. Everybody took time out of their paramilitary exercises to watch.

By the time I was as erect as I was going to get, the Captain had muscled his way up to my ribcage. "You're pushing the limits as usual. We're rolling out in five."

"I'm a pretty face. What do I care about your timetable?"

"One of these days, the boss' tender feelings for you are going to expire. That'll be a nice day. We'll be able to stop having these friendly little chats." He didn't wait around for a snappy comeback.

Before I knew it, Ned, the guy who'd originally stuffed me into the back of a van with Cerberus, escorted me across the center of what I recognized as the Typhon Industries parking lot. I passed short diesel trucks linked to trailers of buzzing harpy hubbub. I passed a cluster of white vans that smelled like carnivore and blood and emitted the tortured howl of Cerberus, the bleat of Dracula, and the roar of Goliath. I caught sight of an orange ponytail through the passenger window of one of the vans. I banged on the glass. The round freckled face that turned toward me made my guts sink.

Abbey rolled down the window. "We're coworkers again."

She'd joined White Industries behind my back. That was why she'd been so mum when I'd last seen her. "You're a turncoat."

"I fell in love. I can't stop thinking about Dracula. I'm his personal caretaker now. He's the biggest bat that's ever lived."

A good person would have opened his mouth and told her to get out of the van. I knew what was coming. I owed Abbey—and I'd dragged her into this whole thing. A good person would have shoved his head in her window and whispered in her ear. I couldn't bend that far. My body wasn't made for sharing secrets.

Ned hauled at my elbow. "Be careful," I managed to stutter at her.

She smiled and gave me a somber thumbs up.

My Humvee spearheaded the convoy. Trucks on either side housed the sibilant chirp of the hydras and the squeaking gremlins. John White—or the Captain, or Charon, or whatever madman was truly in charge of this place—had mobilized the whole army of monsters.

The Minutemen didn't trouble themselves with a lot of preamble. Once I settled in, a couple dozen engines fired up and we rolled into motion. It felt nice to be riding in the front. My seat even had a cushion. Meat Shoulders, the young guy with the harpy sting I'd talked to on my first visit to Typhon Industries, drove our vehicle. I wondered aloud if he remembered me and spent a good couple of minutes laughing about it. Meat Shoulders tried to laugh along at first but ended up clenching the wheel as if squeezing it hard enough could save him.

We filtered single file through the security gate. Some of the less stoic boys in our cavalcade rolled down their windows and yelled words that everybody had heard a thousand times before at the rainbow of protesters holding up their tireless signs. The protesters yelled some words that everybody had heard a thousand times before right back. For some reason, everybody on both sides felt perturbed and insulted, as if they'd never heard anything like it before. Once we'd run the gauntlet, we immersed ourselves in the unspoiled Cibola wilderness, which had been growing for thousands of years longer than any of us had been able to throw words around and feel sensitive about them.

My tired mind jumped like a record being played in the back of a truck on a dirt road. I found myself wondering if Dracula knew he'd sired young. I wondered how many would make it to adulthood and live long enough to suck the blood out of some misfit. Marsupial babies didn't survive in good proportions. Many would die before they even opened their eyes, before their slimy skin ever bore the first tufts of hair, before they realized that they didn't belong to this world. So many of us should have been more wary of being born into a land of normals.

"Is there anything I should be doing?" I asked Meat Shoulders.

"You just relax, Mr. Stick. Enjoy the ride." His eyes flitted from the road to me and back. "You can take a nap if you want to."

"I don't require sleep like the normals do. I'm special."

He chuckled nervously. He poked some buttons in the console between us. "We've got the satellite radio. What kind of music do you like?"

"Polka. Mexican polka." I laughed about that for a while. Meat Shoulders tried to smile along with me, but he wasn't having any fun. After a few minutes of it, I thought I might cry instead.

We fell quiet as the steel centipede of vans and trucks and trailers followed along the asphalt. The setting sun angled across the convoy and it shone like some Yellow Brick Road procession to Hades. We wound through the furrows and frowns of the Sandías. Humans named mountain ranges, but their words did nothing to quantify the eons that had twisted and stretched the land. Humans simply couldn't fathom geologic time. The gravity, the rain, the snow, the runoff. The tectonics at work. The strain of the moon as it creaked by. The plant roots clenching and twining in the dirt. The force of wind and sun heating and shrinking the soil, beating the water into the air like an old lady whacking a rug. Humans liked to talk about the majesty of mountains, using their human words. No words should be spoken in the presence of mountains—or in any of the desert spaces that took so long to form and that we so cheaply reduce to maps, barbed wire, and language. I traveled through the mountains and I saw ages-old beings that had been tortured up from the earth by strife and chaos and were beaten back down by every force known to the universe. They were in a constant intermediate stage between birth and death, between being and nonbeing.

I considered sharing my thoughts with Meat Shoulders but decided it would be too exhausting. Instead, I passed out for a half second and hit my head on the window. I woke back up, blinked, and hit my head again.

"Meat Shoulders," I said.

"You mean me?" asked Meat Shoulders.

"That's your name, isn't it? We'll call you Meat for short. I need caffeine."

"I have a thermos—"

"None of that Typhon Industries swill. It's made of blood. There's a gas station in Cedar Point. Best coffee in the world. Gourmet. It said so on the Styrofoam cup they served it to me in."

"I'm not authorized to stop, except for drive through. And only in Socorro."

"Meat," I said, "you need to listen to me. I want coffee and only from one place. We'll stop, and you'll see. Get out with me. Smell the pines. Use their pay phone. Drink a cigarette and eat a coffee or two. A young woman works there. You'll fall in love with her consonants."

Before he could answer, I blinked a big one. When my eyes opened, we were facing the volcanoes. Buildings sat in low clusters on each side of a freeway that, as my fog cleared, I figured out was I-40. I was confused about what day it was and why I was in a car with another human. I mumbled a little nonsense and then recognized Meat Shoulders. It all came back to me.

"How long have I been out?" I asked. "Did I miss anything?"

"Twenty minutes or so. Go back to sleep. We're only in Albuquerque. It's gonna be a long ride."

I tried to determine our exact location on I-40 based on the superstores we passed at any given moment, but to no avail. Every superstore cloned another superstore. Then Wyoming Mall, a dead shopping mall populated by specters of capitalism, whisked by on my right. Wyoming Mall had been systematically destroyed by its competitors in the cruel battle of commerce. The mall sat like a ghost town in the middle of the city. That's how Albuquerque worked: with unlimited space, you didn't need to renovate or rebuild the structure of a bankrupt business. You gutted it, left the corpse to rot, and moved on. That was the way of the desert.

The motorcade swooped left up a ramp that took us a couple hundred feet above the earth and dropped us onto I-25 going south. We clogged up traffic. People rubbernecked at us as if a crash of rhinos were trying to merge with normal motorists. We blasted our horns and cut people off. Our convoy managed to stay in a relatively unadulterated strand, and only one irritated driver showed his middle finger to our particular vehicle. I got a kick out of it. He'd displayed his longest finger, a fragile appendage of skin and bone, thinking that would somehow change the nature of the world.

The sun began to set, draping the long gentle shadows of the volcanoes over the city below us. On the elevated freeway, we enjoyed the last vestiges of day while the rest of the city drowsed in dusk. It slipped from us inevitably, like a garment gravity tugged from our bodies.

I saw the spotlights first. They dragged their thick yellow fingers across the sky, clutching at the cosmos for help. The universe, a playground of predator and prey, didn't help anyone. It had no favorites. The big top of the Gamut Circus sat in a globe of light at the conflux of the golden beams maybe a half mile distant. I braced myself. I tugged at my seatbelt and checked Meat Shoulders' too.

I wouldn't have noticed the line of vehicles that formed in front of us, shoulder to shoulder, blocking the road, except that the blue hippie van pulled directly in front of us. They packed themselves across all four lanes leaving no space to go around, and slowed down in tandem, as if preparing to execute some acrobatic feat. Meat Shoulders squinted. Maybe he thought the fresh dusk shadows were playing tricks on him. He rode the tail of the blue hippie van. He punched his steering wheel, and the hood of his vehicle bellowed a mighty challenge.

All at once, the back doors of the hippie van and its three friends swung open. Figures crouched inside, roped to the walls, clad in mismatched black trousers, sweaters, masks, and gloves. They looked like bank robbers who'd raided thrift stores for their gear. Several buckets stood lined up above the bumper. The other vehicles held similar figures hovering over buckets, all roped in to keep them from falling into traffic and getting ground to dust.

Meat Shoulders hit the brakes, but too late. Each second-hand bank robber had already picked up a bucket. They poured waterfalls of steel spiked orbs the size of baseballs into our path. I put my palms against the dashboard, and yelled as if I were actually surprised. Our tires turned to confetti. We spun. A calamity of shattering glass and shrieking steel spun with us, first from behind, then from the front, then from behind again, as our convoy had its legs torn from under it. The city did pirouettes around us. The sunset looked prettier with every turn. We collided with another Humvee and careened into a guardrail. Our vehicle stood on two legs for a second, then settled back onto all four shredded feet.

I held myself in place with a hand on the dash and the other braced against the windowpane, my feet pushing hard into the front floor space. The windshield had crackled into one big spider web. The red sunset poured blood into every jagging crack. The engine had died, and our truck sat eerily silent. Meat Shoulders clutched the steering wheel as if he thought the truck would start spinning again if he let go. A mouth of jagged glass teeth yawned through the driver's side window, but I didn't see any blood on him. Outside, hell had broken loose. I knew I'd have to go out there.

Meat Shoulders turned toward me. He looked at me with the eyes of a scared kid. His elbows quivered and his knuckles looked like they might break through the skin.

"You're okay," I said.

He blinked at me. "You are too. Are you?"

I relaxed my body. The crashing and squealing of our convoy turning into a street salad had stopped. Horns and muted shouting blared outside the Humvee's windows. And then another sound cut the air.

"Was that gunfire?" Meat Shoulders asked.

I opened the door, tried to get out, but my seat belt yanked me back. It clung tight against my hips, where it had locked during the accident. I hit the release and blood flowed into a belt of bruise across my lap. I tried to get out of the car a second time. This time it worked, though the world teetered as I unfurled my body to its full height, my head reeling from the impact of the crash, lack of sleep, or both. Our score of vehicles was a helter-skelter blockade of twisted, smoking metal and glittering glass. Beyond it, the southbound freeway teemed with cars as far as the eye could see.

Men had begun to climb, stagger, crawl, and drag each other from the wreckage. Cerberus' lonely howl sailed into the sky from somewhere in the mess. Our Humvee had spun some yards away from the pileup. One of the horse trailers had come unmoored from its cab and lay on its side across two lanes of asphalt. I stumbled toward it. A long high-pitched peal snaked from the shadows inside, sounding like a rabbit's death cry. More joined it. I moved closer. The cries became a chorus. I was looking at the gremlin truck, full of dark rats wearing party favor noses, plated with beetle chitin, and thirsty for human blood. I wondered if it'd be better if they'd been mashed into paste or merely scared. Assassin bugs were tough. I guessed there would be plenty of survivors.

A hundred yards or so away, the Captain limped from the wreckage. A streak of blood ran from his temple, and he brandished a pistol. He waved his arms at me. I walked toward him. He yelled, but I couldn't hear the words over the din of the gremlins screaming their heads off. He waved frantically. I moved my legs. I ate up some yards with my long strides. He yelled and gestured, and I had no idea how to interpret any of it, so I just kept moving.

Off ahead and to the left, another burst of gunfire sounded. Bullets hammered against metal, and some animal or man shrieked in agony.

The Captain was right in front of me. He shoved me in the chest and shouted. "What's wrong with you? Get away!"

I deflected his hand and shoved him back. He staggered and fell to one knee.

He braced himself with the muzzle of his pistol against the asphalt and rose. It looked like it hurt. He faced me again, and I got ready to shove him back down. "Don't you see? Get away! You're making it worse!"

Cerberus howled and howled. I had a vision of him pinned beneath a crushed truck, bleeding and scared. From north to south along the divider between the two halves of interstate, the streetlights blinked to life one by one. A dense form shot up from the wreckage a dozen yards distant, sailed through a cone of yellow light, and swooped off to the west. It trailed the cries of a tortured sheep behind it. The scrabble of claws on metal sounded from behind me, where the gremlin trailer lay overturned. I turned to see carapaces swarming out a hole in the corner. They formed a carpet of gleaming black on the asphalt, spreading toward where the two of us stood.

"God save us." The Captain brought up his pistol arm.

I took his wrist in my hand and raised his arm up, as gently as I could, until the pistol pointed skyward.

"Goddamn you!" the Captain sputtered. He struggled to bring his arm down. He grabbed my wrist with his other hand and tried that out. He couldn't budge me.

"Find your happy place, Captain. They're not coming for us."

He didn't stop struggling, so I continued to hold his arm up. A few of the gremlins gathered around my shoes and tickled my ankles with their proboscises, but most of the swarm passed us by, scuttling under the guardrail and into the weeds on west side of the freeway. When the Captain realized that, I let him go. He almost fell down.

"If they're not after you, then where are they going?" he asked.

My gaze was already on the circus tent. It sat a mile or so distant, pitched in the empty desert that lay to the south of Albuquerque. A makeshift parking lot sprawled on three sides of the tent, packed with cars. Floodlights drenched the sides in light and made playful sweeps across the settling night sky. A winged form sailed through one of them.

My plan was working perfectly. I didn't know whether to feel satisfied or guilty.

"They're headed for a galloping good time at the Gamut Circus and Freak Show."

"Sweet Christ." The Captain turned on me. "Don't stand there! Do what you're here to do! Use your summoning powers and call them back."

"I don't have any summoning powers." My voice sounded a thousand years old. I felt like lying down on the asphalt and waiting for the paramedics to arrive and collect my body. "They like me because I'm a monster—like them. The human part of them can recognize one of their own. But I'm only one guy. There's a tent full of misfits a short scuttle away."

The Captain gave me a disgusted look. "I knew you were a waste."

"We're all waste."

He spat on the ground and turned away. He swung his legs a couple times and set his foot directly on a ball of metal spikes. Letting out a yelp, he rolled to the ground and grasped at his boot.

I'd been lucky not to step on one myself. They littered the highway from one side to the other. There must have been hundreds of them. I picked up the closest, a bunch of long sturdy spikes bent around each other until sharp points stuck out in all directions. Someone had fired a welding torch at the center where all the middles of the spikes intersected, fusing them together. It was a simple little weapon, born of my brain, a foreign invading weed, and some Good Friends with a metal shop.

Meat Shoulders stood beside me. He had a submachine gun in his hands and looked like he wanted his mom. The sky was littered with dipping, diving hydras, their bodies undulating as if snakes had always been meant for flight. They filled the night with their terrible cries. The air hummed with the buzz of harpies, dotting the night in compact swarms. They were a wind of stingers and mandibles and thrumming wings. That wind blew west.

"What do we do?" Meat Shoulders asked.

There was nothing we could do. You can't eradicate an insect population without carpet bombing its habitat with DDT or poisoning its food supply. I could have told him to blow some gunpowder. Throwing lead in the air might have made him feel better. I could have told him that we should try to grab a few of the critters with our hands and stuff them into cages. If John White's theory was correct and I was some sort of beacon, they'd all eventually swarm back to me. I didn't plan on sticking around to find out. Without me, they'd probably disperse into the desert. Since they were all outfitted with GPS signals, it was theoretically possible that the Minutemen could track them down, but it would be Herculean work. Whatever the outcome, my plan had ruined the Minutemen's capacity to sic their animals on any border migrants in the near future.

As we stood looking over the guardrail, Goliath burst from behind a dead Humvee and galloped at full tilt down the freeway. His eely skin gleamed in the street lamps. His big bear body jiggled and danced as he crashed his paws lopsidedly along. He was limping. Black blood slicked his left flank. His tongue dangled from his sucker mouth and his eyes were human with fear. Several goons took positions clear of the wrecked vehicles, aimed their weapons, and let fly. The Captain yelled from where he lay lamed on the street for them to stop, but they didn't listen. Their guns drilled Goliath with a dozen holes and battered the sky with their rattling. Goliath ran until he couldn't. The goons fit a few more bullets into him. When they were done, he was a mountain of meat on the asphalt.

The world housed one fewer unique being. Only a handful of us were left.

CHAPTER TWENTY-NINE

t was time for me to flee the scene and let chaos do its work. As I stepped over the guardrail, planning on walking north until I could hail a cab, I spotted a figure far out on the bare desert between the freeway and the circus. The figure ran full tilt toward where the big top sat in its globe of lights surrounded by a sea of cars. It wore all black like the rest of the Minuteman crew. An orange ponytail bounced between the figure's shoulders. They belonged to Abbey. Her love for a mutant bat was driving her straight toward a blood bath.

Meat Shoulders hovered on the other side of the guardrail. He'd attached himself to me like a scared kid sticks by his mom.

"C'mon," I groaned. "Let's go save the circus."

I slid down the gravel embankment with the grace of an arthritic ogre. The terrain between the freeway and the circus was flat and covered only sparsely with weeds and cacti. Meat Shoulders and I made quick work of it. Halfway across, a hubbub floated up from the tent amidst the lights, but I couldn't tell if it was circus glee or monster terror. We overtook the tide of gremlins grumbling and squeaking and scuttling amidst the weeds. As far ahead to my left and to my right as I could see, the ground twitched and skittered with gleaming black carapaces. In Albuquerque, we were used to cockroaches carpeting the dirt in the summer months. The gremlins were black and shiny and only around ten times bigger. Maybe the city would get used to them. Maybe in a few years' time, we'd wake up and find a rat-bug in our kitchen sink. We'd sigh. Oh, this again. With a cockroach, you rinsed it down the sink or whacked it with a shoe or sprayed it with Raid and watched it gyrate. We'd have to adapt our methods—a hot poker through the torso would do the trick. Or a pot of boiling oil. Or, if all else failed, we could all walk around our houses armed with .22 pistols. Many of us routinely packed higher calibers already, so it wouldn't even put us out.

The gremlins gave Meat Shoulders the heebie-jeebies. His trigger finger looked itchy. I tried to set a good example and appear unfazed as we tap-danced amidst the netherworldly horde. The flying creatures had already covered the span from road to circus. Swarms of feathered snakes circled high in the floodlights. Dracula was nowhere to be seen.

"What are we going to do when we get there?" Meat Shoulders asked.

"Don't ask me," I said. "You're the one who's trained for this."

We crossed a slow and steady rise in the land. The ground crunched with tumbleweeds, dried out over a long winter. We steered around the big ones and marched over the smaller ones. They made good shadows for gremlins to hide under. We had to be careful where we put our feet, and it was slow going.

"Maybe they won't do anything. They might be disoriented. None of them have ever been free in the wild before."

"Oh, they will," Meat Shoulders said, puffing a little from the climb. I guessed it wasn't easy getting around with all the body armor and hardware he had strapped to his body. "They're starving. We haven't fed them for days."

"What possessed you to starve your animals?" I growled. The answer was obvious: to make them hungry for immigrant blood. The question in my mind was whether the chupacabras would see the circus people as fellow monsters worthy of veneration—as apparently I was—or misfits to be singled out and fed upon—as had been the whooping crane, albino rattlesnake, and Esposita the painted turtle.

We were a hundred paces away. Abbey's ponytail had vanished. The circus band fired on all brass cylinders inside, punctuated by bursts of laughter from the crowd. The show went on, apparently. I paused outside the tent and glanced around. It took me a minute. The variation between the darkness low to the ground, the dull glow of the stars, and the floodlight beams made it tricky to see clearly, especially with my substandard human eyes.

A hydra rested atop of the tent. When I saw one, ten more resolved, and then a hundred. I picked out dark ovals among the hydras where harpy clans clustered. The big top was covered with them, thousands of chupacabras, hydra feathers twitching in the breeze, harpies flickering their wings. Not a square foot of the canvas was without little beasties crouching there. They were attracted by the lights, or the smell of the crowd, or the allure of the circus people—or all three. They could have been resting, or they could have been crouching in ambush.

Meat Shoulders saw them too. He held his submachine gun in one hand, dangling by his leg, as useless as an umbrella in the face of a hailstorm. "What do we do?" He wasn't the leadership type.

A few stray harpies buzzed my ears. I felt a presence by my foot. A gremlin nudged the cuff of my pant leg. His pink rat eyes mooned up at me like a puppy longing to climb into my lap. All around us, the quiet tide of gremlins advanced toward the tent skirt. A handful scuttled around the main entrance to the tent. One of them lifted its head and sniffed the air.

"Stay here. Don't shoot anything."

Light and music flooded through the open flaps of the big top. An usher stood with his back to me, watching the show. He was the only one attending the door. Beyond him and down the corridor formed by bleachers rising on both sides, the crowd cheered on the opposite side of the tent. Between them and me, a clown stood in the center ring. He was lacquered in white paint, with a big red mouth and those goofy, spooky clothes clowns like to wear. He grasped a red hoop in one hand and held the other behind his ear. The audience clapped louder and louder as he tilted his ear to indicate that he couldn't quite hear them yet. A little dog dressed in a lion suit complete with a tail that dragged behind it crouched, waiting to leap through the hoop.

High above, amidst the cables and shadows, near an opening in the apex of the tent, Dracula hung upside down with his wings cloaked around him. His mouth gaped partially open. His teeth shone white, and his eyes gleamed. He stared straight at the clown.

Meat Shoulders appeared beside me. He raised his weapon and clicked off the safety. The usher glanced over his shoulder and saw Meat Shoulders with his gun. He saw me. The sight of us must have given him a mild concussion because he stood there showing us his tonsils.

I grabbed the muzzle of the gun and yelled something at him. People in the stands closest to us put their faces over the railing. They probably thought I was part of the show, but they didn't look as sure about my black-clad, gun-toting companion. At the same moment, a little girl in the front row stood and pointed straight up. A loose circle of people around her raised their eyes. A woman screamed. It cut through the music and applause like a cleaver. Dracula spread his wings and opened his maw. His white fangs, black fur, and leather wings came straight from a horror movie.

The place broke apart in people crying and shouting and shrieking. Normals leapt to their feet and knocked each other over. An athletic man grabbed his little darling around the waist and vaulted over the side of the bleachers. He landed on the usher. They tumbled in a mess of arms and legs. Meat Shoulders knocked me away from him—he was a strong guy—and rattled off a salvo toward the top of the tent. His bullets punched some holes in canvas but missed the target. Alighting at almost the same moment, Dracula dropped halfway to the circus tent floor, spread his wings, swooped, and landed ten feet from the clown. He perched on his wingtips and hind legs while grinning at the performer, a petrified rube in white grease paint. The audience screamed in sheer terror. People pushed other people. A grandma fell face first down some bleacher stairs. Across the ring, half a section of people tumbled over one another in a domino game of crying children and clambering parents.

Dracula cantered across the ring on his wingtips and wrapped the clown in a leathery hug. The clown screamed and flailed. His little dog jumped up and down, yipping helplessly. Circus people in sequins and long-tailed tuxedo jackets and leotards rallied from backstage. The ringmaster rode out on a white stallion and cracked his whip. A juggler brandished a gaudy wooden club in each hand. A troupe of acrobats tried to usher people toward the side exits, but the crowd preferred to scream, shove, and generally trample itself.

I charged forward. A carpet of gremlins streamed around my shoes. Some scuttled beneath the draperies that hung down the sides of the bleachers and into the darkness beneath. Others made for center ring. A hydra snaked its neck into one of the holes Meat Shoulders had poked in the top of the tent. A swarm of harpies drizzled in through another. The place had descended into hell, and it was all my bright idea.

I scanned the madness for a red ponytail as I rushed forward. A mob of people had made it out of the bleachers and were at the mouth of the aisle between them, coming directly at me. They made it a few panicked steps toward the entrance before they saw the army of gremlins crawling toward them. The people at the front of the mob tried to stop and scream for God's mercy or whatever. The people behind them couldn't understand why they'd stopped. It seemed unreasonable to them. They pushed and shoved against the front people, who pushed back and did everything in their power not to move toward the oncoming rat-roaches. Some of the front people were strong and held out, others fell forward on their knees or elbows or chins. But eventually, the pressure from behind was too great and a tide of people at in back surged over those in front. The gremlins scuttled, tried to escape, bit, and screamed. They fled for the safety of the dark spaces under the bleachers or climbed the cloth drapes that hung down the bleachers' flanks. One clambered up a woman's long blond hair and took a chunk out of her ear. Another fastened on a child's face and bit his tender little eye. Their hunger and panic had taken over, and they'd become the monsters everyone perceived.

I barreled forward. I had one goal: Abbey. Meat Shoulders, good dumb kid that he was, stuck with me. We shoved and elbowed our way upstream. I tried to be easy with people, but ended up putting my palms on the tops of a few heads, straining a few necks, and shoving people away with a little too much force. Back in center ring, the circus people closed on Dracula. The juggler whacked him on his broad, black back with a wooden juggling club. The ringmaster circled and reared his noble steed. He took aim and cracked the tip of his whip on Dracula's wing. Dracula released the clown and faced off with horse and rider. Blood and foaming saliva smeared his fangs and snout. The horse took one look and fell over backwards. A hydra tangled itself in the boa of the bearded lady. A squadron of harpies buzzed the strongman, while the lobster girl with her tragic hands and cute face batted at a gremlin seeking the safety of her skirt hem. Faced with this onslaught of stingers and fanged beaks, the performers scattered. Dracula squatted in center ring, excreted a pool of lemon urine in the hay, and leapt for the rafters. The juggler let fly one of his clubs. It struck Dracula in midair. He careened into a trapeze platform, where his wings tangled with an older aerialist perched there. They fell together, plunging two sickening stories to the hard ground below. Dracula lifted his head. The aerialist lay still.

I elbowed my way into center ring. Dracula purred at me. The man next to him wore embroidered Chinese slippers and had thick gray hair. His dark eyes stayed closed but the twitch of life pulsed in his neck.

Abbey appeared beside me. Her hair had broken halfway free of its ponytail, and her orange locks were stringy with sweat. She stretched a palm toward Dracula's blood-bearded mouth. "Are you okay?"

"He just killed two men," said Meat Shoulders behind me. "And you're worried about whether he's okay?" He stood a couple paces behind away, pointing his gun at Dracula's head.

"Your job is to protect him," Abbey said.

"He attacked me once before," Meat Shoulders said. "I'm along for the ride if he's helping us track lawbreakers, but when it comes to regular folks, he's a rabid animal."

Abbey moved between gun and bat, spreading her arms out.

Meat yelled, "Get out of the way."

I grabbed his gun without thinking about it, ripped it out of his hands, and threw it under the bleachers. Meat jumped on me. He knew some moves. He got me in a pretty nasty arm lock before I managed to wrench my free hand under his armpit and around the back of his neck. He pushed and I pushed. We grunted and huffed. We both fell in slow motion to the ground. At that point, it became a contest of mass, and I, as the greater planet, prevailed. I wrestled him to a facedown position and put my knee on the back of his neck. He lay there and wheezed. I took some pretty big gulps myself.

"Sorry Meat," I said between puffs. "You're a good dumb kid."

Abbey had wrapped Dracula in a horse blanket and gathered him into her arms.

"Is he hurt?" I asked.

"I think his wing is broken," she said.

"Get him outta here." The vision of Goliath perishing in a stream of bullets was still fresh in my mind. "Take him somewhere safe."

Abbey stood clutching the bundle of fur, wings, and bloody fangs. She was sweat-soaked and her legs quivered. "I don't have a car here. We're in the middle of nowhere."

I fished around in Meat Shoulders' belt for handcuffs. I didn't find any, but I did find some plastic zip restraints. I fastened them around his wrists and ankles and left him face down in the hay. I tried to think of some smart words to leave him with, but couldn't think of any. A gremlin scuttled up and affixed its teeth to the tender veins of his wrist. I figured that'd do just fine.

Abbey and I headed toward the side entrance of the big top. All the people had cleared out and it was pretty peaceful in there. Outside, madness had descended. Typhon Industries soldiers had arrived, clad in black armor, some tending to bodies that had been damaged in the stampede, others directing people away from the tent. A few aimed their weapons at the sky or into the weeds and squeezed off short, controlled bursts. It was pointless. The chupacabras were loose. No one would ever be able to strain the pythons from the swamps of Florida, nor dislodge the rabbits from the Australian outback, nor exterminate the rats from Bermuda. In twenty years, people would say the same thing about the blood sucking monsters of the American Southwest. Someone might be able to knock Dracula out of the sky with enough shotgun blasts, as White's goons had already slain Goliath. But the hydras would scatter to the four winds, and the gremlins would crawl into the sewers and drainage ditches. They'd blend into the river and creep through the grasses of the ranches and kiss the cattle in their sleep. The harpies would soon be as ubiquitous as horseflies, only you'd need a titanium flyswatter.

I shepherded Abbey away from the packets of Minutemen. I didn't want her returning Dracula to them, and she seemed to feel the same. Sirens wailed in the distance. Traffic on the Interstate still stood at a complete halt. The lanes north of our sabotage shone with endless cones of headlights; the lanes south lay barren and dark. Cerberus' barks echoed from far away, or maybe they belonged to another dog, or maybe a whole city full of dogs, forced to live among us without anyone ever questioning why.

Families streamed through the parking lot, searching for their vehicles, eager to escape this nightmare circus. One figure stood still, leaning against a car at the far perimeter of the lot. The figure measured on the short side, even for a normal, had shoulder length straight black hair and feminine curves. They belonged to Tanis, of course. I led Abbey to her. I had a plan in my head to pick her up and carry her into the tent. She might get lucky and be kissed by a hydra.

"John Stick. Time for you to meet your opposite."

"First, you and me are going to take our pals Abbey and Dracula someplace safe. Have you three met? Human, meet chupacabra, meet animal theologian."

The screams and shouts of monsters and humans filled the parking lot around us. The sirens came closer. I wasn't sure if they'd arrive at the freeway or the circus tent first. Either way, they'd be too late. A couple of fire engines and paramedic vans pulled into the parking lot. I half-hoped they'd have Denny, the local coyote catcher, in tow. I would have liked to see his old rumpled face drop open when he saw what his future career held.

"Get in. This place is getting loud." Tanis said. "I'll take you to your destiny, John Stick. And I'll take Abbey and her furry friend to a safe house."

Abbey lingered by the door I'd opened for her. "Who did this?" She looked numb, like a person who's just heard about some historical atrocity. "Who's to blame?"

"Blame is for people of weak moral intellect," Tanis said to her across the top of the car. "This event was inevitable. The greater the weapon you create, the more collateral blood gets spilled. It's a law of physics."

"Funny how you talk about laws, yet you seem to think you're immune to them," I said.

"I am an eagle," she said, "soaring high above it all."

"Watch out for flying snakes up there," I said.

"Just get in the car, zookeepers," Tanis said.

CHAPTER THIRTY

Tanis drove us around to the back of the big top, where a dozen or so smaller tents formed a narrow boulevard. A sign above the entrance read *Side Show Alley*. On each side hung placards advertising the acts found within: The Bearded Lady, Elephant Man, Lobster Girl, the Six-Legged Cow, the Two-Headed Snake. To the chupacabras, it read like either a menu or a list of potential good friends.

Tanis drove in low gear and high speed down a dirt road off into the weeds. The terrain became rougher as we neared the river. Cottonwood boughs arched overhead. Clusters of tumbleweeds gathered among their trunks. We turned on another dirt road that traced the lip of the river gorge, heading north. In the back seat, Abbey cooed at the chupacabra swaddled in her lap. I sat crammed into the passenger's seat beside Tanis.

"So what now?" I asked.

"I take you to the mountains," Tanis said. "It's time for you to fulfill your purpose."

"I don't have a purpose."

"Of course you do. You're an integer. The world is made of math. I already told you that. Why do I have to tell you everything three times?"

"I'm a slow learner," I said.

"The equation was imbalanced. John White has been rounding up immigrants and building his army of men and beasts. He has amassed great wealth and power. He's been exploiting the nature of the universe and wreaking havoc on a relatively stable system, with no one around to check his power. The Good Friends had potential, they had dedicated members, but they're all pretty average." She blew a raspberry. "Useless. The universe needed someone extraordinary."

The dirt road turned to asphalt and led us into the fringes of southernmost Albuquerque, where the houses huddled shoulder to shoulder, coveting their yards full of cast off and weeds, their cars sloughing rubber and paint, their lives of poverty and servitude.

"I'm not extraordinary," I said. "I'm a dullard trapped in a demigod's suit."

Tanis threw her head back and moaned. She fixed her eyes back on the road a second later than I was comfortable with. "You are a very frustrating man. You only see the surface of everything. You see the river and you say to yourself, the water is very shiny. But you don't see the poisonous snake floating beneath the surface."

"There are no poisonous snakes in our river," I said.

"My point is that you haven't learned anything. I've taken you on this journey, and you're still the same myopic man who can tell me the color of a person's eyes, but has very little insight into the space behind them." She sighed. "Have you even figured out the meaning of life yet?"

"I haven't figured out the meaning of my own left thumb," I said.

"You're impossible," she muttered.

We drove quietly across the city, a chessboard of lights and darkness. People lit up those lights to deter burglars, thwart gangs, prevent car accidents. They represented humanity's ugliness, our predilection to prey upon each other. We told ourselves we'd surpassed animals because we'd invented microwaves and tiaras and demolition derbies and fingernail polish. But in reality, our actions served no higher purpose than those of a skunk or a mite or a rattlesnake.

Tanis broke the silence as we shot through Tijeras pass and into the East Mountains.

"I want to give you a compliment. You probably need one."

"Don't strain yourself," I said.

"Here it goes." She took a deep breath. "You're special."

"Great. Thanks."

"You're special because you don't see an animal as a piece of meat. You saw every being that you cared for in the zoo as a luminous being, with feelings and intrinsic self-fulfilled value. You also somehow know that every one of those beings you care for so much is part of a greater cycle of sacrifice and transience. You hold that paradox in your head. You accept it and understand it and fulfill your part in it. That's spiritual wisdom.

"That's what's at stake in our world. We see animals—beings that have as much volition and integrity of spirit as we do—as objects. We reduce their suffering to an entry in a ledger. They have a utilitarian purpose and a dollar value and don't matter beyond that. This is the ideology of a morally bankrupt race.

"John White sees people the same way. That's the risk: we can see all the life on earth, human and animal, as part of a capitalist equation. Or we can see it as the shimmering of God through the ethereal curtain into our crude realm. Once you stop seeing the intrinsic value of life, as John White has, you lose your humanity and your connection to the eternal."

"What am I supposed to do about it? I'm glad you like my view on living things, but what good does that do anybody?"

"He asked me to bring you to him. You"—Tanis flashed her eyes from the road to mine—"have to go in there, confront John White, and make everything better. You're liquid plumber. Your job is to flush away the evil blocking up the universe."

"How?" I asked.

"I don't tell how. I merely put integers together and see what number they make. The mathematician doesn't control math. She solves equations. I believe that you will zero out John White. You're his antithesis. Go in there and be yourself."

"What if you're wrong?" I asked. "What if I'm just a poor zookeeper who only wanted to take extra special care of his dung beetle collection?"

"That's why you're perfect."

We pulled into the dark and quiet parking lot of Typhon Industries. Tanis drove uphill through a checkpoint with a guard post. The guard checked her ID, made a phone call, and waved us on. She parked in front of Mount Olympus' only entrance. Once we'd come to a halt, she left the car running.

"This is your stop." Her black hair gleamed like silk in the soft light of the moon. Her big eyes twinkled and her skin was as smooth, clear, and dark as the desert in the minutes before dawn. I'd only begun to perceive her unfathomable depths.

Abbey sat in the back seat, stroking Dracula's chin. His squeezed his eyes shut, and his mouth curved in a feral smile. His wing would heal up in no time, especially with Abbey looking after him.

"Bye," I said to her.

She smiled and stuck her hand at me. I shook it. She kissed her fingertips and pressed them to Dracula's lips. "I love him," she whispered.

"Take care of him. He's one of a kind."

I walked away.

No animals or humans stirred in the mountain night. No wind shook the pines or rattled the leaves of the aspen. I took a deep breath and then another. Each inhalation reached an icy hand down into my lungs and gripped the core of my body in a cold fist. As I stood before Mount Olympus psyching myself up to enter, a few crickets creaked out their careful noise. A buzz whirled around my ear and landed on my arm. The harpy tilted its head from side to side and washed its hands, one over the other. Its tail ended with a sharp and deadly stinger. Its wings gleamed with iridescent blue and purple, and its big round eyes saw a hundred images of the world, each one the same but from a minutely different angle. I shook my arm gently until it buzzed off into the night.

I knocked on the door, assuming that a camera hidden somewhere was capturing my chest. Before I banged again, an electric mechanism triggered and a bolt sprang back. The heavy doors opened noiselessly. I stepped into a small, featureless antechamber, where I faced off with a set of heavier metal doors. I stood there until the doors sealed and locked behind me, and the ones in front clicked and wafted open.

A humid wave of air caressed my face. It emanated from a hot spring in the center of the chamber. Set in rough natural rock, the pool spanned roughly ten feet in diameter. The dark waters swirled in a gentle but deep turbulence and sloughed steam in lazy tendrils. A slim channel cut under the east wall of the room and trickled over a small falls into the main pool. Where it went from there, I couldn't tell.

The majority of the room looked like a rich Englishman's parlor. The north wall featured floor to ceiling bookshelves, full of finely bound tomes, complete with a wooden ladder on wheels to access the upper shelves. In front of it stood a chaise lounge and two leather chairs with footrests and mahogany side tables. The south side of the room had been outfitted as a fully equipped scientific lab, with microscopes, glassware, and a couple of bulky machines whose function I couldn't guess at. On the west side, beside the pleasant little stream, a matronly woman sat in a rocking chair. A burgundy and yellow afghan lay spread across her legs, and rimless glasses sat on the bridge of her nose. Knitting needles clicked between her hands, and a swath of brown fabric lay in her lap. A cradle sat on the floor beside her, which she absently rocked with her foot. A man stood nearby, with an open book in one hand and his chin in the fingers of the other.

I recognized Charon, with his forgettable face and his average hair, eyes, and build. But colder eyes regarded me from beneath his brow. And the way he snapped his book shut and circled the pool to greet me were the actions of a more decisive man.

"Where is he?" I called out before he was even halfway to me.

Charon spread his hands. His nonchalant brusqueness, his manic insomnia, had vanished. This person walked straight-backed, his face fine-lined and severe—the exact type of man you'd expect to run a corporation like Typhon Industries.

"You," I said.

"I've been watching you," the man said.

"But you're Charon," I said.

He shrugged, a precise movement, as if he'd perfected it. "I am. I'm the head of Typhon Industries. I'm the lead biologist. I'm your new best friend."

"Is John White your real name?" I asked.

"No. It's a blank name, as plain as I am. For my entire life, people kept forgetting they'd ever met me. I changed my name to match."

The central actor in every problem I'd faced over the past weeks stood in front of me. I could have picked him up, carried him to his pool, and pushed him down until it was all over.

"Why?" I asked. "Why make up a name? Or two names, since you're obviously not Jacob Charon either."

"Human beings have names. You and I—we're better."

"I hate to break it you, doc, but we're still human beings even though we have boring names."

"For the moment. But we can be so much more."

"You mean, like being nice to our neighbors and generous to charity and stuff like that?"

"That's not at all what I mean," he said. "Let me tell you the story of my life."

"I can't wait. If I were sitting down, I'd be on the edge of my seat. But shouldn't you be out chasing down the army of mutant vampires your trucks just spilled into the lap of the city?"

He smiled. Every muscle in his face tightened in concert to execute a polite but forced smile. "That is all under control. Everything is unfolding as it should."

Operation Velvet Ant—the meaning of the name hit me in the face. A velvet ant wasn't an ant at all. It was a wasp that disguised itself as an ant, so that it could infiltrate the hives of other wasps and bees. Once inside, it implanted its eggs on their larvae. When those eggs hatched, the velvet ant larvae ate the bees' babies.

"You meant to let them loose. That's why you let me spill information to the Good Friends. You wanted your monsters to escape."

"Yes. I couldn't release them myself; it had to look like an accident. I have to give you credit for your execution, however. Caltrops. An ancient weapon used by ninjas of Japan to deter pursuers." He smiled like a proud but very strict father. "Ingenious."

"Why?" I asked. "Why would you want all of your animals free? They'll get eaten, mauled by cars, shot. You're throwing them under the bus—which I understand is something you industry tycoons do, when there's an angle to it—but in this case I can't see the angle."

He eyed me for a moment, his face tense but neutral. "Do you want to hear my life story or don't you?"

"Mind if I sit?" I asked. "I haven't slept in a hundred years or so."

He led me to the rich person chairs by the monstrous bookshelves. I sank into a cloud of leather and air. Even my body appreciated it despite the chair's normal proportions. It was probably the most expensive piece of furniture I'd ever touched.

"Spill it," I said.

"I was born with a fraternal twin brother." He assumed the other chair. "We were radically different in temperament and appearance. My brother was tall, dark haired, with striking features. People saw him and remembered him. I was average. My hair was mouse brown, my nose average, my eyes gray, my build average, my voice dull. As I grew up, I had to remind people again and again that they'd already met me. When my parents saw me in a crowd, their eyes would pass over me. It wasn't that they didn't recognize me. They simply didn't notice me. My teachers were the same way. I was the last boy whose name they memorized. They never called on me in class. I was a blank space in the universe. A colorless absence.

"Very early in my life, I discovered that while my physical form was absolutely forgettable, my mind was far beyond that of any other human. I was a Hercules, born into the mortal world, but with a god-like gift. His was strength; mine was intelligence. I read voraciously, but I was particularly struck by what Plato said about forms. He believed that everything in the world had a perfect, original form. That's how one knew that God existed: he had created a template for everything from a spoon to the moon. The same went for humans. Man sprung from an original design, but strayed off into all sorts of derivations after that. The original Perfect Forms, though still housed where the Gods lived, were invisible to us, as every tangible thing was an imperfect iteration of them."

John White paused. His eyes lost focus, as if he were peering into the space behind his reflection in a mirror. "In my youth, I thought that I was a perfect iteration of the Form of Man. My intellect was divine—that much was clear. My mind was perfect. And believing that my physical form was so average, so utterly forgettable, because it was a template from which every other human derived—that gave me comfort."

He smiled peacefully, as if that comfort momentarily touched him.

His face hardened. "We live in the Shadow World where only the distorted specters of the Perfect Forms exist. Except for me, I thought. I wanted to see into the realm of Perfect Forms. I wanted to break through our reality into what could only be called heaven, where all is perfect and good and where I might find more beings like myself. I scoured the earth for special places that might be portals into that realm. I learned about black holes and astronomical oddities. I studied paranormal psychology—temporal displacement, out of body experiences, clairvoyance, those who claimed they could touch the astral plane. It was all hogwash.

"Then I discovered this pool, as a footnote in an article in a geographic journal. The writers claimed they measured the temperature of the pool as part of a routine study of hot springs in New Mexico. They discovered that the surface was both hotter than the water from the source of the springs deeper down and the temperature of the air heated by the sun. It was an impossible temperature, subverting the laws of thermodynamics. The writers ran another test the next day and found that the water's temperature was normal. They wrote it off as a fluke—though one that troubled them enough to include in their write-up."

A faint rustling stirred across the room. It came from the cradle. The matron inspected whatever lay within over the tops of her glasses. She resumed knitting.

"I came here. I performed tests and took measurements. Hot springs are often associated with the divine. But this one seemed normal. Then I read the account of a Franciscan monk who traveled to New Mexico during the centuries when Spanish conquistadors were trying to convert the land into a new colony. He claimed that a local healer used the waters to cure women and men of infertility, but this healer only did so on a very specific day. I performed some calculations. It was the same day the geologists measured their impossible temperature.

"Thus, I waited for that day and I took measurements. They were impossible—only by a few degrees. But still. At that moment I knew I'd found my gateway between our Shadow World and the world of Perfect Forms."

"Just because a hot springs gets a little hotter than you'd expect doesn't mean God made it that way," I said. "And isn't believing a monk's description of indigenous rituals a little cliché and probably racist?"

White looked annoyed. "Only to the narrow minded."

"Alright. Call me narrow minded. I believe what I can see. You say you took some measurements. Obviously you found something besides abnormal temperature, since you built this little shrine around your God pool."

His annoyance retreated into a relaxed, almost friendly smile. "I like your ethos, John. Nothing is holy to you."

"Holiness is a word invented by humans to make us feel good about ourselves. It's a comfort blanket so we don't have to be scared of the dark."

"Wrong," he said. "The word describes a perfect quality, of which you can see shadows cast here in our world, but the perfection of which only truly exists in the dimension of Perfect Forms. This spring"—he gestured at the steaming pool—"is one of the few manifestations of that quality here in our Shadow World."

"I'd ask you to prove it," I said, "but I imagine you were already planning to."

He leaned toward me. His eyes gleamed. "I've been proving it for eight years in a row now."

I wasn't a math genius, but the arithmetic was pretty simple. The roof of Mount Olympus had opened eight times. There had been eight calamities on that same day—but I'd only met seven chupacabras. I looked at the cradle. It had high sides. All I could spot poking above those sides was a blanket. I had a sinking feeling in my guts about what lurked down in all that pink and blue swaddling.

"I can tell by your expression that you already know some of this," he said.

"I'm doing guesswork."

"Let me clear it up for you. I'm a geneticist by training. I've been combining the DNA of specific creatures, including a splash of humanity, into an egg and sperm and suspending them in an artificial semi-permeable membrane. I then place that membrane in the pool and subject it to sunlight on the exact day when the anomalous temperatures occur. The sperm activates. It impregnates the egg. The organism grows like kudzu. One can virtually watch it mature by the hour. I incubate it. In very little time a new organism emerges."

"That's how you've made all eight chupacabras. Magic."

"No. I've been stealing the power of Perfect Forms. I've found a crack between the Perfect Dimension and our own where that power leaks through. I've been using it to create new forms."

"I'd call you a lunatic, but I've seen your new forms. But I don't understand why it's worth your while to brew up these new monsters only to chase down Mexican fruit pickers. You must really hold a grudge."

"That's merely part of an economic equation." He waved dismissively. "The government funds my company. I provide them with detainment facilities and innovative technology to patrol the border. I feel the same way about immigrants that I feel about every human being."

"You dislike them."

He nodded. His eyes narrowed and the dark pits at their center glimmered. "Greatly."

"Then why do all this?" I asked. "For science? For fun? For revenge against your twin brother for being better looking than you are?"

"I'm waging a war." His voice was low and sibilant.

"Against who?" I asked.

"Ancient Greece tells the story of Zeus, who overthrew his father to become king of the gods. What followed was an age of Perfect Forms set loose on the earth to do battle—Monsters and Heroes the likes of which we have never seen before or since. Now, we settle for a World of Shadows. I want to bring back the age when monsters roamed the earth. I want humans to prove their worth by performing heroic feats. I want to challenge God's monopoly on creating Forms."

"You have a God complex."

"I don't have a God complex. A God complex is a psychological deficiency. I am on my way to *becoming* a god. I am ripping holes in this World of Shadows. I am letting the light shine in. Eventually, this Shadow World will be teeming with Perfect Forms, luminous and new, and they'll destroy God's shadow forms. For every new form I create, a little bit of God's Shadow World vanishes. The bird deaths were the latest. This well focuses the power of the Perfect Forms. It also imbalances this world. The first law of thermodynamics states that energy can neither be created nor destroyed. Creating a chupacabra requires a huge amount of cosmic energy. It bleeds that energy from somewhere else."

"So, you knew why the birds died all along," I said.

"Of course," he said, "but not in advance. I knew something would happen when I used the pool to create my eighth form, but I didn't know what. Normally, I would have collected and tested a few samples and been done with it. However, when you became involved, it changed everything."

"You're cuckoo, doc. I feel like I should tell you. I didn't change anything. I'm just another piece of biology tripping around in the desert until I die."

John White shook his head. "When I was young, I believed that I was a Perfect Form manifest. I came to believe that less and less over the years. Now I believe that I'm just another shadow, but with the intellect of a god. You are the Perfect Form. Why would God make a small, average man the template for all others? No, he would use you, a titan. I have been on the board of directors of the city zoo for some time. I was struck by your size many years ago. Every other human was an ant beside you. Dracula confirmed my theory. He recognized one of his own, another Perfect Form who didn't belong in this world of shadows. All of the chupacabras see it. They're Perfect, as are you. I realized that I had to have you as my closest ally and confidant, and I set about making it so."

"You could have just bought me a beer," I said.

"You don't greet a titan by buying him a beer. You show him that you respect his power."

"My power is a pituitary gland gone haywire. I'm not perfect. I'm a glitch."

John White eyed the steam billowing from the hot springs and steepled his hands in his lap. "As a young man, I believed in a God who used the Perfect Forms as templates for creating everything in this world. It was an orderly ethos. When I became a geneticist, and I looked at the genome of a human being, all I saw was chaos. Mutation, dormant traits fatal when awoken, diseases inherited through the very fabric of one's being. Death and life, health and sickness were all predestined, not by an orderly God presiding over forms, but by chance. I used to believe God's design was perfection. Now, I believe it is imperfection. He's a dice thrower. And you're the highest number possible."

John White was a lost soul. I should have guessed.

"You know what I'm here to do."

"You're here to make a choice."

I took the pistol out of my pocket and laid it on my thigh. "I'm here to kill a god."

His laugh was sharp. "I'm not a god yet. And I'll never be one without your help. I once believed in heroes. Now I believe in monsters. You've seen seven of them—that's just the beginning. I'm only getting started. By the time I'm done, this earth will face terrors that make the hydra look like a garter snake. And I need the greatest zookeeper the world has ever known to watch over them until they're ready to walk free out in the world. You'll be my Atlas, the pillar who holds the new world aloft."

I sat there with my hand on the gun.

He didn't even look at it. "Before you make your choice—either go back to a world that's cast you out, or become my partner in crafting a new one—I want to show you my eighth chupacabra."

He rose from his chair and walked to the cradle. The matron gave him an absent frown and went back to her knitting. He picked up the bundle of pink and blue swaddling. It encased a form about the size of a loaf of bread. He carried it back to where I sat with the gun and lowered it into the crook of my left arm. I spread my hand to support it. It tilted lightly into my chest, and its warmth spread through me.

I watched its face. My eyes met its eyes. Time slipped away.

"It's a girl," I said after I don't know how long. But she was much more than that.

"Her last name is Stick," White said.

I understood why Marchette had been collecting my genetic tissue at the zoo. I sat with the baby girl—a being unlike any who had ever walked the earth. I don't know how long I held her. When I rose, John White took her from me.

I stuck the gun in my pocket. "I need to take a walk."

"We'll be waiting," he said.

I hiked up the mountain. I walked among the tall spare ponderosas and the waxy needles of the firs and the cheery, bushy spruces. Every creature fled into the brush or cowered in its burrow as I passed. I walked along the Las Huertas Creek, which paralleled the narrow road that led from Placitas to Cedar Crest until I came upon a path that led uphill. The east side of the mountains was gentler than the west, with its steep slopes and cliffs. The grade was easy for the first hour or so, and then the path formed into switchbacks that zigzagged up the tougher spans. Near the top, I crossed a meadow still silent and brown with winter.

Sandía Peak was deserted. I found a rock at the edge of the thousand-foot drop and the mile-high tumble beyond. I sat and dangled my legs over the abyss. A couple chunks of cosmic dust plummeted through the night, leaving fiery trails of destruction in their wake. I didn't make any wishes. I didn't delude myself into thinking they were anything but sad rocks that had been thrown onto a ruinous path. You could call it fate. You could call it design. Or you could call it a series of events and leave it at that.

I sat atop the mountain and understood myself. I'd fallen in love with Melodía because she'd been a new version of my mother—broken, isolated, and sad, just like me. She was another cave for me to hide in. I'd liked my zoo job because it allowed me to bestow all of my human needs for care and companionship onto beings that wouldn't judge me. I was an eight-foot tall cat lady. I understood all that. I'd been shoved beyond the comfort of my routine, and I could look at it from the outside and say, John Stick: pathologically traumatized. Does everything he can to avoid thinking about his problems. Uses all sorts of unhealthy coping mechanisms. Suffers from bouts of severe rage and depression.

The goal of life crises is to see oneself truly and change. I saw myself. I'd learned what and who I was. I was a man who'd been standing in quicksand for forty years. I'd sunk in up to my armpits. It was real warm and snug. I had a long arm-span, and I could reach the bare necessities to survive. The question was whether I had the strength to pull myself out, or whether I'd sink until I suffocated. I had to decide whether to thank John White for showing me that my life was a sinkhole or kill him for not letting me drown in mud.

I sat on my rock at the top of the world. I faced west and waited. The sun rose behind me, far across the flat eastern desert. It warmed my back and inched its yellow blanket over the mountains, casting their long shadow across the city. Slowly, that shadow shrunk and the sublime line of dawn swept across the city and showed Albuquerque that, yes, the sun had risen once again.

The city sprawled brown and flat below. It spread across the river valley to the volcanoes, which were long dead. There was no order to it. The city had sprung into being on the whims of a few men with change in their pockets and the willpower to buy a mule or rent a bulldozer. Down the steep western slope of the mountains, the tumble of boulders, contours of pine forest, and handfuls of cacti arranged themselves in the same way. The structure of the world was a combination of will and chaos, competition and chance. It was purposeless, temporary, and imperfect.

The hike back down to Typhon Industries went faster but was harder on my knees. By the time I'd walked along the creek to where it plunged into Mount Olympus, the sun shone strong, and I'd built up a sweat. Spring had arrived and with it, a whole new cycle of life, perpetuating itself for no reason except that it could. I walked around the front of the building, where I stood in front of a camera and waited for John White to open up.

The outer doors parted. The blank man waited for me in the inner portal, his arms spread wide. Behind him, the pool smoldered in the center of Mount Olympus. The matron sat on her chair, rocking the cradle with one foot. Inside, slept a perfect little monster.

I drew my gun. The metal felt cold and brutal against my skin.

"You've made a choice," the blank man said.

I placed the gun in his outstretched hand.

"I give up," I said.

EPILOGUE

I woke before dawn in Hades. All around me in the great vaulted chamber, the chupacabras slumbered in their enclosures, dreaming of blood. I sat clutching a cup of black coffee in a chair too big for other humans but that fit me perfectly. The chair faced east toward where sunrise would creep into the world. Ralph, drowsy from a night of feasting, sat on my knee. Cerberus leaned against my leg and snuffled at my hand with his tripled-jaw mouth. I slipped a bottle from my pocket and let him suckle at it, telling myself that I didn't care what the bottle held or where it had come from. Nobody out there in the world had ever done me any favors.

An engineer had built a sliding window into the side of Cerberus' cage so I could watch the sunrise. I'd established my daytime workspace there, where I could sit at the first desk big enough to house my legs and under a ceiling that would never ambush my head. After only a month in Hades, everything felt better. My joints and limbs hung looser than they ever had, and my spine had shrugged off its perpetual hunch. My physical self could finally stretch into the size it was meant to be.

An orange halo rose above the eastern horizon, spurring a thrum in the harpy chamber. Even through the greenhouse walls, they could sense the coming of the sun. I'd learned a few hours after handing over my gun that John White had kept a few clans of harpies, a dozen hydras and gremlins, and that his team had rescued Cerberus from the wreckage that had turned Albuquerque into a nexus of new-world monsters. I found the drosophila-mosquito hybrid winnowed down to a few clans as well. John White later admitted to me that he'd released thousands of them after the military convoy embarked.

Harpies were creatures born to fly free during the day, like any pollinator. I'd already gotten to know them. During my first week as the chupacabra keeper, I'd ordered strands of milkweed transplanted into the harpy den. The animals mobbed the pink globes of blossoms, desperate for nectar. They buzzed from plant to plant, spreading pollen. The harpies, just like any other creature, could play a role in keeping nature humming. I'd also started a project that would move the gremlins from singular cubbies to larger enclosures with cage-mates. Rats, I'd learned somewhere down my long history of obsession with animals, like companionship.

A cafeteria worker set a tray outside Cerberus' enclosure just as the sun breached the horizon. She'd received strict instructions not to speak to me or even make eye contact, as had all Typhon Industries staff save for John White. He visited me every morning in the guise of Jacob Charon, and we met in Olympus in the late afternoon. In my new life, I never had to leave Hades, except via underground tunnel to a place called Elis, where I slept. John White had given me an opulent lair there, with a sitting room, kitchen, and bedroom featuring every brand-new luxury I could have imagined—and twelve-foot tall ceilings.

Later, I'd do my rounds. I'd wash and train Cerberus. I kept two cute young bloodhounds in Elis, one male, one female. At night, the three slept on plushy dog beds. Every morning, I rotated the beds. Once everybody got used to each other's smells, the initial face-to-face would hopefully be less horrifying. Eventually, I hoped to coax Cerberus into impregnating the female and accepting the loving embrace of the male. The two purebreds might need to get drunk first, but it was all in the name of progress.

Every day in the late afternoon, I ascended to Olympus, where I took tea with John White. We didn't have much to say to each other. He spent our time combing through paperwork or reading aloud reports of the latest chupacabra attack. The gremlins had thoroughly infested the Albuquerque drainage and sewer systems and used them as a base of operations to terrorize the citizenry. They'd creep up through a toilet or storm drain and sip from the eyelids and lips of babies or old folks in their slumber. Heavy sleepers would endure a day of mysterious sluggishness only to discover circlets of bites on their ankles. The hydras had taken possession of the stripe of forest that hugged the Rio Grande from Colorado to Texas. They terrorized outdoor cats and had massacred the beaver population almost overnight. But the harpies were the worst. They stormed across the desert in a scourge of stingers, speed, and thirst. They'd swarm a cow by the dozens, stinging it into submission, feasting on its blood, and implanting young deep into its skin. They'd attack ranchers and tourists out on the plains. There'd even been a case of a hiker pierced all over his neck and arms until the pain paralyzed him. He'd watched in horror as the wasps drank. John White read these stories with no inflection of pride, disgust, or remorse, but factually, as if they were statistics that required objective consideration.

I barely listened. I had an infant to dandle on my knee. John White could talk for hours and I wouldn't retain a word. Language had little meaning when I was staring into the face of my daughter. Over the month, her eight eyes had begun to focus on distinct objects rather than straying aimlessly. Her large pair, the anterior eyes in the center of her face, would zero in on me for breathless minutes, while her median and posterior eyes would rove around the room, making me wonder what a human with 360 degree vision could accomplish. As I cradled her, she would grasp my thumbs in two or three of her dark hands while her lower limbs pedaled in quadruplet motion. The only thing softer than a baby's skin is the smooth, supple chitin on a freshly born arachnid. Holding her gave me the deepest feelings I'd had since my mother passed away.

Cerberus lifted his head and howled at the new day's sun. Half an hour after breakfast, the first feeding of the day would begin. I stayed upstairs for feedings. After a month, I'd almost become accustomed to the screams of terror that eddied from the vents in the floor.

At least that's what I told myself.

ACKNOWLEDGMENTS

Many people nurtured the long gestation of this book. My fellow MFA students at the University of New Mexico supported the first version, called *Blood Heist*: Melanie Rodriguez, Rudolfo Serna, Chris Boat, Nari Kirk, and Kyle Churney. Jesse Aleman changed the way I think about borderland folklore. Julie Shigekuni taught me about storytelling and connected me with Laurie Liss, who helped me navigate the publishing process. Dan Mueller taught me writerly craft and accompanied me through the painstaking process of the first few drafts.

The following books deepened my understanding of New Mexico: *Pueblos, Spaniards, and the Kingdom of New Mexico* by John L. Kessell; *The Adobe Kingdom* by Donald L. Lucero; *We Fed Them Cactus* by Fabiola Cabeza de Baca Gilbert; *Manifest Destinies* by Laura E. Gomez; *New Mexican Lives* edited by Richard W. Etulain; *Albuquerque* by V.B. Price; *Trees and Shrubs of New Mexico* by Jack L. Carter; and *A Field Guide to the Plants and Animals of the Middle Rio Grande Bosque* by Jean-Luc C. Cartron et al.

Jeff Schrandt, my cousin and closest friend, did field research with me at the Bosque Del Apache, around Albuquerque, and in the Sandia Mountains. My extended family has long supported me, as has my new family, especially Kent and Linda. Mr. Carlson sat with me for many long hours of revision. Colleagues at Normandale lent me their advice, particularly Tom Maltman. Doug Bessette was fiercely supportive of the book throughout its revision, as was Sam Ocena, my writing soul-mate, who gave me endless sage advice. Betty, my daughter, has given me renewed drive to write books that address serious problems.

Above all, thanks to Curiosity Quills, which is taking a big chance on a weird and tragic story, and the editorial dynamic duo of Lisa Gus and Matt Cox, whose feedback improved the book immensely. And to my parents, who financed and inspired the education and empathy necessary to become a writer: a huge and heartfelt thank you. Finally, my deepest gratitude goes to my wife Brianna. She believes in me like no other: she has provided me with space, time, enthusiasm, and encouragement, without which the book would not exist.

ABOUT THE AUTHOR

Dan Darling is a native of Albuquerque, New Mexico. Before becoming a writer, he was a comet, rocketing around the world in long, haphazard, parabolas. While traveling through twenty countries and many states, Dan made a living as a circus performer, bartender, café manager, IRS agent, graphic designer, and magician. In his prime, he spoke Swedish, Spanish, and Mandarin and has studied half a dozen other languages. Dan received his BA in English from the College of Wooster and his Master of Fine Arts at the University of New Mexico.

Gravity having reined him in, Dan settled in Minnesota, where he labors over novels that fuse the language of noire detective fiction with the imagination of magical realism. His greatest influences are Haruki Murakami, Salman Rushdie, and Raymond Chandler. Besides working on novels, he teaches writing and literature at Normandale Community College and is an avid bowler. He lives in the Twin Cities with his wife and daughter.

Archaeopteryx is the first novel of a trilogy about Albuquerque. The next novel, *The Twelve Labors of the Chupacabra Hunter,* will emerge in the near future.

For more news about Dan, including information on public readings, interviews, and more, visit www.dandarling.net.

THANK YOU
FOR READING

© 2017 **Dan Darling**

www.dandarling.net

Please visit http://curiosityquills.com/reader-survey to share your reading experience with the author of this book!

Pop Travel, by Tara Tyler

In 2080, technology has gone too far for J. L. Cooper. He avoids pop travel teleportation, until he stumbles onto a video of a pop traveler who turns to dust. Sparking a series of murders and threats to his brother, Cooper wants to pass off the evidence but knows he's being watched. And who would believe him? With help from the neurotic genius "Creator" of pop travel and a beautiful Southern charmer, Cooper must expose the deadly glitch and shut it down or die trying. No problem.

Unhappenings, by Edward Aubry

When Nigel is visited by two people from his future, he hopes they can explain why his past keeps rewriting itself. His search for answers takes him fifty-two years forward in time, where he meets Helen, brilliant, hilarious and beautiful. Unfortunately, that meeting has triggered events that will cause millions to die. Desperate to find a solution, he discovers the role his future self has played all along.

CPSIA information can be obtained
at www.ICGtesting.com
Printed in the USA
LVHW110811221218
601074LV00010BA/1570/P